CARVED AMIDST THE SHADOWS

A BRANDS OF TAELGIR NOVEL

M.T. FONTAINE

Carved Amidst the Shadows
A Brands of Taelgir Novel
By M.T. Fontaine

Cover Design: Seventhstar Art
Cover Weapon Illustration: Florian Cavenel
Map designed by Tiffany Munro at www.feedthemultiverse.com

To my husband
For believing in me every step of the way, no matter the obstacle.

Pronunciation Guide

CHARACTERS
Aethel: Eh-thull
Aileen: Ay-leen
Andreiyes Lenierz: Ann-dray-yes Leh-neer-z
Aroawn: A-ron
Balliol Lenierz: Bah-lee-ol Leh-neer-z
Chaephren: Keh-fren
Eybah Hirai: Ay-bah H-r-eye
Ghedi: G-eh-dee
Jereown Sertrios: Jeh-ro-inn Sir-tree-oh-s
Kaianne/Ynnea Lyssandre: Kay-ann/Ye-ney-a Lie-sand-dre
Nergail Lenierz: Ner-gay-le Leh-neer-z
Rau Hirai: Ra-oo H-r-eye
Oidh: Oy-d
Ohenor: O-heh-nor
Triunn Lenierz: Tree-un Leh-neer-z

PLACES
Alihuerte: Ah-lee-where-teh
Isyldill: Ih-sill-dill
Gyldrise: Gill-dree-s
Lakoldon: Lay-coal-dun
Lityoll: Lit-ee-oll
Nimedor: Nih-meh-dor
Taelgir: Tail-geer

<u>OTHER</u>
Eidenhail Tree: Ay-den-hail Tree
Elginich: L-gih-nich
Drynn: Drin
Schlenkra: Sh-uh-len-k-rah
Syldian: Sill-dee-an

One

236th Stretch of Gain
Alpha Cycle of the 947th Stretch
Millau Estate - Isyldill

The promise contract landed on the mahogany table with a thump, but Ladyling Ynnea Kaianne made no move to touch it. It was sickeningly thick and something Ynnea wanted no part in, but she was only twelve and that meant she was still under her noble father's thumb. If Papa had listened to her, it never would have been written, but that was far too much to hope for.

A servant uncorked a bottle of ink and placed a quill in her hand. She bit her lip and rolled the stress off her shoulders just a touch, nothing unseemly. She wouldn't want to be called improper and berated for the fragility of her gender's constitution now, would she? Certainly not with Papa, or Lord Pascual of House Bryant, or her future intended, or Princeling Andreiyes in attendance. They all stared as though she were an animal to cage. She dipped the quill and skimmed over the calligraphed words. The ink's bitter scent on the ten crisp pages prickled her nose.

A child half her age could accomplish this task. Initial each page and sign the last to ensure her compliance and bind her and her family's fate on her eighteenth name-day to the Lordling Willik, heir of House Bryant. It gave her five stretches and five moon cycles of freedom to do as she pleased before they forced her to run a household and pop out children like Mama. Oh, so much to look forward to – vomiting, bloating, something growing inside bumping up the skin at odd angles, and the pain. As if to mock her, her mother wailed and whimpered, courtesy of a contraction from her latest pregnancy. The cry echoed from the other side of the manor, and Kaianne winced.

Why couldn't boys be the ones to carry children and help the wetnurses with their chores? Sword training looked like more fun. Other than wearing pretty gowns, being a girl was dull. Sit straight and sew, or read or play an instrument, or dance or fan yourself. The only fun to be had nearby was walking through the markets in Millian – the town attached to their estate – or climbing trees in the Weldolf woods at the estate's edge.

No one reacted to Mama's cries as they echoed through the conference hall. Lord Pascual of House Bryant, northern commander of Isyldill's kingsmen, cleared his throat. His Highness Prince Andreiyes, court witness to the signing, leaned sideways in his chair and stifled a yawn, chin resting on his fist. Even Papa's stern facade only cracked for a grainfall before reverting to marble.

Sweat clammed Kaianne's palm, the quill slipping between her fingers. Normally, the floor to ceiling tapestries that lined the walls brought warmth and comfort, but at that moment they were threatening to wrap and smother her. Her chest tightened in the stuffy stillness.

She pleaded silently across the room for Papa to reconsider, but Lord Thibault of House Lyssandre remained impassive. One blink was all he gave, a silent order to sign. Her two older brothers beside him offered her no further comfort, permanently the faithful sons, and she didn't even try to enlist Prince Andreiyes' help. He tended to be in sync with her brother, Grayson – the two of them thick as thieves. Always with the insults and horseplay, too often at her expense.

Beside her, Willik shifted in his chair. At nearly sixteen, three stretches her senior, perhaps he was just as uncomfortable as she was. Gods knew they could not stand each other. That little hope had her glancing up. He forced a smile below the odd orange fuzz growing beneath his nose and on his chin. Oh little lords, would she really be forced to kiss that one day?

She cringed with a shiver and stared down at the contract outlining her life sentence. A forever with Willik, the pompous dunce who complained of the slightest bit of dirt on his boots. The one who could never be bothered to be seen with her because she was a girl and younger than he. Whose red hair made her wish she could strike flint to it. She gulped. She needed to get out of there, immediately.

Kaianne set down her quill and stood, her chair screeching along the tile. "Pardon me my Lords, your Highness. I need but a moment." Just to escape to the privy for a short while to form a real plan of escape.

"Sit. Down," Papa ordered, his baritone voice promising discipline. His dark eyes were fiery with challenge. "Everyone out. My daughter and I need a moment."

For a moment's hesitation, the air was so still not even a butterfly could have flown on it. Then, her eldest brother Deacon cleared his throat, inclined his head to Papa, and left, trailing her brother Grayson behind him and escorting out House Bryant's members. Kaianne gave Deacon one last pleading look before he slipped into the hallway. The princeling remained, a grin tugging at the corner of his dark face. He waved to Papa to proceed once the doors to the room shut.

"Your Highness." Papa's tone was measured behind gritted teeth. "I require a few sandfalls with my child."

Andreiyes' eyes snapped to meet Papa's, and for a moment the playfulness in his amber eyes that Kaianne hated vanished.

"If you consider her a child, Lord Thibault, then she has no place signing that contract today."

Kaianne gaped at him. She was unpleasantly well acquainted with his jesting nature. The pranks he and her brother played on her were a plague on her life. Being an arrogant arse did not help his cause, either. This serious, supportive side of him was shocking and suspicious. She narrowed her eyes at the boy who was fourth-in-line to the throne of Isyldill.

In all Isyldill, Royal House Lenierz were the closest descendants of the gods – Aethel and Gaia – who had terraformed the land to provide for their people and led them to a prosperous future. Following in their footsteps should be more than enough motivation for a prince, but not Andreiyes. Just past celebrating his fifteenth stretch, the princeling still preferred to frolic and jeer. This was the most dutiful she had ever seen him.

"I may be young, Lord Lyssandre, but I am far from foolish. King Triunn has demanded I bear witness to the signing of this contract and all of its dealings. That includes these conversations." Andreiyes sat upright and entwined his fingers on the table. "Hard be it for me to disappoint my grandfather, and I am certain you do not wish to offend or counter his requests. So, as much as I would rather be anywhere but here…as you were. Proceed."

Kaianne shuddered. He oozed haughtiness like pus from a boil ever since his voice had stopped fluctuating from broken high pitches to a deeper timber than his spindly frame suggested. No one would ever doubt him to be royal born, even if they were blind to his tanned skin tone that was at least five shades darker than hers. Supposedly the god couple had skin black as night, the color carried down in their descendants yet diluted after hundreds of stretches of couplings with light skinned nobles and commonfolk. Not that her own family skin shade was pearl white. Her family's nobility and prestige was tied not only to their wealth and loyalty to the crown but also to their caramel skin. In some distant past, one or more of her ancestors had likely been royal. Unlike the Bryants who were so white they competed with snow.

Papa inclined his head. "As you wish."

Kaianne bit her cheek, eyes bouncing between the princeling's focused gaze and Lord Lyssandre, before choosing to ignore the princeling. It wasn't him she had to convince. She took a deep breath. "Papa, I'm begging you. Willik and I – "

"Are to be married. That is the end of it."

"But Papa, you cannot…I don't want a husband."

"Enough, Ynnea." His tone was clipped. She hated the use of her first name. Its pronunciation was stern, detached, and lacked warmth. "We discussed this. There is nothing further for you to negotiate."

The prince bent forward. She squirmed with unease, staring into her father's brown eyes, begging him to reconsider. Eyes narrowed, Lord Lyssandre slapped his palm against the table.

"Remember your place, girl. My affection for you will only go so far. If you go against your word again, I'll have you locked in your chambers and married in a fortnight. Is that clear?"

Kaianne's breath skipped. She nodded.

"Good." Lord Lyssandre circled the table and patted her shoulder before placing a chaste kiss on her temple. "Make me proud and sign. You need this. We need this."

She stared at his empty seat as he left the chamber, the door clicking shut whilst her mother wailed once more. Her chest tightened. The idea of being pregnant and pushing out a babe, it made her shiver. Never, never would it happen to her. That was a vow. With a shaky hand, she picked up the quill.

"Well," the prince broke her unease. "I certainly did not expect such excitement. Especially not from you."

She shot him a glare. His jesting smile was not in the least bit comforting. "Just because you know Grayson does not mean you know me, *your Highness*."

"Careful, Ynnea. I am not your equal."

"As if you and my brother would ever let me forget it." If only he was the sole cause of her ire. She would certainly love to sear holes through that smug face of his and chip away at the straight edges of his jawline and brows that were becoming more prominent every stretch.

"Little else puts you in your place." The contempt in his voice was as clear as her father's. "This bargain with the Lord, what do you gain?"

"What do you care?"

"What can I say? My curiosity is never sated." He reclined in his chair, the wood creaking from the shift.

Kaianne exhaled and scanned the papers once more. "Five and half stretches. To do as I wish if I accept willingly."

"And if you did not?"

Burning tears fogged up the words on the parchment. She willed them away. "Papa would see me set on the streets without a penny to my name until I accept a quick wedding."

"Well, every woman needs a man. And you are just a girl."

And he was just a boy. She scoffed. That kind of response was exactly why she had nicknamed him Yierd like turd, because that was what his attitude reminded her of: an enormous steaming pile of manure that required a good shoveling.

"That's something only boys like you think to fluff your own feathers. I'd be thrilled to never marry."

His chortle grated her ears. "I almost pity House Bryant. Almost."

The nincompoop winked at her. Kaianne grinded her teeth. Let him mock her. She planned to show all of them her worth. She had the following five stretches and five cycles. That made exactly sixty-five Maiesta moon cycles to disgust Willik and Lord Bryant into abandoning this dumb contract. In total one thousand nine-hundred fifty days to change her fate. There was time – an infinite number of sand grains in timekeepers left to fall. She tapped the quill on the ink bottle's bottom. The quill scratched the parchment as she signed her name on each page. Ladyling Ynnea Kaianne Lyssandre.

While her mother suffered from child pains, Kaianne was the lady of the house. Duty required her to accompany their guests to the estate's courtyard to see them off. As if signing her life away were not enough.

The men ambled from the conference hall to the foyer surrounding the grand marble staircase. Papa, Deacon – her eldest brother –, and Lord Bryant's voices rumbled through tiresome political conversations while Yierd and her brother Grayson regressed to their crude assessments regarding the ladies of court. Her younger brothers Eryk and Adelmo followed behind them like eager hounds. Willik, unfortunately, found it appropriate to wait for her, elbow out for her to hold, lips curled up in a sneer.

She glared into his bland brown eyes and their golden rim around the iris – the same color everyone in Isyldill was born with except for the royals – expecting a deprecating or vain remark now that his father was out of hearing. Nothing about him made her giggle like some of her acquaintances at court might.

His too pale skin flushed with freckles was a reminder that the Bryants were of a newer line of nobles, dubbed only a century before because their coffers were overfilled with gold migs. The royals adored their excessive sycophantic behavior enough to name Lord Pascual and his father before him the Northern Commander. Her family was selling her to the Bryants to further their own wealth and military prowess, nothing else. That twisted her insides. She was no better than kindling for the fire on a cold night.

"Do me a favor, Ynnea, try growing some tits."

She scoffed at the insult. Did he forget she was only twelve? "You dare address your future wife in such a way?"

"My wife should know her place."

"Wow. How much more of a cur can you be?"

"At least I have the decency to feign interest."

"Is that what you're doing? Such a hardship." She waved him forward, desperate to send him and his distasteful slurs on their way and escape the glaring eyes from the portraits hanging along the hall. "Willik, let's be honest. I don't like you. You don't like me, and I will never be your wife. Pretending otherwise is foolish."

His lips twitched into a snarl. "You are a lamb, Ynnea. Always have been, always will be. And I look forward to your slaughter."

Kaianne pulled away and hurried ahead of him, unwilling to deal with him any further. The butler opened the double doors that led to the front courtyard and its greenery. Only then did her tension slacken.

Whiffs of thyme, rosemary and tarragon permeated the air from the vegetable gardens on the edge of the manor's east wing. The heat from the last twelve cycle stretch was only starting to abate, but the breeze caressed her skin beneath the lace of her half-sleeves. It forced a few strands of Kaianne's ash brown hair out of her braided bun. They blew backwards, begging to be as carefree and unrestrained as the wind. She rolled her shoulders and drew back her head. The sky was clearing, clouds bustling by, an ivory waxing gibbous and one sandy sphere hanging on opposite sides of the sea of sunny blue – Taelgir's two moons.

Twenty paces away, along the pebbled passage through the manicured garden hedges, lawn and ponds, their guests' horses awaited with a groom attending to each. Soon, this charade would be over.

"Until we meet again." Willik grabbed her palm. Had she not felt Papa's and Lord Pascual's gazes on them, she'd have torn her hand out of his grasp before he slobbered it with a long kiss.

With a shiver, she ripped her hand away and wiped his saliva on the back of her dress. "You forget, lordling," she hissed through her teeth. "I have no plans to see you for as long as the gods permit."

He chortled with a shake of his head before descending the marble steps and approaching his horse. Good riddance.

"Lord Pascual," she curtsied before the blond noble – Willik's red hair came from his mother's side. "Your company, as always, is a pleasure. We do hope to see you again soon."

"As is yours. I expect to return shortly to celebrate the birth of your sibling. It will be a joyous occasion." His smile reached from ear to ear. Despite her dislike of Willik, Pascual of House Bryant had a genuine charm to his tone and demeanor that always put her at ease. How he got along so well with her brooding father was beyond her. "The day you become a Bryant and we join our two houses permanently will be all the more."

"You're too kind." Kaianne forced a smile.

"You are, as always, welcome at the Zesco Manor. Her Ladyship and I would be thrilled to see more of our future daughter." Instead of a kiss to her wrist, Lord Bryant pecked her cheek and offered a warm smile.

"Please send her Ladyship my best."

As Lord Pascual took his leave from Papa, Kaianne hugged her arms with unease. Pascual held the warmth her father lacked. That attention from a father figure was delightful, almost worth envying Willik for.

The two men locked right forearms, their marks facing in and touching, before pulling each other close for a back-patting embrace before parading down the path to the horses. Absentmindedly, Kaianne traced her own mark – the black outline of a griffin's eagle head in profile, black feathers brushed back, a steely golden eye the exact same color of Isyldill's royal family's, and a menacing pointed beak.

Everyone in Isyldill was born with the same one except for the Flawed. They had none whatsoever, and those few were always exterminated as quickly as possible. Dangerous abominations, they were. They threatened the realm and the Order of Stewards' stability with treachery. Something about them causing dissonance and disarray, all predicted by the gods. Both Papa and Mama had explained it, though Kaianne's attention had wavered within the first few boring sentences of political reasoning and the mention of the traitorous Carved.

Boys' laughter a few paces to her right cut through her thoughts.

"Eh, Kay." Grayson elbowed her. "I bet four gold migs Willik was imagining wetting something other than your hand."

She frowned. "What in Nogo's pits does that mean?"

"Excellent phrasing," Yierd said with a waggle of his eyebrows. Grayson shoved him. Her two other youngster siblings melted into chuckles.

"Your marriage bed, sis," Grayson said. Kaianne blushed at his words. Willik imagined wetting what? "He's most certainly impatient to –"

Deacon smacked the back of Grayson's head. Nearing seventeen and Papa's heir, he was the only levelheaded lad out of her four lookalike brothers.

"Eh, what was that for?"

"Kay's virtue is no laughing matter. Be happy it was me who heard and not Pa, or you'd be yelping from the lashes." Deacon then pulled on Adelmo and Eryk's earlobes. "Was the laugh at her expense worth it? Do you little squirts even know what they're going on about?"

The two whimpered and shook their heads.

"Dea, you don't -," Kaianne said.

"I'm not done, Kay."

She rolled her eyes. For Gaia's sake, why did boys always think that their words were worth more than hers?

Deacon brandished his index finger like a weapon before her brothers. "If you don't know the innings of what is being said, then keep your gobs shut."

"It was only a little humor, Dea." Yierd always acted like it was his right to cut into family talks.

"With all the respect this family has for your position, your Highness, a daughter of House Lyssandre is not sport for wordplay."

"Dea, enough. I can handle myself."

Deacon clutched her by the elbow and ungraciously forced her back inside the manor.

"Let me go." She shook her arm, but he only squeezed tighter. "You're not Pa."

His fingertips dug into her muscle as he dragged her up the grand staircase toward the west wing's upper apartments. With each step closer to Mama's chambers, Kaianne tugged harder against Deacon's hold. He had no right to tug her along like this.

"You're hurting me. Let go."

They stopped in the middle of the hallway, so close to Mama's quarters that Kaianne could hear her panting between wails. The smoky scent of sandalwood and lavender incense wafting throughout the wing didn't seem to be helping to calm Mama. Deacon's grip unlocked from Kaianne's arm, and she massaged the prickling area as a pained shriek pealed down the corridor and left her skin feeling raw. Poor Mama. She'd heard the servants whispering that a day and a half of child pains was already past the norm.

"Look at me, Kay."

She glared up at her brother's straight edged features and into his brown eyes. There was no anger there, but his telltale signs of frustration showed through his pinched lips and shake of the head.

"You think that because you've reached womanhood or because you convinced Pa to push back the wedding, you know best. You don't."

"So, you think I'm useless. Just another girl who doesn't know which way is up without a man's hand."

He shook her. "That's not what I'm saying. I don't know what's best either. Pa always tells me: respect can be given, but most is earned and you have to fight to keep it. If your own brother is permitted to discuss you so crudely, others will too. Then you'll be fighting twice as hard to retrieve all the respect the Lyssandre name has given you. You're worth much more than that, Sis."

Kaianne crossed her elbows, head bowed. "I'm not a fragile little thing. I don't need you to protect me."

"I do because I want to, Kay. My loyalty is to the family, and gods know I love you." He grappled her in a hug and kissed her head. "Not just anyone could have stood up to Pa and changed his mind like you did. Just don't let anyone demean you and your worth."

Kaianne's cheeks prickled, and she dug her face harder against Deacon's tunic. Like water dousing Nogo's flames, she could never stay mad at him for long.

"Thank you."

Another guttural cry from Mama's room pierced the air. The far door clicked open and a woman in her servant grays, hair pulled tight into a cloth wrapped bun, raced through, carrying bunched sheets in her arms. The servant bowed her head and curtsied as she passed, but Kaianne only paid heed to the large, red stains on the flowered fabric.

"Any news?" Deacon asked the servant, who turned to face him midstride.

"No, m'Lordling. The midwife says she not be progressing near as much as she should."

"And the blood?" Kaianne felt a twinge in her stomach.

"I'm sorry, m'Ladyling. I'm no healer." The servant hurried away, somber thuds following her footfalls on the rug.

Two

*P*oor Mama's face was pastier than the palest commoner, despite the sunlight gleaming through the window veils. She had now been in labor for three days.

Purple bags dragged down her almond eyes, lines of tears tracing their edges. Her breathing was erratic, and her cries were filled with more sobs than any other sound. No amount of cold washcloths on Mama's brow calmed the sweating spells. No matter how often the maids aired out the room or the amount of incense that burned, the cloying odor of blood, sweat, and tears overwhelmed the room. Kaianne shook her head, disgusted. Nothing was worth this much pain, not a babe nor even five stretches of freedom.

Mistress Tilde, the midwife, pried up Mama's third nightgown in half a day. This latest one was already crusted in layers of fresh and dried blood. She prodded Mama's belly – top, bottom, and sides. Mama winced, and the old woman rasped an apology.

Mistress Tilde puckered her lips. "The babe's breech, m'Lady."

Mama grunted and whimpered. Kaianne placed her washcloth back into the water basin at the bed's edge and squeezed the excess water out. She pressed it on Mama's forehead once more and dragged it down her cheeks.

"You're almost there, Mama. I'll be meeting my little sister real soon."

"You would like that, wouldn't you? A sister," Mama hissed, face pinched.

Kaianne smiled. "Any more lads in this family and they'll run us into the ground."

"Time to push, m'Lady." Mistress Tilde rolled down the bedsheets past Mama's ankles. "Hard pushes."

Mama grunted and squealed. She squeezed Kaianne's hand without relent. Her knuckles turned white, and she bit back a yelp.

"Almost there, m'Lady. Again, three more."

Once more Mama grunted, then her grip on Kaianne's hand relaxed, and a frozen silence took over. For five long grainfalls – not a word, not a breath, nor even a movement. Until the baby wailed and broke the stupor.

"Well?" Mother asked panting. "Boy or girl?" Kaianne peered around the Mistress' shoulder, just as curious.

"A…a little lad, my Lady." Mistress Tilde forced the barely wrapped babe into Kaianne's arms, all covered in gooey, red muck.

"What?" Kaianne gathered the bundle awkwardly. His arms flailed, wiping himself all over her green gown, as she worked to keep a solid hold on him. The screams coming out of his toothless mouth were deafening. "But I…Where are you going?"

The midwife backed away from them, eyes wide, head shaking, lower lip quivering.

"I must call on his Lordship."

"Wait," Kaianne said. "What am I supposed to do with him?"

To Kaianne's surprise, Mistress Tilde scuttled backward and rushed out the door – bloodied apron, goo-mucked hands and all. Usually, the woman was so methodical that she thanked the blessed moons and stars when she could avoid her. Now, she wanted to beg the woman to come back. If she did, Kaianne promised never to mutter again about how ancient she was.

"He's beautiful," Mama whispered before her eyes rolled to the back of her head.

"Mama? Ma?" Arms busy with the babe that had finally calmed in her bouncing arms, Kaianne nudged Mama's shoulder with her elbow. No response. Bleddyn, Mama's personal chambermaid, lifted Mama's head and fluffed her pillow while her daughter set a clean set of sheets beneath Mama's legs. "What's wrong with her? Why won't she wake up?"

"Sleeping, m'Ladyling. She's tired is all. Long three days, and she's bled her share."

Kaianne wiped a runaway tear against her shoulder. "And now?"

"Less, much less."

"Then why did Mistress Tilde leave? Why is she not here?"

"I'm sorry, m'Ladyling. I don't know."

"Is something wrong with him? Is my brother ill?"

"He sounded just fine. No need to worry now. Just needs a cleaning is all. But go on and hold him a bit longer if ye'd like. Seems he's taken a liking to ye."

Kaianne peered down at the now silent, wrinkly thing cocooned in her arms. Eyes sealed shut, cheeks bunched to make pouty lips. She sighed. Another brother. One more bouncing egotistical, supremacist to the lot. If she had any say in the matter, he would remain forever far from their brothers' irritating influence to become the sweetest, most caring, most loving of them all. If only.

"Baby brother. You need a name." Kaianne gently tapped a finger on his tiny nose and smirked. "I dub thee…Thad." She rubbed the goo off his chubby face and arms. Strange though, his skin was all bare, caramel flesh. She twisted his right arm to the side. "Bleddyn, how long after birth does the mark appear?"

The servants glanced at each other. "It does no' appear, Ladyling. It just is."

But that meant…Thad was a Flawed? How? The servants' unease spread waves of tension that had Kaianne's skin prickling. No wonder Mistress Tilde ran out like the Order's Masters were on her heels. The Order and their trained drynn wielders were a scary few; not even the royals messed with them as the gods' chosen few with the talents to carry out their will.

Gods below, someone was going to come for Thad. Flawed weren't allowed to live. Kaianne shook her head with a trembling breath. Thad's little face looked so peaceful and harmless tucked in the crook of her arm. No snoring, no fidgeting. He was as harmless as a coney's kittens. It just wasn't possible, not him, not this little babe snuggled against her.

"No one will touch you, little brother," she whispered.

She needed to hide him. With Mimsee, her governess, out on holiday, there was a spare chamber in the servant's quarters where he could stay for a little while. Kaianne lay her baby brother over her chest and crossed to the trunk at the end of her mother's bed, the hardwood floor creaking with each step. The two servants backed away to Mama's side on her approach, heads bowed with the occasional furtive glance her way. Neither seemed keen on aiding.

With a tug, the trunk screeched open to reveal stacks of clean cloths and sheets. She grabbed a bolster's case. The servants' hushed whispers grated her ears, worry lines etched in their brows.

"He's only a babe. He cannot hurt you." Kaianne rolled her eyes. She swaddled Thad in the extra layer.

Muffled yells boomed from the other side of the west wing. That meant one thing: Tilde had found Papa. Not good. Usually, Papa waited in his audience chambers to officially be presented with his newborn.

Bleddyn clamped her mouth shut and both maids scooted further into a corner. Kaianne pressed Thad tight against her, his innocent whimper making her lip quiver. A stampede of footfalls drummed through the hallway. Their quake echoed through the stone floor, its hardwood coverings, and rug, all the way up her slippers.

Papa barked commands. *'Double the watch at the gate.' 'No one enters.'*

Still Mama slept, her color unimproved. On the other side of the door, Grayson muttered something, probably a poor joke, and Papa snapped, cursing his idiocy to the pits. A whack followed. Deacon's even tone interfered, yet his calm words had no effect this time.

When the handle clicked and the door opened, Papa was still roaring. Brows furrowed, lips curled, he barged into the room and slammed the door behind him. Kaianne had seen Papa mad, – he often was – but this seemed different. His facial lines were drawn out further than the day before and liquor wafted off his breath and skin.

"Is it true?" he asked, boots clicking against the hardwood flooring.

Kaianne backed away toward the room's center. Her gaze jumped from the room's entrance, to Papa, to Thad, and finally to Mama's dayroom door near the vast windows on the opposite side of the room.

"What will you do to him?"

"Give *it* to me, Kaianne."

"He's not an it, Papa. He's your son. My brother."

"He means the death of your mother and this family's good name."

"Mama just needs some rest. She'll be well shortly."

Kaianne inched closer to the dayroom door, heart thumping in her chest. Less than ten more steps to reach it. From Mama's dayroom, the patio doors led to her private gardens with a winding passageway off the main grounds through which she could reach the servants' quarters. She just had to keep Thad hidden from Papa long enough for Mama to get better and reason with him.

Kaianne darted to the side, but Papa clutched her arm and reeled her back. The jolt forced her down on her rear. A bolt of pain shot up her spine as Thad woke, shrieking.

"Hush now." She bounced him against her chest with a hiss. His wailing would only rile Papa up further.

"Foolish girl."

She didn't see the blow coming. It shot her head to the left. Her cheek prickled with heat. Half the room blurred while one ear rang. Papa had never struck her face that hard before. Tears flowed unbidden, cooling her cheek as he ripped Thad from her grip.

"Why?" she muttered between sobs. "He's just a babe."

"Do not push me further." Papa's sunken eyes warned her.

He was known for his temper, but this wasn't his usual cold fury. There was something unhinged in his gaze that made Kaianne want to cringe and hide. When his stare jumped to Mama's bed and softened slightly, a shaky breath left Kaianne trembling.

"Ready her. She'll be leaving within the next sandturn."

"But m'Lord." Bleddyn's voice was as shaky as Kaianne felt. "Her Ladyship lost too much blood. We move her, she may not survive."

Papa fell to his knees as Thad tumbled from his laid-out arms to the ground. He pounded the floating floorboards with clenched fists until they cracked. Kaianne curled into herself, Thad's wails and screams drowning the thuds that vibrated through the parquet. Strands of Papa's ash hair fell from the band at his nape. Fire raged through his eyes like that of feral criminals escorted to their deaths.

She wanted to grab Thad and hide in a void, but her body refused to respond. All she could do was watch in horror as Papa reached into the bedding that enveloped Thad and grabbed his neck. A tiny snap, and then Thad went quiet. She shuddered and sobbed. That little sound was all it took.

The change in Papa was drastic. One moment, he radiated rage. The next, he clenched Thad's quiet body against his chest. Tears – the first Kaianne had ever witnessed from Papa – drained down his scrunched face. When he rose and made his way to Mama. Kaianne found the courage to unfurl her body.

"Don't hurt her," she begged.

To her surprise, Papa gingerly sat beside Mama and lay a kiss on her temple, soft and gentle. He caressed back her hair, then fluffed her pillow. He proceeded to cover her body with blankets. Kaianne stared wide-eyed at the display of tenderness after the violence from moments before.

"Are you certain she cannot travel?" he asked Bleddyn, voice low, an arm around Mama's head and shoulder.

"Only the healer can give confirmation, m'Lord. We can send for him."

"No, too much time would be lost. It would no longer matter." He caressed Mama's cheek and murmured soft words in her ear.

Kaianne trembled in place, but bit back the stinging tears for the brother she'd never know. Papa still held Thad's bundled body.

"Have her dressed in her finest. Kaianne, order the gardener to pick a mix of her favorite flowers. All violet and yellow. It's what she would want. Have them brought here quickly."

"Why?" The question slipped out, and she bit her lip. She knew better than to question Papa.

Papa sighed, head bowed. He'd never looked so weak and resigned before. "She shall soon have guests, ones even I cannot stop. We must only hope that they shall be lenient with the problem resolved."

Problem. The word for Thad's lifeless body was so cold, it sent a shiver down her spine. He kissed Mama once more.

"I would not change these past two decades with you for a hundred others lived," he whispered against her forehead.

Kaianne tilted her head, breath catching in her throat. "Who is coming, Papa?"

"No questions. Do as I ask, now. Your brothers need to call our guard to assemble. But Kaianne, no mention of the Flawed child to the staff. Not a word."

*T*hree

*A*ndreiyes perused House Bryant's estate gardens on his hunt for Ladyling Lorelai of House Sertrios. Pebbles crackled beneath his boots. The breeze tousled his knotted hair bun, the humidity adding a curl to the loose strands. The taste of incoming rain lingered in the air.

The new season, the Stretch of Gain – with each stretch lasting for an entire twelve Maiesta lunar cycles – was only in its first cycle. Already the overbearing heat from the Stretch of Fervor was abating to welcome a more temperate climate. In the next two cycles, the first leaves would begin to litter the ground, and within a couple more cycles, the Stretch of Gain's vibrant oranges and reds would replace the Stretch of Fervor's green trees and yellowed grass.

He traipsed through trimmed hedges and flower patches, under weeping willows and the shade of white oaks, and in the midst of chattering birds and sputtering fountains. It was far too trite in sentimentality for his tastes, and more than a little pretentious of House Bryant to sport such posh gardens. Were it not for his interest in a certain ladyling that refused to take note of him, he would have been somewhere that projected his virility such as the training grounds, despite his participation being prohibited.

The plan was simple. Stumble upon her during her stroll with Ladyling Istne of House Bryant, seduce her with his endless charm, and take her to bed for a night he would not soon forget. She had experience after all, and who better to show him the ropes than a gentlewoman with skill?

Innocent giggles blossomed from a private alcove surrounded by tall hedges. Andreiyes prowled closer, keeping to the sickly grass opposed to the gravel for stealth. They were alone, not counting the stiff servant in the far corner. Instead of relief, his nerves built and bundled in his throat. He unlaced the top of his tunic to display an outline of the muscles he worked extremely hard to achieve and gripped the vial of blue gods' essence hanging around his neck for support. Now, to approach them. And he had to. That was the whole point of this frittered morning in the gardens.

The two girls lounged atop a blanket on the grass sipping tea and eating grapes as they gossiped over the newest fashions and young men. Ladyling Istne, her voice sweet and innocent, was by far the most alluring. Nearest to his age at sixteen, her fiery red hair took away from her paleness. Her lips were made for sin, and she had a bosom he wanted to bury himself in. Unfortunately, she was also a prude and a known virgin, saving herself for her fiancé.

That was what made Ladyling Lorelai so enticing. Lorelai's face was pleasant enough with blond hair framing skin a few shades darker than Istne's and a face that fell to a teardrop chin. Though her lack of curves called to him less, he would not spit a gift horse in the face. At nineteen, she had yet to recover from the scandal of her affair with a young southern Lord that had not been her betrothed. Her father, Lord Aiofe of House Sertrios, Isyldill's Southern Commander, had shipped her off to Sertrios' northern counterpart, House Bryant, away from family and friends in retribution. If rumors from the guards and maids were to be trusted, that had not stopped her carnal thrills.

He hoped the same favors would extend to him. If they did, victory was his. No matter what, he was going to win the bet against his closest friend, Lordling Grayson of House Lyssandre. He had been working too hard not to be the first to lose his virginity. A sly grin built up his face. Grayson was going to lose.

The bet had only three rules: no using their titles, no being forceful, and no whores. No servants was also implied. Besides, he refused to debase himself to let a commoner be his first. The victor would be awarded prowess and bragging rights for stretches to come. Plus, Andreiyes was looking forward to keeping his favorite hound and taking ownership of Grayson's favored horse.

But how to convince Ladyling Lorelai? He had never successfully seduced a woman before. He had tried four different tactics and failed each time. Two girls had run off from him, red with embarrassment. One had stared at him without a sound until he had felt uneasy and left. The last had remained proper to his person but laughed at his antics behind his back. If he was not a princeling, he probably would have received a slap or two. Perhaps that meant Grayson had incurred at least one red cheek. Andreiyes chuckled at that thought.

The question remained. What could he do to change the outcome with Lorelai? That made his nerves jitter. Andreiyes' mind was already conjuring another rejection scenario.

He rehearsed a few greetings in his head and dismissed them just as quickly. All weak, foolish, naïve. If only he had mastered all the tactics of seduction he overhead from laidback guardsmen during his late-night walks around each estate he was welcomed in. Those men were never ashamed of bragging about their success while hard at play in a card game of Four Fates.

Andreiyes tightened his fists at his sides and exhaled a deep breath. He was a gods' given Princeling of Isyldill. By Aethel's good graces, he could do this. He imagined what Lorelai might look like naked. That was all the motivation he needed. He plucked a purple Gaian rose from a nearby bush, tore off the thorns, and waltzed into the garden alcove where the two women sat.

"Your Highness." Ladyling Istne vaulted from her laid back position to her feet. The V of her corset looked to have poked her belly in the process. She panted, the exposed half of her breasts bouncing with her breaths as she curtsied until the bottom of her gown bunched against the grass.

Ladyling Lorelai slowly joined her on her feet, her dark gaze measured and calculating. Whereas Istne was the epitome of innocence, Lorelai exuded awareness. He bit back his nervousness. Maybe the rumors were wrong.

"To what do we owe the honor of yer presence?" Lorelai asked. An unnerving smile played on her lips as she maintained eye contact. Her southern Isyldillian brogue had him welting.

'*Never show doubt. Be decisive.*' His father's words encouraged him. He turned from Lorelai to face her companion. "I heard your sweet voice on the air, Ladyling Istne, and happened upon a goddess' flower." He presented her with the rose and made a point to avoid Lorelai entirely. "Its delicately veined petals, regal color, and the pearl it hides reminded me of the hidden gem you are. I simply had to present it to you."

Istne's eyes widened, her pale cheeks flushing pink. "I'm to be married in two months, your Highness. You…you witnessed the contract. You saw me sign."

"Does not mean I cannot flatter you as you deserve. Does not mean I cannot state I wish you had not signed." He knew *that* would fluster her.

Her entire face turned red, blending it with her hair. Her eyes jumped back and forth as her breath hitched. "I must go. Your Highness. My father, he requires my presence."

The ladyling spun on her heels with a mere curtsy followed by a one-word apology to her friend before scurrying away from him. Andreiyes smirked. At least he was a master at making women run away. For added effect, he trailed her departure with his eyes and watched her go from the edge of the alcove.

"So, yer Highness," a seductive voice said from behind him. "Was ignoring me yer plan then?"

So far so good. "'Tis working, is it not?"

Ladyling Lorelai's dress ruffled, her steps nearing until she stood at his side, eyes on Istne's retreating figure. "Ye've got more cunning than I gave ye credit for."

"I have motivation to be."

"Aye, I suppose. Men and *boys* are, after all, run by a limited number of desires."

"You speak so informally, Lorelai."

"We both know what ye're after."

"Is this how you seduce *men* to your bed?" He finally turned toward her, tamping down his eagerness.

"Rumors are rarely to be taken seriously. Why, just this morn I heard ye'd lain with four women in less than two nights."

He raised a brow. "Are you denying the reason behind your sojourn with House Bryant?"

"Oh no." She giggled. "I'm quite proud of that shame. Teaches my father well to match me with an old wart. But ye'll not find a mindless whore in my place."

His confidence dwindled. "Nothing I say can seduce you?"

"I did not say that. Ye're a fine young lad who I imagine quite a few will fawn over in good time. But I want a husband, one that I want, not at my father's behest. If ye agree to put a word in with yer uncle and insist on the matter, I'll warm yer bed for one night. More than willingly." She smiled sweetly.

Andreiyes' mouth went dry. Uncle Tellis of Royal House Lenierz, crown prince of Isyldill, was easy enough of a man to convince of many things if he was caught in a good disposition. It was still within the parameters of the bet, but teetering outside with her request, though he and Grayson had not established a rule against nonmonetary exchanges.

"That is all it would take?" he asked suspiciously.

She chuckled and glanced at him over her shoulder. "No, your Highness, that would be too simple. I'll need ye to retrieve a little something for me in good faith first. Just to make sure ye're as willing as I."

❊⇂❊

*A*ndreiyes slapped the heel of his palm against his forehead before swiping his fingers through his loose curls. The tapping of his boots echoed off the corridor walls as he neared the Council Room. This was not how he had envisioned the morning turning out. Retrieve a little something, she said. It means the world to me, she said. Cunning, conniving little minx. Were women in their prime all like this?

Here he was, about to enter a chamber he had never been privy to whether at Castle Ravensten – his home – or any other estate he had visited, to retrieve a family ring Lorelai's father had given to Lord Pascual for safekeeping. She had turned Andreiyes into her own personal stooge. Grandfather would take a cane to Andreiyes' fingers for this if the old king knew what Andreiyes was planning. He should not have agreed to this, but the reward…His imagination sprung free. He grinned. The reward was definitely worth it.

He tiptoed to the nearest intersection of hallways and peered around the corner. Only one guard stood at the Council Room's door. Gaia bless his luck. From the pocket of his tunic, he removed a few rocks collected from the garden paths and kneaded them between his fingers. Four doors down stood a suit of armor preserved from the olden days of Schlenkra, when the gods chose sides in the battle between man and beasts - a treasured relic accumulating centuries of dust.

Andreiyes snickered. Funny how armor ended up as his prey more often than game on a hunt. There was the time he and Grayson had stuffed turf and clay in the top halves of four sets at House Lyssandre's Millau Manor until dirt and grass stuck out from the joints. They had then styled them in different dance poses – pauldrons, spaulders, and gauntlets out to the side or above the head. It was worth quite a few laughs despite the cleaning. Or there was the time he had strung one up by the torso to frighten his sisters half to death. It had worked perfectly. Their guard had even attempted to fight off the faux foe for a few moments.

This time would not be nearly as comical but would serve to accomplish his goal. He took aim. The first stone ricocheted off the wall and clanged against the back of the armor. The guard's head spun in that direction, but frustratingly the man did not move away.

Andreiyes prepared another stone, the helm in his sights. He let loose. The rock collided against the metal with a bang. The helmet tumbled off the gorget's raised neckline and clashed against the shoulder pauldrons on the way down. The rest of it followed suit in glorious cacophony.

The Council Chamber's guard jerked at the sound and hustled to the pile of scrap metal.

"Nogo's pits," the man cursed. He turned down the corridor, his calls for servants echoing off the walls.

Andreiyes chortled, hand over his mouth to limit the noise, and gave himself a pat on the back. Almost too simple. He slunk toward the door. The latch clicked, and the door opened without a creak. He slipped in and closed it soundlessly behind him.

There was not a window in sight. Not a single torch was lit, but the room was far from stale. A whiff of smoke and floral scents lingered on the air. How in all Taelgir did they hold half-day meetings in the dark? Were Council Chambers at the castle and each estate always this shrouded in darkness? He patted along a wall. No sconces. This challenge had suddenly become much harder. He advanced further inside, arms stretched out. Four steps in, his fingers met a polished and grooved surface that descended downward to a cushion and then further to the ground. His other hand met the same textures. Chairs.

Feet shuffled to his far left. A heavy sigh was released. Andreiyes froze. There was someone else in the pitch-black room with him. As his eyes finished adjusting, he craned his head in search of the interloper. Along the floor to his left in a straight line and up opposite walls, a soft light shined as though the chamber was separated in two with a thick drape.

"How much longer until the shift change?" a feminine voice asked, void of the general lilt of the Isyldillian accent.

Only the disciples of the Order of Stewards spoke in that manner – the Greenlings, Mentees, Foremen, and Masters. They were the gods' guardians. They had the ability to manipulate and wield drynn – Taelgir's life source present in everyone and everything – in order to enforce the gods' will. There were rumors of people in the general population of Isyldill having minute drynn wielding abilities, but never had a royal born since the Apostate War five hundred stretches before shown signs of having any talent whatsoever.

Nogo's wrath be on him, what had he gotten himself into? Lady luck had damned him if there were Masters here. Grandfather would hear of this, and not even Father would be able to save him from the lashings.

"A whiner is rarely sought after," a deep voice replied. "You're not going to be reassigned to the Temple anytime soon, Greenling Faina, if you can't handle a simple watch here."

Andreiyes frowned, utterly confused. Light on his feet, he approached the curtain, careful to feel the surroundings with his hands for any obstacles. Curiosity beat out the threat of punishment as he gently pried aside the thick cloth. A puff of concentrated incense made his eyes water.

Spots marred his vision from the sudden lighting. It was not bright, more like a tapered glow that illuminated the little corner in a yellow hue emanating from the middle of this closed off section. Hundreds, no, thousands of specks shined there, floating horizontally up to his hip in height. In some areas, the dots were clustered, their glow dense. Most of those clusters were located throughout the center stretch of the plot, ranging from one side to the other. Some of the dots shifted snail-pace in different directions, but most were unmoving. A firm, golden line surrounded them all, crevassed and curved into a shape he recognized but could not put his finger on.

A shiver crept down Andreiyes' spine. A Master's wielding of drynn he could somewhat predict. Their types of talents were known and established. This, whatever it was, was unnatural in its appearance and secrecy. He had never even heard a rumor of this floating mass of speckled golden light.

He stiffened as a hooded figure in a gray robe snaked around the glow. Another figure in a similar garment, a yellow that melted into the light, meandered through the display without a single disturbance to the arrangement. No blue robes meant no Masters. Tension released from Andreiyes' shoulders. These two were far lower on the Order's hierarchy. Yellow robed Greenlings were closer to the regular folk than any other of the Order's representatives, and gray Mentees were only one grade higher, their manipulations of drynn limited as far as Andreiyes had read.

He trailed their movements. If caught, those two underlings could still cause him some trouble.

Pressure condensed against his chest as a cluster brightened in the middle of the floating mass of specks for a few grainfalls before the light flickered away and undulated in ripples over the other specks in waves.

"Mentee Tilson, do you see that?"

"Yes. From where? Where did it emanate?"

"Here." The Greenling woman pointed to the epicenter.

"Keep your finger there." The Mentee rummaged through a case of scrolls in the far corner. He pried one out and unrolled it directly beneath the glowing, horizontal mass. "The Millau Estate."

Breath caught in Andreiyes' throat. Now he recognized the shape of the dotted spectacle – an unruly line at the bottom to reflect the southern coastal line, the curved inward lines around lakes that belonged to the Lakoldesh kingdom, the sharp contours that delimited the ridged borders with Gyldrise, and the straight edge at the top that ran along Telfinor. This was a map of Isyldill. But what in all Taelgir did House Lyssandre's manor have to do with this?

He squinted to better observe the clusters of specks. Strangely, each dense glow mirrored the placement of Isyldill's largest cities and large estates. He had been forced in his royal studies to memorize enough material on Isyldillian geography and topography to plot their locations on a blank map. A few of the dimmer clumps of dots, he recognized as towns and small settlements. It stood to reason that the range of brightness reflected population size, which meant that each speck was a subject. '*We are all chattel to the realm like cattle with their brands,*' Father had once said. The words made more sense now, yet had him gulping with unease. Absentmindedly, Andreiyes rubbed the griffin head mark on his forearm.

"We are the closest watch," Faina said with excitement.

"And with the Commander of the North. Send a falker with news to the Archchancellor, then notify Lord Bryant. He needs to be ready to receive word from his King." The male Mentee bent over to gaze at the ripples' point of origin while the Greenling woman tapped her fist to her chest.

"For the Faith," she said and bowed as she turned to the curtain.

Andreiyes scrambled away, following the length of the curtain in the darkness to the other side of the Council Chamber. His foot bumped a chair, its scrape on stone barely a whisper, yet he froze. The curtain was pulled away, dousing the room with a faint glint. Sending a falker to the Order's head in Telfinor sounded urgent. The rare mixed breed between falcon and raven were used to relay messages in only the direst of circumstances.

"Faina." The woman turned toward the speaker. "*This* is how you get your work acknowledged. Attention. Patience. Duty."

"Yes, Mentee. Thank you."

The woman bounced forward with a skip to her steps as the curtain swerved back in place. She paid Andreiyes no attention – not when she passed an arm's length in front of him, not when she opened the door and torchlight from the corridor flooded the chamber, and not when she gave a last glance toward the curtain, face hidden in the shadows of her hood. Still, Andreiyes did not relax. Instead, he cursed himself as a monstrous fool.

In the corridor, the guard stood once again at his post, the armor distraction at its end. Not only had he not retrieved the ring, but Andreiyes had no blithering idea how to pass by him unseen. The Council Chamber's door clicked shut. This time, he welcomed the encasing darkness.

Four

The Order's Temple - Telfinor

The mausoleum was graciously empty that morning, giving Master Rau Hirai the peace of mind he craved. No one to pester him. No duty to be done. He could mourn the length of his long, long life in silence.

Birdsong filtered in through the open ceiling of each mourning alcove, a note of happiness in their tunes contrasting with the whistling breeze through the winding corridor. Floral fumes lingered in the air from incense burned the previous night. It nearly overwhelmed the aroma of wet soil. His boots clacked against the marble tiles as he followed the curved pathway past dozens of family alcoves left and right, a grieving tree growing in each.

Rau's sapphire robes ruffled behind him. At the sixtieth alcove on the left, he knelt and placed the bouquet of blue forget-me-nots clenched against his chest at the base of his wife and daughter's grieving tree.

He whisked dried leaves and fallen twigs off the plaques embedded at the base of the tree trunk. His fingers lingered over their engraved names – Moira Ly Hirai (born 429, died 434) and Tilnee Ly Hirai (born 405, died 435). His daughter's face had been chiseled onto the plaque, but after centuries of visits, the embossment had eroded almost entirely. All that remained was the curve of her nose and the dips of her mono-lid eyes that mirrored his own. Five hundred and twelve stretches had passed since he had seen her smile, heard her voice, or held her tiny figure in his arms. Five centuries since she had plucked the petals off her last forget-me-not.

Her tree should have withered and died two centuries ago like most of the grieving trees that had been planted that fateful stretch, like he himself should have long before that. Whereas many Stewards had replaced their original family grieving tree with a fresh seed, Moira's had continued to flourish, its black bark firm, its blood-red leaves flexible and forever unaffected by the seasons. Its secret was the same that prolonged his own ageless lifespan.

The waters from the Well of Unity were blessed by Gaia's tears. They strengthened and renewed the flow of drynn within everything they touched. Every few stretches, Rau sprinkled some of the Well's waters on the roots to prolong its lifespan. With it, a part of her was still with him. It gave him a reason to keep on going. To ensure that what happened to her would never happen again.

"One day soon, my little greenling." He pressed his fingers to his lips and returned them to the plaque. "We'll be together again."

In the distance, heavy steps pounded their way over the tile. Rau shook his head with a sigh.

"Master," a young winded voice called. "Master Rau. You're…you're needed. His Eminence… requires your presence."

Rau spared the messenger a wry glance as he shoved his skeletal hands into the sleeve of the other arm. Bent over and gasping for air was a Greenling in yellow robes, hair shaved to indicate his recent induction to the Order. Either he was the son of another Steward or this young man was one of the rare few in Telfinor discovered with talent.

"Your name, Greenling?" Rau asked.

He rubbed one of the grieving tree's leaves between his fingers, careful that his sleeves covered his hands. The veins were plump, the blade soft. It was healthy and would not need more Well's water for at least another two stretches.

"Greenling Cliof, Master. I am Master Ilor and Foreman Telef's son."

Now that was an interesting lineage. As Rau observed the young man, he honed onto the aura of drynn around them. The particles encompassed everything and everyone, more present in some than others, but were constantly in motion. The more one could take in, the more likely they were to have a talent. This Greenling had them in spades, glowing the Telfinorian silver as it streamed through his body. With practice, diligence and time, Cliof could become a Master like his mother. His drynn's flow had not yet stabilized and moved erratically without rhyme, making it difficult for Rau to decipher his talent. It was not unusual for new inductees. Once their talents began to show on their twenty-fifth name-day, it generally required a month for them to adjust to the strain of strong drynn flow.

"I've been eager to meet you. Mom and Pop speak highly of you, but you didn't come to my initiation ceremony."

Rau grunted. He no longer held the patience to attend any more of those, rare as they were. Watched one, watched them all. And they were dreadfully tedious.

"When the Archchancellor ordered for you to be found, I jumped at the opportunity. It's an honor. I can't wait to learn from you. Everyone says your classes…"

The fellow went on and on. Rau rubbed his brow, a headache taking root, then traced the deep scar on his left temple that stretched down his sunken cheek to his chin. Before Cliof ever became a Master, he would need to learn when to hold his tongue.

"Greenling." Rau held up a hand and gritted his teeth. "Get to the point."

"Sorry, Master. There's a Flawed. I mean, the ripple of a Flawed was spotted."

Rau's brow furrowed. "Why does his Excellency require my presence?"

"He didn't say."

Rau rubbed one emaciated palm against the knuckles of the other, tugging on the skin. Each Flawed birth was a potential threat to the Order's hold on the balance of power across the realms, and this was the third Flawed birth in the first twenty-three days of the stretch. As the population in the realms increased each decade, it was expected that the ratio of Flawed births would follow suit, yet the rate was growing exponentially.

But he wasn't needed to handle these Flawed – there was no point while he remained perpetually in Telfinor at the temple. Besides, Archchancellor Aroawn always commissioned the local rulers of the realms concerned to deal with it and its mother. That was far more effective than sending out a Master to ride days into another kingdom.

Perhaps this Flawed had escaped. That would be troublesome. It had happened before, but those had always thankfully been caught. Or, maybe this was in regards to all the whisperings he had noticed of late between the Archchancellor, Master Aileen and Master Ohenor.

With a heavy sigh, Rau rose to his feet and strode through the mausoleum's winding corridor, not waiting for Cliof to match his gait. Best not to keep his Eminence waiting too long.

Once outside, he pulled up his robe's hood. The wind beat the cloth against his face as his features fell into the shadows. He shielded his hands inside his sleeves, their gauntness a reminder of his unending sacrifice. Only a handful of the Masters remained from the era of the Apostate War. The younger Stewards thought it appropriate to gawk at, whisper about and praise the old ones. While Archchancellor Aroawn and others like Master Aileen adored the reverence, Rau found it taxing and burdensome. What was there to praise? It was the reason he preferred to wear the sapphire robes of a Master with his face hidden instead of his Steward High Council blues, with the Eidenhail tree embroidered in white along the front. He blended in better this way.

He strode past the strip of land between the mausoleum and the Temple used for crops and nodded a greeting to a farmer who wished him well. This land was one of the few places in Telfinor where the soil remained fertile enough for crop growth, but it wasn't enough to feed all the mouths between the Temple and the towns nearby. Continued hunger across Telfinor made the food offerings to the Order from the other realms that much more crucial. At least here, the crop field was sheltered by the mausoleum from the harsh Telfinorian winds.

The building was arranged in a crescent moon shape around the rear of the Order's temple. It housed two hundred fifty-three family graves and their grieving trees, which fed off the obsidian rock that covered the landscape. It also protected the Temple by surrounding it with a wall of stone and a sea of red leaves so that potential attackers were detoured to the Temple's front gates. Never again would the Temple's defenses be breached.

At the gates, a long line of Telfinorians awaited admittance to the Temple despite the morning hour for either worship, work, or a ration of food in their overalls and loose dresses of muted colors. They occupied every inch of space and blocked Rau from rushing his way through unseen. Their conversations were heavy on the air, a patchwork of different voices and words.

As the most gifted Hefter currently alive, he could manipulate the flow of drynn in all things living or inanimate. With a simple thought, he shoved aside a column of drynn from each man, woman and child in line. Like a dance, they each stumbled one step to the side in unison. Silence now reigned as he charged forward through the gates, the lower courtyard and gardens, and into the foyer inclining his head in quick nods to his fellow Brother and Sisters.

"Master Rau," Greenling Cliof called, only two steps behind him. He had almost forgotten about the young man. "What you did back there was simply amazing."

Rau ignored the eager inductee and headed for the floor to ceiling stone doors that barred passage to the Chamber of Concords where the council usually met. The left door depicting the goddess' sculpted form was ajar, but no sounds filtered out. Rau forced it open further. All twelve seats were empty, and the fireplace was unlit.

"The way you displaced an entire row of people without them feeling even the slightest twinge of pain and without breaking a sweat, that's just-"

"Greenling," Rau scolded. "Where? Where am I summoned?"

"Oh, yes, sorry. He instructed for you to meet him in the Remembrance Tower."

Rau winced. "Are you certain?"

The young man pounded his chest with his fist. "As sure as the Faith."

With apprehension, Rau climbed the steps up the southeastern tower to its highest room, now ordained 'Remembrance Tower'. Over five hundred stretches had passed since the events that lent credence to the tower's name, yet his gut still twisted at how easily the memories returned as fear dug into the pit of his soul. He remembered the smell – the sweetened stench of new rot. He gagged and scaled the winding stairs. Aroawn's gravelly voice carried in an echo from the chamber above. Back when the massacre had occurred, the stillness of the air and the lack of noise had made Rau lose all hope. This new commotion made his ears ring.

On the last step, Rau took a deep breath and glanced around the chamber. The circular room's exposed stone from centuries ago was covered in black clay, smoothed to perfection, atop which the names of all those lost in the Apostate War were painted in white cursive. Plush rugs shrouded the bloodstains on the flooring that deep scrubbing could not remove. An armchair and footrest were pressed against one wall. Two side tables cradled the chair – an empty chalice on one and a half-eaten plate of food on the other. The far side of the room was adorned by a four-poster bed so out of place with the chamber's history of violence and a trestle table littered with dozens of scrolls. The only thing that had not changed was the view from the room's sole window.

From it, the long entry line through the Temple's gates was on full display. Telfinor's barren land stretched as far as the eye could see, villages carved into the volcanic obsidian stone. It was difficult to imagine from this view that all of that black stone and dead earth vanished and transformed into lush greenery once the borders with Isyldill or Lakoldon were crossed.

Despite the changes to the chamber, the image of the bodies arranged in two rows – adults and children – haunted his memories. Moira's body had been so cold, so pale. Touching her lifeless hand had chilled Rau to the bone, a sting that he could still feel every now and then, like an old wound.

"Good of you to join us, old friend," Aroawn said

Rau swallowed the bile that threatened to come up and snapped his attention to the Archchancellor's gaunt face. Stretches of taking the Well's Waters had not fared any better on his old mentor's physique than his own – sunken cheeks, his dark skin speckled with discolorations, and features taut except for distended frown lines around the forehead and eyes. Nevertheless, Aroawn did not look over sixty stretches old. The shine of the Archchancellor's raven black hair particularly contrasted the health of his face, braided to the crook in his back.

Master Aileen was hardly more appealing, her femininity turned skeletal. Master Ohenor was the healthiest out of the four of them in appearance, with fatty skin despite his aging features and peppered hair. He had worked hard to wean himself off the Well's Waters for over four decades, little by little, after receiving Aroawn's approval. It was a great feat to overcome the addiction and welcome aging and death. Another five to ten stretches and Ohenor would join his family in the mausoleum. Rau envied him for that.

He cleared his throat. "Another Flawed, I heard. That takes precedence over my unease."

"Yes." The Archchancellor inclined his head.

"Where?"

"Isyldill," Aileen said. "We're near positive it belongs to House Lyssandre."

"Has it escaped?"

"No."

"Then, why the reunion? The methods we apply go nearly without fail. What's different now? You're not planning on letting it be, are you? After what was foretold-"

"No, my friend." Aroawn held up his hands. "It shall die, like all of them. You know very well I'm not lenient."

Rau eyed the three of them warily. "What is it then?"

With a nod from Aroawn, Ohenor stepped to the trestle table and unrolled the scrolls one by one. "For decades now, we've been mapping Flawed lineages as far back as ten generations to find a way to predict their appearance. At first, we thought they were at random, but it's become clear they appear in families with ties to the gods."

"You mean to say, in other circumstances, they would have become Brothers and Sisters of the Order once maturity was reached?"

Aroawn crossed his arms as Ohenor cleared his throat. "No, no, of course not. They're aberrations. A Flawed never existed before the Apostate War, and therefore none were ever admitted to the Order. To be honest, what they are is not clear."

"What *exactly* are we here to discuss?"

Aileen leaned over the table on her fists. "Ohenor and myself have discovered a correlation. Flawed descend from godly lineages. Weak or strong, bland or blessed skin, it doesn't matter. The murky part is that not every god lineage produces a Flawed. Yet, once a Flawed appears in a family, others in that lineage are far more likely to produce another one. There's at least a twenty percent increase in the likelihood the Marked sibling of a Flawed will have Flawed progeny within their next two generations."

Rau's throat dried as his gaze jumped from one to the other. "Tell me you're not suggesting what I think you are."

"End the lines and the rate of Flawed births will decline drastically. It's a good plan." Aileen sounded so proud of herself. She'd always been quick to jump to action, but this…this went beyond preservation and stability.

"You're implying a massacre. If we do this, if we annihilate entire lineages, how are we any better than the royals that killed hundreds of us?"

"We're nothing like them," Aileen spat. Her lips curled in disgust.

Rau shook his head with disbelief. "You've already decided."

Aroawn gave Rau's shoulders a few reassuring squeezes. "We must be ahead of the enemy, my friend. For all the horrors the royals committed, many in this very room. What they did to your Moira, to my sons and all the others, and for the damage they tried to inflict on the foundation of the Order and the power they sought, we must do *everything* we can to prevent it from happening again. This is what we've survived for. You know this."

Chest tight, Rau glanced around the room. His gaze fixed on the foot of the bed. There, right there was where he had cradled his daughter's lifeless form.

Aroawn tapped Rau's cheek. Those dark brown eyes with Telfinor's silver ring around their irises mirrored his pain and melancholy. It stretched into compassion and tenderness. "We are Brothers for a reason, old friend. We are the bridge between the gods and the people. We are the balance between the realms. We must maintain the stability the gods established. It's our mission, and we have all sworn to see it through. Yes?"

Rau nodded. Aroawn was right. It was for the good of all. What they were doing was just. They needed to preserve the Order and keep the royals sedate. It was the gods' plan, their will, their hope for all Taelgir. This was the easiest way to accomplish their goal, but that didn't make it the right choice. All that violence, all the blood spilt. It seemed never-ending. There had to be a better way.

'Have I ever led you astray?' Aroawn's voice echoed in his mind, the pull of the man's Sayer talent opening a drynn pathway between their minds for a private discussion.

Rau shut down his doubt. He would need to think on it later, when his thoughts were less exposed. *'Why not tell me before?'*

A soft smile played in the corners of Aroawn's pinched lips. *'Because there are times, I and others fear you've gone soft. You tend to prefer watching without taking part.'*

'Observation is crucial.'

'So is reaction.'

'I'm not one to abandon my duty.' Rau held back an eye roll out of respect for his old mentor. *'This is why you instructed we meet in this tower. To force my hand.'*

'Yes.' The answer was so readily given. It made Rau's stomach churn.

'But why tell me now, and not with the remainder of the council?'

'Because I need your sway with them. I may be Archchancellor, but they listen to your voice of reason as much as they do mine. They will need to be persuaded for future Flawed. We can do it together, old friend, like old times.'

"The longer we stand around here without his Eminence giving the orders, the longer the Flawed has to escape." Aileen scowled. She had ten more stretches in the Order than Rau and despite their long collaboration, never let him forget it. Her belief that seniority played into favoritism with Aroawn had made Rau sigh with exasperation on more than one occasion. She tapped her foot with impatience. Ohenor, to her side, nodded in agreement.

"You chose me for the council for a reason, Aroawn." Rau ignored the other two Masters, his gaze fixed on his old mentor. "Matters like this should be discussed, the pros and cons weighed. Logic comes from all sides."

Aileen scoffed. "Pretty words from someone who hasn't crossed Telfinor's borders in more than a century. Cowards discuss, Rau. Risk-takers achieve."

"Violence is not always the key."

"Enough," Aroawn grumbled. "In the future, yes, I shall be more mindful. We all shall. For now, King Triunn must announce this new edict before any further time is wasted. I trust the three of you to keep watch."

Without waiting for further responses, Aroawn crossed the room to the armchair, adjusted his white robes as he sat, and closed his eyes. Silence fell on their small group, and unease settled in Rau's chest. Whenever Aroawn used his ability to project himself outward and transfer his consciousness into one of the rulers of the four other realms, his body was at its most vulnerable. It became a shell, and while Aroawn was one of the most capable Stewards of the Order, he had no defenses if an attack came while he was under. It made the choice of this room for these types of dealings more...understandable.

The moment Aroawn disconnected from his body, a shockwave tremored through the drynn in the room, tickling up the soles of Rau's boots. The drynn in Aroawn's body quivered with each inhale and exhale. Some of the particles shot out of Aroawn and incorporated with bundles of drynn formed in the air, walls and floor. The longer his mind lingered away from his body, the more erratic the drynn movement became and the more particles he lost. Aroawn often spent sandturns in this condition, sometimes days depending on which matters needed his oversight. In those situations, the Archchancellor was force-fed Well's water while under to restore and steady his drynn flow.

The sun reached midday before the stray drynn that had left Aroawn snapped back into its owner. The Archchancellor opened his eyes, new rings beneath them marring his already dark skin.

"It will be done." Aroawn rubbed his temples. "Now the four of us, we work together to convince the council of this continued course of action."

Five

Millau Manor - Isyldill

*A*t past midday, news spread throughout the estate that a force of one hundred strong were marching on the horizon. All that for tiny little Thad. Kaianne couldn't wrap her head around the concept as she stared listlessly out the window at the pelting rain. At least the weather could feel what she couldn't.

What was the point? Thad was already dead. She had swaddled his tiny form in a blanket embroidered with their 'L' and House emblem of a feather crossed with a griffin's talon. No other funeral service would be given to him, Papa had said, so she had applied herself to the task far more diligently than necessary. Doing and redoing until it reached perfection and Thad looked like the sweet sleeping babe he should have been.

As for Mama, she still had not woken. A fever had set in, and the healers were far from optimistic. Kaianne had heard whispers from passing servants. Rumors of a Flawed child in the estate were spreading despite Papa's wishes. The staff spoke of the blight the Flawed were on the land and their families. They also spoke of the fate generally bestowed on the mothers that dared to birth one. That chilled Kaianne to the bone, and she prayed the rumors were exaggerated.

The rain battered against the window and ground with determination and vigor. It blanketed the horde of kingsmen in the distance and blurred the estate's front gates. Papa was out there, in the courtyard with Deacon and Grayson. His silhouette alone advanced toward the dark mass while Lyssandre guards pried the gates open.

She prayed for his plan to work. He would hand over Thad's wrapped body as a measure of goodwill with the optimism that his act and their family name held enough weight. It had to be sufficient to demand leniency for Mama. She had not chosen to birth a Flawed. Mama was no traitor.

A sole figure on horseback greeted Papa halfway. For a while, nothing happened. Kaianne gripped the curtain, wishing she could hear the conversation. When the outsider lunged and Papa slumped to the ground, not moving, her breath caught in her throat. In the courtyard, coordinated cries ordered the men on the ramparts to rush into place. Deacon hauled Grayson's yelling and kicking form back to the mansion, the words overridden by the torrent. She watched, unable to pry her eyes away.

The mass of intruders filtered in through the gates and filled the courtyard in sandfalls. Their swords slashed at anyone resisting, four against one in most cases. This was not how things were supposed to happen. The Lyssandre reserve of twenty guards was no match, one by one falling.

Kaianne strode to the chest at the foot of her canopy bed. She had never unsheathed the dagger Grandpa had gifted her as part of her dowry on her tenth name-day. It was a family heirloom, the Lyssandre 'L' carved into the blade and its silver sheath. No one had ever bothered to show her how to use a weapon, but now was as good a time as any to learn. Girl or not, she refused to be taken against her will or killed without a fight.

She crossed the room to the door, her steps more confident than the thumping of her heart and crept into the hallway. The clanking of swords was muffled and distant, giving her a boost of confidence. A quick prayer for Mama — there was little to be done for her now — then she hurried for the west wing in search of her brothers. Deacon and Grayson might be able to handle themselves, but Adelmo and even Eryk needed looking after.

Heavy thunder growled as she reached the foyer's stairway. She clutched the handrails and paused. There was no movement in the west wing's hallway – not a single maid, not a guard for the boys, nor even a half-opened door for them to peer out of. If her two youngest siblings had followed Papa out with Deacon and Grayson, they wouldn't be in their chambers. She peered downstairs where servants scurried to hide as the fighting neared. The rain no longer drowned out the clatter. Where could they be?

A body crashed through the front doors. Glass shattered. Wood splintered, the panels dangling from their hinges. Kingsmen in Isyldillian amber and brown colors spilled in through the damage and surrounded the guardsman sprawled on the ground and grappling for his weapon. For a moment, Kaianne breathed easier – they were saved – until an incomer impaled the Lyssandre man. She muffled a scream with one hand and ducked behind the balusters. Heads snapped upward in her direction, and a group of three neared the bottom steps. Nogo's wrath. She ran.

Their steps pounded up the stairs as she rushed down the west wing, her pants louder than her soft soled footfalls. She entered the first room on the right, an antechamber. It connected all the way across Papa's suite from his chambers to his parlor and thankfully, the gardens. Hopefully the others didn't know. She slammed the door behind her, no pause in her strides, then crossed to the side door that led to his dressing rooms. She barreled past three more chambers before the first clack of a door sounded in the distance. Sprinting the last five paces, she locked the parlor side door behind her and slumped against it for a few grainfalls.

Papa used his parlor as a private study, his desk and chairs occupying the bulk of the rug covered floor while bookcases lined the walls. Floor to ceiling windows replaced one wall with a panel serving as an access down to the lower floor and gardens. Right now, there was no better safe haven than outside. She scurried to the door, hand on the knob, when a sniffle and sob made her freeze. In the shadows beneath Papa's desk, a small figure moved.

"Who's there?" she whispered.

"Kay?" a little voice croaked. Adelmo crawled out, a fist wiping tears from his chubby cheeks.

Kaianne knelt down and crushed the five-stretch-old in her arms. One kiss on his head for the relief of finding a sibling, two more for the worry he'd put her through. She brushed aside his bangs. "You had me worried, Adi. I had no idea where to find you."

Another door clacked, not too far off.

Kaianne jumped to her feet. "Take my hand. We cannot stay here."

"To where?"

"To find the others. Dea will know what to do."

She clutched his little fingers in a tight grip and tugged him through the opened glass door, onto the stone terrace and down the steps, ignoring his whining protests. Finding their siblings was her mission. Beyond that, she refused to think on it. Papa was dead. Mama was dying, and who knew who remained standing. Slain by Isyldill's own. Where was the logic in it?

The amber and bronze tunics had always made her feel safe and secure. They had escorted the Lyssandre carriage on numerous visits across the realm. They had been the ones to rescue her after climbing too high in trees, and they had been the ones who returned Eryk safely after a bandit's ransom. Now they were her family's murderers. She smeared a runaway tear across her cheek.

When she and Adelmo exited Papa's private gardens into the estate's rear courtyard, she still had no idea where to search for her brothers within the three acres of land, forest, and buildings. Rain plummeted down at them from an angle and fogged away anything more than ten steps ahead. Within moments, she was soaked head-to-toe, gown fused to her skin. Water fell from her hair into her eyes, more coming from the skies. No amount of wiping was enough to see. Perhaps climbing a tree for shelter would offer a better vantage point. Kingsmen were also less likely to find them up there.

"Where are they?" Adelmo asked.

Kaianne pressed a finger to her lips for silence and crept around bushes, dragging Adelmo's little shape behind her. Pebbles ground underfoot, digging into her soles. The goal was to reach the great oak tree that stood alone between the masterpieces of trimmed hedges, flowerbeds, fountains and ponds. From there, she would have a view of both the manor and woods when it stopped raining. If necessary, she and Adelmo could wait the attackers out.

She turned a hedged corner and smacked into the chest of another figure. His tunic was darkened from the wet but still amber and brown. Eyes widened in horror, she shoved Adelmo backward.

"Here men. Lyssandres," the kingsman cried as he clutched and twisted her arm until she shrieked and dropped the dagger.

"Adi, run. Find Dea," she screamed, tugging and squirming, over her shoulder. Adelmo did but toward the mansion, where too many of these Isyldillian traitors were probably stalking. "No, not that way."

His little figure kept going until he vanished in the rain. Blurred shadows were approaching throughout the gardens. She was trapped, her little brother soon to be as well, to be ransomed or killed like Papa and the man in the foyer.

When the kingsman drew his weapon, she lurched her knee into his groin like she had once done to Grayson when he and Yierd had harassed her into a corner. It had worked then, and it surprisingly worked now. Free from his grasp, she retrieved her small dagger and left the man to crumble to his knees on a groan.

"Serves you right."

Her feet squelched in her thin shoes as she raced to the manor. She had to find Adi. The squelching footfalls behind her quickened her steps. When playing hide-and-seek, her youngest brother never picked the same hiding place twice and teased Eryk when the eleven-stretch-old got discovered repeatedly in the same place. From that logic, Adelmo had not returned to Papa's chambers. Running from danger, Kaianne reasoned he would have picked the nearest entrance instead of hurrying further down the exterior of the east wing to Mama's access. The service entrance fit. Out of all the lower rooms, she rushed toward the kitchen. Even frightened as Adelmo was, his sweet tooth was likely to win him over if any lockleberry nutted buns remained from yesterday.

"Psst, Kay. Over here," his soft voice whispered.

Kaianne bit back a chuckle. The sly little one was comfortably holed up in a kitchen cupboard, hand holding a bun, chewing with one cheek rounded.

"You got away?" he muttered in between bites.

"Of course." She furrowed her brow. "Nothing was going to stop me from getting back to you. Now, come on. We cannot-"

Shouts and a scuffle echoed down the corridor leading to the pantry, larder, and storeroom. Besides climbing up the oven's chimney alcove, the kitchen had no other hiding spots. Without a tablecloth, the table offered no shelter, neither did its benches. Adelmo might have fit in one of the large banquet pots, but she never could. And she was not about to leave him alone with men after them.

"*Scooch*," she whisper-yelled to her brother. They could both fit in his cupboard. "Now."

She shoved him to the side and scrambled in after him, hauling the excess of her soaked gown with her. A puddle remained where she had been.

The cabinet door was left ajar, just enough to see whatever came their way. Surprisingly, it was Deacon that raced into the kitchen, sword drawn.

Her eldest brother's tunic was torn and stained red on one arm and the left side of his torso. His hair was disheveled but dry, stuck to the rivulets of blood on his face. He panted, his wide-eyed gaze jumping from one corner of the room to the next. Kaianne gulped. Deacon had never looked this unsettled and savage before. When Adelmo moved to call out his name, Kaianne stifled the sound with her palm against his mouth.

Rushed steps resounded, and Deacon faced the incomers. She couldn't see how many from her sliver of a view, but Deacon's defensive posture implied it wasn't a fair fight.

Kaianne pushed the cabinet door open a little further. Three attackers – their faces ranging from sneers to pity, weapons at the ready. Nogo swallow them all, three-on-one were poor odds.

"Give it up, lordling."

Dea tossed jars, pots and pans at them, but it merely slowed their advance. Kaianne winced at the clanking and shattering racket that echoed off the walls. Two lunged and Deacon parried their attacks. His movements were inspiring. A step here, a duck there, a well-timed thrust, a block, a side-step. It was a dance, and he was showing more skill today than he had displayed in practice swordfights with Papa and the guardsmen. She held back a cheer and watched with pride as he stabbed one through. The second, a mountain of a man, charged. Deacon went on the offensive, swinging strong, forcing the kingsman back against the opposite wall. She squeezed her fists with excitement. He was doing it. He was winning.

A shadow stalked before the cabinet, legs blocking her view of Deacon. Gaia forsaken, she had forgotten the third man, and Deacon's back was facing her. The incomer prowled toward the fighting duo, a bastard sword in one hand, a short sword in the other, while her brother stayed oblivious. Gods below.

"Stay here," she ordered Adelmo. She ignored his grumbles as she thrust one side of the cabinet open and lunged for the man's legs.

She had never before so much appreciated the baked clay tiles in the serving quarters until that man tumbled and smacked his head against them with a bounce. His weapons clanked across the ground from his grip. She crawled over his form, dagger still sheathed, the stench of ripe sweat on his attire crinkling her nose. The man lay still, sprawled out, not making a sound nor even twitching. Her shaky breath stifled a chortle. By Aethel's good graces, she had done it and saved her brother – her, a girl.

A sputtered grunt pulled her gaze up. Deacon glared at her, horror in his rounded eyes. His snarling attacker stood at his back. That's when she saw the tip of a blade protruding from Deacon's chest. When the kingsman wrenched his sword out,

Deacon fell to his knees, his eyes never leaving hers. She shrieked. Blood trickled down his tunic. He mouthed '*run*' before crumpling to the floor. Deacon was dead. This was not how it was supposed to be. She was supposed to have saved him.

Deacon's murderer gave her no repose for the sick that pushed its way up. He pounced after her and slipped in the puddle, his fingers only grazing her dress while she vomited her morning meal and crabbed away. With the table separating them, she scrambled to her feet.

"Don't come any closer." She unsheathed her dowry dagger and pointed it with a trembling hand. Tears trickled down her chin unbidden. She trembled.

Why did this kingsman have to be so large? He stood almost two heads taller than her, shoulder width nearly double her size. Half an ear was missing. A knotted scar ran up one side of his neck to the corner of his mouth. His sneer worsened his look.

She went left, he mirrored. Right, he matched. She feinted one way and ran the other as he circled the table in the most heart pounding, terrifying game of chase. Once, twice, then with one roar of frustration he upended the table, which careened against the cupboard with a thud. It caught her foot, and she fell.

"Now I've caught myself a mouse." The kingsman fisted her hair and tugged her to her feet.

He glared at her with dark eyes that promised death. Fear twisted her gut, and she swerved the dagger toward his neck. With a tug on her hair, her aim went wild. The blade plunged instead into his shoulder through cloth, skin, and muscle easier than a knife through warm butter. Sick threatened to come up once more.

"So, it's suffering you want?" He wrenched the dagger from his shoulder and drove it into hers instead.

Her scream did nothing to dull the pain – the pulsing, burning heat that radiated from neck to fingertips. It wrecked through her skull and took over everything else. She barely felt the hand that squeezed off her airway, or the brush of her skirts being pulled up.

"Drop her," a familiar voice bellowed. Despite its anger, it soothed her, calmed some of the throbbing. Safe. Rescued. Behind her blurred vision, she could not make him out.

The kingsman loosened his grip but did not let go of her neck. "My Lord, this traitor caused me injury. I am only returning the favor."

"We are not monsters."

With a sickening thunk, the pressure on Kaianne's neck fell away entirely, but the pain remained. She flinched when a grip clenched onto her injured arm and shrieked when the blade was ripped out of her shoulder.

"Ynnea, dear child, I am so sorry." A large finger wiped away tears from her face.

She blinked away further tears. Lord Pascual stood before her, Willik wasn't far behind with his usual glare of annoyance, and her assailant lay on the ground.

"Oh, thank the gods." She threw herself in his arms and sobbed through the pain and relief. Her father's closest friend was the best sight she'd seen all day. His arms cradled her slowly. "They killed Papa. And Deacon. Mama's upstairs. I…I don't know if they got to her. I've no news of Grayson or Eryk. But Adelmo. At least Adelmo's safe."

He grabbed her face with both hands, the hilt of her dagger pressed to one cheek. "Tell me. Where is your little brother?"

His voice was gentle and calm. The crease of his eyes and soft smile were reassuring, yet his words were rushed. She shoved aside the unease and pointed to the cupboard and table blocking the cabinet doors.

"Here, help me get him out. Adi, we are going to get you out."

But Lord Pascual's grip around her tightened. Her arm ached from it.

"Hurry, Kay. It's dark in here." Adelmo's little voice shook.

"My Lord, please. My brother. Before more kingsmen come."

"Forgive me, Ynnea," Pascual whispered as he tugged her closer to him and kissed her temple. "I swear I would have loved you as a daughter. May the gods forgive me. For glory and realm."

Intense pressure, discomfort, and breathlessness struck her before the shock of pain hit – fiery and barbed, worse than the shoulder stabbing, far worse than being thrown from a horse. Her body threatened to keel in half. Still, Pascual did not release her. Liquid seeped through her gown, trickling down her undergarments to her feet. Her vision whitened and spotted with black, but she looked down for the source of her pain. Her dagger's hilt protruded from her lower belly. It hurt too much. Her legs gave out.

"Kay, please. Get me out." A stray tear barreled down her face at Adelmo's plea.

Forcing her head upward, she glanced at Lord Bryant. The same calm he always exuded remained fixed there. Placid, tender and deceitful eyes. His kindness had been too good to be true. She had thought so before. Now she knew it for certain. He gestured Willik forward, and without any remorse, her betrothed piled bags of wheat and flour against the upturned table to keep Adelmo captive in his cupboard.

"No," she grunted, reaching aimlessly as shivers wrecked through her. "Please. We trusted you."

Pascual laid her down on the ground. The tiles felt warm to her skin. Her fingers were numb. Her body shook. The scent of copper rested heavily on the air, yet she could not look away from him.

He caressed her head. "Trust me now when I say this pains me more than it does you."

His words did not register right away. When they had, he had already left and Willik stood above her with a horrible sneer on his face.

"Now you know your place." He hawked spit – her skin was too numb to feel where it landed – and turned away on his heels.

Adelmo rapped against the cabinet and table, screeching for freedom. Deacon's lifeless eyes stared right back into hers. Would events have changed if she had not demanded five stretches of freedom? The thought haunted her as blackness took over.

Six

S moke billowed on the horizon as Andreiyes pressed his horse into a gallop toward Millau Manor. A coincidence, he convinced himself. At each pulling stride, the stallion's strength and power recoiled up Andreiyes' calves. The rain had nearly stopped, the sky cracking open in sections to let light through. The sun was pushing past midafternoon. By the flooded hoof and tread marks loitering the Midway Highland Road, Commander Bryant's kingsmen had passed this way; more than seventy had already crossed him earlier on their march back to Zesco Manor.

An entire family for one Flawed – to think Grandfather had approved such measures. Someone was making a poor quip, or more than likely he had misheard the reading of the King's letter Lord Pascual had received by falker. He might have been able to convince himself of that if his Lordship had not left the Council Chamber unguarded in a rush, long enough for Andreiyes to slip out unseen while orders for the kingsmen's assembly were conveyed. That chamber *never* went unguarded.

The closer he drew to the Millau estate, the larger the black clouds seemed to blanket the fields in the distance that were in the midst of a last tillage and seeding before the Stretch of Gain's cycles grew too cold. The air smelled of ash, charred roast, and wet dirt. He slowed his pace on a hilltop no more than a mile away. It was a viewpoint that surveyed the land without the obstruction of forests or villages. He should have been able to see Millau Manor from there, but its location was marred in the smoky darkness that sparred with surges of orange flames. The only thing he could make out between the hilltop and the estate was a company of nearly twenty kingsmen headed his way. Andreiyes shook his head in disbelief, no words coming to mind, and pressed hard onward.

At the manor's gates stood a line of five kingsmen, the remainder of the commander's retainer. The Lyssandre banner had been torn from its pole on the ramparts. The buildings on the estate were engulfed in flames, the grounds blackened, some parts still ablaze. Despite the distance, a wave of heat made his brow sweat as ash rained down in black sludge.

"Move aside," he ordered the footmen, strain tugging at his words. "On order of his Royal Highness Prince Andreiyes."

"Your Highness, welcome," a familiar voice replied, self-importance and amusement dripping from Willik Bryant's tone. Gods, it grated his ears.

Andreiyes groaned inwardly as the redhead trotted toward him on horseback. The lordling sported a toothy grin, the happiest reaper in these parts by the look of it. The sadistic chump.

Andreiyes zeroed in on the lordling's smirk. "Why in Aethel's good name are *you* here?"

"Orders from His Majesty. It surprises me you're unaware, Your Highness." With an ego as large as Willik's, of course that little tidbit was going to swell it. "We've put an end to a Flawed's line, you see."

May Pyre piss on his grave, that tone. Andreiyes gritted his teeth and tightened the squeeze on his reins. Not worth it, not right then. If it were any other day, the lordling would be sucking the mud at his feet. A glorious day that would be. To see Willik on his knees, thoroughly humbled and unable to do anything but tuck his tail in and retreat like a good hound. That, or maybe a duel to the death, if only to see all the distasteful humor vanish from the lordling's face because *no one* accepted a challenge against a royal. No matter the outcome, the opposing party always ended up the loser. One lethal strike triggered Aethel's curse and annihilated the regicide's entire line and those of any nearby.

"The Lyssandres, where are they?"

"Dead." So simply said, not a trace of regret in his eyes.

Willik pointed to the finials at the top of the Millau manor's wrought iron gates. A head hung on a tip, mouth drawn open, white of the eyes on display. Andreiyes gulped and rubbed a hand down his face. His stomach churned, his head swam with unease. Lord Thibault had not deserved that fate.

"What of your bride-to-be?" Andreiyes scanned the courtyard for even the smallest sign of life.

"I would thank Gaia's fortune for avoiding a union with a Flawed's relative." The lordling tittered.

"How is that amusing?"

"Forgive me, Your Highness, but as you yourself found it difficult to entertain the girl, I am certain you would find yourself just as relieved were you in my position."

The words were crude, but he too had narrowly avoided an arranged union with that gullible Lyssandre girl before her Lord father had settled on the Bryants. Grayson had always called his sister frail and ridiculous. He agreed wholeheartedly, but he would carve his mark out and forsake his realm before he admitted to sharing any opinions with Willik.

With a shake of his head, he forced his horse between Willik and the kingsmen. He needed to see the Lyssandre's bodies himself, if only to come to terms with the truth.

Another stepped in his way and grabbed his horse's reins, stopping the animal short. Andreiyes' riding gloves scrunched as he tightened his fists.

"You have heard then?" Lord Pascual asked.

The man looked weary, eyes drawn, long hair disheveled around his face. Blood stained his yellow doublet. There was a small tremor in his hand, as though he held the reins more to balance himself than to stop the prince.

"Your entire estate was abuzz with the news." Not entirely a lie.

"You shouldn't get any closer."

"Do not presume to tell me what I should and should not do, m'Lord. You forget I am your prince."

The man had the decency to incline his head. "Forgive me, Your Highness. I simply meant…you are young. It's not a pleasant sight."

"Hardly younger than your son. House Lyssandre will receive my respects."

A ghost of a smile haunted Pascual's face, his eyes downcast. "Then I request you keep my men as guards."

"No," Andreiyes snapped. He glared down at the man who had dared call himself friend and ally to a House he had helped murder. "No. I intend to keep vigil over their souls for as long as the gods take to fetch them, and I will not be disturbed."

"Of course." Pascual sighed dejectedly as if he were the most affected by the situation. "Your wishes are to be respected, but for the sake of our King and your father, one man shall remain at the hilltop should you have need of him. And if I may request you abstain from approaching the fire. Royal or not, we all burn the same."

"Your concern and loyalty are as always so inspiring."

Without a care if the man understood the jab, Andreiyes tugged his reins free and spurred his horse down the pebbled pathway of the front courtyard. Since Lord Pascual did not want him near the fire, that was precisely where he would go.

He rode by the first body, a guard by the man's leather cuirass, pauldrons, and collar. No armor meant House Lyssandre had not expected the massacre. Andreiyes adjusted himself on the saddle and forced his steed onward. The roof of the stables on his right crumbled beneath the flames, a section of stone wall tumbling beneath the weight of fallen beams. No horses shrieked inside. He shook his head with a scoff. Of course, Bryant had turned a friend's death into a profit and filled his own stables.

The garden house's roof was long gone, the roses and vines that used to creep up the walls charred onto the walls. Where there once was a door, another blackened corpse lay. Despite the creaking wood from the raging fire, the patter of rain and the squelching of mud beneath his horse's hooves, an eerie quiet rang.

The manor stood beyond, its front door turned to ash, flames licking up the stone to trace black slaver in its wake, yet its roof still held. Through the window, despite the dance of red and yellow, he saw the destruction was limited; the second floor had not plummeted down. He had no plan, but he jumped off his horse, ran inside Millau Manor, and jumped over the corpses felled by swords, wood and flame alike. The smallest hope of finding survivors subsisted.

"Grayson," Andreiyes yelled as if the dead could respond. Sweat drizzled down his brow. The fire promised to cook his skin. Smoke prickled his eyes and clogged his throat. He coughed.

A dismembered thin body littered the main stairwell, dressed in fine male clothing and too tall to be the youngest Lyssandre. Little Eryk then, he presumed. Andreiyes covered his mouth with the back of one hand while the other clasped the vial of gods' essence suspended against his chest. These deaths made public executions look like child's play.

Andreiyes remained downstairs, unwilling to step over the morbid spread of limbs. Instead, he searched both lower wings. Most chamber doors were open, and after a rash decision that ended in a sizzled palm and singed hair, he avoided any closed rooms where smoke billowed beneath the doors.

The servant quarters were littered with bodies. Young, old, commoner and noble – the kingsmen had not discriminated against the condemned family's household. Andreiyes did not have the courage to turn them over to check who they were. He pinched his nose and ran for the nearest exit, swearing himself off pork for the immediate future.

He leaned against the door frame of the service entrance and took long drags of the fresher air. This was madness, all of it. His family did not approve this. They could not have. That letter had been forged. It had to have been.

A new sound from within the mansion pulled his attention. It had been a cry… or perhaps his mind was twisting the fire's crackling and the building's creaking into hope. He waited.

There it was again, soft but shrill. He rushed back inside and followed the mewls to the kitchen.

Pots and pans were scattered about. Those exposed to the flames were red hot while all the wooden furnishings were blackened or smoldered to ash. Four bodies were splayed on the floor. One whose embroidered tunic and ash colored hair in a top knot braid had him running to check a pulse against lukewarm skin despite the raging inferno. It was Deacon, not Grayson, but that brought no comfort. Grayson was not half the swordfighter his eldest brother had been.

Something squeezed his ankle, and he nearly kicked off his boots as he scrambled away.

"Nogo's pits."

"Adi," a girl moaned, her hand tainted with blood, right sleeve burnt off to the shoulder. She was curled on her side facing the other direction, drenched in her own dark puddle. Stained or not, the fabric of her gown was too fine for that of a servant. "Help."

Ynnea. He groaned in frustration. It figured the most obstinate, irritating lass in all Taelgir would survive such an ordeal when her brothers did not.

The beams above creaked and popped louder this time, before the entire manor wailed. Part of the upper level crashed into the storeroom and larder next door. A cloud of dust battled for space with the smoke. He cradled Ynnea's form against his velvet doublet, a dagger still planted deep in her gut, and rushed out the service entrance to the outer courtyard before the ceiling crushed them both.

Her weight dragged him to his knees as he panted clean air. The manor roared its upset as the roof followed the second floor downward until only the stone husk remained standing. It cracked and sputtered. Sections of wall broke free and collapsed. The stone hissed and sizzled now exposed to the drizzle. Aethel be praised, they had gotten out just in time.

Ynnea moaned and sobbed weakly. Her blood was soaking through his doublet faster than the rain and soiling it worse than the ash ever could. The dagger needed to come out, he supposed. He jerked it out. The wound poured her lifeblood out faster. He pushed on her belly, stuffed her gown's bottom into it, and begged her to make it stop. Still, it continued to gush. Her whole body quivered. Her breath quickened.

"Come on, Ynnea. You survived blade, fire, and conquest. Survive this too, you stubborn mule."

Her large, round eyes fluttered open, but quickly her dark irises vanished beneath half-closed eyelids. He tapped her chubby cheeks and pinched her arms. No response. Gods below, she was dying. There was only one choice. It irked him to use all he had left on her, but he had not carried her out for nothing. No one else was going to die today.

He uncorked the glass vial that dangled from his neck and poured its remaining two drops onto her wound. The gods' essence derived from Eidenhail trees glimmered bright sapphire one second before blending with her blood and vanishing completely. Her breathing evened. The outpour of blood ebbed to a trickle, but the gash in her lower abdomen did not close. He racked a hand down his face. It was not enough. He wished now he had not exhausted his reserve of Eidenhail leaf oil on a sprained ankle and some bruises across his face moons ago.

When the master-at-arms at Castle Ravensten had lost a fight with a boar during a hunt several cycles earlier, healers used needle and thread to sew the lacerations shut. Andreiyes held no needle in his pockets, and he did not have the skill to unravel the thread from his clothing. Instead, he unclipped three brooches that adorned the lining around the buttons of his doublet.

The punctures he made through Ynnea's skin were not delicate nor symmetrical, but she did not move or shriek. Of course, *she* would sleep through this and make him suffer the work alone, though maybe that was better than hearing her wailing and cries. Andreiyes guffawed at how ridiculously gaudy his stitchwork looked. Here was a girl impaled on the King's command with gold brooches adorned with gems and the royal griffin crest jutting out from her gut.

He laughed until his belly seized and tears streamed down his face. What was wrong with him? Princelings did not cry. They were strong, fearless and domineering, but he felt so alone and unsure. He squeezed Ynnea's cold hands and gazed back at the manor. One alive out of so many. One entire House wiped nearly clean off the map. The *map*. Its specks of glimmering amber. '...*Like cattle with their brands.*'

It reminded him of an event from nine stretches before. Around his sixth name-day, soon after his mother had joined the gods. He ran away and was taken captive by bandits attempting to ransom him back to the crown. Kingsmen rescued him the same eve the ransom note was sent, but the how had always worked at his thoughts. There had been no markers or villages nearby to spot their location in the wilderness, but he had been relieved enough to accept his Father's words of reassurance: '*Where you are is always known and watched, son. Remember that.*'

Now, the memory no longer held its soothing touch. It fit with other odd things Father had said over the stretches. About his hunts or wishes to travel south to the sea: '*If you desire to go somewhere out of the ordinary, make sure to render it a habit.*' Or about the griffin crest of the Royal House: '*We may be the royals of the sky, but the watch of its people is shared.*'

Andreiyes pulled up his sleeve and exposed the black mark on his right forearm. The griffin's amber eye glared back at him. Everyone had the same one, he knew that. Grayson and he had compared theirs for sandturns on end in an attempt to find any differences to no avail. This mark had to be the key to that map the Order's members watched over. The Flawed had no mark. Therefore, if marks were a tracker of some sort, Flawed were untraceable; yet logic dictated those ripples the Greenling had seen were for the Lyssandre child. Is that why Flawed were hunted?

Andreiyes rubbed his mark absently. There had to be more than that as to why they were considered traitors and dangerous if left to age. If the lack of a mark meant no trace on the kingdom's map, it made sense why bandits carved theirs out. There would be no trail of their movements, no accountability toward the realm. If so, that meant the mark's trace only lasted as long as the bearer's life. Gods below, that meant Ynnea remained a glowing speck on that map.

Andreiyes puffed out a lungful as he pulled her right forearm toward him. The tatters that remained of her sleeve were blackened and crumbling off while the skin underneath from hand to elbow was angry and swollen. It ranged from a violent pink to red with unsightly blisters. Her mark was still there, the black lines resembling more a porcupine than a griffin's head on the bubbled skin.

The mark had to come off or else any surveyor of that map would know she lived. He gripped the dagger drenched in her blood and neared it to the brand. Easier said than done. His hand shook. He had sparred against enough training mannequins to deal some blows, but this was so far removed from that. Slashing or stabbing were entirely different skills than slicing. Cracking his neck, he shoved down his insecurities, settled on the image of an uncooked boar's leg, and carved away the front of her forearm as deep as he dared.

⁂✝⁂

*Y*nnea did not stir while Andreiyes cleaved through her arm, nor did she when he cauterized the new wound with the same dagger that had impaled her. She did not wake when he hauled the dead weight of her body into a wheelbarrow, arms and legs jutting out. It was nerve wracking to see this little imp keep mum and limp for so long. Her slow pulse and shallow breaths were not comforting.

He wheeled her through the rear courtyard, past the limits of what had caught fire, to the small service gate that had not been used since he and Grayson had been caught sneaking off estate grounds two stretches ago. It was not their fault an abandoned door buried behind tall hedges and weeds had been built into the stone wall surrounding the estate. Honestly, with how furious Lord and Lady Lyssandre had been, one would think young lads never went on adventures.

Those had been the good ol' days. With a heavy sigh, he tugged weeds free, hacked through vines creeping up the wall, and applied all his ten-stone weight against the stone egress. The wall's door grated along the ground and its stone encasement until it groaned open. Plants snapped free on the other side. What a ruckus. No wonder he and Grayson had been found out so quickly. By any sliver of luck, Lord Pascual and his entourage had long since departed and not heard.

The vegetation on the other side concealed the secret door more than flowered weeds and hedges ever could. Andreiyes spent so much time cutting a path through thorns and vines that by the time he had finished, the sky was clear of rain clouds, the sun was setting, and the estate's blaze was more charcoal than flame. His tunic clung to his skin. This was far too much work for a prince. He gazed down at Ynnea's chubby, soot-stained face and huffed. There was not one bit of amusement in this for him, but stopping now equaled retreating. Princelings did not surrender.

Precaution made him wheel her body a hundred paces into the Weldolf Woods adjoined to the estate. He set her down on a plush bed of moss, his doublet folded as a pillow beneath her head. Still, she did not rouse. His stomach growled loud enough to wake a bear. Besides some bread and a few strips of dried meat he had liberated from the Zesco kitchens, there was nothing to eat. Her sleep was Gaia's blessing; there was no genteel need for him to share.

Stomach still grumbling, he rummaged through his pockets only to find Ladyling Lorelai of House Sertrios' prized ring. He squeezed it in his palm, nails cutting into his skin. This small trinket represented all that had gone wrong. Of the prodigious night he could have had and the squandered time spent finding the jewelry after Lord Pascual had left the Council Chamber. If he had not wasted the time, he might have arrived here earlier. Perhaps he could have saved someone else or stopped this entirely. How could Grandfather have ordered this?

Dusk turned to night. Quickly, the presence of the two moons in the sky sucked the warmth from the air and shrouded the lands in dim shades. Half the Maiesta moon shone its white glow as the alpha cycle, the first thirty days of the new stretch, grew to its end. And with the new stretch having only begun, the Persefin moon's golden aura muted the stars.

A shiver racked through Andreiyes. He rubbed his blood-stiff sleeves. An orange glow flickered in the distance. It was a sure indicator that flames still persisted at the estate. He arranged a few stones in a tight circle and cleared the ground of kindling and dirt. Time to steal some warmth and find his horse.

Seven

A night in the woods was bloody uncomfortable. Twigs dug into Andreiyes' back. Rocks poked his ribs. Roots lopsided the ground. Critters scuttled about. The breeze rustled leaves. His horse snored and puffed breaths. It all set Andreiyes on edge.

Even during hunts he had more comforts – at least a tent, cushions and furs. His small fire pit provided minimal warmth. Seeing as the ladyling owed him as he saw it and she had not deigned him worthy of her conscious company, he snuggled into her form for a little heat. Her burning skin and confused mutterings made the experience less than pleasant. When she finally cooled, it was only for her to turn into a mop of sweat. By daybreak, he had not slept a wink.

He and his horse left the ladyling where she slept and cantered back to the estate. Only ruins remained of the main house and its annexes. The place could not look worse if Nogo's dragons themselves had descended upon it. The well at the rear of the grounds was intact, its waters unaffected and refreshing, but the vegetable gardens had not fared so well.

At least Lord Pascual had foreseen to Andreiyes' needs. The kingsman meant to keep watch on the far hill rode through the estate's gates once dawn had cleared. The man handed the princeling a basket full of loaves, cheese and dried fruits prepared by the Bryant's kitchen maids. Not a proper breakfast, but decent enough all things considered.

"Forgive me, your Highness," the kingsman said gruffly. "I've been commissioned to request your return today before moonsbreak."

"No." Andreiyes regarded the foot soldier. "You may inform Lord Bryant that I meant every word spoken."

For a moment, Andreiyes considered asking the kingsman for help in his day's chosen task but thought better of it. Which of the murdered souls here had this man plunged his blade into?

"But I should require a shovel. And before you urge me against it, know I choose this burden. I shall not be deterred, nor shall I appreciate your aid unless called upon." The last thing he needed was someone discovering the Lyssandre household was missing one corpse.

The man left shortly thereafter to complete his errand. Andreiyes scavenged the grounds for anything that might be of use. Only an outbuilding close to the rear wall remained standing. Inside, a great many tools either hung along the stone walls or were organized on shelves – some sharp, some dull, wooden or metal. The collection was vast, and it seemed very little if anything had been pillaged despite the broken bolt. Not that Andreiyes could be certain. Most of these tools were a mystery to him. He doubted the estate's armory collection had fared half as well.

The rest of his time was spent unearthing whatever charred corpses he could find beneath the manor's wreckage while maneuvering about fallen beams and brittle stone. Moving beams did require the kingsman's aid. The rest he did on his own. At least the Lyssandre brood were easy to identify by the jeweled rings that adorned their blackened fingers or the gold chains with 'L's encased in amber melted onto their chests. Andreiyes eyed his own bedecked hands and hoped it was not an omen.

It took three days for Andreiyes to pull free what he could of their bodies and drag them to the rear courtyard, out of sight from the kingsman's hill – the servants in one corner, the

Lyssandres in another. Another two further days passed whilst he bound their heads with strips of his sodden clothing where their eyes would have been and built a combined pyre as was Isyldillian tradition for all the Lyssandres over a grave for their ashes to fall in. The cloth offered the gods their respect for safe passage to Iltheln, the sacred realm where desires came true. The servants' and guardsmen's eyes he bound as well, but he speckled them in mounds of dirt, unable to gather the energy to do more.

When Andreiyes finally finished and collapsed drowning in sweat, ash and fatigue, he swore to the earth, sky, and bloody weather that Grayson owed him a great debt he planned to collect the day he also crossed over to Iltheln.

The kingsman on the hilltop changed every other day, always offering him a new basket of goods each morning. Each one petitioned his return to House Bryant's manor. Andreiyes' refusals grew sterner and more brash as the days went by. It would take the King, his uncle, or father to command him, not some petulant guard or Lord that was inconvenienced by his wishes.

After those five days, his self-appointed tasks at the manor were completed. The gods were bound to have fetched the Lyssandres' souls. Only one problem remained. Ynnea had yet to wake.

The first few days after the massacre, Andreiyes watched over Ynnea's sleeping form, sponging her forehead with the hem of her dress and checking her pulse often. That was far more tedious and aggravating than digging graves. Her fever broke twice. He fed her water and milk. There was little else to give her that she would not choke on without chewing. Her wounds, he left as they were. With no healers at his disposal, there was little more he could have done anyway. She just lay there, eyelids shut, not even the twitch of her lips in guise of a smile or frown. Not once did she respond to the prodding and taps he gave her limbs with his boots. Not once did she even mutter a thanks for all his hard work in that lyrical voice of hers. She obviously refused to die, but she would not wake either. Ridiculous. She was the worst company he had ever had.

He chopped wood by himself, celebrated his first fire sparked by himself, ate by himself, and entertained himself. He pretended to be in avid conversations and shared imagined food with ghosts of his own creation. By the fifth night, Andreiyes was quite certain he was nearing madness. Grayson would never have subjected himself to this absurdity were he in his shoes. Why Andreiyes had willingly allowed it to go on for this long and so far from comfort was beyond him. He kneaded Lorelai's ring in his pocket between his fingers as he glared at Ynnea's prone body.

It was high time he returned to civilization and collected on some well-earned repose. On the morrow, the morning of this ordeal's sixth day, the equivalent of a quint in number of days, he would return to the Zesco estate. Whether Ynnea lived or died, that was up to her stubborn self.

⁛↓⁛

*Y*nnea was still firmly unconscious when he departed the next sunrise. Out of the goodness of his heart, he bound her eyes in case she passed on and left his canteen behind were she to finally wake. After that, he declared her on her own.

The birds chirped. The skies were clear. Fresh morning dew brightened the meadow between the Weldolf woods and Millau manor. There was a bounce in his step as he neared the hidden door at the back of the estate. What would his basket from the Zesco kitchens hold this morning? A bottle of fresh milk, hot buns, lockleberry jam? His stomach growled. Once he returned to House Bryant's manor, he planned to demand eggs with sides of beans, pancetta, and sausages, all steaming hot with a cup of spiced wine. Six days was far too long since his last warm meal. And a bath. His hair had lost its volume, the curls greased and fixed against his scalp. Grime and ash coated his skin. His first order of business: a good meal. Second: a long soak in a bath.

He grappled the handle ring on the secret doorway, whisking aside hanging vines that tickled his neck, ready to pull the stone egress shut.

A throaty yell resounded, some further shouting, and then what sounded like a woman's sobs. What in Aethel's good name was going on? Forgetting the door, he raced through the rear courtyard and what remained of the manor's west wing.

"I tell you again, Madam," a surly male voice said. "Leave."

"Ye have no right," a woman cried, still too far away, her southern brogue carrying. Her voice was high-pitched, almost shrill, definitely familiar.

"By order of his Lordship of House Bryant, Northern Commander of Isyldill's kingsmen, none are permitted on these grounds. Begone with you or remain on pain of death."

Andreiyes followed the crunch of gravel to the front courtyard where the two figures wrangled – one, the latest kingsman down from his hill with the daily basket rations plopped on the ground beside him and the other, a heavy woman sitting on the pebbles. She was twisted away from him. Her hair was pulled taut into a bun, a kerchief pinned atop it. Her dress had no gold or silver to indicate descendancy of a noble House, but the embroideries and combined green shades were too fine to belong to a common servant or wench.

"I mean only to pay my respects. All the dead deserve that. Have ye no heart? No soul?" The woman scrambled to her feet as the kingsman drew his falchion, curved tip gleaming in a ray of sunlight. She did not flinch and instead brandished her finger in rebuke. "Ye should be ashamed, threatening a woman who means ye no harm. What would yer own kin think, were it them watching from Iltheln hoping for a little love and respect after such tragic deaths?"

"Quiet, woman. I'll be showing—"

"Enough," Andreiyes said, approaching the two. "I hardly think that such behavior shall counter the Mistress' scolding."

The kingsman bowed his head, dropping his sword hand to his side. "Forgive me, your Highness. I did not wish to trouble you with this simple matter."

"An execution is hardly simple."

"Your Highness." The woman curtsied, head lowered before daring to meet his gaze and hold it. "I did not expect to find ye here."

Andreiyes pinched the bridge of his nose. Now it made sense why the pitch of her voice had seemed so familiar. With the number of times Mistress Harleston, or Mimsee as the Lyssandre brood had called her, had chided him and Grayson and ended their pranks before they began, her voice was commonplace.

"Mimsee." Andreiyes pulled his shoulders back. "It is with sorrow that I inform you that House Lyssandre shall no longer be in need of your services."

Omga Harleston, the Lyssandre governess, eyed the ruins and nodded. "Yes, I'm quite aware."

"Why are you here?" he asked, standing straighter. He would not be intimidated by her harsh stare, regardless that she was almost three times his senior.

"Dear laddie, ye may not have been my charge, but yer ears did not escape my tuggings for ye to disregard sensitivity where due."

Andreiyes clenched his jaw, with a tinge of embarrassment. "Return to your hill," he ordered the kingsman, gaze fixed on the governess. "Leave the basket. Mistress Harleston will return it to you when she departs."

It took a particular woman to address him so informally, especially in front of a pledged soldier, but this was Mimsee. The woman who had read him stories on nights he spent at the Millau manor as a young boy. The woman who nursed him back to health while he lay in bed for days on end with a bad case of erysolio. He still remembered the waft of the honeyed milk and gingerbread she had patiently fed him. No others had visited him, save for the doctor, Grayson kept away by his mother. Grandfather had not even permitted his transport back to Castle Ravensten. It was her lessons and remarks, even as aggravating as they might have been, that kept him straight and made Father compliment his demeanor.

He sighed, resigned, surveying his guard's retreat. The kingsman had already reached the estate gates. "It's not safe for you here."

"Nor ye I would imagine." Her hands massaged her chest, directly over her heart. "I did not think the rumors true."

His nod was instinctual, the feeling mutual. There was no justifying this massacre, Flawed or not. No matter how long he stared at the ruins, the shocking reality of it did not change.

"M'Lady had a Flawed, they say. All this for one child?"

"Yes."

"Did none of them survive?" Mimsee wiped away a stray tear.

The kingsman was trotting back to his hill, growing smaller and smaller. Andreiyes signaled with a jerk of his head for Mistress Harleston to follow him as he traipsed around the rubble to the ash grave he had dug.

Rain over the past couple days had packed the dirt and flattened the mound. To any onlooker, it might appear as a random patch of freshly tilled dirt. Covering his nose with a handkerchief to keep the reek of rotting corpses at bay, he gestured to the tomb that held the ashes of every Lyssandre family member except for Ynnea and Lord Thibault. Unfortunately, Andreieyes had lacked the courage to take down the decaying body parts spiked along the estate's wall.

"Oh, M'Lady. Oh m'dearies. Gaia be with you." The governess fell to her knees beside the plots and wept. She grabbed a handful of dirt, then padded it back down and mumbled a prayer.

Andreiyes fidgeted in place, massaged his neck and counted the birds flying overhead in formations followed by the manor's number of rows of stone still standing that formed its 'L' shape. Over the last four days, he had done his damnedest to avoid spending time hunched over that grave. He spared it a glance, pulling his eyes away just as quickly, but it pried his attention back. He clenched his teeth and worried his palms against his trousers.

A sense of finality crept up his spine. That mound of dirt made it all too real, unavoidable, and certainly not an occurrence he could pretend away. They were all gone – there was no changing that - all except one. Guilt squeezed him. He should check on her, just one more time.

"Why?" Mimsee asked, her words shaky, back still turned to him. "Why kill 'em all? There's no sense to it."

Unable to find an answer, Andreiyes shook his head and gazed at the hedge, behind which the stone door lay hidden.

"Were you there, dearie?" Mistress Harleston now stood before him, a hand holding his cheek.

He flinched away from her pitying touch. "I could not save them."

"And none would've expected ye to. Ye're only a boy."

"I am a princeling."

"Andreiyes Xander Lenierz. Ye may be higher on the gods' ladder, but that does not spare ye from feeling as we all do. Ye feel pain, loss and wretchedness the same as any other. And ye are permitted to give way to them from time to time." She cradled his face and when he did not pull away, she pulled his cheek to her shoulder. Then she caressed his head.

It was affectionate, tender, and Gaia grace him, he needed it. His tension, stress and worry bubbled to the surface and burst out in a sob as his shoulders trembled. A tear trekked down his cheek and moistened her sleeve. It felt good showing weakness, just this once. When he calmed, Omga gently pried his face upward and wiped the wetness from his face.

"What's done is done. Nothing can change the past, but never bury yer heart. Ye're a caring lad. That's what'll mold ye into a fine man, a righteous princeling." Her soft smile reached her dull brown eyes to form crow's feet at the edges.

"I burned and buried them." The admission tore from him as though it could burn.

She caressed the hair away from his forehead. "I suspected as much. Though I don't see why the servants were forsaken a pyre. Surely, yer men might've spared—"

"No, you do not understand. I did it. Alone."

Her eyes widened before glancing over the grave and the jumble of servants' bodies. "Why in all Taelgir would ye do so?"

"You cared for the Lyssandres, yes?"

"Ye very well know so. They could've been me own and I couldn't have loved them more."

"Would you care for them still?"

"Andreiyes, m'boy, I've no notion of what ye're asking."

His mouth went dry as he opened and closed it, words suddenly lost. This was a leap of faith. A quint's worth of fretting and worrying over Ynnea could all be for naught if he had misunderstood Mimsee's affections.

"Well, don't keep me waiting. Spit it out. I've no access to the torrent of yer mind."

He clenched his fists to stop the nervous tremors of his hands. "Not all the Lyssandres are here."

"Not here?" Her eyes widened. "Who?"

"Ynnea." Andreiyes could not risk anyone hearing more. What if the kingsman had doubled back? He led her toward the secret doorway. "Come."

"Ye better have taken good care of her, I hope."

He winced, considering he had just about been to leave Ynnea behind. "As good as I have been able."

Eight

*K*aianne's head pounded. Breathing hurt. Her mouth was powdery and dry. A few strands of hair tickled her nose in the breeze. Someone had left the window open, yet smoke lingered in the air. She winced from the slightest motion. Her eyelids begged to stay closed, her heavy limbs needing a few more sandturns of sleep, but the incessant clopping sound nearby was far too annoying to ignore. Servants were generally more mindful of waking hours.

Her eyes fluttered open to find a canopy of sticks and leaves overhead in the semblance of a shelter. Trees and bushes surrounded her. Nearby, a small fire crackled in a pit of stones. This was definitely not her bedroom.

With effort, her arms escaped a wooly blanket. She tried to rub her eyes, but her right arm flopped down against her chest, aching terribly with the movement. Her hand slapped her chin. That was graceful. Her brothers would be cackling their heads off had they seen.

Her brothers. She jolted upright and gasped at the burning pain in her lower abdomen. Adi, Dea, the kingsmen, Lord Pascual, the fire. Her breath caught in her throat at the assault of memories. It wasn't true. It couldn't be. None of her family was dead. No, this wasn't real. This had to be a nightmare. It had to be, but her belly throbbed like needles were stabbing at her gut while feeling hollow with hunger at the same time. Every bit of her ached. And her head, it spun. Gods below, it didn't feel like it was on straight.

She was in the woods, wrapped in a strange blanket. No, not a blanket, a cloak. With a shake, it tumbled off her shoulders to her thighs to reveal trousers and a basic, linen tunic tucked inside. Other than riding breeches, she owned only dresses. Panic bubbled in her chest as her eyes darted about the woods, the steady clop, clop, clop in the distance not calming her one bit. If she made it out, someone else in her family must have.

She tried to get to her knees, but her right arm gave out and the skin on her stomach pulled taut. Nogo's pit, there was no strength in her limbs. She rubbed her marked arm, the throbbing concentrated between the wrist and elbow, to find it bandaged with torn, linen wrappings. That didn't make sense. She had no recollection of damaging it. Perhaps it really was all in her head.

She tore at the front of the tunic to pry it up. If the stab wound wasn't there, if that hadn't happened, then…Her heart dropped at the sight of more bandages wrapped around her lower abdomen, her pelvic bones jutting out unlike ever before. She stared at the red scars, unable to move, unable to think. No, it wasn't possible. Pascual would not have betrayed them. Kingsmen would never have killed Papa. And there was no way Deacon had been bested. He was so well trained. She shook her head in denial, the word 'no' bouncing repeatedly in her thoughts. A drop of water plopped onto her hand. Then another and another. She was crying, which was absurd because it had not happened.

Movement caught her gaze, a shadow amongst distant trees. The rhythmic sounds had stopped. She wiped away her tears, lay back down, and pried the cloak back over her body.

Her mysterious keeper wasn't quiet. Footsteps trudged closer. They crinkled leaves and snapped twigs. A male voice muttered to himself. She caught what sounded like a string of curses as he approached, dragging wood in a wheelbarrow. The gleam of an axe's blade lay over his haul. His face was hidden in the shadows of his cloak's hood. The material was a rich brown with a velvet sheen despite the woodland debris stuck to it. His boots were made of fine leather, the shine lost but not worn through. This was not the attire of a poor man.

Once he reached the fire pit, he began unloading the wood – logs, branches, and twigs into three separate piles.

"Who are you?" Her voice croaked.

The yelp that escaped him made her jerk and the load he carried went flying. Would he hurt her now? Bash her head in with one of those…When his hood fell back as he plummeted to his rear, she gaped.

"You?" She couldn't believe it. It was Yierd of all people. Not a pauper nor a good-intentioned person, but a pitting arrogant arse of a princeling whose family's kingsmen had killed hers. Surely this was a cruel farce.

His hair was disheveled, the curls knotted from one side of his head to the other in plump volumes, leaves and debris stuck within. His face was marred with streaks of dirt. He looked awful – tears in his clothing, eyes stretched with fatigue, cheeks sunken in slightly – no better than a peasant after a long day of work. This entire image of him was simply wrong and unfathomable, but his amber eyes were unmistakable.

"You are awake."

"You're observant. What're you doing here? And dressed like that?" Her eyes darted around the woods. "Where are your kingsmen?"

"Finally, *finally* you awaken and those are the first words out of your mouth?" He dusted himself off, glaring at her. "Do you realize how long you have kept me waiting?"

"What on all Taelgir are you muttering?" She pushed herself up to her elbows, wincing from the strain in her abdomen and shoulder. "Why are we here? Where is Grayson? How-"

The flash of pity in his eyes made her words go silent. Oh gods, it had happened. All of it. Her lips quivered. Tears gathered in her eyes. It wasn't right. Dea, Adi, Grayson, Eryk, all of them. They were really dead, and it was all her fault. If she hadn't distracted Dea, if she hadn't told Adi to hide and stay in that cupboard. "No. No. It's not true."

"You cannot be that daft."

Anger boiled in her veins, turning the quiver of her lips into a teeth-chattering tremble. "My family is dead. The least you can do is not be an insensitive arse."

"Why in all Taelgir do you think I am here, and you are still alive? No one else was willing to help, so I have more than earned my 'insensitivity'."

Her eyes went wide. "*You* pulled me out of that fire? *You* bandaged my wounds?"

"Do not forget I also fed you, watered you, kept you warm and safe."

Really? Watered like a plant? What a bloody turd. "By your lonesome?"

He nodded. "I am perfectly capable on my own."

She chortled. "Those are not words I would have used to describe you."

"Do you see anyone else here?"

Kaianne huffed at that. There was no movement about, no one that she could see. Still, she couldn't believe it. Here was the young royal she had always assumed would not mature until he reached forty. For Gaia's sake, he and her brother had hidden toads in her bedding only a few Maiesta moon cycles ago.

"How long have I been here?"

"Nine days." He tossed a log onto the dwindling fire in the pit.

Her jaw dropped, her breath catching. Nine days…She was thinking sandturns, maybe a day at most. How was that possible?

"Who else made it?"

Yierd shook his head, the arrogant look in his eye faded.

"Oh gods, they're really gone." Breath quivered from her lips. "Did you…find them?"

His amber gaze looked past her as he plopped a handful of yellow lockleberries into his mouth and chewed.

"Well?"

His throat bobbed. "I built their pyre."

Somehow, she believed that. For all his haughtiness, he wasn't cruel. "Will the gods grant them passage?"

"I hope they have. I spent enough time wrapping their eyes and saying the prayers that they should."

That was more than she ever expected of him. "Thank you."

One of his brows raised. "You're an odd one, Ynnea."

It felt wrong to hear that name spoken, like it belonged in another life, another time. "Don't call me that anymore. Kaianne. That's all I am now."

"Because your brothers used it?"

She nodded, silently counting the fragments of tree bark laying on the ground. "If I'd have had a choice, Papa would have stopped calling me by my first given name altogether. He refused to do so or let anyone use my second name outside of our family circle. Now my family's gone. If my memories and my pride are all I have left, I'll hold onto them with the name my mother gave me."

He scoffed but kindly did not comment further. When her stomach growled loud enough to rouse a bear, he tossed her a cloth bundle.

"Eat. There is no pride in starving to death, and I did not waste my time laboring to keep you with the living to have you die from hunger."

She sat with a groan and unraveled his charity. It was bread, the center hardened, the crust tough. At least two days old. No wonder he had not eaten it, but her belly cramped and ached to be filled. With a sigh, she wrenched off a bite. Beggars could not be choosers after all. Gods, is that what she was to become – a beggar? At the whims of someone else's charity and alms? Surely, no one would let a young girl like her starve. Then again, she had seen starved children in the villages huddling behind their mothers. Was one orphan girl like her really any different?

"Whose clothes are these?"

"Yours now."

"I mean where did you get them?" Last she remembered the manor had been on fire, and the material was too rough to have been his.

He stuffed a few more lockleberries into his mouth and poked the fire. "Your governess."

"Mimsee? She's here?"

He rolled his eyes at her. "Yes, she is camouflaged with the bushes waiting to be discovered."

"You don't always have to be so contemptuous."

He shrugged. "With you, it comes naturally."

If glares could kill, she hoped hers would have stabbed through the arch between his brows.

"She was here though. Checked on you once. More than that would have been dangerous."

"Why?"

"They are always watching." His eyes glazed over for a moment, but before Kaianne could ask who, he slapped his knee and continued, "I did meet back up with her at your estate for supplies and clothing though. You could not swallow much more than broth, so she supplied thicker soup."

"And these clothes. Tell me she changed me."

He simply shook his head as if it were no big deal. Kaianne's eyes widened. She pulled the cloak to her chest and glared at him. He had dared?

He barked a laugh. "What? 'Tis not like there is much to see. Honestly, as is, you could pass for a young lad."

Kaianne's cheeks burned with embarrassment. Fully developed or not, she was still a girl and he a boy. "Is nothing sacred to you?" She tossed twigs, dirt, even her cloak at him. "It's not proper. I'm to be a lady."

"Not anymore." His tone was firm, harsh. It sucked the last bit of hope from her because he was right. Everything had changed. The life she knew was gone. "Is there anything you wish for me to request of Mimsee when I meet her at sundown?"

"Can I see her?"

He lay back against a trunk. "You cannot risk being seen, by anyone. Not only are you a ghost, but a Carved as well. Expect no one's mercy, save hers and mine."

"A Carved?" she screeched.

He explained the wound on her right forearm, how he had inflicted it and made her into less of a person, how the skin would probably forever stay disfigured and scarred. He was under the impression she should thank him for the mutilation, that somehow she was safer this way as an outlaw. By his regards, a mark made her traceable. That with it, the King and the Order would have known she was still living and would have continued to hunt her. The explanation was vague and missing the how he knew or why others would care enough to pursue her, a young girl with no wealth or family anymore. It was one more reason to turn her insides numb. Her life had ended.

Everyone knew the Carved were a vile lot – heartless and savage. They would sooner turn on their family and kingdom than raise a finger to help those in need. What did that say about her now that she was one of them? She stifled back rising nausea. They also said the Carved were hardly better than Flawed. One mutilated their bodies; the others were abominations.

Thad's little face came to mind. Nothing about him screamed vicious or dangerous. Perhaps these known facts were false. Part of her hoped not, otherwise her family had died in vain. The other part of her, the selfish part, wished with all her might that the lack of a brand did not change who she was.

Oblivious to her inner turmoil, Andreiyes kept on talking. He even made commentary on bits of his monologue without being prompted. At times, it sounded like things Grayson might have cut in to say. She raised a brow in concern. Yierd must have really been lonely the last nine days. And that was the mind-boggling bit. He, of all people, had cared for her for nine days.

He spoke of her wounds and how he had tended to them. When he went into detail about removing the brooches, she almost hurled the few contents in her belly. He described the first few days after her family's murder, giving her far too much detail about the bodies. While she hyperventilated, he spoke with pride of his good deeds and how he had rebuffed Lord Bryant's demands he return to Zesco manor. She got the sense he needed to get this out in the open so that someone might know he had not stood idle after the slaughter. Nevertheless, the part of his tale when he had nearly abandoned her three days before did not go unheard.

"You would've left me here?" The nincompoop.

"Consider yourself fortunate that no one has fetched me back to the Bryant's estate and leave it at that."

"From what I gather, I should thank Mimsee for my good fortune."

His head dropped with that rebuke, shame silently rippling off him. From her experience, that was an uncharacteristic reaction on his part, but from what he had said, it was the truth.

Knowing the woman, Mimsee had most likely chastised Yierd, then guilted him into delaying his departure until Kaianne was awake and lively. Classic Mimsee. Thankfully, Mimsee had taught Andreiyes how to feed a sleeper more than water. Considering how thin Kaianne's wrists were, the lesson had come just in time. And despite everything, he *had* taken care of her. Perhaps – and this took a lot to admit – the princeling was not all bad.

Andreiyes' long winded tale came to an end, and a comfortable silence engulfed them. Birds hooted and sang in the distance. Sunlight was still far reaching, despite the woodland cover making it impossible to tell a more specific time of day. The fire crackled and danced. Combined, it was almost peaceful.

"Do you think anyone will rise up in protest against my family's murder?"

"No."

"No one? What about the nobles who were allied with our House, or the peasants that worked our fields?"

"No one will rise up against their King and the Stewards."

Tears fogged her vision. She blinked them away furiously. There had to be someone who cared. Someone had to be willing to help.

"What does the Order have to do with this?"

"I have not the faintest idea, but I know they are involved."

"So, all this was sanctioned?"

Andreiyes nodded, and Kaianne's heart dropped further. It was hopeless. A long silence engulfed them. When the fire dwindled, he dropped another log carelessly into the pit. He hissed, shook his empty hand, then placed it to his mouth to suckle his finger, his face scrunched.

Kaianne couldn't help the chortle that escaped her as she watched him. He looked utterly ridiculous like that. "Dainty now, are you?"

"Quiet, my hands are not fit for this labor." He shook the appendage more, nearly growling at it as though the embedded splinter had chosen to pester him.

Now she was in full laughter, her stomach tightening around her wound. The twinge of pain was worth his expression. Poor Yierd, bested by a splinter. That made the laughter come even harder.

"I'm certain the log regrets impaling your delicate finger."

"As if yours are any better."

"But I fully admit their daintiness. Do you?" She grinned at his scowl. "Pass me the water and I swear to stop teasing."

His grumble as he handed over the waterskin was worth another chuckle. An unsettled Yierd was amusing.

"You swore."

"I know. I can't help it."

"Then you get a challenge." His wicked smile was disconcerting. "Chop the wood in my stead."

Her jaw dropped in horror. She didn't know how to swing a sword, let alone an axe. How was she supposed to hold it up? "I couldn't."

"You shall very well have to if you care for a fire and warmth. I cannot stay out here forever. I am dying to dive back into civilization. I mean, look at me." He tugged on his clothing. "If it were not for my eyes, no one would think me royalty."

"And me? What will become of me?"

"That is for you to figure out."

"Such a gentleman. No wonder the nickname Yierd suits you so well." She rolled her eyes and bit her cheek. Maybe she could find a way to stay with Mimsee in the village despite her carved-out mark.

"Is that what you call me? Does not sound flattering."

"It wasn't meant to be. What did you expect? You're always an arse to me, even here, now, during our conversation."

"Grayson was never any better. Did you give him the same dashing epithet?"

"My brother…" She hiccupped a shaky breath at the thought of him. There would be no more disagreements with him. No more anger and frustrations at his stupid attitude. She blinked away her blurry vision and straightened her back. "Grayson wasn't a member of the royal family who the people have to look up to. You are. You're supposed to hold yourself to a higher standard. Do more. Be better. You helped me, so you have it in you. You just need to pry it out."

"That was almost motivational."

"And that almost sounded like a compliment." She grinned, but when he winked, she ducked her head to gulp from the waterskin, her cheeks flushing with warmth. "Did you know Papa tried to negotiate our union with your father before he turned to the Bryants?"

"Aye, but father and I had already agreed on our stance toward such a match. Good thing too."

"Right. All the better for the both of us." She pinched her lips shut and tucked her knees to her chest, itching for the uncomfortable silence to end. "If you must know, Grayson and I didn't shy away from name calling. Idiot, dullard, halfwit on my end. His personal favorite for me was gnat." A lump lodged in her throat. Those screamed exchanges, the tension, and hateful glares were not something she'd ever thought she would miss.

He snorted. "Well, you have to stop calling me Yierd. That name picks at my mettle and virility."

"Good thing you're not a man yet." At his grumble, she giggled. "Alright, I promise when you've earned it, I swear to no longer think of you as Yierd." Oddly enough, she was already beginning to think the nickname wasn't as fitting as she had assumed. "How about you start by showing me what I need to know to survive?"

*T*hat request was easier said than done. It surprised her how quickly Andreiyes agreed – whether to help her or be rid of her sooner, she wasn't sure. Before he showed her how to hunt and some basic defense with a blade, he said she should first be able to cut her own wood and make her own fire to fight off the cold nights and the frigid temperatures promised during the Stretch of Gain's later cycles and the following Stretch of Blight's frost and snow.

That was all good and logical, but she wanted to learn to defend herself. Never again did she want to feel as helpless as she had that horrible day. Alone in the wild, fighting for survival was going to be a necessity, but Yierd – the name stuck since he was being stubbornly ridiculous – said there was no point in teaching her the uses of a blade if she could not build a fire to last long enough to need to defend herself. That made her grumble.

"You have to start with an axe."

"And what exactly do you know, your Highness, about hard labor?"

"More than you."

Her irritation flared as he pulled the axe from its cart and strode to her. The hard-edged tool thumped to the ground. Little lords, it was massive. Its metal gleamed in stray rays of sunlight. Its curved edge was sharp and stretched to a large triangular head fitted on a wooden handle. She had no idea if that meant it was worth anything or good enough to use. This was the first time she had ever seen one up close.

She wrapped a hand around the handle that spanned the entire length of her lower body and lifted the blade. Or rather, she tried to. She pried it not more than an inch off the ground before her shoulder screamed in protest and the head clunked back to the ground. Yierd's raised brow made the whole situation mortifying.

Not only did he think her weak and incapable of providing for herself, but now she had proved it. She gave it another attempt, this time with both hands, though the right one was slow to respond. She had to squeeze her left fingers over the others for leverage. She raised the axe maybe a centimeter higher, but swinging it up was out of the question. Her shoulder sockets were bound to pop out if she tried, and lifting it had her arms burning and body shaking.

"That is bound to complicate things." The prince scratched his head. "Pile these over there with the rest. We shall have you on logging duties then."

She wanted to bury her head between her shoulders but did as told. She carried log by log from the wheelbarrow to a pile underneath the canopy of twigs and branches Andreiyes had assembled into a makeshift shelter – the shelter which might crumble at any moment with the wrong gust of wind. At first, her abdomen and shoulder muscles jerked in protest around the healing scars. By the time she finished her chore, they were only a murmur of pain in the back of her mind.

"Now place them all here." He was standing on the opposite side of the little encampment where the wheelbarrow had been.

She wiped her brow, jaw clenched. "Do it yourself."

"'Tis for your endurance, not mine. You continue this way, with a little luck in a couple days, you should be able to deal at least one swing of that axe. So, on with it and be done before I return."

"My company not stimulating enough for you?"

"Surprisingly, I prefer it to your silence."

She cocked her head. Was that a compliment? Surely not. It did not fit their dynamic. "You leave just as I do your bidding? How often have you and Grayson pestered me to obey your demands? Are you not prince enough to gloat?"

"I will, no worries." He grinned and secured his belt and scabbard around his waist. "But Mimsee awaits. Princeling or not, that woman is not to be trifled with. Besides, I need some fresh air."

Fresh air? They were surrounded by nothing but fresh air. As if to emphasize how ridiculous his statement was, he winked before walking away. Was it a clue about something in regards to her? With a groan, she picked up the first log for the new arrangement.

By the time she finished replacing the wood in its new pile, sweat drenched her tunic. A pungent smell wafted around similar to that of the gardeners after a long day's work or the guardsmen after training. She raised her arms and gagged. Oh little lords, it was her. She had run off the prince with her stench.

She chortled and chuckled, but quickly that mirth turned to heart wrenching sobs. She had run him off, and no one else was here. She was alone in the world. Forever a Carved, an outcast, no family, no friends. Tears poured down her face.

Everything had been so simple before. Convincing her father to push back the engagement had seemed like the most difficult task she could ever experience. If only she had known then what the future held. Kaianne blew her nose into a leaf.

Wallowing would not change what had happened. She needed to grow up and survive. Those who had murdered her loved ones had to be held accountable, and only she could do it. Lord Bryant, Willik, the kingsmen, the King, the Order. Only Yierd deserved to be spared. She shivered at the thought of killing, of blood and dead eyes, of sinking to their level. It was too soon for all that. She was far from ready, but one day her vengeance would flame. She picked up another log with a grunt and continued her task.

Nine

By the time Andreiyes returned, Kaianne barely had the energy to swallow the bread, soup and berries he brought before slipping into a dreamless sleep. She woke from a forceful shake of her shoulder while nestling further into her cloak for more warmth.

"Ynnea, wake up. I need to meet with my guard."

"It's Kaianne. Get it right," she muttered and turned on her side to avoid seeing his face. There was something rather humbling about being cared for by someone she had sworn herself to loathe for all eternity.

After he left and with the risk of embarrassment lessened, she worked at her axe-wielding ineptitude. Another failed attempt at a swing left her sore arms burning, but at least she could now sway it like a pendulum for more than a few grainfalls. It was an improvement, and just the motivation she needed to do more.

She worked at shifting the log piles, holding two or three at a time in her arms. In short time, she imagined herself impressive with newfound strength and skills, but after three pile relocations, her newfound thrill was thoroughly bored out of her. Since Andreiyes had yet to show his face, she searched for something to eat.

A coney lay beneath the lopsided-twig shelter, its cute ears and stumpy paws limp, its furry head unmoving. Poor thing. She knew little about surviving in the wilderness, but her naivete did not stretch far enough to believe coney was cooked with its fur on. She gagged. The thought of skinning it made her want to hurl.

Not far from the coney lay a double-edged knife. It was sharp enough to do the deed, but so short she would have to touch the meat with both hands. She gulped but steeled her spine. She wasn't a ladyling anymore. Not after little Thad had been killed for being born. Adi burned in a cabinet. Dea, Papa, Grayson, Eryk, even Mama. She was all that was left of them. For her family, she had to survive, and this gruesome act was part of it. With a deep breath, she bit her cheek and plunged the blade deep into the thick of the coney, then cursed herself when the knife could not wiggle to either side.

Her second attempt had her pining the top of the fur down with her right elbow. It was gory business and exhausting. It took so pitting long to detach one small section, and she quickly felt as if coated in the coney's blood from head to midriff. Several times her fingers cramped around the knife or her entire right forearm went numb. How did the cooks and servants ever manage to provide enough meat for banquets if one animal took this long to prepare? When the skin finally gave way, any flutter of excitement evaporated at the sight of her work. Instead of smooth texture, chunks of meat were dug out of the skinned creature and remained attached to the pelt.

One more thing she was useless at. She tossed the knife away and buried her face in her hands, only to jolt backwards with a groan. Now her face was painted in coney muck. Everything was so bloody difficult.

That was when she noticed the chill and lack of wood crackles. Nogo's wrath curse her. The fire had dwindled to embers. She hurried to the pit and blew hard on it like what she imagined a bellows would do. Ashes billowed in the air, but no flames arose. She spat, bits of ash stuck to her tongue. She piled log after log in a rush, but the fire never took. In fact, the embers buried beneath the dry wood faded.

Rocks, that was the solution. She had once seen the servants start a chimney fire while hitting two stones together. After wiping the coney muck on her trousers, she selected a few rough-edged rocks.

She collided two together…with no result, other than her fingers tingling from the force. Again, and again she smacked them together, failure after failure until the embers turned black. She hurled the rocks away with a scream and buried her tear-streaked face in her hands. She was terrible at surviving.

"Those were never going to work."

She cringed at Yierd's presence. Gods, how mortifying. She ducked her face to the side and wiped it clean on her sleeve. "How long have you been there?"

"Long enough. You have tenacity. Fits your stubborn self." He gave her a half smile. "One piece of advice-"

"What do you know about woodland living?"

"Not much, granted. But following the same course of failed actions will not yield you positive results. Call that princely knowledge."

She was not in the mood for his arrogant demeanor. "Nothing works. I can't do it. I'm bound to fail and die."

He laughed at her, bent in half chortling a fit. She wanted to strangle him. "I never pegged you for a fatalist. That would have made our task to tease you so much simpler."

Forget the coney, she was going to skin him. Actually, that meant too much effort. She settled for hurling dirt and twigs his way until he cried for a truce. His scowl was appeasing.

"I do not remember you being this vengeful before."

There was that fateful word. Before. Before the massacre at Millau Manor. Before her life changed. Before Andreiyes went from prankster to savior. She eyed the princeling warily.

"Why do you help me? We've never even liked each other." She flung dried pine needles aside.

His nod made her shoulders sag. "Grayson would have done the same for my sisters."

Of course, this all was for Grayson's sake. Her life didn't matter to Yierd in the long run. This was only about the here and now, a way for His Highness to bury whatever guilt he felt with an act of contrition.

Her stomach mocked her with a growl, loud enough to make her flinch in embarrassment. Without a word, Yierd handed her a baguette garnished with cheese, vegetable spread, and bits of cured meat. She took it without protest and wolfed it down in a few bites, nearly forgetting to chew. Sauce dribbled to her chin. She wiped it with a sleeve. It wasn't the ladyling thing to do, but she wasn't one of those anymore and hunger aches weren't pleasant new sensations. One more tally to her newfound disgrace. More were to come, certainly.

Yierd scratched a nail down the young stubble of his chin. "You know, I expected to either be grated enough to need to abandon you for my own sanity or give in to your begging to put you out of your misery."

"I would never beg." Not for that. Him leaving though... "And I'm not weak minded."

He grunted. For a long moment they stared at each other until he dropped a pair of stones at her feet.

"You need those. Flint stone and pyrite. Now try again."

Glancing at him skeptically, she tapped the two together again and again. A lone spark fell to the dirt and died out, but her surprise stifled the air in her throat.

"I did it." She laughed, smacking the stones repeatedly. When another flash of red tumbled down, happy tears came free. "I did it."

"Of course, you did. You only needed the correct tools."

That made the tears flow faster. She wiped at them with abandon, flashing him a heartfelt grin. "Out of everyone in Taelgir, I never thought you could make me feel better about myself. Thank you."

The rare smile he gave in return felt like the start of something new. That day, he taught her about building a fire, how to prepare the tinder to receive the spark, how to tend its fragile beginnings and mold it into what their pit could hold. It took three days for her to perfect her technique to working order. During that time, he demonstrated a couple snares with rope and sticks he had learned during hunting parties or while touring the realm.

None of her snares were fruitful over the following days, but at least she held a better idea of what she needed to do. For the skinning though, she was on her own. The prince had never come close to doing that or watched it being done; the indignant look he gave her when she requested his help was worth a very un-ladyling-like eyeroll.

Each day, he left once in the morning to return with food and once near sundown to meet with Mimsee. Every time, he asked her to stay behind and hidden. As if. Princeling or not, he had a better chance at acquiring a drynn talent than making her obey. She snuck through the shadows of the evenings to get a glimpse of Mimsee, the last hold on her past life.

Over four more days, Andreiyes filled every corner of their encampment with blankets, clothes, tools, a sharper knife for skinning, and even a bow with arrows. He scrimmaged with invisible enemies and showed her a couple sword-fighting stances. Throughout that time, she strengthened her arms enough to wield an axe one or two swings at a time. There was a thrill to each swing that made the weapon feel powerful and reliable. One day, she planned to be able to throw it with precision and strength.

Other than her survival training, their discussions grew longer and more playful, often ending in laughter and teasing. They told stories around the fire until the moonlight was at its brightest. Every night, Andreiyes fell asleep first and she listened to him elegantly snore – only a prince could manage that – with a smile on her face as she counted the streaks of moonslight through the trees until her eyelids fell shut and the nightmares of that day came back to haunt her. It was his presence at her side that calmed them, that made them disappear. Here, with him, she was not alone.

After their fifth day together, she no longer thought of him as Yierd but as a friend. It made her wonder if perhaps, had events been different, Grayson, Andreiyes and she might have made a good trio. If only she could keep him forever.

†

She had been conscious with Andreiyes for a quint and a day, seven days total, before someone came looking for him in the Weldolf woods. It was past midday, during a game of catch the lockleberry as they each tossed the fruit at each other's mouths when a familiar male voice cried out Your Highness and Prince Andreiyes. The echo through the woods sent chills down her spine, but she hefted her axe nonetheless.

Lord Bryant's calls made reality snap back into place. Her family was dead. Her mark was carved out. Pascual and Willik needed to pay. And all this time with Andreiyes had only been borrowed. That last thought made her bitter.

Andreiyes shook his head and jerked his hand down in a command for her to lay the axe on the ground. As if. She had trusted Pascual before he had stabbed her. She refused to be so naïve again. The prince's face contorted in frustration and annoyance – she was getting good at reading his expressions – as he mouthed '*hide*' and strode away toward what remained of Millau manor.

Kaianne shadowed his paces, clinging to the trees for cover. The need to wipe the fake kindness off the Pascual's face fueled her bravery, but she wasn't stupid. She was small, young and still weak from her wounds and lack of muscle. Almost anyone could overpower her in this state, but she refused to be left behind while her family's murderer was nearby. Her arms burned from the weight of the axe, and quickly she went from carrying the weapon to dragging it.

"Your Highness." The bellow was closer, followed by rasped mutterings from several male voices.

Twigs snapped in the distance. Birds batted their wings erratically and scattered. The leafy bushes rustled which meant the incomers were traipsing through whichever way they could. Clearly, they didn't know the cleanest passageways through Weldolf. Too bad for them. She knew them like the back of her hand, having played in these woods since she could walk.

She caught a few of their aggressive curses and flinched. Her heart thumped wildly against her chest. She slumped against a tree for a moment, fear overriding her senses. She rubbed at the pain in her abdomen she had not felt since waking days before. It throbbed like a new wound. The dead look in Dea's eyes stared back at her. Adi's screams echoed in her ears. She couldn't confront Lord Pascual, not yet. She wasn't ready.

"What in Aethel's good name is the reason for this ruckus?" Andreiyes' voice was a balm to her jitters. She crept one tree closer, the princeling's figure in sight, whoever else concealed by distant trunks.

"Your Highness? Are you…are you well?" Pascual asked.

"Are you implying I look ill, Lord Bryant?"

"Of course not, dear princeling. I simply, had you but told my guard –"

"Told him what?"

"That you required new attire, my House might have better accommodated you."

"Ah yes, I do look quite feral. Pray tell me that is not your excuse for disturbing my peace."

"No, your Highness, the King demands your return."

Lord Pascual came into view. His blond hair was tied in a knot at the back of his head and contrasted with the woods' brown and greens. Despite her erratic heartbeat and numbing fingers, Kaianne could not look away. His pale skin looked lighter than usual despite the wood's shadows. His eyes were drawn. His posture was stiff, and his demeanor was the most reserved she had ever seen on the man. He handed Andreiyes a scroll.

"'It's regarding your uncle. The crown prince is dead."

Kaianne smothered a gasp with one hand. Poor Andreiyes. He had always spoken so fondly of his uncle to Grayson, but never once had she overheard him mention the crown prince was ill. If not sickness, then what? Everyone knew about Aethel's curse: the ten royals in line for the throne born with the rare amber eyes were untouchable unless the assassin was willing to sacrifice the lives of their entire lineage, all those within fifty paces, and those of another line at random.

Andreiyes snatched the parchment from the Lord, cracked the seal, and unraveled it without a word. Long moments stretched, the whispering among Pascual's men the only sound aside from the crawling of critters. From her position, the script on the vellum was impossible to decipher. Whatever the message said must have confirmed Pascual's announcement. Andreiyes crumpled the parchment and sunk to the ground, head buried in his hands.

"My deepest condolences. Crown Prince Terris would have made a fine king."

"Yes, he would have." His sniffle made Kaianne's chest clench.

"Did the King mention in your scroll the cause of the crown prince's demise? We were not aware he was ill."

"If the King did not inform you, it is not my place to." Andreiyes' tone brokered no argument. He stood. "Ready my carriage to depart from Millau Manor's gates by a quarter past midday, and a set of fresh attire. Now leave me."

"My men will assist you." Pascual waved them forward.

"I said leave."

He tossed up his hood and left them without a glance back. Then, he passed her without the slightest sign of acknowledgement. Well, whether he was grieving or not, she hated being ignored, especially since he was going to leave her soon, all alone with no one in the world. She peered over her shoulder in Lord Bryant's direction. He and his men were already gone to do the prince's bidding, and that further built her frustration. It seemed Pascual was faithful to the crown's power but not to his lifelong friends.

"Are you truly leaving me?" Kaianne caught up to Andreiyes and panted. No answer. "Is Lord Bryant trying to trick you?" He shook his head and accelerated his pace. "Do you want to talk about your uncle?"

"No." It was a curt response, but at least it was something.

"I always liked Prince Terris. He always made time to play with us children during visits to Millau manor, even though most other visitors only cared about talking to Papa or Mama."

They arrived at their encampment. Andreiyes drank his fill from a waterskin and wet the bottom of his tunic to wipe his face clean. Still, he added nothing to the conversation.

"There were so many games we played. Hide-fetch, chase, weave the flower. Sometimes he brought treats and shared them with us under the willow tree."

It was unsettling to not have Andreiyes respond. He dug through bushes, branches swishing and rustling, to pull out his belt, sword and sheath adorned with gems and gold. A pouch followed that he emptied into his hand: the livery collar with his Royal griffin insignia that he rarely wore.

"I think he would have liked having children, but he never married. Do you know why? He would have made a good father, I think. Better than mine. Perhaps that way, he would not have been so sad. I think he meant to hide it, but whenever he walked our gardens alone, he looked worn down and unhappy."

"Enough." Pain laced his tone. His face was scrunched, his eyes searching the branches high above for lords know what. His shoulders were tense, almost quivering.

She stepped forward and did a very unladylike thing. She embraced his tall figure, her arms circling his thin waist, her hands on the crook of his back and pulling him toward her, her head against his chest. For a moment she froze, horrified by her actions, until his arms bent around her and his chin rested on her head.

"I'm sorry." She considered asking how his uncle had died, but it seemed even more inappropriate than hugging a royal, especially as his shoulders shook, wetness moistening her scalp. "You'll get through this. If I can do it, so can you."

For a long moment, they stayed like that. It was peaceful and warm. She didn't even mind his three-day old rankness since their trip to the frigid stream. This moment was simply pleasant and right.

"I wish I could keep you," she whispered.

He flinched and pulled away. Papa would have given her two lashings of his belt had she ever lacked so much propriety in front of him. By Andreiyes' reaction, maybe she deserved their sting. It took all her self-control to keep her gaze from plummeting to the ground, dejected.

"I should have left a long time ago."

"Of course. I'm sorry my troublesome nature kept you occupied."

She helped him pack his few belongings. Almost everything was staying behind with her, and it felt surreal to think that he was leaving just like he said he would days before. He had a very valid reason, and she had known it was going to happen sooner or later. It just didn't seem fair. She forced back tears that threatened to come as she handed him the waterskin.

"Keep it." He pushed it back to her. "There will be another for me. And this is for you." The dagger gifted by her grandfather lay sheathed in his outstretched hands.

"You kept it," she accused.

Not a speck of blood remained on it, as if the memory of the hilt protruding from her gut had been only a nightmare. She rubbed her fresh scar absently, the skin prickling.

"Why give it back to me?"

He shook his head. "It belongs to you. 'Tis a symbol of who you are. You will always be a Lyssandre, even if you can no longer use the name."

She shrugged. "It's just a name."

"As is Yierd, but you give it meaning. Lyssandre can mean anything you want it to in here." He pressed a hand to her heart, then her forehead. "And here."

"How is it you can sound like the worst arse in one moment and the kindest lad the next?"

"How is it a ladyling like yourself can curse like a lordling?"

"Haven't you heard? I'm not a ladyling anymore." She winked and relished in his smile, despite how quickly it faded.

"These are also for you." From the inside of his cloak pocket, he fetched the three gold brooches that he had used to keep her wound closed and placed them in her hand.

Accepting the dagger was only natural, it was hers after all, but these felt like too much. "I wasn't aware we were exchanging gifts. Otherwise I might have gathered some shrooms for your voyage."

"These will trade for a good sum. You need to afford food while you learn to fend for yourself."

"Oh." The metal and gems cooled her skin, looking far less stunning and elegant than they had moments before. "You'll never come by to see me then?"

"No, I will." That had her smiling. "Give me two, perhaps three cycles at most, and I shall return. I promise."

He pressed his lips to her temple. So soft, so gentle – her skin tingled, warmth spreading all over her face.

"I shall hold you to it, Andy."

He regarded her coolly for a moment, his bright amber gaze searching her dull brown eyes. "Andy?"

She shrugged. "Yierd doesn't seem so fitting anymore."

He fastened his belt along his waist and adjusted his weapons, then tossed his travel sack over his shoulder. "Never stop smiling," he said with a wink and a nudge to her chin with one finger.

Then he was gone, leaving in the same direction he had gone twice a day for the last seven days. Only this time, he was not returning. Even with all the gold in her hands and the memory of his kind words and his kiss, she had never felt so alone.

Ten

The Order's Temple - Telfinor

With the tap of a gavel that echoed against the Chamber of Accords' marble walls, Archchancellor Aroawn proclaimed the council session adjourned. Rau slumped back into his chair and rubbed at the emaciated skin and tendons of his hands. Nine of his fellow High Masters pounded their fists on the table in approval. Apparently, Aroawn had overestimated Rau's influence with the High Council, and Rau had underestimated their bloodlust. A Flawed's birth officially sentenced its family to die with it, not just the mother.

This was unbecoming of the Order. They were better than the enemy. They held a higher purpose. W*hy* were they debasing themselves by employing such tactics? Rau had said such and much more throughout the session and implored them to see the error of such a way. It had been pointless. Their anger remained too great. Their pain from long ago still festered.

Before the Apostate War, the Order and the realms were a unit. The royals of each kingdom made their own laws and verdicts while the Order checked and balanced their power and acted as mediators between realms, but that had not been enough for the royals. They wanted it all and waited until a volcanic catastrophe weakened the Order to attack. The peace

Aethel and Gaia had founded was rammed through that day, the pieces crushed to dust the day of the Truce Treaty. The Order had won the war, but the royals, ever the deceitful bastards, had not accepted their defeat. Under the guise of a new peace, the Order's strongest met the Isyldillian, Lakoldesh, Nimedorian, and Gyldrit royals at the Well of Unity to sign a treaty while unknowingly leaving the Temple open to a bloodbath.

The burn of betrayal still raged in Rau as if the massacre from five hundred stretches past had occurred only a cycle before. To never forget – another curse courtesy of the Well's Waters – but even in his darkest hour, he had never considered a tactic similar to what Aroawn had implemented.

Chair legs grated against the tile as his Brothers and Sisters rose from their seats in a blur of blue-white robes. They filed toward him. His seat was closest to the doors, opposite Aroawn's. It was a highly sought-after position, and one he had held for centuries. One it seemed he might finally lose. His fellow members chatted amongst themselves – tidbits of gossip reached him concerning their classes, prayers, or the harvest. The session's topic was already filed at the back of their minds. Aileen sneered at him as she passed. Always one to gloat, and gloat she may. Her argument had prevailed. A sigh escaped Rau as he rose to follow suit.

"Rau," Aroawn called from his carved Eidenhail tree chair that matched his white robes. "Stay. We have matters to discuss."

The Archchancellor was bent over the oval desk, quill scratching his signature on parchment after parchment. Disappointment was clear in his lack of eye contact. The thud of the Chamber's stone doors closing behind Rau was ominous, yet he regretted nothing. He had spoken from the heart during the council session, knowing his logic and explanations were sound. Only Aroawn's Sayer talents could have changed Rau's mind. His drynn wielding talents were unique in their potency just like Rau's ability to see drynn instead of only feeling it, but influencing the mind of his subordinates was a line Aroawn would never cross. He was a good man, a great Archchancellor, even if at rare moments misguided. Rau sat and waited.

"You spoke against what we had discussed." Aroawn spoke flatly.

"I was never convinced it was the right way to proceed."

"And now?"

"The Council has proclaimed it so, and therefore it will be done. There is no other say to be had. That's how the vote functions."

"You would follow it?"

"You doubt me?"

There was a moment's pause, too long to Rau's liking.

"No." Aroawn buried his face into the crook of one hand and traced his features downward. "But I've ignored others for too long who've accused you of placing too much stock in tempting words."

Rau raised a brow. "Wordplay is beneath you, Aroawn."

"Chaephren once said you would be my voice of reason. Now at every turn, you seem to attempt to take that role."

Rau shook his head in disbelief. To bring up Chaephren – his once closest friend, the one person he had had more trust in than Aroawn, the man who in the end had shat on him and everything they believed in – it gutted him.

"You compare me to a traitor?"

Chaephren's duplicity had burrowed a hole in his soul. It had come so soon after his wife, Tilnee, had taken her own life when Rau had held onto his faith by a thread. Yet he had stayed the course. For Aroawn to doubt him now, it was a shock that shook the little sanity he clung to.

"Contradicting you doesn't negate my duty to the Order, nor my oath to you. A system can only thrive where there is determination, discipline, and the discussion of ideas. You taught me that, one of the first things I ever learned from you. Now you deny it?"

Aroawn rubbed his temples. "No, it remains a good principle. I know you're not Chaephren, but your vision of this world is based on the now. As Archchancellor, I cannot confine myself to that outlook, and this infernal situation has gone on for far too long. The threats against us are ever evolving, and we must adapt or perish. Our numbers continue to decline. Our Masters are stretched too thin, and Flawed births are increasing.

"Three Flawed in the last moon cycle, another four in the three cycles before. The gods guided our hands to catch them and their helpers, but under your airy ideals, the day will come when we will not be able to subdue them all. What happens then to everything we have strived for? To the charge the gods entrusted us with? To the Faith as it was meant to be?"

"There are other ways, Aroawn. We could create an edict that forbids them from reproducing."

"No."

"Or…Master Xanthra could alter an animal's sense of smell to track specifically Flawed. That would reduce the risk of them —"

"No," the Archchancellor bellowed. His fist struck the table, the bounce reverberating on Rau's end. "You said you would follow. Now follow."

Rau flinched.

"You refuse to understand." The disappointment hung in his old mentor's tone. "And how could you, secluded in our temple for two centuries. You have grown complacent, and that must be remedied."

Rau leaned over the table, the loose flesh of his forearms flattening along the wood. "I've fought by your side for every war, every rebellion since this began. I teach many of our Brothers and Sisters. I help in the growth of our gardens by distributing drynn through the infertile soil. I'm on the High Council by your designation when you were ordained and have advised you well hundreds of times. By Aethel's good graces, I've even forsaken my desire to rest with Moira and Tilnee. What else can I possibly give?"

"You've done much good here, but it is past time to broaden your horizons."

Aroawn rose from his throne and circled the table to Rau's seat, robes swishing. Rau straightened as Aroawn stopped behind him and bore down his weight against Rau's shoulders.

"Four Masters are to depart to each of our four neighboring realms. You will be the one to head to Isyldill."

"Are you silencing my voice? We're part of a whole, Aroawn. That's why there is a council. Does my opposition threaten you so much?"

"Do not challenge me, Rau. I promise you will *not* like it."

Rau stiffened. It was unlike Aroawn to throw around idle threats. Aroawn patted Rau's shoulders – a patronizing touch that set Rau further on edge – and sat beside him.

"Your views and opinions are crucial, as always, but I mean to redirect them. To show you what we see. I know a stay in the lower realms will demonstrate my point far better than any conversation could."

"And what am I commissioned to do in that Pyre stricken realm?"

"Observe, instruct, discipline, protect. There's news that Isyldill's crown prince threw himself off the tallest tower of Castle Ravensten. What was left of him needed to be scratched off the bottom of Gaia's Butte. His brother, Prince Balliol, is now next in line, and we need him primed. King Triunn is too old for me to task with the readying of the new crown prince. See to his firstborn as well, Princess Edmira. She seems to be a willful, prissy thing."

"Those are tasks a Foreman, even a Mentee could handle."

"Stuff your pride, Rau. I force myself into their heads all the time. A little presential time with them will not damage your soul half as much."

With a huff, Rau nodded.

"You'll also take note of rumors. There are reports of Carved gatherings across the four realms. A small outpost in Nimedor nearly fell to one such group, and others are said to have been spotted throughout Taelgir. We need to know more. They need to be squashed before another attempt is made against the sanctity of this institution."

"Who else are you sending? Are any other High Council members privy to this special mission?"

"None of their views matter to me as much as yours."

What a load of rubbish. The words lay on the edge of Rau's tongue as he narrowed his eyes at his old mentor – older naturally by nearly twenty stretches when they had first met – before he smoothed his features into indifference. None of his thoughts were free from invasion if Aroawn wished to delve deep into his mind, Rau reminded himself. It was a worry he had seldom if ever had. It was a line Aroawn had never crossed, but now Rau felt the necessity to tamper down his thoughts and bury them deep. Already he had not been careful enough to avoid Aroawn's touch – tactile memory of a person's drynn imprint was necessary for a Sayer's gift to function – and Aroawn's threat weighed on his mind. After all Rau had done for Aroawn, for the Order, it was an insult in the face of all their centuries of brotherhood.

"At the next council session, who will decide my vote? You?"

"For it to cause that sort of dissent among the council?" Aroawn's thin lips curled as he shook his head. "No, your vote shall go to no one."

"My voice is not to be heard? Even by falker?"

"No."

Rau slapped his hands, palm to back. The sting was a reassurance. "If I am to be in the presence of Isyldill's royal family, you could still bring council matters to me through Triunn."

Aroawn squinted, lips pursed. "To be seen."

Those three little words crushed him, like a boot to an ant before smearing the insect's entrails as far as they could go. All these stretches, all his hard work, all he sacrificed, just for him to be pushed aside as an insignificant. Guiding Aroawn and the Order had been his purpose, his reason for surviving. Now...Aroawn was snaking it out from under him. For centuries emptiness had tugged at his insides as he fought to keep it from consuming him whole. What was the point?

"We will be a council of eleven throughout your absence."

Rau sighed and stared at a painting across the room. "How long will that be?"

"However long it takes for you to gain some perspective. Four stretches should do it. More, if needed."

Four. Stretches. Over fourteen hundred days. Rau tapped his hands together listlessly.

"I want you by my side again, old friend. When you return, we will once again accomplish wonders together."

Rau grunted. "I'll do as you ask. I'll be what the Order needs me to be. But when I return, I want the same courtesy you approved for Master Ohenor."

Before, he never would have deigned to ask Aroawn for it – the hope being Aroawn would offer it on his own – but it was time. He had done all he could for the Order, and he was tired. So very, very tired. If even his opinions no longer mattered, long life meant little to nothing. Death held the only joys he held onto. He wanted to hold his family once more. He wanted to walk through the gardens of Iltheln with them.

"No," Aroawn whispered so low Rau nearly missed it.

Rau squeezed his fists shut. "I've earned it. Far more than Ohenor ever could."

"Ohenor was never as crucial as you."

"Yet you send me away."

Aroawn slammed his palm on the table, the bounce reaching Rau.

"No." There was no hesitation in the word this time. "I need you. *We* need you."

"When will the need end?"

"You know our task is unending."

"All the more reason to keep me close. Take my counsel and let us find a way without the taking of innocent lives marring our minds."

"There are no innocents. There are those who would follow the gods' edicts and the godless, and you will whittle them out while you set Isyldill's royals straight."

Rau sighed and rubbed at the skin over his bones. This was fruitless. "I'll go as you wish, but the Master you knew will not be the one to return."

"Nogo's fire on you. Is this your grand plan? An ultimatum?"

"I seek peace, Aroawn. An end to the suffering. I want to rest and go by choice so that there is no grieving tree to my bones."

"We are not finished."

"I *need* to be. By casting me out, you prove I'm obsolete. Give me hope. When I return with your...perspective, I want to wane off the Well's Waters."

Aroawn's fists balled. His jaw clenched, teeth grating teeth, rage paling his dark face. The Archchancellor tended to mask his emotions better than most, an aspect connected to his talents Rau always supposed, yet here he was as agitated as he had been during the first rebellions after the Stewards had reestablished peace. With a lurch, the Archchancellor upended his chair. It clamored against the tile, snapping a few more strings of their long friendship.

Rau nonchalantly glanced at him, burying tumultuous thoughts. This was a show, one where Aroawn wanted to show him his place if he so much as flinched. But Rau's ideas were all he had left. He clung to them like Moira's grip had been around her dolls. If Aroawn no longer required his aid, then his time had come. Aroawn simply did not realize it yet.

⯒✦⯑

*P*acking was a simple affair. He held very few possessions in his bedroom on the fourth floor – the same chamber he had occupied since his ascendance as Master. The paintings Tilnee had forced him to purchase at a bazaar early in their marriage still hung above his lone dresser. He had long ago donated her clothing and jewelry to the less fortunate. Only Moira's chimaera doll decorated the furniture top with its vibrant colors, one for each part of a different animal.

A smile tugged at the corners of his lips when he found a few of its seams undone at one paw. No matter how many times he sewed it shut, at the slightest tension those same ones always unfastened. Always in the same spot where Moira had held and lugged it around. It was coming with him.

Next his clothing went into the traveling bags, all sapphire robes. He was not a High Council member where he was going, and there was no point in trailing along the ones embroidered with the white Eidenhail's tree.

He said his goodbyes to his Brothers and Sisters – from the ones like him who had lived too long to the youngsters who had yet to understand real pain. They had coalesced at the gates to bid him and the three other Masters safe travels. Some he embraced while with others he exchanged a handshake or smile. Aroawn's friendly pats on his shoulder were more than the Archchancellor gave the three others, but not enough to deter Rau's mind. He had already given too much of himself to the cause. Physically he resembled an underfed thirty-something, but his mind had felt the passing of every single stretch.

Rau tapped his fist to his chest. "For the Faith."

The carriage creaked as he climbed into it. It was a gaudy thing, so contrary to his meager possessions that were strapped to the railings at its top. The exterior had panels depicting scenes of Aethel uniting his Stewards to form the Order with the Eidenhail tree at its center. The interior was gold trimmed, velvet lined and dyed vibrant colors that hurt the eye, and had pouches with frilly ends against the sides of each cushion.

It made him cringe with unease – he who grew up with little to nothing and then spent his life at the temple where wealth did not reflect on status or rank. With the collection of the rents over the five kingdoms, the Order's coffers were filled, and whereas the temple did not need it, it made sense to display wealth on visits to realms where riches meant power. Rau huffed in annoyance at the thought of spending almost thirteen days in it, only two days shy of an entire bilial. At least he would be alone.

The carriage door clicked shut behind him with a certain finality. It seemed to cut him off from the chatter outside. The first pull of the carriage lurched him to the back of the cushion. Slowly, the Temple fell from sight under the crush of small stones beneath the wheels. It lulled him with a steady, jolting rhythm into a rare state of repose.

On the seat across from him, two large trunks were strapped in, a clip lock on each in the form of a well as the only decor. In total, they held ninety-six flasks of Well's water, enough to supply his addiction for eight stretches. This far from Aroawn, Rau gave in to the hilarity of the situation. He chuckled to himself, with no care that his driver might hear his sudden lack of nonchalance. A minimum of four stretches away from the temple, Aroawn had said. Oh, Rau would gain perspective. That was a certainty, but he doubted Aroawn would be very pleased with the result.

He flipped open the case and plucked up one flask. After a moment's hesitation, he dumped its precious cargo out the window. Tomorrow, his journey toward abstinence was beginning.

$\mathcal{E}$leven

*I*t was a long eleven days of travel back to Castle Ravensten. Andreiyes swore the days were stretching longer and the nights were shrinking the further they went. He spent the first in the carriage. No one was to see him disheveled, dirty, and dressed like a pauper in rags. After a bath at an inn, he abandoned his carriage to the rear of the procession and rode with the men, leading the way.

The King's missive had been succinct and disturbingly blunt: *You are hereby ordered to Castle Ravensten for the ceremonial burial of Crown Prince Terris following his self-slaughter.* No beating around the bush, no care in the wording – it was cold, even for Grandfather.

Uncle Terris ending his own life...Andreiyes had felt shock at that announcement – another bright light in the world burned to ash. Uncle knew how to drink his weight in mead and remain mirthful. He never snitched to Father when he caught Andreiyes mid-prank. Uncle had taught him to hunt and where the best hideaways were to spy on the servant maidens when they dipped in the underground springs for a bath. Why in all Taelgir would one of the most powerful and richest in the realm do such a thing? He had had everything to look forward to, and yet he had thrown it all away. Perhaps Ynnea – no, her name was Kaianne now – was right. There had been sadness lurking beneath the surface only a gentle soul like hers could have seen.

Gentle soul, who was he fiddling to? Irritating, obnoxious soul was more to the point, but the thought was half-hearted. How was she going to get on without him? He swiped a hand down his face. Gods, if the kingsmen escorting him could read his thoughts, they would be falling off their horses bent over in fits of laughter. She was fine. She would be fine. He repeated those words to himself whenever she popped into his head. After the next three cycles at the Castle, he would find an excuse to spur himself away from his confinement and go south for a visit.

In the meantime, he relished in being surrounded by men. The first couple nights were bleak as the gloom of the prince's death dangled over everyone's head like a noose. That tension quickly lessened. Their banter the subsequent evenings, whether in a dining hall of a great House, camped in fields or at an inn made Andreiyes feel like who he had been before the slaughter at the Millau estate had stolen a sliver of his soul. He joined in, conjuring a tale of his imaginings that boasted his prowess and hid his inexperience. The men patted his back in approval and drank to his continued good health, not another care in the world. It reassured him, but stray worries of Ynnea's well-being stubbornly filtered in. Kaianne, not Ynnea. Pitting Nogo. This name change was hard to keep straight.

On the eleventh day, with the temperature already holding a light airy chill though only in the Beta cycle of the Stretch of Gain, they entered Lityoll. Isyldill's capital city was built at the base of Gaia's Butte where the King's castle stood ever unchanging. Up on its perch, Castle Ravensten attracted the eye like an elaborate dessert among a table of fruit from moldy to ripe. That was Lityoll. Its best homes and merchants lay along the main road toward the castle to disguise the rest of the city that declined into shacks of clay piled one atop the other and squeezed between the next. Andreiyes had only once traveled deep into Lityoll past the refuge of the middle-class homes as a prank to his guards. He would forever remember the cloying stench of all types of secretions that had his eyes watering and the loss of his purse after a beating in a darkened alley. Even as a royal, it was clear not all parts of the city were open to him.

His empty carriage bounced along the cobblestone street, its ruckus a clear sign for the villagers to stay clear if the clopping of horse hooves was not explicit enough. And the people did. A few lined the edges of the road, their heads and bodies tipped in a bow as the procession passed through.

They traveled up the butte's switchbacks – fresh air blowing away the city's ripe scents – along the homes of lower nobles that did not have their own estates but lived in mansions carved into the mount's side instead. It was considered an honor to live nearest to the top of the butte that had risen when Gaia's mortal body had been buried beneath it. The first ruler of Isyldill, Lenierz Jonah, second born of the gods, had forever seen to that glory by building his castle atop his mother's grave. Sordid thing in Andreiyes' opinion. In his ancestor's place, he would not have rested above his late mother – no matter how much soil separated them – without forever losing the ability to sleep.

The castle was guarded by parallel watchtowers on either side of a portcullis and two sets of curtain walls. The first ringed the butte's edges. Guards in Isyldill's amber and brown paced the old age battlements that spanned the mount's cliffs, a remnant of a history when men watched the skies for dragon attacks. Now they were pointless, some might say decorative, but it remained tradition to renovate the wall whenever stone crumbled or was dislodged.

Sentinels in the watchtower rang coded bell signals for each type of approach. With the rhythmic two beat knell to announce a royal's nearing, Andreiyes and his kingsmen plodded through the last stretch of lower noble Houses and beneath the raised portcullis. Never in his life had he seen the barbaric gate closed, yet a lump lodged in his throat as though it menaced to keep him locked in these walls forever if he was not mindful.

The second curtain wall was far younger, having been built in the last century. The stones were lighter, with less exposure to moss and the elements. It cross sectioned the first in a crescent moon along which the families of high ranking kingsmen resided. Their homes, taverns and merchant stalls littered the space with bright colors and sounds that contrasted the rigid constraints of castle life.

The rest of the butte's plateau belonged to Castle Ravensten and its courtyards. Once past the second wall, the laughter of children, the music and barking calls of vendors faded into the stone, the crunch of gravel on their approach taking over. It was solemn and mirrored Andreiyes' mood. He had hoped to stay away longer.

From the exterior, the castle had changed little in the centuries since its completion. It was a relic of a bricked fortress impenetrable by sight if not by force, though none had ever tried. Imposing, formidable – that was the intention. Its large bay windows, roofed battlements and cone towers were the only indications of renovations since its earliest constructions. The interior, on the other hand, reflected modernity and comfort with open spaces and rooms fit for multiple kings that put manors like Millau and Zesco to shame. Every inch was filled with the finest furnishings and embellishments, the mortared floors and walls covered in tile, hardwood, curtain, or tapestry.

That richness however could not hide trauma. How Andreiyes' mother had perished inside, tumbling down stairs while heavy with child. Or how his stepmother, Pearle of House Adel, had overtaken and remodeled every corner of his mother's old chambers with his misfit, petulant, contemptible, ridiculous half-brother of five stretches in tow – Nergail – whose skin was a pitting shade darker than his and his sisters. Or how his Uncle had now ended his life somewhere within this space. The lump in his throat thickened. His chest tightened as his fists squeezed the horse's reins to command a halt. Welcome home.

※↓※

*F*ather met him in the circular entrance hall with his two sisters standing on either side of him. No sight of the great and honorable Pearle nor her whining urchin. Andreiyes' shoulders relaxed a sliver, but the castle air remained oppressive. Despite only seeing his three family members in the hall and the guards posted at the entrances, distant conversations reverberated from each side into a cacophony of murmurs. It was a reminder that privacy and secrecy were a luxury only granted in the countryside.

"Welcome home, my son." The pain in Father's voice was hard to miss.

Andreiyes first exchanged a peck with his eldest sister. Edmira forced a smile, her face hard-edged and stern, posture stiff despite her elegant figure. Her gown was the typical mourning amber, embroidered with threads of silver and black to shape a griffin's torso and head along the bodice. It circled her shoulders, draped down her arms and hugged her shape like a sheath.

"Welcome back, brother." Even her voice had hardened over the past few cycles. Only two and a half stretches his senior, Edmira somehow managed to appear as jaded as Grandmother Sajra had before her death after ruling at King Triunn's side for nearly three decades.

"Has no one given you a reason to smile in the last three cycles? No fun in the castle, or is it my lack of companionship that has turned you hard and stale?"

A roll of her amber eyes relaxed her features. "Do not think so highly of yourself."

Hardened maybe, but she had not changed too much. "Of course not. Just the right amount."

"Yes, you would think that. Interesting how it takes a family tragedy to force you back among us."

"Enough, the both of you," Father scolded.

Andreiyes tittered internally and winked at his sister. "I missed you, Ed."

"Ditto, An." Her lips twitched.

Without a brother – Nergail, the halfling, did not count – Andreiyes had enjoyed playing pranks on Edmira and teasing her. Her outspokenness and reactions had always made it worthwhile, and she had never been shy in returning the favor. The time he had poured a bucket of ale over her head shortly before being presented to a suitor had to be one of his favorites, though that had earned him in return some embarrassingly snipped attire that had left his rear on display during a banquet of Lords.

He squeezed her hands in his. "'Tis good to be home."

"You might just wish you stayed away."

No teasing in her tone. He cocked his head, waiting for her to elaborate, but when she simply shrugged and kept silent, he moved around to his other sister.

On Katheryn's forehead, he tapered a kiss and sighed at how timid and demure she remained even with him. Her amber eyes met his for an instant before they plunged back to whatever mesmerized her in the rug. The curls of her hair fell over her face to hide it further. It was odd to think Kaianne and her were practically the same age. Whereas he could never imagine Kaianne being so passive, the image of Katheryn attempting to build a fire was downright preposterous. He stifled a chuckle and bowed before Father.

Prince Balliol had the same amber eyes as Andreiyes and his sisters. Only ten of the Lenierz royal line had those eyes, and only those ten could ever aspire to the throne in the order of their birth. Father's eyes curved down in an unusual display of fatigue. New stress grooves marred his forehead. His black hair lay past his shoulders, untied despite Balliol's past preferences, and a shadow of a beard darkened his skin several shades further.

Despite those changes, what shocked Andreiyes the most was the oval heartstone newly embedded in the livery collar that adorned Father's black doublet and tunic. The amber gem glimmered beneath the silver that encased it and spiraled into an 'L' for Lenierz, his family name. Made of a dragon's fossilized heart, Aethel was said to have divided the artifact into five gemstones, endowed it with his own drynn and talents, and handed it down to each of his five sons that each ruled over a realm. Old tomes made references to its ability to enhance a ruler's talents, sanctify royal weddings, and accumulate drynn. The first was conjecture as far as Andreiyes was concerned, since not a single royal had been endowed with a talent for centuries.

Nevertheless, the heartstone was revered. Only a royal with matching eyes or their blood-sworn spouse could touch it – not even the Stewards could lay a claim to it without burning to a crisp – and it obeyed the hierarchical birth line. As far as Andreiyes remembered, Grandfather had never laid claim to it, but Uncle Terris had worn it over all formal wear. Once, Andreiyes had been foolish enough to try and steal it from Uncle's chambers as a prank. His arm had tingled from numbness for sandturns afterward despite only grazing a finger along it.

Now Father wore it, and that made the reality of Father's newfound position all the more real.

"'Tis true then? About Uncle? You are now the crown prince?"

A strained pinch of Father's lips etched grief into his eyes.

"When is his pyre set to burn?"

"Tonight, son. They are removing Terris from the crypt's doldrums casket as we speak. He will soon take his place amongst our ancestors in Iltheln."

"Are we not to wait for Uncle Dagrun?"

"His husband has caught a fever. He will not be joining us, but I am glad you are here."

Father tugged Andreiyes into a firm embrace. Andreiyes stood stiffly, unaccustomed to such blatant affection. Father had not gathered him into his arms since before Mother passed. A few stretches before, he craved such a show of tenderness. Now, it felt bloody awkward. Girls needed that sort of thing, not a young man nearing his prime. To make matters worse, Edmira shrugged at him with resignation, as if this display were now the norm. Finally, *finally*, Father pulled back and gave the usual squeeze to his shoulder and tap on the cheek. That was the loving father he knew.

"Do we know why Terris did this?"

Father sighed dejectedly and squeezed Andreiyes' shoulder harder. "His woes, his pain, we cannot judge. If I…if I did not have the three of you to think of, I cannot say I would not follow."

Andreiyes reared back. "You cannot mean that."

In the shadow of his father's figure, Edmira shook her head, mouthing '*do not push*'. Like the pits, he would not. He sure as the gods themselves was not about to accept this self-deprecating, resigned version of Father.

"Tell me that was a poorly made quip."

"Oh son." Balliol shook his head and tapped Andreiyes' cheek. "There are things you do not know yet. Things I must tell you, but if I held a choice in the matter, never would I pass this curse on to your sister or, gods forsaken, yourself."

"What are you going on about?"

"Later. Come, midday meal with the King awaits, but I am relieved you are well. Commander Bryant sent troublesome reports in your regards."

"Not surprising." Andreiyes raised a brow at the conversation change but let Father guide the way through the mirrored double doors near the stairwells' base. Their boots and heels clacked against the vestibule's tile, echoing down the hallway to the gathering chamber.

"Yes. Apparently, you stayed behind after an assault," Edmira added with that arrogance of hers. She slipped her arm around his elbow. "Unguarded, without regard to life, in the woods of all places. Like a bandit."

"You should try it, Ed. Moss makes a softer cushion than down feathers. And the freshness of it would save you hours on skin care."

Balliol bellowed an aggravated sigh. "What you did was reckless, and your reported demeanor is unbefitting of your rank."

"I hardly consider Bryant's report worthwhile since he was the one that perpetrated said assault. No, not assault, massacre." Andreiyes stopped midstep. "The Lyssandres, their servants, Millau mansion, gone. All of it."

Katheryn gasped while Father whispered, "I know."

"Grayson?" Ed asked. When he nodded, she lay her head against his shoulder. "I am so sorry, An."

"Father. Tell me Bryant was overzealous in his charge. Tell me the King's letter was a ruse."

"A Flawed birth cannot be disregarded. You know that, son."

"This was not only one Flawed. This was an entire family of loyal Marked. Guardsmen that were protecting their sworn duty. Servants who had done no wrong. I saw it all burn. I dug through the remains. I had their ash under my nails."

"You what?" Ed asked.

"One child, unable to walk, talk or even lift a spoon, could never be evil enough to merit all those deaths. This sort of devastation is what the realm should be protecting its people from, not causing it."

"Hush, *hush*," Father's voice grated in his ear. Balliol gripped his son's doublet collar. "You are never to utter a word of such ideals before the King. Never. If ever he were to…Promise me. None of you, not a whisper."

The grief had vanished from Father's eyes, a severity carved in them instead. These jumps in emotional extremes were a stark difference to the Father he knew. Thank the moons he had not mentioned Kaianne. He nodded, unsure of what else to do.

"Good." Balliol released them and inhaled deeply. "You have questions. You need answers. I know. We will speak of this after midday meal, during the King's garden stroll. In my study."

⁜⊥⁜

*L*unch was uneventful. The clanging of utensils and the scratch of knives against porcelain made up most of the conversation if not for Grandfather's open-mouthed chewing and Nergail's tantrum at refusing half the meal presented. From the other side of the twelve-foot table, the King seemed as stoic as ever and unaffected by the death of his eldest son. Then again, Andreiyes had rarely seen even a frown on the man's square face in his fifteen stretches. It made him wonder how in all Taelgir the wrinkles on Grandfather's face came about.

Father sat stiffly next to his wife-in-title, Pearle of House Adel. Considering her black hair, heart-shaped face, constantly red tainted lips and objectionable age – with only eleven stretches on Andreiyes – it was not beauty or youth that kept the married couple apart, but deceit. She had managed to trick Balliol, who had still been grieving his first wife's death, into a blood oath marriage while inebriated. Their one-time union had spawned a half-brother for Andreiyes and his sisters. Father had never forgiven her. He and Edmira had sworn to do the same.

At least the food was delectable. After his stay with Kaianne and travel rations, Andreiyes dug in with fervor. Steaming pots of leeks, carrots and parsnips buried in gravy. Venison roasted in jam. Fresh-baked sweetened bread. And two roasted qualves, a bird primarily found in the realm of Lakoldon that on occasion flew through Isyldill's borders, Grandfather's favorite.

The King broke off a qualf thigh and seemed to suck the meat right off the bone until it was clean and smooth. Considering Grandfather's age…impressive. Grandfather reached for a second leg, a gleam in his eyes that put Andreiyes on edge. Andreiyes had never been certain if Grandfather actually preferred qualf meat to other poultry or if instead the King took pleasure in the risk hunters took retrieving a bird for him while trying not to touch the invisible border between the two realms and disintegrating to ash. Now, after recent events and Father's stern warning, Andreiyes was close to betting on the latter. That ended his appetite.

※ᛪ※

A guard knocked on the door to Father's study while Andreiyes waited in the hall. This was the third time and Father had yet to answer. Andreiyes cracked his neck and rolled his shoulders.

Grandfather was off in the gardens, surely enjoying his afternoon stroll beneath dry but cloudy skies, cane shaking in his grip while a maiden on each side provided 'moral' support. Therefore, Father had no excuse to delay the discussion he promised.

"You are certain the Crown Prince is within?" Andreiyes asked the guard. A shiver raced down his spine. Gods, it was odd to refer to Father using that title.

"Yes, your Highness. He entered his sitting room with Princess Edmira not long before your arrival. Should we try him there?"

"No." Father had said to meet in his study. Time for a fourth try, Andreiyes' way.

He stepped forward and pounded his fist on the door repeatedly until his fist ached. He had never been the patient one in the family.

"Father. You summoned me. Here I am, in the hallway. Waiting, like a good son. I know Ed is in there with you." He did not, but he assumed.

The handle clicked. The door creaked open, and Father ushered him in, lips pinched.

"I expected more decorum from you, Andreiyes." Balliol slammed the door shut behind Andreiyes.

"And you had it. For three announcements without response."

Andreiyes eyed his Father's study. The curtains were pulled shut but since the outer shutters remained open, light filtered through the layers of cloth. Burning candelabras replaced the sun. That was not half as odd as the piles of old tomes arranged along the 'U' shape of Father's desk and across the floor – tomes that were normally tucked away on shelves in the Archive Chamber. By the look of it, Father was becoming a hermit, ready to drag him and his sister into it. Actually, she appeared already at ease. Edmira lay in a chaise, one such tome open atop a cloth on her lap. She rolled her eyes at him and returned to her book. Andreiyes raised a brow. She had never been an avid reader before.

"That poor guard certainly believes you furious with me, denying me entry, your poor son you have not seen in three cycles. All that to find you reading…" He rubbed off the dust from the cover of the tome on the nearest pile. "'*The Brands of Taelgir*'. In old Syldian? What is this? What sort of mythological nonsense have you buried yourselves into?"

"Historical, not mythological," Edmira corrected. "These books were scribed on past recounts and events."

Ancient events. Syldian had not been used in Isyldill since the Apostate War more than five hundred stretches before. The treaty between the Order and the five realms had made Elginich the universal language, and slowly the realms' own languages had died off. Only a rare few outside the royal family were still taught the old tongue.

"And buried behind more recent works in what I suspect an attempt to hide them," Father said as he pried Andreiyes' find from its pile and delicately opened it. The spine cracked. The pages crackled and dust swam in the air, tickling Andreiyes' nose.

He sneezed. "I find myself lost to the importance of this conversation."

"Somewhere, in one of these, may lie the key."

"The key to what?" This was particularly cryptic even for Father.

"To our freedom."

"Very much *still* confused."

A chair was dragged along the hardwood floor, bumping past each dent and crevice in the wood. "Have a seat and let me explain."

Andreiyes sprawled himself into the armchair, staring ahead at Father as the man settled against the edge of his desk. If Andreiyes was to have an unplanned tutoring session with the crown prince himself, he would bloody well be comfortable for it.

"What have you retained about our history?"

Was Father testing his attentiveness to his tutors? "The little Sir Microlf felt necessary for my education. Our creation through the gods before the onset of Schlenkra and the war with dragons that followed, the division of the five realms to their birthed offspring. One of which was Lenierz, the start of our royal line. Also, Aethel and Gaia's blessing when they chose to leave their physical bodies behind. Sir Microlf mentioned nearly nothing of importance between the centuries that followed and the Apostate War, except to mention the societal structures that came about and the prosperity that followed. Have I absorbed well enough, Father? Do I pass your test?"

"The Apostate War. What do you know of that time?"

"Our ancestors, along with the other royal families, grew too greedy while the Order was too ambitious for power."

"Sir Microlf never spoke of the Order in that manner," Edmira interjected.

Andreiyes shrugged. "I read between the lines. We went to war because the Order was sidelining the royal families and needed tempering after continually overstepping their advisory duties and attempting to rule in the stead of the gods' pure descendants."

"Again, not the version we were taught."

"Of course. But if I took heed to every word that spewed from Microlf's mouth, I would almost believe us royals were Nogo's spawn and that at any moment, we might smite our own lands. Is that truly what you wish me to believe?"

"You just enjoy twisting words."

Father pinched the bridge of his nose. "You both try my patience."

"As we always have. It takes the both of us to counter Katheryn's excessively subdued nature." Andreiyes dusted off a white trail on his trousers. "So, what does this history review have to do with freedom?"

"Tell me who won the Apostate War."

Andreiyes sighed in aggravation and leaned his head back for a view of the ceiling's dentil molding. "It ended in deadlock, no faction stronger than the other, heavy losses on both sides. Negotiations went underway and each agreed not to overstep over the other."

"Ah, that is where the story goes askew."

Andreiyes sat up in attention. "Oh please Father, do contradict Sir Microlf. I would love to see his face when I tell him the crown prince himself finds his history lessons horseshit."

"You kiss with that mouth?" Edmira reared at her own words. "No, no, do not give me an answer to that."

Andreiyes chuckled.

"Andreiyes," Father stood, "you cannot, under any circumstance, mention anything of what I am about to tell you. You are not my heir. You are not supposed to know. I should not yet even be informed, but Terris told me the truth of it the night of the King's coronation. I thought it a farce and laughed at him when he begged for my help to find a solution. I was only a lad of ten at the time. What was I to think?"

Father paced the room. "Terris had been informed of his future fate the day our grandmother died, and her crown was passed on to her eldest, your grandfather. For quints, Terris kept it to himself, obsessing, not believing until the Order's Archchancellor touched his thoughts and made an impression on his mind. It was a warning of sorts of what was to come. That is when he came to me, and I disregarded his concerns."

"You are not making sense, Father."

"There was no deadlock to the war. The royals lost. All of us. And in turn, the Order took over. For five centuries, they have ruled, not us."

Andreiyes snorted. "You are forgetting Grandfather sits on the throne, not a Steward."

"He may sit there, but it is not his mind that dictates the laws and systems of Isyldill. The Order controls him like a puppet, as they have done so with each ruler since the end of the war. I am not even certain anything of the father I once knew remains."

"How would that even be possible?"

"The closest explanation Terris could deduce was that it could be a combination of two drynn manipulation talents used simultaneously: a Sayer and a Planer. But the manipulator would have to be an exceptional wielder to maintain a connection over such long distances." He handed Andreiyes a smaller tome, which Andreiyes flicked closed guarding the open page with his finger for a glimpse at the title: '*Mastering Drynn – A Talent Guide*'. "Sayer talent allows the reading of drynn pathways in the minds of others. If the wielder is gifted enough, they can influence those pathways and alter ideas or behaviors. The Planer talent permits the projection of oneself outward, though there does not seem to be a mention of that talent permitting the incorporation of such projections into another body. But take a look at this notation."

Andreiyes skimmed over the passage then read the handwritten note on the corner of the page.

'Sayer + Planer ≈ occurrence P. Shawna described (Battle of Hamlin). Possession forced surrender?'

"It lends credence to Terris' theory, yes?"

"The Apostate War's Battle of Hamlin?" Andreiyes asked cautiously. P stood for princess, since Queen Shawna inherited the crown a decade after the war. When Father nodded, his mouth went dry. The implications of this were terrifying. He read the descriptions of the talents once more. "And we are certain Stewards have this possession capability?"

"Based on this note and Terris' experience and research, yes. It would be impossible to tell how many."

Andreiyes let the information sink in, his gaze shifting from his sister to father. "The edict that sentenced House Lyssandre. Was it Grandfather or the Order?"

"We cannot ever truly know," Edmira said.

"Your guess. Father, you were here. What did Grandfather say when he ordered it? How did he command it? His behavior, his words."

"He has been King since before either of you were born, and far too long for me to remember what kind of a prince he was before. The only oddity was that the King cut off mid-sentence. His shoulders were tense, unlike their usual hunched bearing. Terris and I argued on the behalf of Lady Lyssandre with his advisors, but he added nothing until he bellowed for silence. That was when he made the decree."

"Nogo's pits," Andreiyes muttered. "If the Order–"

"You should have seen your uncle." Father spoke over him, lost in thought. "Terris, he was so stricken. Poor Margrit. I should have known Terris would not stand for it." Father scrubbed a hand over his beard, his eyes glazed.

Edmira sat up, a brow raised to match Andreiyes'. "What are you saying?"

"Your Uncle never would have sealed a blood-sworn union by his own free will. He was adamant that he never wished to sire a Lenierz heir. But he did once give his heart. After refusing to take her hand in marriage, she wed Thibault Lyssandre. She was the reason he took it upon himself to accompany you to visit Millau manor so often."

Andreiyes' mouth gaped.

"Lady Margrit?" Edmira asked.

Father nodded. "He took the King's decree of House Lyssandre's fate poorly. Sequestered himself for seven days before he…It was the final weight his soul could take."

"So because he was too fragile to handle it, you must?"

"Andreiyes, guard your tongue."

"No. This was his responsibility to bear. I cannot forgive him for passing this to your shoulders, and then Edmira's."

Father grabbed him by the shoulders and shook his head with a sigh. "You have never yet known hardship. You cannot fathom his emotional pain."

"Then explain it to me. Had you been in Uncle Terris' shoes, would you have followed in his footsteps? Would you have chosen never to have us? Would you have killed yourself to leave the crown to Uncle Dagrun?" He had not seen his youngest uncle in two stretches, too busy and happy holed up at his estates in the southeastern Isyldill province of Alihuerte with his blood-sworn spouse. Free, that's what he was. Fortunate grandfather had banished him from Ravensten for taking a secret, male bride.

"Those are impossible questions. Ask me again in three decades and I may have a better answer."

"No. That is not good enough." Andreiyes thrust aside his father's arms. "An entire high house was slaughtered. I want to know what they died for, what my closest friend in this entire forsaken realm was butchered for." He tossed the talent describing tome over his father's desk. It skidded along the hardwood flooring. "I was there. The carnage. Thirty-seven bodies. All of that over one Flawed. Are Flawed even harmful for the fate of the realm? Or is it another of the Order's distortions to keep us under lock and key?"

"Oh, An." Edmira's arms circled him from behind, her head pressed against his back. "Is that why you secluded yourself in the woods?"

He pried himself away from her hold, holding his Father's dimmed eyes. A few cycles ago, making such a fit would have earned him a red cheek. Now, only resignation stared back at him. "I want to know. Are Flawed a threat to Isyldill, or a threat to the Order? What have all these old tomes told you?"

"Andreiyes, you are in pain. I understand that. The Lyssandres, your uncle..." Father approached him gently. "Knowing who is responsible will do nothing but ease your conscience."

"That is already better than nothing. I need to know. Does it not bother you that perhaps all those put down for lacking a griffin's head and for birthing a Flawed die not for the betterment of the realm, but for the Order's own goals?"

Father shook his head. "There is no certainty on the matter. Every record that mentions a Flawed notes their danger and the chaos they would bring if left unchecked. But for all of those, there is no mention anywhere of a Flawed until a decade after the Apostate War's end. Only assumptions can be made for that."

"Then we should make assumptions."

There was pity now in Father's gaze. "Have you ever noticed, son, how people rarely ask the whys of a situation unless they are directly affected? Would you have troubled yourself with this if it had not touched a family you knew?"

"So...I should be shamed into acceptance for not thinking on this sooner? What does that mean for you?"

"Careful, son," Father said slowly. "I have been tolerant because of our losses. That does not mean I accept your disrespect."

"We cannot sit here, reading about the Stewards and their power over *our* realm, discussing it like gossiping ladies and do nothing. Uncle did nothing. Look what that brought him. There must be a way to end this. We must act."

"Yes, An. Because no one else has ever thought of that before."

Andreiyes glared at his sister. "At least let us inform Isyldillians that these actions against their families are not our doing. That we mean no harm against our own."

"To what end? To inspire riots and unrest? What good would revealing our impotence be for Isyldill?"

"We could fight them. The people might assemble. With an army large enough, we could push the Order-"

"How?" Aggravation rose in Father's voice. "We have no measure of how many talented make up the Order's ranks, and Isyldill has none to counter their power. A regular army cannot stand against the power the Order wields. And who would fight against those blessed by the gods? Not a single new royal has been blessed with a talent since the Apostate War. The people might see the gods' work behind that. Can we reason that our own people would not desert us for the Stewards when the gods have seemingly shunned us from their gifts?"

"You cannot believe Aethel and Gaia have chosen the Stewards to rule in the stead of their proper descendants."

"Of course I do not. If that were the case, the Order would not need to go through us to rule the realm. You are thinking emotionally based on your hurt, not on your logic. If there is a way around this, we will find it somewhere amongst all of this." Father waved his arm over the stacks of tomes brimming his study. "A direct confrontation will not be the answer. In this, you are still too young to understand the consequences of such actions."

"I am not the youngling you think I am."

"Actually," Edmira interjected, "that raises a good question. What need does the Order have of us? Why control the realms through proxies? Why not take over the realm themselves?"

Andreiyes raised a brow and crossed his arms, fingers gripping the muscle to counter his frustration.

"The only reason that your uncle and I could ever unravel had to do with the Tying. Before Aethel and Gaia ascended, they divided Taelgir into five sections, one realm for each of their five sons, and tied their lives to it. And although Flawed were not initial creations of the gods, the marks have existed since the Tying. If ever the royal line of a land came to cease, the land and its people were cursed to perish with it. Our guess is, was, that controlling the ruler of a realm gives the Order some measure of control over the land and its people."

Andreiyes immediately thought back to the Zesco manor's war room where two Stewards had stood guard behind a curtain. "Like the map," he whispered.

"You know of that?" Father asked.

"What map?" Edmira glanced between them.

Andreiyes shrugged. "Fell upon one at Zesco by inadvertence."

"Tell me, what map?"

Father rubbed his brows. "There is a drynn produced map generated by our King in three War rooms across the realm: one here in Ravensten, one at Commander Bryant's estate, and the last at Commander Sertrios' estate. On it is represented every Marked Isyldillian and their movements."

"To what end?" Edmira looked positively confused.

"To herd us like cattle. Is that not what you once said, Father? That we were chattel to the realm like cattle to their brands? Animals to manipulate and bend to the Steward's will."

Heavy knocking resounded on the door in an adjacent room of Father's suite, his reception chamber.

"Forgive the intrusion, Your Highness," a muffled voice called.

Father sighed, buried his forehead into his palms, and traipsed past the doorway into the next room. "What?"

"The King has requested your presence in the chapel before the start of the ceremony," the messenger said from the hallway.

"Very well. I shall be along shortly." Father returned to his study. "It is time. Let us put aside all these notions and discussions. Tonight we honor Terris. Knowledge and discoveries may wait until the morrow."

"That sounds dreadfully like doing nothing."

"An, do you think I want to inherit his mess? To be controlled by someone else?" Edmira held his hand, her eyes pleading. "Before any change can happen, we have to find the way, no matter how long it takes."

"Then I shall will it, not read it." Andreiyes strode to the study's door, jaw clenched, tension building in his limbs. He wanted to pummel something, anything, and render it as useless as he felt.

"Andreiyes," Father said as Andreiyes clicked down the door handle-lock. "A Master is on his way to the castle. 'Tis not the time to be reckless. Keep your anger in check. Watch your words. Now more than ever."

"See you in the courtyard." Andreiyes slammed the door behind him.

He kicked the wall for good measure. The thud bounced through his boot, an ache building in his ankle. Father and Ed wanted him to sit, lean back and wait for a solution to present itself all while their people were dying believing their rulers were the cause. And he was supposed to accept that? How could they? Too many had already died. Good women like Lady Lyssandre. Babies who had done nothing and might never do the realm any harm. Carved folk whose only crime was hiding from certain death. People like Grayson caught in the storm. Hundreds, maybe thousands of people. All while he and his kin sat on plush cushions and ate their fill believing in the fantasy of royal supremacy. He volleyed out another kick and another and another until his ankle screamed louder than his voice.

"Your Highness? Are you well?"

Andreiyes shoved the guard aside, avoiding the gazes of the kingsmen that awaited outside the crown prince's chamber. Their tension was clear. One even held a hand to his hilt. Andreiyes stifled a chortle. As if he of all people would go after Father. As if they would survive an encounter against him.

He strode down the too bright hallway, light shining through windows at either extremity and swaying from sconces reflected off mirrors and glass frames. He turned corners and climbed stairs, barreling through with a limp. The ache distracted him enough to focus on reaching his quarters. At least for today, Father was right. Nothing could be done right now. Nothing could be changed at that moment, and certainly not when their thoughts might be a buffet for the incoming Master. But he would find a way to free Edmira, if not Father. There was always a chink in the enemy's armor somewhere, no matter how small. He had not studied strategy and realm dynamics since early childhood for nothing. He would bide his time and –

"Got you," a shrill voice cried as something hard pummeled into Andreiyes' gut and scraped downward. Another strike landed between his legs.

He crumbled to one knee, struggling to breathe, eyes fogged. His midday meal threatened to come up. His throat burned, but he swallowed it back and pulled back his fist to fight back. His attacker laughed, high pitched, childlike. Nergail, the little twit, was bent over in a fit of laughter with a wooden sword dangling from his chubby fingers.

"I bested brother, Mama," Nergail yelled between laughs back through the open doorway to the little freeloader's chambers. "Best princeling in Taelgir. Me."

"I." Andreiyes tore the toy from the boy's fingers. "Am. Not. Your. Brother." He tossed the shaft into the room. It clattered against the tile. "You are nothing. We all are nothing. There is no such thing as the best prince. Better to disillusion yourself now."

Without another thought, he shoved the boy into his rooms. The child tumbled on his rear, his squalling already beginning as Andreiyes slammed the door shut. He left the wailing child behind and rubbed his temples. How in all Taelgir his father had sired that irritant was beyond him.

❉⭣❉

*T*hat evening, under the glow of another Maiesta moon leaving its peak, Uncle Terris' corpse burned. The pyre's flames soared up into the dark night, the smoke blending into the sky's leaden depths taking the rot and decay with it. Uncle was free – not tied down by an unstoppable future, not worried, not hopeful, not happy nor angry – just free. And Andreiyes found he could not hate him for it. The man had been broken from the inside. A prince reduced to being a pawn in an endless game with no outlet.

Andreiyes glanced at Father and at his sisters on either side of the crown prince. Their faces were warmed with firelight. If the tomes did not hold a solution, would Father break like Uncle? Would Edmira follow suit? His future niece or nephew thereafter? He choked on that worry and tightened his fists. It would end. By Aethel's good graces, they were royalty. Pitted or not, he, if no one else, would make it end.

Twelve

Northern Isyldill

Rau squeezed his eyes shut and pressed the back of his palm to his mouth as if that could suppress the nausea. His breathing was labored. Sweat trickled down his brow. His ears rang constantly. His fatigued body weighed him down to the carriage cushion in a slumped mass. The carriage swayed and lurched. Too much.

"Stop," he croaked to his driver, Greenling Averill. "Stop. Stop."

The carriage slowed, every bump in the road more pronounced, but not fast enough. He tumbled out of the still moving transport, his knees crunching against rocks buried in the mud and heaved his morning meal until he was empty and drained. The nausea remained.

Rau crawled to the nearest bed of grass and rested. The lack of obsidian around him in Isyldill was almost surreal. Not a touch of the volcanic stone that covered half of Telfinor was to be seen. The dirt was a deep brown, drynn plentiful within, instead of the beige mulch that passed as soil in the Order's homeland. The grass was vibrant with yellows and green, not washed out like the crops grown behind the Temple. A droplet of rain pelted his cheek. He flinched with the need to take cover, but his flesh did not burn. Another droplet hit the corner of his lips – pure and refreshing. How long had it been since he had felt clean rain on his skin?

"Master?" Averill jumped off the now still carriage and rushed to his side, yellow robes trailing behind him. "What do you need? How may I be of service?"

Rau waved him off, exhausted. "A moment."

He needed a few grainfalls for his stomach to settle. Nogo's wrath it ached, and his throat burned from constant heaving. Eleven days on the road and he still had yet to find the appropriate withdrawal dosage from the Well's waters.

He wanted to wallow in self-pity – him, a battleworn five hundred forty-four stretch old man. Oh, the humor in that. He had forgotten to account for how much additional Well's Water he ingested every day while at the temple on top of his tri-quintly dosage. It wasn't common knowledge Well's water was used in cooking and mixed with their water supply, and he had forgotten to add that in his calculations. Plus, Rau suspected that Aroawn had supplied him on this journey with the bare minimum needed to sustain his body. He groaned. The bastard had read his intentions. Yes, bastard. While Rau lay tortured and rolling on grass and dirt like an injured animal, there was no better word to describe his old mentor.

When the Order first began dispersing Well's water to its members at the end of the Apostate War, a vial's worth every two days had been enough to sustain their drynn and talents. Taking that in account, Rau had planned to push that to every four days. Terrible plan, far too ambitious – the paralyzing, gut-wrenching pain and tremors by the fourth day of travel had proven that. A span of three days was also too much – his skin dried, cracked and bled while he nursed high fevers. Then he had tried a vial every two days, twice in a row in case he only needed time to adjust. The vomiting and cold sweats were far from the worst symptoms of withdrawal, but he could not take this much longer. His stomach ached for food nearly as much as it needed to expel its contents. And water, he felt capable of draining barrels. Too often during this trip he considered drinking both trunks of Well's water flasks dry to stave off his thirst.

By his latest estimates, for these sort of symptoms two days apart, his routine dependency relied on a vial every half day. To the pits with Aroawn. The Archchancellor had made unsupervised withdrawal nearly impossible with this level of dependency. If Aroawn expected him to live four stretches off this supply, it meant he would be required to drink a vial's worth a day. Rau needed to get used to that first before reducing the dosage to minimize withdrawal symptoms. That adjustment alone could take several cycles at the very least, if not an entire stretch, but he would do it. And in record time, if only to prove to Aroawn that this was what he wanted.

"Averill?" he called.

"Yes, Master? Water?" The man knelt at his side, a waterskin extended. In the yellow robes of a Greenling, Averill's hair was shaved only up top while the rest of his head was covered in long, black hair tied at his nape, a few white strands mixed in with the rest. The man had seen quite a few stretches as a Greenling, but despite his loyalty could never aspire to more. His talent was simply too weak. It was amazing he had any at all considering how pale his skin was. "You've been so ill, Master Rau. You must drink."

"Fresh water?" When the man nodded, Rau took a gulp, then another. "What do you think of my illness, Averill?"

Averill retrieved the waterskin. "I'm not sure I get your meaning, Master. You've been sick since we left the Temple with varying gravity. Is it a healer you want me to find in the next village?"

"A tonic to settle the nausea, yes." Rau surveyed the man who looked older than his own frozen age. No visible deception in his demeanor. The edge of concern in his eyes did not appear faked. This was not a Steward privy to the Well's Waters or the meals prepared for Foreman and Masters, so one could reason he had no knowledge of what lay in the carriage's trunks. "What's your purpose on this journey?"

"I am to be your aide in all matters you require for as long as you're abroad. An honor, sir. I've never traveled outside the Temple."

"But you're to report to the Archchancellor on our arrival?"

"Well, yes. I doubt he'll find what I have to say of import–"

"You are not to mention the severity of my symptoms. If he asks, I was weak, pale, nauseous, and ate half my rations. That's all."

"Master, I swore an oath." Averill's eyes widened. The water in the skin sloshed. "I can't lie to the Archchancellor."

"This won't break your oath. There is no lie. I've had the symptoms mentioned. I've only eaten half of my allotted provisions. I simply ask that you not mention anything else. If the Archchancellor was to worry about my health, we may be recalled home." The man's brown eyes softened. "I ask this for the good of the Order. As a High Master, this is where I am needed most. My health should not interfere with that." Rau's muscles cramped for a brief moment as he stifled a chuckle at his own words. Who would have thought *he* would push to remain in Isyldill?

"And if you get worse?"

"I am already on the mend. Am I as ill as the first few days?"

"No, Master," Averill straightened his posture.

Rau nodded briskly. "Help me up, would you?"

Rau's bony fingers gripped into Averill's fleshy, soft palms. The man pulled him up with ease. Long ago Rau had had hands like the Greenling, filled cheeks and muscles like him too, and he missed it dearly. Now his skin was a wrinkly, see-through barrier between bone and air, the fleshiness sucked dry from consuming regular doses of Well's water.

He settled back into the carriage. Averill clacked the door shut behind him. The curtain swung in place. With a sigh, Rau measured out a vial of Well's water and drained it.

The carriage jerked forward. There were two more days of travel until they arrived at Castle Ravensten. Two more days until he was surrounded by pompous, haughty royals who gorged on their own arrogance. For four gruesomely long stretches. He groaned. The thought of it worsened his blooming headache. He rubbed his throbbing temples.

As the carriage swayed and bumped along Aethel's Highway, his nausea returned with a vengeance. Bile rose to his throat. Not again. He needed a distraction before he begged Averill to stop once more. He pried a map from the carriage's side pouch and spread the velum flat on his knees. All of Isyldill lay before him, like an oblong stain a child had fingered with at the edges.

The cities and towns were drawn as grouped blocks, one square per hundred inhabitants. To the north nearest the border with Telfinor stood the ruins of Salost where only an outpost remained and a few homes that now housed only those loyal to the Stewards. They had made a stop there three days before.

Lityoll represented the largest bundle of blocks, located five finger spacings lower than Salost. The city encased Gaia's Butte in a crescent moon, Castle Ravensten depicted atop with a crown. Millian, the town attached to the now-burned Millau Estate, was in the map's dead center with Zesckar less than half a finger width further north, but smaller in size. To the southeast there was Alihuerte nearest to the Gyldrise border, larger than Zesckar by two squares followed by Misthall along the coast and Ollin in size located southwest near Lakoldon's border.

What held his interest were the red circles marked around smaller villages whose names needed a handlens to be read, a few wooded areas, and Ollin. They were locations of Carved raids. Some were far inland, a couple near Millian. So far, the Carved had avoided extending their raids further north. Given the number of sightings, they were growing bolder, perhaps more numerous, and there were rumors that more than an entire hamlet on the coastline had gone rogue. Their motto 'Carved Forever, Free Together' was certainly causing unrest against the Crown. Poor, deluded folk risking infection or death for permanent mutilation and societal rejection.

Rau bit his lip at the irony of the situation. The Order controlled the Crown, and therefore did not tolerate civil unrest against the royals. Tilnee would be rolling in her grave if she knew his mission was to protect the Crown's image and contain the threats against the family of those that had murdered their daughter.

Now he willingly wished to retch, but the nausea was gone. The Well's waters had kicked in. He gritted his teeth and tapped at his hands. More than ever, Rau doubted he could gain the perspective Aroawn wished of him.

*H*is carriage reached Castle Ravensten late on the thirteenth day. The castle was gaudy and enormous just as he remembered and blocked any sight of the Persefin moon in the northern sky. Nothing ethereal or delicate about it. That was the royal way. They had to be seen, acknowledged and worshiped for their wealth and arrogance.

A minimal staff greeted him, but he took no offense. The king, his family and his retinue were already in bed. Praise the gods and the Mistress of Dreams for the peace of mind. He had yet to take his Well's water dosage for the day. Exhaustion made his eyelids droop. His stomach was holding out, but it was only a matter of time before the withdrawal symptoms took over the little control he had left of his cramping body. Already his skin itched, the scar on his face worst of all.

A personal attendant led him to his chambers where Greenling Averill extended his farewells and left Rau alone. His sleeping quarters were oversized for his needs: twice as large and brassy as any he had slept in throughout the voyage and thrice the size of his room at the Temple. Furnishings lined every wall, a bed to fit three, an attached sitting room, and a delightfully private bathing chamber. Excessive was an understatement.

He stripped off his robes and sank into the tub's warm water. His head pressed against the cushion of towels on the tub's edge. His long hair floated around his shoulders. The dust and stress from the day's journey dissolved off his skin.

On the morrow, after drinking his dosage, he would meet with Aroawn through Triunn to discuss the plans to ready the crown prince and the Carved. That would make it a day and a half since his last take.

"Every day, I take my draft," he whispered to himself, eyes closed. "Every single day."

He imagined himself swallowing the water every morning during the travels before slipping back into his carriage. It was the truth he wanted Aroawn to see if he read Rau's thoughts. Freedom was tenuous. Castle Ravensten was another cage of duty, but here his choice to die was going to blossom. He repeated the words over and over until his skin pruned and he believed them.

Thirteen

Six sets of stairs. That's how many Rau needed to descend in order to meet with Aroawn the next morning. His legs were shaking after the fourth set. His old mentor could not have possibly met him in the throne room. No, it had to be the Lenierz crypt where the royals stored their family urns.

The crypt extended into a vaulted corridor that spanned the entire castle estate. Sconces were lit throughout. Every footstep clapped against the expanse of stone. There was no mix of air, no wind, just a suffocating staleness in an echo of footsteps and whispers. Pillars jutted from the walls, each sculpted with a mix of vines and griffins in flight. Their purpose was decorative, Rau assumed, yet the lack of color did not make the place any less bleak. There was not a single grieving tree to be seen, not that any would survive underground.

His feet carried him forward. The sides of his robe's hood swayed in and out of sight with each step. He squeezed his wrists with the opposite hand within his sleeves, eager to get this over with.

The royals were even colder of heart than he previously believed – to burn their dead and bury the ashes so deep underground that no one would care to visit. Any love they might have for their ancestors was sucked out by the chill of the stone. The only memory of the person entombed was their chiseled name under a sculpted face on the façade of the stone veneer – eyes closed, lack of stress lines, obvious replications made from a deceased face – behind which lay their urns. It was eerie to pass by a volley of dead faces in sets of three between pillars.

A group of two dozen people had huddled four pillars ahead. Their gold and black garbs among robed Stewards added another level of gloom to the crypt amongst its torchlight. A chorale filled the crypt, reminding Rau of a ballad sung after a battle centuries ago - solemn, tender, but hopeful.

The smoke of incense tickled his nose. He stopped mid step, assessing the scene. A chiseled stone cover rested against the nearest pillar. The castle's appointed Mentee in his gray robes set a gold rimmed porcelain urn into its hole in the wall. Rau's eyes widened with realization. This was Prince Terris' inurnment.

Nausea built in his throat, and his nails dug into his forearms. He should not be here. This was highly inappropriate. Grief was to be respected. Had he known…Rau squeezed his wrists. If Aroawn intended for him to be uneasy, he had absolutely accomplished that.

Rau glanced down the way he had come, the procession of stone faces daring him to pass them again. Aroawn could call on him later, even if the gods sent him to the pits for it. He turned to leave as footsteps on approach scraped against dirt.

"Master Rau," a female voice whispered. A Greenling in yellow, hair reaching her ears beneath her hood, bowed. "It is an honor to meet you. The King requests your presence beside him."

Rau raised his brows at the obvious disrespect Aroawn was showing the royals and shifted his weight. Decline and Aroawn might consider the refusal another mark against him. Accept and a clear message of power was sent to the royals. Gods, Aroawn knew how he felt about times of mourning. This was a test of the worst kind.

With a nod, he followed after the Greenling and reached the group as the tune ended. Two of the singers embraced. No, not singers. Their eyes were golden amber – Isyldillian royals, and young ones at that. The boy could not have passed his sixteenth name-day and the little lady with her rounded cheeks and button nose appeared a few stretches younger. Two royals actively participating in the service? That surprised him. Another royal joined the embrace. This one was slightly older, her posture more rigid, her eyes cold and calculating. Behind them, a middle-aged royal spoke in hushed tones to an elderly man sporting a silver crown gleaming with amber stones – King Triunn by the looks of it. He filled a large ebony throne, the legs of which were tainted with the crypt's dust. Rau pitied the poor soul chosen to haul the throne down and back up the hundred steps, hopefully empty of the king and his heavy paunch.

The man had not aged well compared to the three decades old portrait of Triunn that hung in the Temple. Back then, one would have called Triunn handsome. Now his eyes sagged with wrinkled creases above and below the lids. His skin hung under his chin while taut over plump cheeks. Bald spots appeared like lattice work among the patches of black and white strands combed into a small bun. All together his features held a permanent look of disdain. When Triunn's gaze fixed on him, there was no sign of Aroawn's signature twitch of the lips or even a spark of recognition in those amber eyes.

"So kind of you to join us, esteemed Master, in this arduous moment." The King's voice rumbled in the back of his throat.

Rau raised a brow. He blocked out his regular sight and focused on his sensation of drynn brimming within the space. The crypt turned blindingly white, drynn movement stifled with the lack of airflow. Trapped in the hundreds of urns hidden in the walls, specks of amber drynn flickered, mirroring dying embers. The particles exiting Rau's body enveloped him in a purple mist, the color of his birth realm, Gyldrise. The group, though, they all shined and pulsed with flowing amber, the royals far more concentrated and brighter than the others. Drynn flowed in and out of them, suffusing the air with puffs of gold until it faded to white while their bodies absorbed more and converted it to amber.

Except for King Triunn. His body was a platform of Isyldillian amber molded with a flow of Telfinorian silver that shaped a second figure within the man's large body. Rau made out the form of Aroawn's sunken cheeks, curved eyes and thin lips within the silver accumulation atop Triunn's face. The silver lips twitched up. Rau released a sigh.

The entombment lasted long enough for Rau's shaky legs to recover and for his unease to switch to impatience. The urn was placed. The prayers were spoken. The stone face was sealed over the hole. Embraces were exchanged amongst the crowd. Condolences were muttered one over the next in this echoing crypt. Endlessly, the rite went on until abruptly it finished.

The Greenlings and Mentees dispersed the royal guests to the opposite end of the crypt from where Rau had entered in a cacophony of conversations and clacking steps. By the time the group reached the stairs, they were but a blip of shapes. Only Triunn remained, along with the four royals and a few servants.

The middle-aged royal was older than the three youngsters by at least twenty stretches. The Isyldillian heartstone gleamed on his livery collar. Several times the man had glanced at Rau during the rite, posture tense, the lump in his throat bobbing repeatedly. Square jaw, high cheekbones, wide set eyes that matched Triunn's. This was the new crown prince, Balliol, which made the three others his progeny.

The oldest two upturned their noses at him, and Rau smirked at the insolence. Royals never changed – always believing respect was due because of a title they never earned. Rau tapped his palm against the other hand. His skin may be withered and flaccid, but at least it was a few shades darker than the lot before him. That in itself was consolation.

"Who are you, sir, to infringe on this private moment?" The young princeling stared him down. Paired with the boy's unmatured features, the look was far from menacing.

"Master Rau," King Triunn said gutturally, "is a revered Brother of the Order, and here at my request. You shall all respect him as such. That is a command. Now, Master Rau, introductions. My only surviving son, Crown Prince Balliol. And his heir, the willful Edmira, my prideful grandson Andreiyes, and my bashful little Katheryn. There's another little bird, Nergail, but at only five name-days, you must understand he does not have the temperament or understanding for these…matters."

There was so much pride in the King's voice at the mention of his descendants. How, by Aethel's strength of will, did Aroawn make Triunn's attachment to his brood sound so true? Did the words spout from Aroawn, or Triunn? And that begged the question: how much control did Aroawn truly have?

"Master Rau will be a guest here with us for the foreseeable future, and we are all to make him welcome."

"What is the purpose of your stay, *Master*?" Andreiyes asked, the title drawn out.

"I'm here to serve as a liaison between the King, the Crown Prince, and the Order."

"Are the Foremen and Greenlings we have shared our hospitality with not sufficient?" Princess Edmira's bluntness matched her stern gaze.

"Please overlook my children's lack of propriety, Master Rau." Balliol bowed his head, but his eyes remained fixed on his offspring. "They were taught better manners than this."

"Why do you wear a hood?" Katheryn asked, her voice gentle like a breeze through chimes.

"For comfort, your Highness." Her genuine smile and bunched cheeks made him melt – the epitome of innocence.

Triunn cleared his throat. "Master Rau shall also be dealing with the Carved raids occurring in the South."

"What Carved raids?" Andreiyes asked.

Rau rubbed his temples. This princeling was already giving him a headache. "Whether you're ignorant or choose to be uninformed about the occurrences in your realm, royal, I suggest you remedy that on your own time."

"How dare you? We are the rulers of this realm. You serve us."

"The Order has *never* served royals, and we never will. You would do well to remember that."

"We, not you, should–"

"Enough." The crown prince squeezed his son's arm and bent over to his ear. "Pick your battles."

The crypt's acoustics made the whispered words echo, and Rau clapped his palm against hand before swiping another glance over each royal. Their hostility, except from the little one, suffocated the air. Four entire stretches of dealing with this. It made his stomach churn, and not from the lack of Well's waters.

"Sir, Master?" Little Katheryn looked up her lashes at him as she swayed in place. Rau pinched his lips to stop the smile that tugged at the corner of his lips. "Do you have a talent like Mentee Tilson?"

"Katheryn, quiet." The eldest scorned.

"No, that's quite alright. I do, Princess, but mine is far stronger than Mentee Tilson's. Have you seen him control his before?"

The girl nodded and bit her lip. "Not on purpose, but he slipped in a puddle as I was turning a corner. His robe went from soaked to dry in seconds." Her honesty was refreshing.

"Yes, he is an Aquer. He can manipulate small quantities of drynn in fluids." There was more to it than that. The elemental talented could generate or negate the element they handled by forcing a change on drynn particles. Most importantly, only the descendants of a royal line could inherit such a talent.

"Master Rau…" Aroawn warned through Triunn's lips.

Rau caught the silver gaze of Aroawn's drynn outline.

'*They need to understand why royals of this age cannot rival a Steward. Why the gods chose us, why they should respect us.*' He let the words echo in his mind, eyes fixed on the shadow of Aroawn's. The silver lips twitched in silent agreement.

"Do you know what drynn is, Princess?" he asked. She nodded once more. "Well, those little particles that make up everything around you, I can displace them at will, whether one little particle or millions at a time."

Her amber eyes widened while the other two siblings exchanged quick glances.

"And we are honored to host the Order's most prominent Hefter," the King added. "Is that not correct, my son?"

"Yes, Your Majesty. A true honor." Balliol inclined his head and snapped out his fingers for his children to follow suit.

"Now that we have that settled. We must discuss your plan for the Carved."

Rau focused his attention on Aroawn's drynn face. "I intend to settle here for a Maiesta cycle. Such will give me the time to adjust to Isyldillian politics and to get acquainted with your heir. Then I shall visit the Southern Commander. I want to know what he has done to protect against these raids."

"Very well. Take Edmira with you to the South. It would do her well to learn more of her future kingdom and how to handle traitors amongst her people."

"Grandfather, my nuptials are to be finalized," the princess said.

"What nuptials?" Her brother's brows furrowed.

"Ah, yes." Triunn rubbed the edges of his beard and sighed. "That does cause an issue. Edmira wed Lord Dresden's eldest son by proxy one cycle ago. By gods' law, her betrothed has a full stretch to retrieve her hand at her home estates before the nuptials are annulled…and shame ensues." The withering glance Triunn threw the girl did not deter her.

"A patriarchal, old-fashioned tradition if you ask me," Edmira muttered, arms crossed.

"You married? Truly?" Andreiyes pulled his eldest sister aside.

"Yes, An. Alright? I married." She shrugged him off.

"And neglected to tell me? Or you, Father? Why was I not informed of this? I would have returned for you."

"I wanted the small ceremony kept private in case…" Edmira's eyes fell to the floor.

"Oh, come on. In case what?"

The princess glanced up with reddened cheeks – an image Rau would never have associated with her attitude – as she whispered, "In case he refused me."

"And you think he would? You, the heir after Father?"

"Well, you know how much persuasion Arkov needs at times. This was what I could devise with his Lord father to force his hand. I could not let him slip away." Ah, there was the royal haughtiness Rau was accustomed to. "Grandfather agreed."

"But I did not," the crown prince interjected. At least, someone in this family had some sense.

Andreiyes pulled his sister aside by the arm. "You forcing his hand will not make him love you."

"What do you know, An? At fifteen, you cannot even fathom the meaning of the word 'love'. But I do love him. I want him. And this will make him mine."

"You would make your Lord husband a possession?"

"Men claim to own their wives frequently. As future queen, why can I not do the same?"

"You are being foolish."

She shrugged off her brother's grip. "Perhaps. But I would rather be foolish in love than foolish on the throne."

"Children, enough." King Triunn pinched his nose and shook his head. "Rau, *Master* Rau, how long would you need for your tour of the south?"

Rau was surprised at Aroawn's quick slip of his title. "For travel, passage to each town and village concerned, and then time allotted to track the traitors down near each, a minimum of four cycles, perhaps double that."

Triunn grunted, still massaging the bridge of his nose. "Take Prince Andreiyes with you instead."

"Me?" The prince's eyes widened. "To help the Master handle Carved? And how exactly are we to *handle* them?"

"In the manner all traitors must be dealt with," Triunn said dismissively.

Any wider and Andreiyes' eyes might have popped out of his head. The princeling squeezed and released his fists. His chest nearly pulsed with an acceleration of his breathing.

Rau left his thoughts open to Aroawn, '*The princeling appears…conflicted.*' Rau turned to Archchancellor's silver face. '*Can you read him?*'

'*I've never made contact with the boy,*' Aroawn snapped in his thoughts, '*so how do you expect me to read him while projecting? You are there in person, you discover his secrets. We'll speak more of your plans on the morrow.*'

With that, Aroawn's silver glow dissipated, leaving behind only Triunn's amber drynn. Rau stayed transfixed on the King. Aroawn had admitted to a limitation of his combined talents. The implications. Aroawn could only project into the body of another as long as he had touched them once, but Rau had never thought that limited his ability to experience the minds of others. To Plane and Saye were separate talents, and yet it seemed, from what Aroawn had divulged the restrictions of one affected the other. Which meant – quite possibly – that Aroawn could not hear his thoughts without line of sight from the Archchancellor's projected form.

"This has been a trying moment for us all. Now, if you would all leave me. I need a moment with my son." Triunn rose with shaky legs from his chair and hobbled toward the stone guarding the ashes of his first born. "Alone."

"Grandfather, I beg you. Do not send me—"

"I said leave. Now." The King was already caressing the sculpted cheeks of his son in the stone.

The royal offspring all bowed, and much to his disdain, Rau mimicked. Pretense needed to be upheld for diplomatic reasons. By Nogo's wrath, he hated pretenses.

Their footsteps echoed against the crypt's vaulted ceiling, but they did not muffle the King's shuddered sobs. It built an all too familiar ache that had Rau absentmindedly rubbing his chest. Beside Rau, the new crown prince turned to watch his father press his head to the stone facade. Whatever burdens Prince Terris' heart had held, his suffering had now transferred to his loved ones. They would carry it for the rest of their lives along with the guilt of not having known, of not having seen the signs, of not having done anything to prevent his death. Just like what Tilnee's suicide had done to Rau for centuries. Triunn and his family were fortunate this torment would only haunt them the short remainder of their lives.

Rau turned away and focused on the burn in his calves that increased with each step up the stairwell. It crept up his legs and fired into his lungs by the fourth set of stairs. Just as he reached the top of the last set, bent over, huffing and puffing like the old man he felt like inside, his title echoed from behind.

Footsteps pounded in a racing procession. The princeling appeared, all his youth smarting through an accursed lack of panting.

"What?"

"I wish to discuss our travel plans." Contempt oozed from the princeling.

"The itinerary has already been decided and at this time is none of your concern." Rau strode down the hallway, heading for the nearest exit to the gardens. Nothing sounded better than a stroll to absorb some fresh air after the stillness of the crypt.

"Who chose the itinerary?" Annoyingly, the prince kept pace. "Because it certainly was not me, my sister, or father. I know for a fact you have not met with the King until just now. As a prince of this realm, I demand you tell me your route, and if it is not satisfactory to my wishes, it shall be changed."

The princeling demanded. Rau was not sure whether to laugh or rub his temples. Arrogant, foolish royals. It was always about their needs, their wishes, their desires. Rau accelerated his steps.

"Master. Master Rau."

To Rau's irritation, the princeling stuck to him like a fly to sap even when he crossed the threshold to the gardens. He ignored the boy to take in the pleasant breeze, the sway of the trees, the chirp of the birds and the scent of pine in the air. None of it appeased him, not with the royal yapping in his ears.

"Please." That grumbled word made Rau pause. "I only ask that we pass near the Millau Estate on our way south."

"You ask?" Rau bit down a scoff. Millau Estate, the name rang a bell. "I was not aware anyone remained there."

"No, no one does. Not since House Lyssandre…"

Rau cringed within the darkness of his hood. "Why would you concern yourself with a vacated estate?"

The princeling cleared his throat. "I was there when I received the call to return for my uncle's burial and left behind…some possessions in my haste. I must recover them before bandits pass through."

"It's my understanding Isyldill's northern commander resides in an estate nearby. Have his men recover your possessions."

"No. You see, Master, these are items sensitive to the crown. It must be me."

Rau raised a brow at the princeling's demure behavior. "Are you suggesting the Northern Commander doesn't have the trust of the royals he serves?"

"Of course he does. To suggest otherwise-"

"Then send him your request. Our itinerary is not changing."

"And when," Andreiyes asked through gritted teeth, "if ever, are we to pass near Millau Estate?"

"The town of Millian will be the last stop on our return voyage."

"I ask you *humbly*," the princeling forced out the last word. "Make it the first on our descent."

His posture was tense. He was hiding something, just like he had in the crypt. Rau held no doubt of it, and for that alone he would go against the boy's wishes.

"If you refuse to call on your realm's Northern Commander, pray the gods keep your possessions hidden for the next half stretch." He turned on his heels and left the princeling behind. To his relief, the boy did not follow.

Fourteen

After thirty-four days of slow travel along the Western Highway, stopping to butter and charm every Lord from Castle Ravensten to Iltheln's great beyond, Andreiyes had already had his fill of this excursion. His thighs were sore. Clothing burns itched on the inner sides up to his groin. His back ached from the constant upright seating and bounce of his horse's trot, and exhaustion from the days of riding and dealing with minor Lords was feeding him constant, blistering headaches.

The next stop was the Tirnsh Manor, home to the Southern Commander Lord Sertrios near the town Tirnabit. Finally. It was the first crucial stopover in this long, unending route. With less than a day's travel left ahead, it was time to try and share the carriage with the pompous Master. It simply would not do for him to arrive at the Southern Commander's estate crusted with dirt and crumbling with fatigue and wobbly legs.

To his dismay, Master Rau had not shied away from riding long hours on horseback and spent more than half of the journey alongside him and his men and tended to his own horse every eve. That did not mean the Steward made any attempt at civil conversation. Then, every second or third day of travel, the

Master hired local stagecoaches arriving later in the eve before taking his place upon a horse the next morning once more.

Ten paces away from the carriage, Andreiyes steeled his nerves. This coach was mediocre at best – no adornments on the outer wood, worn and indented cushions in the interior, and lacking curtains for privacy. Still, it would provide the rest needed so that he might arrive at Lord Sertrios' manor with a regal demeanor.

Storm clouds riled overhead. Humidity was heavy in the air, almost bitter on his tongue. His fists clenched, released and reformed as he glared at the shrouded figure within.

Master Rau was bent over scrolls and parchments that crinkled as he moved. Always uninterested by those around him, his quill scratched against the papers as he whispered words in monologue. His hood was down for once, his hair in a top knot swaying at each movement, the long-jagged scar along the left side of his face on full display.

Andreiyes had not forgotten the Master's blatant dismissal of his wishes to pass by Millian on their way south, especially when a quint and a half ago – nine days before – it would have been only a day's worth of a detour. He had even considered sending word to Mistress Harleston in case she remained close to Kaianne, or whatever the pits her name was now, only to decide against it in case his correspondences were intercepted.

Andreiyes' thoughts churned at how to turn their upcoming proximity to his advantage. Befriending the man seemed far-fetched, even if he overlooked their staggering age difference. There was nothing for them to relate to there. Perchance a mutual agreement of some sort, if they could see eye to eye on something, anything, at least until Andreiyes found a weakness or a crack in the hold the Order held over his family.

He blew out a breath and tramped to the carriage's door. The handle was cold in his hand as he turned it. The Steward was just like any other Lord to be negotiated with and appeased. And that was a skill that had been coached into him since before he could talk.

The door creaked open. Master Rau lifted his eyes from his task, an eyebrow raised halfway up to his hairline's widowed peak.

"Dear Master, good morning." Andreiyes forced a smile. "I thought I might partake in the comforts of your coach for the day."

The man's jaw clenched, every flex of muscle and tendon visible under the gaunt skin, before his attention returned to his paperwork. "As his young Highness demands."

The scoff escaped him before Andreiyes could stifle it. The man was already in a twist. It was not the good start he was hoping for. Andreiyes rested his head against the back cushion, and the rickety door clicked shut as the captain of their troop called forth the advancement. The carriage jostled him with every bump, but it was the kind that did not burden his sore muscles. Silence reigned in their enclosed space, every crushed rock beneath hoof and wheel amplified. The sun rose a finger width in the sky without the Master attempting conversation or even deigning to glance at him. That made Andreiyes grind his teeth.

"I predict by midday it shall rain." Andreiyes stuck his palm out the window. No response, not so much as a twitch on the man's sunken face. "How are you liking Isyldill? I am told you have never been to visit our lands."

Master Rau snorted but did not raise his gaze. "Not in the lifetimes of any you know."

Andreiyes frowned. That…that was an enigmatic answer. Perchance the Master was jesting, and he needed to play along. "Has it changed much?"

The Master scribbled notes on a parchment, then unrolled a map without giving an answer. Yes, jesting, Andreiyes decided, in the Master's typical boorish manner.

"You like horses," Andreiyes stated. He nearly clapped his hands in success when Master Rau raised a brow. "You tend them well. Is it a practice that Stewards learn such a task?"

The Master cocked his head at Andreiyes whilst tapping a palm to the back of his other hand.

"What would you say your favorite breed is? Do you own any horses? Or does the Order own them for you? What are the stables like at the Temple?" Not that Andreiyes cared, but he was fishing to find anything the Master would respond to. The ride was becoming incredibly dull. "In fact, I'm curious about your Temple. I found an old engraving of it. Doubt it does it justice, and I would very much like your perspective."

Master Rau turned toward the window. "No."

"No?"

"No, I'll not be drawn into this with you," the man said nonchalantly whilst observing the countryside.

Andreiyes clenched his jaw, grating his teeth together. "Is being mute a trait forced on you to become a Master, or did you simply acquire it to explain your lack of rapport? I cannot imagine the ladies find it appealing. Or is celibacy a require-"

Saliva gurgled in Andreiyes' throat as he felt its walls close in on itself. He gasped, but no air came through. He grappled at his neck. Water bubbled in Andreiyes' eyes. He felt them bulge out. His head swam. Air, he needed air. With a free hand, he tugged at the Master's robe, calling for help. The Master was already glaring at him, cold and distant, no trace of humor on his face. Gods below, Master Rau was doing this to him. Displacing his body's drynn without even raising a finger. Andreiyes was going to die. He knew it, but pits all. It wasn't supposed to be like this, never like this. His vision blurred with black dots. He smacked the ceiling, the walls, and the side panel in search of the door handle. He was too young to die, had done nothing worth anything. He was a royal. This was not supposed to happen to him. The consequences to the Master, to those around them if he died a violent death...Did those consequences not apply to Masters?

The swelling vanished as quickly as it had come. Air plummeted back into his body, fresh and full of hope, as he twisted the door handle. His body flipped out of the now stopped carriage, smacking the step ladder and thumping thankfully against the open ground. He coughed and lay his head back, rubbing his neck in relief. Distantly, the voice of the coachman and other kingsmen called to him, but he focused on Master Rau's looming figure that filled the coach's doorway.

"What in the pits is the matter with you?" Andreiyes rasped. He tugged at the neckline of his tunic. "It was simple conversation."

"My silence was answer enough." The Master's words were measured. "But of course, someone like you does not accept a 'no' or silence to their arrogance. Raised on privilege and your own zeal. Find your own carriage, boy. You're not welcome in mine."

The door slammed shut with finality, leaving him embarrassed and dejected before his men. Andreiyes raked a hand through his hair and repressed the urge to spit on the man's carriage. If only a Master's lack of civility were a punishable offense.

⁂

*H*is men helped him up and dusted him off. They brought him a fine horse with a regal coat and trappings, offered him water and a new cloak, then bowed before leaving him be. A few stood guard around him should the Master make another attempt – not that Andreiyes thought he would – but that was the extent of the devotion his men showed him. No kind words. No outrage. No camaraderie. That made him uneasy. This was all a show of duty and obligation because a Lenierz was needed on the throne in order for the drynn in the land of Isyldill to thrive. What about their dedication, fervor, and deference? Did they resent his family? If there was a choice, would they have turned their backs and sworn fealty to another instead? It left a sour taste in his mouth.

Andreiyes adjusted himself on his horse at the head of their procession next to Captain Dalton as the long journey continued. He held his head high, shaking off the neck tingling stares of the kingsmen at his back. Out of them all, he only knew firsthand of Captain Dalton – three times his age – because as a Lord, the captain often came to court functions with his heirs, who were good companions of Andreiyes' father. He recognized no other man in the entire troop, and that would not do. He needed these men, along with all the other kingsmen of Isyldill. One day he might need to call on them to unite against the Order. Their absolute loyalty had to be on his side. They needed to see him as one of them. The question was how.

"Archers," a soldier barked to his left. An arrow whizzed by Andreiyes' head.

"Protect the prince," Dalton bellowed. Three took formation in front of Andreiyes and three behind while seven others galloped for the tree line where shadows crept over branches. One kingsman tumbled from his horse, an arrow's shaft sticking out of his neck.

"Bow and arrow," Andreiyes commanded. "Hand me one, quick." It was not his best skill, but he refused to wait here uselessly. He was young, not incapable.

Another arrow flew close and a guard yelped, the arrowhead embedded in his shoulder. Andreiyes and two others aimed at the shadows in the tree line and let loose. One assailant hollered as he fell from his hideout and landed with a disagreeable thump before two kingsmen finished him on the ends of their swords. There were still at least two other sets of arrows being released. One more kingsman fell dead down the tree trunk his fellow soldiers were climbing. This was getting out of hand. Andreiyes let loose another arrow. No hit.

"Enough of this," Master Rau's voice grated as he stepped down from carriage, his features etched with irritation. His eyes looked past them to the targets. He barely notched his head to the side before screams dragged Andreiyes' attention back to their attackers.

The two remaining assailants were whisked to the side off the tree before plummeting to the ground. Andreiyes' jaw dropped. Such skill, such power, and from at least a hundred paces away. That simply...how did one fight that? Andreiyes' men slew one of the Master's victims. The other ran, his silhouette dissipating through the grove before the kingsmen had time to mount their horses to give chase.

Reining in his stupefaction, Andreiyes glanced back at the Master, wondering what the man's face might show, but his hood was firmly in place again, cloaking the man's face in shadow. He was so concentrated on capturing some form of emotion beneath the Master's hood that Andreiyes almost missed the figure nearing at a sprint behind the Steward, hatchet raised in the air.

"Behind you," he yelled, rearing his horse around and bypassing his lines of guard.

His warning went ignored. Master Rau did not even glance backward. The attacker grew closer. The hatchet was released. Andreiyes' horse had reduced the distance enough. He jumped off, tackling the Master down. The hatchet flew overhead and hit another horse. The unlucky beast screeched as its front legs collapsed.

The miss did not halt the attacker's advance. In the bat of an eye, he was before them, short sword and a second hatchet ready to strike. Andreiyes diverted the sword's blow with the tip of his bow against the man's arm. He unsheathed his sword just in time to cut short the enemy's double-handed strike. His arm shook with the heavy clang of metal on metal. The man raised his weapons once more.

"Stop," Andreiyes bellowed.

The man faltered. Recognition of who Andreiyes was dawned in his widening gaze, of what killing him meant. The man's eyebrows strained high on his bald head. The indecision lasted all but a moment before rage scrunched up his features once more, his hatchet and sword posed for a fatal strike.

One moment, Andreiyes was seeing his life about to end, the next the assailant dropped his weapons and stumbled back a few steps. The man lifted his hands to his throat, mouth gaping like a fish for air, eyes bulging in panic. The crack of broken bone seemed to echo as his neck twisted unnaturally. His body slumped to the floor, lifeless. His eyes, that grainfalls before were filled with rage, then panic, now looked empty.

Master Rau sighed deeply and stood with a grunt. It was alarming how daunting a figure buried beneath a cloak could be, hovering above him like Pyre's shadow of death, especially after that display of control.

"There's hope for you yet, young royal." Master Rau said as he slipped away toward the dead attacker, robes swishing over tufts of grass and dirt. The kingsmen that had stayed with them gave the Steward a wide berth. Several quickly made themselves scarce to scout and round up their dead comrades while the rest avoided glancing in the Master's direction.

Master Rau squatted beside the body and ruffled up the sleeve of the man's right arm, seemingly nonplussed by the lack of a mark or the near-death experience. It gave Andreiyes pause. That body could have been him. The Master might have stolen his life with only an afterthought. Andreiyes swept a hand down his face. His family, all Isyldillians for that matter, did not stand a chance if the Order sent a company of fighters like this Master. Wrestling back his kingdom's freedom from them might be a tad more difficult than he had envisioned. Gods below, he needed one pitting hell of a plan to change the fate of his family and the realm.

When Master Rau placed a cloth over the body's eyes to afford the man's soul safe passage to Iltheln, Andreiyes raised a brow and approached. It was unexpected for a Steward to show mercy, especially to a Carved. He had never dealt with Carved before, heard of them yes, but to see their savagery and rage up close, that was a different matter. It could not be all Carved though. He certainly could not imagine Kaianne attempting such murderous follies – hollering in anger, brandishing a hatchet over her head, rushing to her death, battle paint staining her face. It was almost laughable.

The Master muttered words Andreiyes did not grasp before meeting his gaze. The sun shone directly into his hood and lit up his vicious scar and dark irises rimmed with purple. The color shocked Andreiyes. It was the first time he had noticed it. Gold circled the black eyes of Isyldillian non-royals. That meant this Master was not Isyldillian, and yet he crossed the kingdom's border without burning to ash like any good Marked person. It was another enigma to add to the list regarding the Order and its Stewards.

Master Rau cleared his throat, eyes stern, and Andreiyes shied away, squeezing his fists at having been caught staring.

Not his most diplomatic moment. He settled on the body instead.

"What was the point?"

"It was rather obvious he wanted us dead," the Master said slowly.

"Yes, clearly." Andreiyes rolled his eyes. "But he had to know death would follow."

"I imagine he had nothing left to live for. That, royal, is when anyone is at their most dangerous."

"There is always something to live for."

Master Rau snorted. "Naïve. Oh, some will find a reason in their darkness. Others use what's left of themselves to do what most have no courage for. When you have lost all you hold dear, you will understand. Until then, bask in your ignorance. You do it so well."

Andreiyes shook his head as the Master sauntered back to his carriage. There was very little he understood about the man. Andreiyes stared at the dead Carved. Did it really matter what horrors had forced him onto this murderous path?

⌗⫯⌗

Whilst the rest of their day's travel went quietly, the change of expression in the Carved's eyes plagued Andreiyes through the drizzle of rain. The pain, fear, worry, resignation, and finally anger. All of it in mere grains of time. And it followed him along with the Master's words and display of drynn control. What was he compared to that Carved who wore his passion on his sleeves for all to see? Or his men's courage to race headfirst toward possible death? How could he protect his family and people from a force as strong as the Order with no drynn control of his own? Gods below, perhaps Father had the right of it.

When the first shacks on the outskirts of Tirnabit came into sight, followed by the first stone homes and the scent of meat stew and fresh baked bread in the air, Andreiyes sighed in relief. The day's exhaustion had worn him to shreds. He sagged in the saddle, the rocking of his horse's pace soothing. No longer did he care if Lord Sertrios greeted a filthy prince. Tonight, he rested. Tomorrow, there were two pyres to build for his dead kingsmen, and he planned to add the first logs. Some Carved might not have anything left to live for, but his kingsmen did. Andreiyes would show them he cared.

Fifteen

*K*aianne leaned against one townhouse shadowed by another, shawl firmly pinned around her head at the neck as she swayed her head to the music. Her boots tapped to the rhythm. Millian's villagers laughed, danced and bantered, their troubles drowned in spiced wine and the yeast of ale and mead. Children were boisterous in play. Meat sizzled and squash roasted over pits built for the occasion throughout the town. Ribbons clung from balconies, lamp posts and awnings in shades of red, orange and yellow. They twisted through the air in corkscrew formations and mirrored the wisps of clouds in the sky. A child ran past her, trailing a kite that ruffled the first fallen leaves of the season in whirls that had been scattered over the cobblestones like bronze slag and gold mig coins.

Millian hosted the Red Medley Festival every fourth Stretch of Gain for all the towns and villages within a day's ride, the last time having occurred five stretches before her birth. Never in her wildest dreams had she imagined witnessing this festival. Papa had always been adamantly against any such thing. He had always stated too many vagrants wandered the streets and pickpocketed during these events for it to be fit for a family of high birth. No, her family held stuffy balls with nobles that forced their laughter and mirth followed by an equally uptight meal.

Here, merriment brimmed the air without restraint. There was so much life, so much fun – the opposite of the cycles of seclusion she had lived since the massacre. She had been watching the townspeople set up the festival for days from the outskirts of town, waiting impatiently. Gods, it was worth all the fuss. She wanted to jump out there, join in and forget all else for a few sandturns.

Families, young and old, indulged with their neighbors from nearby villages in a motley of conversations. All the women were dressed in their finest frocks and shawls, and the men in dusted-off waistcoats and trousers. If any were affected by the death of their nobles, they had long since stopped showing it. That gave the festivities a bitter edge, especially with the nightmares that haunted her and chased away her sleep.

A boy her age embraced his parents before grabbing hold of his two siblings and darting off to join a circle of dancing children. Kaianne's arms itched to feel the warmth of an embrace. It had been nearly four cycles since the princeling had left her behind. The days had long ago melted together. She had waited and waited for him, ready to show off her new skills with an axe, to have discussions by moonlight and laugh in his company again, until finally the hope of him returning had drained out of her. His promise to visit was nothing but a lie.

Kaianne rubbed her palms, imagining contact. The press of Yierd's lips on her temple. The warmth of a brother's hand in hers. The feel of Mama's chin on her head while Kaianne buried hers in the crook of her neck. The perfume that clung to Mama like a second skin. The stern looks from Papa. The banter with her siblings. The gossip of the maids. The clatter of practice swords in the courtyard. Mimsee's stories. She missed all of it. And this, this was a chance to feel again.

Even with a dagger strapped to her calf, she was more than ready to partake. A procession line of adolescents shuffled past, and Kaianne jumped into the fray. They let her, not a hint of worry on their faces at the sight of a stranger buried in a hood's shadow. She clutched her right sleeve in her palm, lest it ride up and take their kindness with it, and shuffled like the others. When the wind instruments changed their tune, the procession changed to lines divided by gender for a new dance. She smiled at her designated partner across the lane, a boy no older than Yierd, skin tanned from the sun and features lean and set for someone so young.

The hand-on-hand contact was pleasant and warm as he skipped with her around the other pairs, but quickly the dance demanded closer contact. The lad's hand fell to her waist, too close to her scars. She flinched out of reach. He went for her arm, and she yelped. The mark wound had long since healed, but the new stretch of skin was sensitive. She twisted out of the lad's hold and tumbled to the ground. Her shawl fell back.

The gasps of those closest to her had her scrambling to cover her face once more and make certain the pouch attached to her waist remained in place. Did they recognize her? Is that why everyone was staring? Her clothes could not be more common: gray chemise, high waist wool skirt, and a plain brown shawl. Had the scar on her arm been revealed? Or had she not washed up enough in the creek to look clean enough for their party?

"What's a pitting blue-blooded girl doing here?" Her dance partner loomed over her.

She mumbled an unladylike curse. Her skin tone set her apart, and now she'd gotten herself noticed. Precisely what Mimsee had warned her to never do.

The lad jerked her to her feet, his friendly smile replaced with pinched features. "Well? Not enough fun in your manor, dear lady?" he sneered. "Have to come take over ours?"

She wrenched her hand away. "If my skin makes me a noble, then your attitude makes you a bandit. Fumbling idiot." She stomped away, tears fogging her eyes. She wasn't allowed even a modicum of fun.

Five paces out, an older man blocked her way. Shaggy hair, cleft chin and brutal eyes, resting his weight on a crooked cane. Gods below, why had she not been more careful to avoid notice?

"Ye're bad news, ye are," he ground out in the southern brogue. "My niece has no need for yer sort of trouble."

She stared at him a moment, not sure whether to reply or run. Perhaps he was visiting for the festival, but he certainly was not native to Millian. "Your niece? I'm sorry, sir. I don't know you or your niece."

He grunted, lips curling, then flicked his head twice to the left. Kaianne followed the motion. A woman in a neck-high dress stood across the street under the archway of a shop's shade and beckoned her forward. Two steps closer and Kaianne recognized Mimsee's heart-shaped face and the stress lines around her lips and eyes. Her hair was elegantly braided atop her head in a twist. By the time Kaianne turned back to the man who had introduced himself as her uncle, he was tottering past her toward the festivities, as if they had not exchanged words. She sighed. Rudeness was the least of her worries.

"Mimsee." Kaianne nearly jumped into the middle-aged woman's arms and gripped her tight. "You have an uncle?"

The man had not looked older than his supposed niece.

Her governess' eyes followed the man while caressing Kaianne's unruly hair behind her ears. "Youngest of ten on my mother's side. Not more than a five-stretch difference between us in his favor. A decent man under that hard shell."

Little lords, it was good to hear the fruity cadence of her voice.

"Come." Mimsee sauntered from the town square onto one of the village's axis roads, not once turning to make sure Kaianne was following. Kaianne tried not to let Mimsee's inattention pierce the bubble of happiness she felt at seeing her, but that didn't work. Not one bit.

Mimsee led them past the outer shops, through a street of wealthy merchant homes – some made to mimic the Millau Manor in miniature – and into a small lane barely wide enough for a horse-drawn buggy. It was lined with cottages casting their shadows along the path on one side and weeping willow trees overlooking the river on the other.

"Please don't be cross with me." Kaianne hurried to match Mimsee's steps. "I should've been more careful. I just had to see the festival. You know how much I've always wanted to."

Mimsee stopped and cupped Kaianne's face. She thumbed Kaianne's cheeks. "I know, dearie, but nothing in yer life will ever be simple anymore. Ye have to be mindful of others at every turn." She pulled her into a hug, just like the ones Kaianne fell into whenever Mama was too busy with banquets or guests to give her any comfort. "Oh, I missed ye."

Kaianne relaxed her head against Mimsee's shoulder, tension thawing. Arms cradled her further into Mimsee's warmth. The scent of 'home' – lockleberry pie and ink on parchment – that lingered on her governess' clothes drew her in like a moth to a flame. Mimsee was here, with her, a bit of her old self. So close, so warm.

Mimsee had stayed in Millian for Kaianne's sake – she was fairly certain – since Mimsee's late husband's homestead was in Tehial, a village northwest from there. One of the brooches Yierd had left behind had paid for Mimsee's new cottage with enough left over to buy a seamstress shop near the center of town, as well as better tools and necessities to ease Kaianne's woodland lifestyle, and a couple cycles of food.

Since then, Kaianne's food reserves had dwindled, and her axe and knives needed sharpening. Her hunting skills were improving, but if she made a kill once every few days that was a miracle. Her skinning and curing of fur and meat still needed much improvement. Most of the meat turned rancid before she finished her attempts. Much of her clothing had irreparable tears and holes. Only her current attire was in a good state because she purposefully avoided wearing it. And she wanted new books, plus a few items to style her hair with. After all, she was not a barbarian.

"Could you sell another one?" Kaianne removed the treasured brooch from the pouch hanging at her waist. Its gold and gems gleamed.

"Hide that." Mimsee thrust a neckerchief from her dress' collar over the brooch. She glanced about them, then propped open a curtain of weeping willow branchlets. Its leaves were tinted in a medley of green, yellow, and orange that reflected in erratic swells in the river's flow. "Through here, dearie. Now."

Kaianne followed Mimsee's gaze down the street and across the river. There were onlookers, but most were headed toward the town square. Only a handful seemed to be paying them more than a glance. No guards. No memorable faces, except perhaps Mimsee's uncle. Apparently he hadn't returned to the festival like she had thought and had followed them instead. His scowl was as distinct as his cane as he met her gaze, but he limped past their location without a word. Kaianne shook off her dislike of the man. If he was Mimsee's uncle, he was practically family. There were no other dangers that she could see. With a shrug, Kaianne strolled into the tree's enclosed freshness.

"Dearie, ye must never expose such treasures." The veil of branchlets swooshed closed behind Mimsee's figure. "Ye never know who's watching."

"I've been careful thus far. With my face cloaked and my arms sleeved and gloved, there's been nothing untoward from any of the villagers, no matter how often I visit the market exchange."

"What of today? What ye did was reckless and foolish." Mimsee crowded her, hands on her hips. "It only takes one dastard to recognize ye before Lord Bryant calls kingsmen down on ye. Ye must be leery of everyone."

"Even you?"

Mimsee ignored the taunt and embraced her again. Kaianne melted into the soft touch. "Oh m'sweet dearie, I wish there was more I could do to preserve yer innocence."

"Innocence is for the weak. It won't bring back Adi, Deacon or any of them. It won't help me avenge them."

"Oh shush now. That be no talk for a ladyling such as yerself."

"But I'm not one anymore, now am I?"

"Ye'll always be one to me."

Kaianne shook her head. The little girl who had embroidered, read books, and played the harp died with her family. There were no more carefree games with her siblings, boring tutor sessions, or frivolous dinners to prepare for. It was just her, in the woods, with one sole purpose – draining the life out of Lord Bryant and Willik's eyes like it had gone out of Dea's. Every day she trained for it. She threw her axe at trunks from further and further away, honing her aim. One day, she would be ready to avenge her brothers. Not yet, but soon she hoped. She lived for this purpose as her penance for surviving, but Mimsee never needed to know that.

"Please, dearie, reconsider sharing my home. I keep a room made up for ye. Always ready."

A true bed sounded lovely, with four walls to keep her warm and sheltered. The thought of an indoor bath with water warmed by hot stones was almost enough to make her moan. But then what of her training? What would happen to Mimsee if Kaianne were ever found out? Temporary comfort wasn't worth it. She had gone four cycles without it and had adapted. It was no longer a hardship. This arrangement worked as it was. Kaianne was far from truly hungry, and she felt stronger and freer than she had ever been before.

Kaianne smiled warmly. "I like my corner in the woods. It suits me."

"'Tis no place for a young lady."

"Now you sound like Papa."

Mimsee whisked her neckerchief against Kaianne's rear in mock outrage. "Oh, I'll have ye know I'm not near as severe as his Lordship is. Was."

Kaianne's smile dissolved, a sudden pressure pushed at the back of her eyes. She blinked it away and offered out the brooch.

"Will you manage to sell this? Like the last one."

Mimsee sighed. Her shoulders sagged as she hid the trinket up her sleeve. "We'll need to wait on a traveling merchant. It might be another half cycle. The blacksmith will grow suspicious if I ask him to melt another one down, seeing as Millau Estate has long been picked clean. I'll get it done though. Don't ye worry on that."

"Thank you, Mimsee. That's all I ask."

"Just be more careful, dearie. I'll not be losing ye too. Come see me again soon, ye hear, and I'll have a squash pie ready for ye."

Kaianne embraced her in a tight hug, relishing in Mimsee's closeness once more. It was almost enough to reconsider the offer to live in town. Almost. How long before the craving for contact weakened her resolve to shreds?

*T*he festival remained in full tilt when Kaianne parted ways with Mimsee, the music louder than ever, the cheer and savory scents spreading to each part of town. While the governess returned to the festivities, Kaianne began the walk back to her nook in the Weldolf woods. Her stomach growled. She patted its upset, head hung. No roasted squash for her. No dancing or fun of any kind. Just her luck.

A few stragglers swaggered down the road toward town or to groups gathered off the beaten path around their own fires, their singing too loud and off-key. Once the main road joined Aethel's Highway, she was alone. A little further, the sight of Millian vanished beneath the green fields of corn on one side and the ripe squash fields on the other. She eyed the orange crop, licking her lips. No one would miss one or two out of hundreds. To an extent, it was owed to her. She had thoroughly been swindled out of roasted squash by that dancing villager.

It was settled then. She planned to roast her own and feast, perhaps dance with an imaginary friend or two. She unfastened her skirt, slipped it down over the breeches she wore underneath, and strode into the field to harvest her meal.

The sun lowered three finger widths by the time she reached her camping nook and home. It wasn't luxurious, but had much improved since Yierd's departure. Furs covered a den of beams and sticks with bundles of blankets inside for a semblance of a bed, and a bucket of water for bathing. At the very least, it sheltered her from the wind that soughed around it in irritation and gave her some semblance of privacy from whatever lurked in the woods.

Fire started, squash impaled on skewers, she picked up her best axe and brushed her thumb along its blade. Not a single nick came of it. The blade was too dull like all her other weapons except her dowry dagger. Her young arms lacked the strength and dexterity to sharpen them correctly on a honestone. She dug the heel of her palm against her temple. Half a cycle – Mimsee had said – until funds came in for her to replace her axe.

Only seven more cycles of the Stretch of Gain remained before the Stretch of Blight's cold cycles began. Each day already grew more chilled than the last, the winds more violent, the nights longer. Rain drizzled through the foliage more often, making a blinding fog in the early mornings. Some leaves overhead remained green and fresh, but most had started to wither into yellow and reds that once upon a time she found beautiful from the view of her ivory rooms at Millau Manor. Would she freeze to death once the Stretch of Blight began? Catch consumption, erysolio, or any other life-threatening disease? Live long enough to enact her vengeance on the Bryant lords? It was still unclear if Yierd had done her a favor or cursed her by saving her life. This was *all* his fault, she decided.

Mood soured, the squash tasted no better than stringy leaves. She lay it aside for the next time her stomach growled and took up her axe instead. She ground it along the honestone. It wouldn't help its sharpness much, but that didn't matter. It felt good to rasp metal on stone where she imagined Lord Bryant's or Willik's neck were.

Little lords. She dropped her axe and reeled backward, gagging at the darkness of her thoughts. The wood's shadows pressed in on her as she buried her face in her palms and shook her head vehemently. This wasn't her. It couldn't be who she turned into.

A branch snapped, then another. With a tear leaking down her face, she brandished her axe and faced the sound. Shadows writhed through the trees, surrounding her. More cracks, snaps and leaves crinkling. Whispers cackled around her – front, rear, sides. Chuckling joined in. The hairs on her arms rose. Her legs trembled. She craned her neck to follow their movements.

Seven, she counted. One voice pitched high, the rest men or boys. Guards? Villagers? Bandits? No option was better than another. Her palms turned clammy, the handle gradually slipping down her hold.

"Aw, look at this mozzie of a thing," a lilting voice to the side said in an accent she'd never heard before. "It actually thinks it has a chance."

"She, not it," Kaianne snapped back.

"Let's give it a bone and make it dance," the sole woman taunted. Kaianne could almost hear the sneer in her voice.

Their steps brought them into arcs of light. Their ragtag tunics were plain but well maintained, no griffin emblem in sight, no armor. On their belts hung weapons. She had gleaned enough from spying on her brothers to know these weapons – from their handles and sheaths – were at least of decent make. Most were certainly too costly for the average villager. It was the scars on some of their faces that gave them away, and two were missing a hand. Bandits. Kaianne gripped her tired tool tighter.

"I'm no thing, toy or pet. I demand a modicum of respect, whomever you might be. My father and brothers will be along shortly. Begone with you. I have an axe, I know how to use it." She swung it once as a warning, hoping she looked more menacing than she felt.

Another hmphed and the group pressed in closer on all sides. "A prissy little noble demanding and threatening. Nothing new about that. We just love dealing with little nobles and their brood, don't we lads?"

"I'm no noble." She gulped.

"Forego the fibbing," a third said, his southern brogue recognizable compared to the others' accents. "Yer words' timbre and yer skin tell right enough."

"Papa," she yelled with a prayer. The group stiffened. A few turned away from her to survey the woods. "Harold. Zain. Jeyr. Come quick."

She begged some large animal to make noise in the hopes that might scare the bandits away. One of the one-handed men met her stare, left arm gripping the stub of the other, – cut three-quarters up the forearm, just past the griffin mark – his stance domineering. His tight curls were shaped in square angles, firmly resting an inch over his equally angular face. His large nostrils flared as his eyes flicked around her camp while the others worried themselves over the woods.

"Family, is it? All I see is enough for one. We're not blind, little biscuit." There was a calming sense to his slow words. His clipped accent was different from the first two male speakers, every syllable over pronounced as though he might otherwise swallow them whole.

Another shadow traipsed forward, the same scowl on his face from earlier in the day. "Aye, that's her."

Kaianne's jaw dropped and her eyes widened at the sight of Mimsee's uncle, walking just fine with no cane. "But…she trusts you."

The uncle shrugged. "What Omga don't know, will do no harm."

"Did you hurt her?" she gritted through her teeth. "I swear if you laid a hand on her-"

His guffaw of laughter cut her short. "And what would a wee thing like ye do? I've no quarrel with family. Ye, on the other hand… Give over the gold." His hand went to his sword.

Gold? What gold? She stared at him in confusion. Oh, the brooch. He saw it before Mimsee had pulled her beneath the weeping willow.

"There's no more." Her voice shook. She had no idea how long the money from the second brooch could carry her for, but without the funds of the third, she was quite certain she would not survive the Stretch of Blight. "That's all there was."

"Where'd you get it?" the woman asked, sashaying forward.

"Pillaged it. From Millau Manor. Moons ago. Soon after the… Lyssandres died." It sounded believable to her. After all, the Manor had been raided for quints once the last guard had vacated the surroundings. Every beam picked bare, every item worth a grain of salt gone. Even plants that survived the fire had been dug out and stolen.

The one-handed man approached closer, the strain of his life visible in his permanently furrowed brow and wrinkles, yet he could not have been older than Papa. They called her a noble – regardless that they would have been right cycles ago – but his skin was only a shade or two lighter than hers. What did that make him? "See, that's a hang of a problem, little biscuit. We do not like being lied to."

"I'm not. Now, off you go."

"So tenacious. So proper. A walking contradiction." He chuckled and waggled a finger at her. "Search the camp. There's something here biscuit does not want us to scale."

The man spoke strangely, his words an unwelcome riddle while the bandits leapt to the task. But this was not searching. This was ruining. In pairs, they tore down the hides of her den, hacked the sides down with their swords, and pillaged through her tools, blankets and clothes. All her privacy, gone. All the care gone into shaping her solitary home, wrecked. Moons of hard labor destroyed. The leftover squash vanished down one bandit's mouth. Her favorite trousers were tossed aside and landed in the fire pit, searing to ash. A half-burned doll she'd found in the ruins of her ancestral home was trampled. Her blood boiled. They had no right, just like Lord Bryant had had no right to take her family from her. She saw red and lunged at the nearest thief – the one-handed instigator – axe raised.

In seconds, her ribs throbbed from an elbowed jab. Her axe thudded to the ground, and she ended in a half-armed neck hold against his chest with a dagger pressed to her belly. The man tsked in her ear, the gamy reek of his sweat filled her nostrils while the ransacking of the camp continued without pause.

"I doubt you a dof, kinder, but that was a foolish thing to do." He pressed the blade's tip harder against her skin and her breath skipped. "Do you know how fluidly your life could end?"

Kaianne watched the destruction this bandit's followers wreaked on her life. Her fingers shook, but not from fear. "*Yes,*" she hissed.

"One eensy shove and your life gone."

"You cannot do worse than what has already been done."

"Well look at this, fellas," the youngest of the group called out. He was less than twice her age, blond hair cropped to his ears, and as pale as the Bryants. He paraded her family heirloom in a circle for all to see with a snarky pride. Cheers and wallops followed him.

Kaianne's eyes widened in horror. How? She had buried the dagger beneath roots a couple trees away from camp to avoid precisely this. She elbowed her way out of her assailant's hold and raced toward the thief. That dagger was all she had left of her family. All she had left of who she had been. It was a piece of them, a piece she had to keep at all costs. Never mind the plan to use it for her revenge.

"Give it here." She jumped for the jeweled weapon the bandit held over his head. "It's mine. Return it."

A hand was shoved over her face, and she tripped into the grip of another bandit as the thief vaunted her dowry dagger to their one-handed leader. She struggled in vain. If only she could rip their grins clean off their faces.

"It's not yours to take." Her voice quivered. "Please, anything. Take anything but that."

"Fine make," the leader said as he examined her dagger. "Better than a gold brooch, I'd say."

"No, no it's not. I beg of you, I need that. It's…" *Special*, but she could not admit that to them. "The only weapon I have that's still sharp."

The leader smirked, taunting her. "Then we'll leave you your honestone."

Kaianne stomped and shrieked a gritted cry as she squirmed to get free. Her assailant's grip tightened, the calluses on his hands catching on her sleeves. "An exchange then. We can trade."

"You have nothing we want, little biscuit. Know when you've lost."

"There is another gold brooch." She gulped, hoping beyond hope this worked, that they would then leave her in peace.

The one-handed instigator cocked his head and held her stare silently. The others spoke in his stead, their colorful language ranging from simple questions like 'where' to insults with detailed profanity. His silence among the uproar of the others made her balk, his calm seeming more dangerous.

"Do you agree?" she asked slowly, never dropping his gaze. She straightened her shoulders, held her neck higher and willed her fear into a heavy ball in her gut. This was a negotiation after all. If she had learned anything from Papa, it was that the weak never gained footing against the strong.

"Show me."

"Pinned in the center of that bush." She gestured with her chin.

While her uncertainty of this tactic plagued her, the bandits held back no hesitation. In moments, the brooch was found. Their excitement was deafening, and her assailant loosened his hold on her arms.

"Now return what is mine." She shrugged off her attackers and held out her hand.

The leader tsked, a corner of his lips twisted up. "I never agreed, biscuit."

"But you…" Her mouth gaped. There was a momentary lapse of time before her fingers crisped inward with anger. No one was taking advantage of her today. Never again. Her assailant still stood close. Kaianne unsheathed his short sword and pivoted to face the leader. She brandished it to attack, her stance balanced like Yierd had shown her. "I demand satisfaction."

The man had the gall to laugh at her – a full body guffaw, head tilted back. Kaianne's cheeks heated in outrage. She advanced, but the female bandit swept in from the right. Her sword handle thumped against Kaianne's hand, the shock and pain forcing her grip loose, while a fist met with her other side and knocked her down. A blade was pressed to her throat. Tears escaped her. From pain or anger, she didn't care.

"Enough. Weapons down."

"But, Ghedi," the female bandit said, "she meant to murder you."

"And you think she could've?" His smirk was enraging. "In any case, we do not harm our own."

Kaianne glared at him, her side and wrist throbbing. What on all Taelgir did that mean? With the gods as her witness, she was nothing like them. Nothing. She spat at him, satisfied at her unladylike display.

Mimsee's uncle stepped forward "She's not-"

"She is." Ghedi, the leader interrupted, hand raised. "Even if she does not know what that means. We will overlook her actions. This once." He winked at her, and she gritted her teeth. "Away," he barked.

Slowly, the bandits melted back into the shadows while Ghedi kept her eye.

"Stay away from m'niece." Only her frustration kept Kaianne from chortling at Mimsee's uncle as his shadow bobbed through the trees.

Soon, only Ghedi and the bandit holding the blade to her throat remained. As if to scorn her further, the bandit leader flipped her dowry weapon through the air and caught it.

"We thank you for such a fruitful scale."

"Give the dagger back." Her lips trembled with rage as she watched the dagger arc through the air once more. "Or I swear, by Nogo's wrath, I will hunt you down."

That made the man smile. *Smile.* Her hackles rose. Her life wasn't the strings on a harp to be played. She jerked an elbow into her assailant's most sensitive spot – her short height an advantage – and shoved his blade aside. He doubled over with a huffed groan, but not before pain cracked against the back of her skull. Black spots marred her vision. Her knees met the mossy ground. Her ears rang as she tumbled forward. Before the darkness took her completely, hot breath fanned over her ear and cheek.

"If you have the will, biscuit, find us."

Sixteen

'Find them', the bandit had said. Easier said than done. Following paw prints in mud or piles of droppings was easy. Footsteps in moss and leaf-covered forest beds the morning after, not so much. The trails Kaianne did find were spaced out from one another and nearly nonexistent – a broken branch here, an indent there. No trampled paths. No clothing caught on branches. No general straight lines. No speech or unnatural woodland noises, only uncharacteristic quiet and several throngs of birds making their escape. A full day of this frustration with a pounding headache throbbing from her nape. Gaia forsaken, it seemed it all led her in circles.

With the sun's last rays vanishing, she crashed against a tree. Silent tears trekked down her face. What did her family think of this from Iltheln? Did they think her frail as she fumbled through her new life like a newborn foal? Better if Dea or Grayson had survived instead of her. They would not have wasted cycles learning how to survive, or debated the best course of action. They would have found their targets and set a plan in motion. Why could her mind not work like theirs? She cradled her knees and imagined each of them alive and well, unlike in her nightmares.

†

A snap of a branch woke her, but the whispers on the breeze rendered her alert. Her fingers strangled her axe's handle. That medley of accents, she would recognize them anywhere. Moonslight littered the forest floor in patches. Her fatigue evaporated, limbs tensed. She crept forward in the darkness, boots testing the ground with each step before her weight shifted. Gaia bless her, Kaianne hoped it was them.

A fire crackled thirty paces or so ahead. It flickered behind shadows that shifted with the pacing men. There were at least twice as many as had cornered her in the Weldolf woods. She recognized a few lit profiles and their builds, but no sight of Ghedi, the ringleader, despite there being six one-handed men and women in the bunch. Kaianne chewed on the inside of her cheek. Their numbers made this more difficult. She would only get one shot at this, but she needed a better vantage point than a bush. Elm trees surrounded the campfire, bark perfect for climbing grips. Their thick branches stretched over the group invitingly.

Thank the gods for trousers. Kaianne made quick work of the ascent up the nearest one and settled onto her stomach along the thickest branch on the outskirts of the assembly. The view was certainly better – a few more faces discernible, dozens of bedrolls strewn around, a handful of scouts standing guard at the edges of camp. For once her young stature was an advantage. If only Mama could see her now. Oh, the rebukes she would have received. She stifled a snicker. Those stretches in the safety of the Millau estate had been a veil of ignorance over her eyes. This was how the real world worked – thieving and killing to survive. Tonight, that naïve little girl of her past was bound to die completely.

The bandits spoke in hushed tones. They ate and they drank, the brew of ale lingering in the air with the roasting of meat. They scrubbed their clothes in water buckets filled from a nearby stream and hung them on a line. The lookouts guarding the outskirts switched out as more bandits trickled in from all directions – one even traipsing through her previous hideout in the bushes. Their numbers swelled from one dozen to two dozen. Sweat beaded on her temple from the sight of it. Her odds of getting in and out with the dagger unseen were dropping fast. No matter what, she had to try.

†

She caught sight of Ghedi edging into camp from the opposite end as most tucked themselves into their blankets and furs for the night. Lucky brutes. There they were, all cozy and warm while she was trembling against the chill, cursing the gods for allowing so many stragglers to arrive this late.

By the time everyone had settled for the night, a grand total of thirty-one bandits rested below her with two extra on watch. Their snores were loud enough to scare off any beasts nearby, and more importantly cover any sounds she made. She'd faced worse odds at Millau Manor and survived. That was the only reason she did not abandon this obscenely poor plan.

Nobody sounded the alarm when she landed in a bed of moss and dry leaves with a lack of grace that would have made poor Mama shiver. None woke when she tripped over an errant leg and crawled around occupied bed rolls. She froze, heart beating in her ears when one whimpered and blabbered in his sleep. And she splattered to the ground, teeth knocking dirt, when another sprang to sitting before crumpling back to sleep. Neither lookout seemed fazed by the occurrence, but fear stiffened her limbs.

"Brave, you're brave," she whispered to herself. "Bravely foolish."

She crept through the center of camp, around the crackling fire pit whose light put her in plain sight – because of course, her target had chosen to rest for the night in the most visible spot around. He couldn't have chosen a more remote area. Aethel forbid that.

She steeled her resolve for the last couple meters. Almost there. Ghedi lay asleep - his aggressive nose and deep wrinkles relaxed, his arm stub hidden beneath his furs, the rectangular edge to his coif an extension of the contours of his face instead of a contrast.

Kaianne pried her axe from the straps that held it to her back and gulped when looking down at the man. There was no coming back from this. Whatever the outcome, she would never again be the demure little girl Papa had tried to marry off. She glanced around the sleeping camp, not a stir in sight, the lookouts' backs to her. A night owl hooted its encouragement among the cricket's song. She pounced.

With a dull axe blade to his neck and her timid hand over his mouth, Ghedi's eyes shot open, warning violence…until they saw her. They softened as a wistful smile formed beneath her palm and tugged at his cheeks and eyes.

"Biscuit," he said. His voice, lulled by sleep, vibrated against her hand. "What took you so long?"

"My dagger," she hissed in a whisper, eyes darting around in case any woke. "I want it back. Where is it?"

He tugged at her palm, smile still in place. Rather than flinching away, she put a tad more pressure against the axe which made his breath hitch. His arm splayed out in surrender. "Eish. That's not very nice."

"Not meant to be. Now, give it back." His fingers turned clammy around the hilt. "And no loud proclamations."

He chortled. "The little not-noble kinder makes demands? Nigh. Any thief may claim property. It's not yours any longer."

"I had it first." She was practically shaking.

"And my crew took it. The bounty is ours now."

"Laws don't abide by the rules of thieves."

"Ja, but we live outside the law. Even you, biscuit."

A bandit stirred two bed rolls over with a groan. This was not going at all like Kaianne had hoped.

"My dagger for your life," she gritted through her teeth.

His eyes fell to slits. "You would kill an unarmed man?"

"You're not. I can see the handle of your short sword under your headroll's bundle. My dagger, now, before you regret it."

"Strong words for a kinder. Did you not wonder why I've not used it?" he asked, volume raising. "Try your worst, I dare you. I'll not even move to stop you."

His hand remained spread open, pressed down beside his head roll. More than one head turned in their direction. Bandits wiped the fatigue from their eyes despite the poor moonlight, the Persefin moon a dull yellow and the Maiesta moon hidden behind clouds. Murmurs spread throughout the camp. A few blades reflected the fire's gleam. Kaianne swallowed hard.

Ghedi lay there immobile, just as he had said, but held his palm out as though to stave off his companions. His stare held no anger, no pity, only a strange pride she dared not decipher. Her blade was right on his neck, so close to the vein that it bounced with his pulse. A bead of salty sweat rolled down her forehead to the edge of her lips, the breeze chilling its trail. One swipe was all it would take. Gaia forsake her, the blood it would spill. How his skin would take on the same ashen color as her brothers and his eyes would dull. Her free hand spasmed. She shook her head. This was wrong. He was supposed to give in to her demands, not agree to this, not call her bluff. She could *not* do this.

"Thought not." Ghedi tossed her axe aside with an ease that surprised her. She stumbled backward onto her rear as he raised to his knees. "Killing is nasty business, and you, biscuit, are far too innocent for it yet. Oh, you will kill, but your first will be in defense."

Her first? Kaianne's eyes jumped from Ghedi to his approaching crew, searching for the blade that would strike true and end her pitiful excuse of a life. There was little she could do to defend against their bulk without a weapon. Trouble had found her and she had dived headfirst into it. She shut her eyes and took in the forest air full of moss, pine, and their Gaia forsaken sweat. She bit into her bottom lip. Soon, she would see her family once more. The fire cracked and sputtered. An owl hooted.

"What are you doing?" Ghedi growled.

Kaianne snapped her eyes open. No one had swung their blade. Actually, those looming nearby had lowered theirs.

"I thought…Are they not…I tried to kill you."

"Poorly, but you couldn't have."

"Yes, I could've," she sputtered under his condescending gaze. "It just…wasn't enough of a challenge."

That earned a few chortles and the shake of Ghedi's head.

"If you're going to kill me, just do it."

"Brave little kinder. Nigh, you'll not die today."

"Just get this over with," a woman's voice called from the side.

"Are you to threaten me instead?" Kaianne asked, her nerves fraying bit by bit with the wait.

He cocked his head. "Were you not a kinder, yes."

She hardly believed her good luck. "Then I want my dagger back."

Ghedi's round eyes widened to marbles before his shoulders began to shake and laughter bellowed out of him. He smacked his thigh, wetness gathering on the corner of his eyes. Others joined in, a cacophony of sounds so out of place with the woodland's calm. Kaianne held her head high and glared daggers at them, fist clenched and shaking. It was *not* a laughing matter.

"You've got some spirit there," Ghedi said with a wheeze. "I have a proposition for you."

"I don't want anything from you except my dagger."

"Tell me its importance."

She shook her head.

"You are making this harder than it needs to be, biscuit." He considered her a moment. "A kinder on her own, a fixed camp in a neck of the woods, walking distance from a large town. The Stretch of Blight nearing." He clucked his tongue. "It was only a matter of time before you starved, froze or got caught."

"I was doing just fine before you pillaged my home."

"That was not a home." He crossed his arm, looking taller and more intimidating if possible. "But we, all of us, could be."

What had he just said?

"Ghedi, mate, whatcha doing?" The shock of another voice from behind made her flinch. Ghedi's group had circled around them, rallying to their leader.

"Join us. We are all the same here. All of us have lost. All of us are Carved."

Whispers and mumblings rose. Kaianne regarded the stump that remained of Ghedi's right arm, a hundred questions swarming her head. Movement in her periphery caught her eye. Bandits – men and women – were all rolling up their right sleeves, while looking thoroughly inconvenienced and disgruntled. Even in the poor light, she made out the irregular scars on several arms where the mark should have been. Others were not so easy to discern by firelight, but she could guess.

So many Carved. So many traitors to the crown in one spot, surrounding her, addressing her. Papa would have called on his men to chase and eliminate them all, but she was one of them now too. Had they betrayed the crown? She hadn't, as far as she knew, until Yierd carved out her mark. Was that what being Carved meant? That they were first forsaken by the royals? And why not betray the crown after what was done to her family? But then, what about Yierd? Where did he fit in among this mess? Why would he have nursed her back to health if her existence was a betrayal to his family? Little lords, her head was spinning.

Ghedi gazed at her expectantly, but Kaianne had hidden the scars for moons now – exceedingly cautious to not let anyone catch even a glimpse. Even before that, as a ladyling, her skin was rarely on display, always wrapped in lace and fine trappings from neck to ankle. It felt unnatural to show them now. She eyed the edges of their camp, expecting a group of kingsmen to jump out from the shadows and slaughter them all. There was nothing but stillness. No reason to hide it any longer. A Carved was who she was now, there was no denying it. At least here, among this group of degenerates, she could accept it.

She rolled up her sleeve exposing the scars of melted flesh that extended from wrist to past the elbow, along with the indentation of carved tissue along her forearm. The skin was a mottled pink she recognized even in poor light without a single dark line from the mark in sight. Its bumps and taut skin felt thin and vulnerable, every touch to it a shock to her system.

The group whispered and muttered words like 'burn', 'wretched', 'butchers', 'shameful'. Cheeks burning, she shoved down her sleeve, ignoring the jolts up the nerves in her arm and back, and glared at Ghedi. She blinked away the building tears and clenched her fists. This was all his fault.

"Stop gawking. Would you like it if it were your stump?"

"Not an insult." His tone was calm, almost soothing. His facial lines had smoothed, sympathy in his eyes. "We admire your bravery. One so young surviving fire and a carving. You should be proud."

"Proud to be alone? To have lost everything and everyone I cared for?"

"Nigh." He spat at his feet. "Proud you can live to avenge what was done."

Her breath caught.

"Join us, and you will learn to fight, to survive. You will have a family again. And when the time comes, you will be ready to face your fears."

Kaianne wiped away an errant tear.

"Why not tell me this at my camp? Why wait until my axe almost cut your neck?"

His lips curved up one side as he shrugged. "If you had no will, no one could have helped you."

"A test?" Somehow, that they thought her worthy of a test made her swell with pride. "But I'm not a bandit."

"Everything can be learned. I cannot promise you a future, but I do promise no innocents are harmed in our doings."

"Then who is?"

His smile turned cruel. "The true criminals of our stories. Kingsmen. Royalists. Stewards."

His words resonated in her chest. To stay with them meant her vengeance could be enacted. On kingsmen like the ones who murdered her household. On royalists such as Lord Bryant. They deserved everything coming to them. Five moons earlier, she would have agreed the Carved were the vilest criminals of the lot. Now, she knew there was much worse. It was astounding how quickly perspective could change.

"What do you do to them?"

"Take their pride. Their joy. Their lives." Ghedi's crew cheered at each word.

This…this she could do. Well, except the lives part. For now. Her vengeance demanded she learn. "Do you make them suffer?"

"Is that what you want?"

She stared at the ground and shook her head vehemently. That's not what she had meant.

Ghedi grunted and closed in on her. Before she could stop it, his arm wrapped around her and tugged her to his chest. His warmth cocooned her. The firmness of his arm around her back. The male stench after a day's exercise. It reminded her of Deacon's hugs after a day of sparring in the training ring. Safety. Caring. Hope. Family. She didn't want to move.

"You are still young, but should feel no shame. We are who we are. We will feel what we must. All of us are forged by the tides of our lives, our fates carried by the wind. You have strength, biscuit. Strength that needs nurturing. So, what will it be? Will you join us?"

He didn't pull away, and she made no effort to pry her cheek from his chest. "You'll teach me?"

His chest bounced with his nod. "We all will. We are to each other the closest to a family people like us can have."

She wanted this. So much. They could give her more than a furtive trip to town to visit Mimsee ever could. Kaianne gulped. Mimsee had left behind a chance to reunite with family for her sake. Now, she had left her out-of-work governess behind. "I have someone in Millian. I can't abandon her."

"She helped you?"

"As she could."

He pulled her back, his eyes bouncing between hers. "She will always be separate from you. Never able to give you the support and help you need. Despite her attempts, as much as she might try."

"I know, but she lives there for me. I could not leave without saying goodbye."

"My niece? That who ye speak of?" Mimsee's uncle's curt voice shattered the little peace Kaianne felt as the mountain of a man shoved his way through the circle, aggression rolling off him like waves of heat. His gaze withered her down to a lump of coal. "Why would Omga be…Oh, that's who ye are. Bogging noble dobbers-"

"Oidh. That's enough." Ghedi blocked the man's stampede. Oidh, even his name was burdened with curtness. Come to think of it, he reminded her of a bull, ready to charge at the slightest misstep. "She's a Carved now, old bru. And a kinder at that. Hate her from afar if you must, but keep it civil."

The brute huffed. "Not what I'm known for."

"And yet, you will deliver a letter to your niece on biscuit's behalf." Ghedi's amiable disposition would have fooled her if not for the death grip on Oidh's arm that scrunched up the bull's tunic. "Ja?"

Oidh glared at her, nose flaring. "Aye."

"Good man. Have we got an extra bedroll and fur for biscuit here?" Ghedi called out.

"Catch," a woman hollered as a bundle hurtled toward her. It thumped against Kaianne's chest, stealing her breath and sending her to her rump while the rough fabric punished her chin. "Your reflexes and stance need much work, girl."

Kaianne ignored the burning in her cheeks and rose, clutching the bedroll for dear life. This was a chance. To be more. To do more. To take their help and knowledge and forge it into what she needed to accomplish her oath to her family.

"I want to learn the same as if I were a lad, not a lass. I want to know how to fight off men like him." Kaianne gestured in Oidh's direction. "But I won't hurt anyone undeserving, no matter what. And I want my dagger back."

Ghedi's lips curled upward. "How about you earn it in time?"

She narrowed her eyes to hide the thrill of excitement building within. Ghedi did not make demands of her. He did not force her will or choices. He negotiated. With her – a lass, a young lady, a child in his eyes. Never had Papa ever done that, or her brothers, or even the guardsmen that followed Papa's orders. She had always been told what to do and been expected to follow or be reprimanded. That was a woman's role, they had said.

Not here, by the looks of it. The men might be larger, but the women in this band of misfits looked just as fearsome – jaws set, armed to the nines, sleeping and eating in no better conditions than the opposite gender. Kaianne suppressed the smile that itched to be displayed.

"How much time?"

"Until you are ready to take hold of your fate. But that will depend on you. We each do our fair share. No laziness tolerated. If you want to be with us, you put in the work. If not, you leave. Do you accept?"

She gulped, but nodded.

"Good. Tomorrow, you write your letter and start. When Oidh returns, we move out. Get some rest, biscuit, you will need it."

With a wink, he left her standing amidst the grumbling of his comrades, yet no one argued. Yawns spread throughout, followed by muffled cracks from stretched limbs before the majority stumbled back to their rolls for the rest of the evening. Like a fool, she stood, turning her head about, hoping for some sort of indication as to where to go until she realized she did not need direction to find a patch of earth to rest on. She scuttered to the nearest bare spot and laid out her bedroll before anyone questioned her decision. When she settled in, surrounded by strangers encasing her in a fortress of rhythmic breathing, sleep took her faster than any night in the last four moons. And not a single nightmare disturbed her.

Seventeen

Ollineol Estate, Ollin, Southwest Isyldill

A fter sandturns of charming his way through Lord
Welnit's caprices to within the brink of his sanity,
Andreiyes took comfort strolling the Ollineol's estate gardens
alone under the sun's warmth after days of gray skies. The
possibility of getting lost amid the maze of hedges, fountains
and trees was the only thrill available to him, and he took it to
task. Welnit was a presumptuous arse. The last half-day in his
presence wore on Andreiyes harder than the three days ride it
had taken from Tirnabit to Ollin after a bilial's stay – fifteen
days were not a long enough reprieve.

The Ollineol Estate was twice as large as Lord Bryant's or
Lord Sertrios'. It made a mockery of the town, Ollin. The estate
could have swallowed the town tenfold. The garden went on
past the horizon, and the manor – more chateau than grand villa
– had battlements and a moat. It housed no less than forty and
was built with large stones in the olden style from before the
Apostate War, set in a mosaic of gray, brown and orange.

It was rumored that before the war the Ollineol Estate was
used as an ambassadorial home between Isyldill and Lakoldon.
After five hundred stretches of closed borders, who knew the
truth of that anymore. The opulence of its modern gardens

trimmed and primmed to perfection contrasted the brute architecture. The same was true with the barracks, separated from the manor by a long hedge that did nothing to hide the grunts and clashes from training.

Andreiyes followed the sounds to the centuries old building and its yard. There were men running laps, others worked on core exercises or hefted weights set nearest to the barracks. Most trained in hand-to-hand combat or weapons sparring. They used the entire yard, splashing in puddles and some slipping in dirt as they maneuvered. The master-at-arms hollered instructions and corrected positions as he weaved between the groups.

Andreiyes had observed enough training sessions at Castle Ravensten to know the routine. Envy spiked in him nonetheless. When the men attacked each other too roughly and fell, it did not cause a scene. Their partner extended a helping hand and they grunted or laughed it off before beginning again. If a little blood was spilled, no one panicked. The castle or manor healer did not sprint to them. If anything, it spurred on a cordial rivalry.

He leaned against a tree. The bark grated against his cheek like he imagined dry sand and gravel might if he were to fall while sparring. Gods below and beyond, he wished to be in the thick of it with them. Being a Lenierz was stifling. Everyone was constantly worried they could cause his death – blood loss, stabbing, head injury, the list went on – and therefore ignite the curse that would end their line. So, they avoided him. Aside from Grayson, no one had dared spar with him once his skills had surpassed the need of a wooden sword. Grayson had made entire theatrical tournaments out of their skirmishes. The memory gave him a tight smile.

It had been three stretches since he had been forced into solo training, imagining his opponents while his trainer spat instructions but never partook. It irked him to rely on others and be unable to defend himself should the need arise. Besides, if the men were to follow him willingly, he needed to gain their trust. What better way than on the sparring field where they might see that even though he was a princeling, he was one of them?

Andreiyes sauntered to the master-at-arms, Sir Felgrim if memory served, and crossed his arms in casual observation until the older gentleman noticed him and stopped barking criticism.

"Your Highness, welcome to the training grounds." The southern brogue was thick in these parts. The man bowed his head, a muffled annoyance at the interruption evident in his tight jaw. Strands of his salt-and-pepper hair not tied back cascaded down the side of his face. "To what do we owe this honor?"

"I am in need of an adequate partner and a *genuine* weapon. I will be partaking in this afternoon's session."

Normally, horror such as that reflected in Sir Felgrim's bulging eyes would have been comical to Andreiyes. Something to be pushed and prodded. Here and now, it was downright aggravating and insulting.

Sir Felgrim shook his head. "Begging yer forgiveness, yer Highness, but 'tis simply not done. For the safety of all concerned."

Andreiyes turned toward him, gazing upward, jaw clenched, eyes nearly twitching. Pits. He only reached the master-at-arms' nose, embarrassingly enough – his need of another growth spurt or two working against his intimidation tactic.

"I insist."

The man gulped with unease. "Yer Highness, I implore ye. Royals and the training yard, they're not to mix." Andreiyes narrowed his eyes. "Ye must understand–"

"Felgrim," a voice called across the yard, another Southerner by the brogue, and far too familiar of late. Pits. With his luck, the Southern Commander's youngest son, the one closest to his own age, had certainly overheard him begging to train.

Keeping his gaze focused on Sir Felgrim and the vegetation beyond him, Andreiyes clenched and released his fists to stave off the embarrassment. While Lord Aiofe Sertrios, his heir and spare had remained behind at their estate in Tirnabit, the youngest son Jereown had agreed to shadow Master Rau and Andreiyes' journey through the kingdom.

"Lordling," Sir Felgrim greeted with a bow of his head as the Sertrios lad's shadow sprawled over the ground at Andreiyes' feet.

"I'll spar with him." The Sertrios lordling clapped a hand on Andreiyes' shoulder. "If he can handle a blade."

Andreiyes' eyebrows shot up at the Lordling's audacity. A smirk painted the lad's angular face. In the last three quints since their visit to the Sertrios manor, the two of them had shared little interaction.

"Is that wise m'Lordling?"

Andreiyes shook off Jereown's hand, which only made the lordling's grin grow. He wanted to wipe it off. "If the lordling is willing, what does the rest matter?"

"Oh, we'll be getting along just fine," Jereown said with a wink. "I've a feeling our princeling is gagging for a lil' wallop."

Throughout his fifteen stretches, Andreiyes had perhaps met the lad once or twice. Jereown had rarely accompanied his father and brothers on gatherings at Castle Ravensten. The lordling had been too busy making a name for himself as a swordfighter – already champion of the southern sword tournaments at seventeen. Jereown Sertrios had long ago shed any preteen chubbiness. His jaw was set, his shoulders were broad from constant exercises. To worsen Andreiyes' envy, Jereown towered a few centimeters over him. His blond hair was clasped at his nape, a few stray strands clinging to the sweat on his face. With that rugged appearance, it pained Andreiyes to admit that Jereown probably worked much less than him to catch female attention.

"As ye say, m'lordling, but let it be known, I advise against it."

"Well noted."

Sir Felgrim nodded at Jereown, and Andreiyes simmered in his own boiling stew at how easily the man had acquiesced to the lordling, but refused him.

"Stay in yer own circle. No others are to join ye. Strike to disarm only. Those are m'terms, or Iltheln forbid I'll grab ye both by the scruff of yer necks and toss ye out to the gardens on yer rumps."

Andreiyes raised a brow at the old man's lack of respect, not quite certain of the warning's sincerity.

"A hard bargain, sir." Jereown inclined his head, smile still in place. "But most heartily accepted."

The lordling sauntered off with a bounce to his step, picked up a pair of sheathed swords from a rack, and gestured over his shoulder at Andreiyes. "Better follow me, princeling, if the need for a walloping still tempts ye."

Andreiyes shook his head in surprised amusement and followed. There was something disarming about the lordling that put him at ease.

The yard had grown quiet. Jereown led Andreiyes to the opposite side of the training square away from the others, but every eye was on the two of them. Jereown stopped beneath the shade of a tree near the bridged walkway over a pond to the estate's chapel, secluding them. Yellowed leaves and the prickly burs of fallen nuts littered the ground, crunching underfoot, the thorns of a few nuts digging into his soles.

"Why here, Sertrios?" Andreiyes asked, eyes roaming their shaded corner before looking back to the men. They were slowly returning to their training. "Why so far from the others?"

"Ye're a danger to them, to yerself, and neither Sir Felgrim nor I know the extent of yer skill. If ye want to spar it'll be with me, and far enough there'll not be any risk of a stray blade taking yer precious royal life, your Highness." Jereown mocked a low bow.

Andreiyes narrowed his eyes. "Are *you* not worried?"

"I'd not be much of a swordsman if I was, but I get my thrills where I can." Jereown slapped a palm against Andreiyes' back and pressed one of the weapons into his hands.

When pulled from its sheath, a steel blade reflected Andreiyes' face. "Not wooden?"

Jereown shrugged. "What's the point of living without a little danger? Compared to the prim and proper lordling life, 'tis much better."

Andreiyes adjusted his grip and stance. "Ah, so you intend to use me for your own amusement."

"Absolutely." Jereown struck a slew of obvious blows that Andreiyes parried. The clash of blade on blade echoed down the prince's arms and untrained muscles. "Call it mutually beneficial, princeling. Ye need this. I want this. And no others are willing."

"Tell me. How many suffer fatal wounds while training? How plausible is this fear you all have?"

"'Tis rare, but happens. Kingsmen don't join to prance around."

Andreiyes blocked another four attacks, cursing the strain in his arms. His boot slid in a track of mud and nearly made him fall.

"Widen yer stance for better balance, and don't hold yer sword so high." They exchanged a sequence of strikes and parries. The lordling was hardly panting at all while Andreiyes' lungs burned. "Good. Again."

Andreiyes followed the instructions and repeated the sequence, almost relishing in the sweat trickling down his brow. He was participating – no longer on the sidelines. It was a step in the right direction, a chance toward achieving his goal. And he would make it. He would earn the loyalty of his people. He would free his family from the Order's grasp if it was the last thing he did.

A shadow in his periphery caught his attention. Before he knew what had happened, he landed on his rump, side sore from the jab of a sword's pummel, back and butt soaked from a puddle. Jereown chuckled and extended his hand to help him up.

"Always keep up yer guard. Distractions serve no purpose other than getting ye on the right end of steel, or in this case on yer royal arse."

Andreiyes' lips thinned as he glanced over Jereown's shoulder at the shadow that had stolen his focus. Master Rau stood beneath the overhang of the chapel's roof, face obscured as always in his hood. How many identical sapphire robes did the man have? He almost pitied the Master for the degrading lack of individuality in his uninspiring attire. Almost. Less so after the Master dismissed Andreiyes with a shake of his head, his robe undulating from the movement before he shuffled out of sight.

"I will make you a deal, Sertrios." The lordling had followed his attention on the Master and glanced back at him. "I will be your wry amusement on any training yard if you convince Sir Felgrim my place in the training yard is with them. Not here."

"For what purpose? Ye want yer kingsmen to challenge ye?"

"No. I want them to see me fight. I want them to know I am with them."

"Oh, ye're more fun than I gave ye credit for, princeling." Jereown nodded with a grin. "Ye have yerself a deal, but not 'til ye've drawn blood. If ye want 'em to respect ye, ye need to be better skilled. Now, let us see how long it takes for yer attacks to reach me."

Eighteen

Misthallen Estates, At the Fist, South Isyldill

The imperious young royal was doing well for himself, Rau remarked from the balcony of his rooms that oversaw Misthallen's training yard. Andreiyes' swordsmanship had improved, enough to convince the master-at-arms in the last two and a half cycles since leaving Ollin the princeling was less of a danger to himself and others. The princeling was more tenacious than Rau had given him credit for, breaking thousands of stretches of tradition and royal bigotry for a chance to play warrior. As much as he would have liked to admire the boy's determination, this development made Rau all the more wary of the princeling.

It had now been almost six cycles since he had left the Temple. From the crenelations of his balcony, Rau oversaw the grunts of hard-worked soldiers, the scuffles of boots sliding on dirt and the clang of weapons, but also the wonders of the open sea. Salt was palpable in the air from the spray of crashing waves against the cliffs at the estate's edge, clinging to his skin despite the cloak over his Master robes. Misthallen manor differed from the other estates they had visited in that the gardens and training yard were within the manor itself, not separate. The villa extended in a figure eight punctuated with two circular atriums along a knuckle of the cliffs known as the Fist for its shape.

It had been two centuries since his last journey to a coastline on the Taelgirian continent. And being here, near the ocean, basking in its sounds and smells like he had every day of his childhood before being sent to the Temple, felt right. For the first time in a long time, his pain and heartbreak crashed against his heart and ebbed with the soothing beat of the waves down below. Peaceful, there was a measure of serenity here that he wanted to sink into.

He downed a vial of Well's Waters, the first in two days – cheers, Aroawn. Unwelcome symptoms were not going to disturb the calm of his thoughts.

A knock on his door broke that hope. He sighed. There was never a good moment alone, a curse if ever there was one.

"Master Rau," his guard said at the door. The fact that anyone believed he required a guard for safety might have made one of his Brothers or Sisters bark a laugh, but he paid it little mind. Let the royals and the rest of the non-talented believe he required the help of a guard, if it made them feel better.

"There is a missive, your Grace."

Rau forced a wave of drynn out from him and pushed it toward his room's door. The clasp clicked, and the door creaked open. Rau cringed from the noise. Salt spray – it was a balm for his skin, but an irritant for hinges and his ears.

Too quickly, the guard was invading his personal space, a rolled parchment in hand. The missive was barely the length of his pinky and still held its wax seal. He unfurled it and scanned its contents. More Carved it seemed - more of them sprouting up and plaguing the realms as the stretches went by. By the looks of this, a group of seven had been spotted thieving in Misthall before daybreak. Attacked a few inhabitants that tried to detain them, two citizens dead and one Carved. A hunter tracked their whereabouts to a cavern nearby, and the townsfolk were requesting aid for justice.

Rau rolled the missive up and tapped the back of his hand. He had been forced to trail along the princeling on this voyage. It would not do to exclude him now, unfortunately. Besides, Rau had yet to see if the princeling had the stomach for what needed to be done. There was still the matter of Andreiyes' initial hesitancy in regards to this journey's mission against the Carved.

He returned the missive to his guard. "Gather half your kingsmen. See to it Prince Andreiyes receives this before I have reached the stables. It is imperative he makes haste. The people have need of their royal representative."

With a bow and quick words, the man retreated. Rau glanced once more over the soldiers below, over the rooftops where seagulls had landed for shelter squawking against the rising winds. A storm was brewing on the horizon, dark and dangerous over distant water. Infrequent lightning blazed in the sky, far enough away that no thunder could be heard. Whether the change of weather would drift toward them or not, only time could tell.

*T*he tracker – dirty, disheveled with exhaustion lines dragging down his eyes and hardly old enough to be considered a man – met their party of over twenty outside the estate walls. The young lad led them over the knuckles of the Fist and down the cliffside through a passage hidden between jagged rocks. Two men stayed behind with the horses. It was on foot from there on out, single file. The cliff was angled to push them over the edge onto the punishing rocks jutting from the waves far below while the beating wind threatened to make good on the cliff's threat. The water spray chilled Rau to the bone and weighed down his clothes, and yet it was peaceful.

Despite the approaching Stretch of Blight, here the climate was temperate. The pull and crash of waves drowned the Isyldillian's chatter and the scratch of their boots. The algae and wet stone against the salt masked the reek of their training sweat. If Rau could have closed his eyes without the threat of falling, he might have believed he was alone. And perhaps he would have accepted the darkness – closed his eyes, had a misstep and fallen to the dangers below – if the lingering resentment and pain from Tilnee's suicide did not make him strive for an honorable death.

Too quickly, they arrived at a curve in the cliff, the yellow rock fading to black. Frustratingly, as the group lit torches, the captain of their little troop signaled him to the rear of their party with the princeling, like he needed their protection, but Rau did not argue. Those up front would soon know how it felt to burden their souls with the death of another. Then they would understand what duty truly meant. Rau's soul carried more than enough weight already.

They filed into the cavern that widened the further they went. The crash of the waves thundered in an echo, and the drip of water and their whispers filled any lulls. The musty air was stifling. Their torchlight flickered against the jagged stone walls and uneven slates of stone at their feet as they crept in further. The princeling beside him clenched his fists then spread his fingers out and repeated the action – a chronic habit, it seemed.

The cavern veered to the right. A soft light emanated from the distance, the first indication the grotto was in use. Swords were unsheathed. The blades softly rasped on the metal top rim of their scabbards.

"What's that?" a voice echoed from the alcove.

"Douse the fire," a woman ordered. With a hiss, the orange hue vanished from the alcove.

"In the name of his Majesty, King Triunn of Isyldill," Captain Dalton recited over the beat of waves as he and his men blocked the alcove's exit, "you are hereby under arrest awaiting the verification of your status as citizens of this realm. Lay down your weapons and no harm will befall you before trial."

"Liar." The woman's voice echoed.

Rocks were thrown. One hammered into Rau's temple. Another rammed his shoulder. Screams and hollers rang. He sank to his knees, head swimming and pounding. Blood trickled down his brow into the curve of his scar. He vaguely heard the order to halt from the princeling and then the clash of fighting ensued. Blurred forms fought each other as Rau wiped the sticky liquid out of his eyes. Cries, grunts and clanging muffled the waves. The iron of blood – whether his own or others' – blotted out the cavern's heady mustiness.

A figure sprinted toward him with long frizzled hair, roaring at the top of her lungs. Pinpointing the drynn in her movements worsened Rau's pain. He had no weapon except his talent. Now, his ability to manipulate drynn was smothered by the throbbing in his head and the blood loss. The cavern was fading from sight. Ha, of all the things that could have killed him over five centuries, it was a rock, a gods fated rock that would send him to Iltheln to join Tilnee and Moira. And he would let it. If he'd had the strength, he might have raised his arms to welcome her blow.

A body barreled into him, sprawling him to the cavern's stone floor. "What in Aethel's good name are you doing?" the lad over him yelled. No, not lad, the princeling, that haughty voice discernible as ever. "Get up."

A snort escaped Rau. As if he would let the boy command him now. *May the world fade and me with it.* The princeling's form raised off him and swung at his attacker. Once, twice before impaling her through.

"Maha." A child's cry forced his eyes wide open. Rau twisted his head toward the girl whose voice turned urgent with uncontrolled whimpering.

A little figure was running into the alcove, her face lit from fallen torches. Chubby cheeks, innocent diamond eyes, dark black curls down to her shoulders. Moira, it was his little Moira running toward him from Iltheln. He reached out a hand for her, his lips twitching into a smile. Soon he would hold her again. But Moira was sobbing and a shadow was reaching for her, blade extended.

Not again. He refused to see her die again. If this was the price the gods required from him for passage to Iltheln – no, absolutely not, he did not accept. With all the strength he could muster, he thrust drynn at the shadow and its weapon. The sword was wrenched from the shadow's grasp with muffled snaps and anguished cries before it plunged into the cavern wall with a deafening crack.

Black crept further into his vision. His head bobbed in a struggle to keep it up as he stared at his little girl. He was too weak to protect her here.

"Run, little greenling," he whispered. "Run."

And she did. He would soon see her again. The escaping pitter patter of her little feet was all the reassurance he needed to succumb to the darkness.

*R*au woke to mutterings, thunder and pelting rain overshadowing the crash of waves, and candlelight. His head pounded despite the plush pillow and mattress that cradled his body. He smacked his dry lips together, tongue nearly sticking to his palate. A wet rag covered him temple to eyelid, partially obstructing his view, but the coffered ceiling remained identifiable. This was *not* Iltheln.

Disappointment hit him and moistened his eyes. Had he not been close? Moira had come to take him and he thought, no, he could have sworn he had felt the warmth of her little body embraced in the crook of his. That…that had to have been real.

"Hush. He awakens."

The group sat, assembled like spectators around his bed in his Misthallen's chambers. The rag cut off the tops of their faces. Four…five…eight sitting in total, while the princeling, his recently self-appointed personal guard, and the Sertrios lordling leaned against a wall. There were too many in his room, around his bed.

"Leave," he ordered, voice unnaturally hoarse and scratchy.

An older man with white streaked through his bushy red hair bent forward – the princeling's personal healer. He pried Rau's eyelid open and flashed a candle's flame in front of Rau's face. The heat seared Rau's eye, and the light blinded him. Without a care, Rau shoved the man's drynn away until the healer was back in his chair and hissing from a drop of hot wax on his hand.

Dizziness overtook Rau. The coffered ceiling twisted as the panels melted together. Exhaustion crept back, pulling his weary eyes down as nausea threatened. Aethel curse him. One use of his talent and he felt depleted. He must have been very close to passing on to Iltheln for it to drain him so. So close, yet so far away.

"Is he well enough?" the princeling asked.

"Responsive to say the least," the healer croaked.

"Good. Leave us, gentlemen."

Most filed out quickly, seemingly relieved to not be forced to stay. A couple stragglers showed their reticence by darting gazes between Rau and the princeling before receiving an extra nod from Andreiyes. Only the princeling's trio remained.

"You as well, Uslan."

"Is that wise, my prince?" Uslan stiffened, standing half a head taller than Andreiyes. The young man had at least five stretches on the princeling, but it was hard to tell exactly behind the shaggy beard and busheled red curls he sported. He was a good swordsman though, one of the best of Lord Sertrios' bequeathed men, and the princeling had managed to gain his favor.

The need to parch his throat grew urgent. Rau grabbed the cup on the tray at his bedside and downed the liquid. The itch in his throat demanded another and another.

"The Master and I have matters to discuss. Alone. No worries, Uslan, he appears too weak to do much harm. Jereown, follow him out, will you?"

The Sertrios lordling snorted as he shoved a dagger into the princeling's hand. "Your risk, not ours. Best of luck then."

The two left, and Rau groaned. Now he was going to have to listen to the princeling enjoy his own voice. The gods were testing him, surely. Why could he not have joined them instead?

"You caused quite the stir." The princeling pushed himself off the wall. "Many hoped the gods would leave you to rot with your eyes uncovered. Fret not, I would have gone against that wish of theirs."

"Why?" Rau shuddered at thought of dying without safe passage to Iltheln.

"Even a Steward deserves a measure of kindness in death, whether or not he can give any." The princeling faced the balcony windows, looking far older than his fifteen stretches and a little wiser for it. "You should know the kingsman you harmed will live."

Rau cleared his throat. "What kingsman?"

"The child also escaped." The princeling dug the heels of his palms into his temple. "That day…everything went wrong. There was supposed to be no bloodshed, not yet, not until they had been tried." The princeling raked a hand over his face. "You once spoke to me of desperation. They would never have surrendered. It was obvious from their faces, and I was foolish to hope so. One man dead from my lack of foresight, and you ruined another from ever lifting a sword again."

Rau scrunched his brow, even that small motion hurt. "I seem to recall receiving a blow to the head before the battle began. That is why I am restrained to the bed and forced into this discussion, is it not, your Highness?"

"You think I wish to have this conversation?" The princeling faced him, dark circles beneath his eyes. "I have had to deal with appeasing my kingsmen while you recovered. They wanted your arm in retribution. Quite frankly, you should feel fortunate you still have it. Intact and untouched. If not that, it was your life some wanted instead."

"You didn't give in to their demands." Rau forced himself to raise his gaunt hands in the air, pivoting them for reassurance.

"Obviously. It helped that missives from both my grandfather and your Archchancellor – who bears as charming a disposition by hand as you have in person, I might add – motivated the physicians to be *extremely* diligent with your care."

Rau snorted.

"You need to understand, Master Rau, that no matter how much time we spend together on the road, you are the outsider here and every man in our party feels it. You have kept to yourself, addressed no one save when mandatory, and looked down on any display of authority. I understand my family and the Order have an…agreement."

Rau raised a brow at that.

"I am not the fool you think me. I am young, yes. Used to luxury, of course. Frustrated that your Order and my family work hand in hand, most definitely. Your death or even harm to you under my care would only cause friction with the Order that my family does not need. You saved my life nearly three moons ago. Now I have saved yours. We are even."

"It would seem you've given this quite some thought."

"Overseeing your care for the last moon take-a-quint has afforded me the time."

Rau started at that. Twenty-four days – an entire bilial and a half – of unconsciousness. And for what?

"You should have left me to die."

"Perhaps." The boy nodded. "Iltheln tried to claim you several times. You broke fevers, had tremors, almost choked on your own vomit, awoke spouting delusions. Your eyes were blood red at the time. It was quite ghastly. One might think you did not want to live." The princeling cocked his head as if Rau were a curiosity. "Are you at your most dangerous right now, Master? You certainly do not look it."

Rau tittered at the reminder of their conversation in his carriage. The ache in his head pulsed with the slight shake. His fingers grazed the new groove on his forehead, the freshly knitted bone and skin tingling under his touch.

His even thinner than normal arm ached and shook from the strain of lifting its weight, as if what remained of his muscles had been eaten away. The sensations were worse than when he had awoken from a coma after diverting the lava flow around the Temple during Mount Haphaeus' eruption shortly before the Apostate War. At the time, the healers had been gorging him on Well's Waters. He glanced at his two trunks nearly full of the liquid. One clip lock was unfastened.

"Did you rifle through my possessions?"

The princeling scoffed, catching the addressed look at his trunks. "You should feel so fortunate. Your Archchancellor demanded that we administer a vial from those trunks every day. If it were not for his threats to my men or the worry I read in his missives, I would have wondered if he truly wanted you alive. Why *do* you carry trunks of poisons with you?"

"Poison?" Now Rau was amused.

"The Lord's healer could hardly administer a treatment he had no knowledge of. The poor man tried a drop of it and fell deathly ill. Took three days for him to recover. Needless to say, that substance was not fed to you."

Twenty-four days without Well's Water. The luck of it. The fevers, the tremors, the vomiting and back-splitting pain of withdrawal. He had not felt a bit of it, not that he could remember. No wonder he still felt drained after so much bedrest.

"Care to explain?" the princeling prompted.

"Not poison, not for Stewards." A half-truth. Any descendant of the gods with sufficient drynn naturally accumulated in their body could drink it without taking ill. The princeling, for example – not that Rau would tell him. Rau could hardly contain his outwardly nonchalant demeanor. This turn of events was riveting. Ilthein was in his grasp. He could finally age. "Does Aroawn know?"

"Know what?"

"That you did not give me the waters."

"Why in all Taelgir does that matter?" Rau gave the princeling a pointed look to which the boy rolled his eyes. "No, I did not include that in my responses."

Emotion riled within Rau, bubbling to the surface. After all this time, all this effort, and it was a rock to the head that he needed. A chuckle escaped him, then another, until he was laughing so hard his belly ached. He pressed a hand to his head's new scar to suppress the pounding. He even took to the nausea with a smile.

"Fortunately one of us finds the situation amusing."

Rau stopped himself short of asking the princeling's forgiveness for his outburst. He was feeling oddly thankful. That shook him out of his good humor. Andreiyes was a royal through and through – arrogance and selfishness personified. There would be no thanking him. Rau cleared his throat and tapped his palms against each other.

"Your kingsman, will he recover?"

"Look at the pair of us having a decent conversation. Who would have thought?" The princeling winked, and Rau grunted from the boy's inability to remain mature. "But no, 'tis unlikely. I will admit your talent is frightening. You fractured his sword arm in thirteen places, managed to crush his thumb and index nearly to dust, cracked three of his ribs and popped out the joint from his shoulder. The physicians debated taking his arm. So no, dear Master. You have effectively stolen away that soldier's future. It was far harsher discipline than I would have administered."

Rau grimaced while Andreiyes lost himself to the night sky beyond Rau's balcony doors and raked a hand through his hair. There was a weight to the boy's shoulders that he had not noticed before.

"I think I would have demoted him to guardsmen if circumstances were different. Whether your actions were driven by delirium or your own righteousness, that child did not deserve the death he would have given her. Not without a trial at least."

"Child?"

"The girl. The one you attacked the kingsman to save."

Rau reeled back. The girl – he shook his head – no, it had been Moira. He would have known the difference between his daughter and another. It…She…He had been so sure. The chubby cheeks, the crescent eyes, the dark hair and curls, but that wasn't much to go on. That rock, that Nogo forsaken rock.

"Master." The princeling snapped his fingers before his face. More proof this youngster was only another entitled royal. "Master Rau, have you heard a word I said?"

Rau had saved a Carved child, injured a Marked, and damned his soul in the process. Aethel forgive him – there was no other prayer he could think of.

The princeling frowned. "Too much excitement for one day it seems. Rest up then, we need to resume our journey. The sea air does nothing for my hair but pack it into a bushel of curls."

Rau nodded numbly. The more he focused on his memories of the girl's face from the cavern, the more he tried to distinguish her features, the more his recollection blurred in fog. He barely registered the tapping of the prince's boots as he crossed the room or the squeak and click of the door as the boy left.

A Steward traitor had long ago foretold Rau had a part to play in the Order's doom. Rau had secluded himself so long at the Temple, he had simply forgotten. Aroawn had as well, it seemed. If his assistance in this child's survival was the start of the end predicted, he needed to find her and fix this.

⁂

*R*au sat in a lounge chair in front of his closed balcony doors as rain pelted against the glass in the dead of night. The manor was silent, not a rodent scurrying about. Everyone else had found comfort in their beds for the night, but not him. Whether it was the three-quarters of a cycle spent unconscious or his churning thoughts, sleep was unlikely to find him.

Out of sight, the sea raged and battered against the cliffs like a battalion at siege, the violent crashes shaking his core. It pounded with his heartbeat. The skies lit up. Thunder burst with an echoing clap. The gods were telling him something, but only they knew what.

"You're awake."

The soft voice startled Rau. He bolted upright and spun, ready to thwart an attack with a thrust of drynn, but a sudden onslaught of dizziness gripped him. His room tilted and vanished behind spots of white. His knees crunched against the tile. Bile built in his throat as he braced one hand against the floor.

Little fingers dug into his shoulder. "I got you," the voice whispered. Soft, gentle, and soothing like the pressure those fingers applied. More tiny fingers caressed his temple before digging through his long hair undone from its usual topknot. The little stranger's hair tickled his nose and cheek. "You're safe. We're safe."

Rau breathed those words in. They were a lifeline, words he had not wanted to hear or accept in centuries. The tempest in his head calmed. The beating in his ears receded. His vision cleared, the shadowed angles of his room brighter, the aureoles framing the candles burning at his bedside flickering with a steady wobble.

It was a child that comforted him – a little girl with a head of fibrous dark hair, untamed and knotted in every direction.

On his knees, her eyes were level with his chin. She had downcast crescent eyes, ones that showed far too much history for her young lifespan, yet she could not have seen more than four or five stretches. Chubby cheeks, dirt stained but smooth and round despite the protruding outline of her collarbone beneath her oversized tunic. A scar on her chin. A button nose with a slight upturn. Her skin was far from the palest he had seen in this realm. For the life of him, Rau could not figure out who she was. A servant's child? A young squire's sibling? Did the children of Misthallen's guardsmen remain at the estate with them?

"How did you get here?"

"I'm a good climber. Always have been, always will. And you can't stop me."

He supressed a chortle. Her parents must have a thrill of a time reeling her in. "Why are you here, little one?"

"I always come to make sure you're alright. Every night." Her gentle voice lulled his restless soul. It called to him and tugged his lips into a smile, muscles he had not been certain he still knew how to use. Why did she care? "I don't like the bad man with you."

His forehead creased. He caressed the hair out of her face, wanting desperately to take away her fear. "No one here will harm you. No bad man can get to you inside these walls. Flower, where are your parents?"

Her little hands went around his nape. She buried her face into the crook of his neck as her little shoulders shook with sobs. She fit snug. Warmth tingled from his collarbone to his chin.

"He's always here. I don't want him to hurt you. He can't take you like he took Maha." Her hold tightened around the collar of his robes, the cloth cinching his skin. She trembled and let out a whimper. "Can't lose you. Need you."

Confusion and unease hit him hard and rolled in his stomach like a stone tumbling downhill. No one had truly *needed* him in a very long time. Rau pried her arms off him. Streaks of tears trailed down the grime on her face. "Child, where are your parents?" Her eyes met his. Why are you here? In my rooms? Don't you know who I am?"

As she wiped tears away, she did the most unexpected thing. She pressed her tear-soaked lips to his cheek. "You're my hero."

His throat closed in on itself. Those words…Moira had called him that, so long ago. They weren't words he had ever expected to hear again. He gasped away the emotion building behind his eyes and blinked away the tears. Warmth spread in his chest. It had been the small things with Moira that had made her utter those words. For this girl…he held not the faintest clue as to what he had done, but he liked the effect those words had, more than he cared to admit.

The girl dropped her head in shame. "I didn't bring enough bread. I didn't know you were awake." Bread? Certain he had heard wrong, Rau's eyes widened when she unraveled a quarter loaf from a scarf tied to her waist. What else did this child hide? She cracked a chunk of bread off and handed it to him, her fingers grazing his palm ever so lightly. Her smile in turn made his lips twitch. Such a simple act, and yet far more than he deserved.

"Little one, I appreciate –"

"Eybah." He cocked his head. "My name, silly." She shoved his shoulder with a little laugh and went back to her bread.

Sensation pulsed in his shoulder. How long had it been since a child had been playful with him instead of cringing back from his brick facade? Since someone had treated him as a person, not an authority figure or threatening force?

"Eybah, do your parents know you're here?"

Her eyes jumped over his in confusion. "They're gone. You saw Maha leave. You told me to run."

Rau flinched back, tendrils of ice creeping over his chest. He picked up her right arm, the sleeve of her tunic ending past her fingers, while she traced his facial scar with the other hand. Such a small gesture. It tickled over every inch of his face, the tingle of it remaining long after her index had continued further down. He wanted to be wrong about her, but he already knew what he would find when he pushed her sleeve to her elbow. Scarred, mottled skin on her small forearm dipped where the mark had been removed. He hissed and forced his eyes closed, despair wriggling back in.

"Does it hurt?" she asked.

The pain in her voice made his mouth go dry. The fact this little creature thought she had hurt him when he was the one that needed to end her life made him want to cave in his own chest. "Not in a long time."

"Mine either. But it itches sometimes. Like ants walking on it."

He nodded absently and tried hard to ignore the smile that bunched her cheeks. She was a Carved, a potential threat to the realms and the Order. Perhaps not now, but when she aged, when she was old enough to conspire with others like her. She was not just an innocent child, she was a traitor in the realms, a future malcontent, a potential murderer. This gentle soul she held was bound to vanish with time. If he did nothing now, any blood she spilled in the future would be on his hands. Child or not, he had a duty. He had to. It would be quick, he would make it so. She deserved that dignity, a flower as she was among the rest.

Jaw clenched, he reached out with his senses for the drynn within her. A splitting headache consumed him. He saw her particles, purple like his own. She was a child born in the realm of Gyldrise like him, and that chilled him further. His breathing turned ragged. He didn't have the strength to do more.

He turned his attention to his own drynn. Purple particles normally swarmed him to the hilt. Now, there was only a scattered mess of them flowing beneath his skin, and only minute quantities permeated his system from the air as the grains of time drained by. No wonder he was exhausted with his reserves so dwindled.

Now, what was he to do with her? A quick death with a snap of drynn at her neck was one thing, but his hands upon her for the same effect…he shuddered. Bile rose at the thought of squeezing the life from her and burned his throat. Rau collapsed onto his rump and scratched at the tingling sensation remaining on his facial scar. What a righteous mess.

"You alright?" The worry in her little voice tugged at him.

"I'll be fine, little flower."

Her giggle made him feel all the worse. So innocent, so joyful. "I like that. I like Gaian roses best. Because they're purple like my eyes."

Purple like her soul, he wanted to say. A Gaian rose, what a cruel joke. The goddess was not blessing her, but Eybah's beaming smile was undeterred by his depressing thoughts.

She yawned and stretched her little arms above her head. "I'm so happy you're awake. I was worried. So worried."

This little child, who had no idea he had tried to end her life moments before, wiggled into his lap and pressed her head to his chest, wrapping her arms around him. The warmth of it. The thrum of her pulse through his robes. Her breathing blew ripples into his robes and brushed his skin. No one ever worried about him. And yet, this little rose of a Carved did. Her breaths evened out. Her arms dropped to her sides. Unsure what to do, he wrapped an arm around her.

Her trust was humbling and so undeserved. He should have peeled her off but couldn't. He should have called the guards to take her, but the words never came. Eybah reminded him of Moira so much. Too much.

"Sleep, flower," he whispered as he lifted her in his arms to lay her on his bed.

Tomorrow, the strength and courage would find him to do what needed to be done. Yes, tomorrow. For now, she could live a little longer.

Nineteen

"Never lose sight of your target," Ghedi whispered beside Kaianne, his tone so contrary to the gruffness of his voice. It somehow wasn't out of place with the breeze through the leaves, the chirping of the birds or the bristling of water down the creek. "Breathe its movements. Glean what it intends to do from the strain of its body. Let its tension flow through your arm and into the arrow."

The roe, thirty paces away, lapped at the water hidden by low foliage. It was big-headed with spotted fur that shone in the sunlight. Its round dark eyes that normally would have made Kaianne smile held a gentle soul. It was so dreadfully adorable, and therein lay one of her problems. She didn't *want* to kill it. That didn't mean she didn't *have* to. It pried up its neck, the corded muscles rippling over its torso. So much meat right at her fingertips. So many people it could feed in their traveling band of Carved. So much responsibility. All Kaianne needed to do was aim true, and that was bloody hard to do. Her fingers squeezed around the grip of the bow.

It wasn't going to be her first kill. Enough kizlins had met the edge of her axes and tip of her knives in the last few moons that she was no longer prissy – Ghedi's words, not hers – about taking an animal's life or the sight of blood. Sometimes the nightmares of her family's deaths returned if she stared at the dying birds too long or if she let remorse in, but they were fewer and farther between since the first one she had woken screaming from. That night and every eve since, Ghedi and a few others nudged her between them until their warmth and strong frames calmed her to sleep. Oidh, despite his dislike of her, even whistled through a lullaby that Mimsee had often sung to her. It was a semblance of peace she dared not linger on for too long.

Now, according to Ghedi, those flightless birds with necks and wings twice as long as their bodies had served their purpose. She needed to hunt more than simple kizlins. Three quints before, he had handed her a bow she had seen him carve in the eves, along with whittled arrows appropriate for her kinder stature – as he so often put it, before rubbing his knuckles over the top of her head – and demanded she learn. So, practice she did, every single wretched day. Even after her arms and legs were already drooping from carrying her packs and treading however many tens of thousands of paces Ghedi had dictated for the day. And little lords, she didn't care for it one bit.

Pulling taut a bow felt like battling against herself the entire time – pull the string, push the arc. That was without the reminder of the string's whiplash when released against her cheek and fingers that stung nearly as bad as the stinger from a gray hornet. Those little beastlings caused welts that lasted for days, just like a bowstring. And the strain it put on her scarred skin and muscles made her tremble at each draw and hold – not good for aiming. It didn't help that a few of the group had taken to placing bets on how many shots she missed in a practice.

Why couldn't Ghedi let her polish her burgeoning skills with hatchets and knives? She had gotten quite good. Most of her knives met their targets now. Her hatchet throws were more forceful, imbedding deeper, and Maarin – one of the one-handed women built nearly as robust as half the men – had only begun to show her a few stances and offensive tactics for close range. Kaianne found safety in the weight of a hatchet in her hands. The feel of its swing rippling down her arms made her feel stronger than the thirteen name-days she had celebrated.

When she reeled and released, it was power that thrummed through her body when the blade thunked into its target in the exact spot she had aimed. She could achieve anything when wielding that weapon. Not once when holding one did anyone think of her as a ridiculous frilly ladyling. With it, she commanded respect. She walked through camp with her head held high, and her companions nodded in greeting. That was smile worthy.

If only Ghedi saw it that way. Poor for stealth, he had said when she argued against learning the bow.

"It's for those who want to hide," she had responded. "I don't want to hide more than we already do."

"Ja, but sometimes that'll save your life, biscuit."

"I understand that. I swear I do. But I want to be in the thick of it. I want to be the hand that bleeds dry the Nogo infested dungholes that betrayed my family. I want them to look in my eyes with my blades stuck in them and know who they wronged."

"Careful. Those are the words of the bloodythirsty."

She ignored his jab. "A bow just won't have the same effect. I cannot do right by my brothers by hiding all the time."

"What'll you do? Run head on into a fight you cannot win?" Kaianne shook her head absently. "Agman, it sounds like you intend to. You need to be smart. Learn to think, devise a plan where every angle is covered. You learn the sword for its stances even though many will surpass you. You learn the knife for the agility and close contact. The hatchet for strength. A sling for aim and versatility. And you learn the bow for sight and stealth. All of these give you options. That is your arsenal." Ghedi forced the bow into her arms. "Live now, die later. Let there always be a later."

She pouted, knowing the discussion was lost. Nothing was going to change his mind. "I just want to be the best at wielding a hatchet. Let me do that. Please."

With an infuriating slow twist of his head, his lips curved up on one side and broke his stoic features. It was something he did just for her. Never for the others. "Stop tunning me grief. Did you think trekking this merry crew through thick and thin tickles me silly? We rarely get to do what we want in life. The question is how to make what you have work for you."

He rarely if ever raised his voice at her. He never had to. His tone and imposing demeanor, a hand less or not, commanded her respect. She wanted to please him. She needed to earn her place in this crew, to abandon the title of the kinder that had been so grievously tied to her.

So here she was, a thousand paces from the day's camp with only Ghedi, Oidh, and Isane as company, to test her newfound proficiency at missing a target's edge only one time out of seven. That merited an unladylike eye roll, not a participatory hunting celebration.

"Track its gait," Ghedi muttered. "Almost, almost. Let it turn its head."

Gods, her neck ached. The hold on the bow strained her shoulders. Her wrist and fingers were still bloodied from the recoil of the bowstring from the practice shots earlier that morning. Her arms shook hard. Pain in her forearm echoed to her elbows. She winced with a flinch. The bowstring slipped from her grasp and released.

Her arrow flew off and missed by a long shot, arching far to the right. Kaianne bit back a slew of unhappy terms. That shot was shameful. The arrow snipped through foliage, and the roe perked up, ears twitching. Before she could blink, Oidh stepped up beside her, drew and released. There was a gentle whistling before the roe thumped lifelessly to the ground.

"What in Nogo's arse was that?" Isane hissed at her with a dark glare, the blonde braids from the unshaven half of her head obscuring one eye. Kainne imagined Isane had once been pretty and dainty before the scar down her forehead to nose was drawn. She had the build for it, despite the muscles the hard life her twenty-or-so stretches had given her, but sometimes the woman's motherly nature came through if the men weren't around.

"I got distracted," Kaianne muttered. Discussing how uncomfortable and how painful the position had been would get her nowhere here, or with any of the Carved for that matter.

"Aye, ye did." Oidh's input was never welcome regardless of the esteem Ghedi held for him.

"Well, go on and fetch it then. You don't have enough of those arrows to be wasting them about."

Kaianne glanced at Ghedi for confirmation of Isane's instructions. His nod and lowered brows were enough to send a chill down her spine. Not a word of encouragement or reprimand, not even the simplest smile or frown. Gods below, he was not happy or upset, simply disappointed, and her chest sank at the realization. Despite the four-dozen other Carved under his care, Ghedi was personally training her. She had grown to look forward to his silent approvals and rare praises. She worked hard for them. Even his harsh rebukes drove her to do better. It was more than her own father had ever done for her. She cared what he thought of her.

Right now, his blank expression screamed shame. Shoulders tucked, she ducked her head and plowed away in the direction her arrow had flown.

Twigs cracked beneath her footsteps, and she kicked tuffs of weeds to release her irritation. She should've done better, fought the shakes and stiffness harder. That's what the others would have done. She had never truly fit in as a ladyling, and now made a lousy Carved as well. A disappointment, that was all she was. To everyone.

With a deep breath, Kaianne forced away those thoughts. She could be better. She would be. She needed to become the best. Disappointment pointed at her would never grace another face. No, people would look to her with pride, awe, and if she did well, fear. Perhaps the thrill of excitement she got at picturing a trembling Willik of House Bryant before her should have been worrying, but she was no longer the cowering, naïve little girl who had thought a delayed marriage contract was life altering. With determination, she swatted at ferns and bushes in search of that Gaia forsaken arrow.

"What do we have here?"

Kaianne whipped around as a hand clamped around her arm. Her eyes widened. A man towered over her, jaw clenched in disgust as he eyed her male attire. That was not what sparked a tremor of fear in her. No, that was all the sigil's doing, of crossed griffin wings and its yellow and brown colors on his doublet. Her mouth went dry. She shuddered as flashes of the kingsmen's attack on her family's estate clouded her vision. It didn't matter that it wasn't the same guardsman. Or that the sigil over his torso was not her family's griffin's eye nor the Royal's spread winged griffin, nor even House Bryant's griffin's head with its talon peering out on the sides. This man came from another Isyldillian House altogether, but that did not make him any less dangerous.

"What's a wee girl like yerself doing this far in the woods? A bit far to be lost, no?"

"I could say the same to you, dear sir." She did not try to pull free, but she glanced around nervously. A bird hooted in the distance, but everything else seemed still. Too still. Had the others seen him?

"Brock," he called over his shoulder. "Reckon this wee one's not who shot yer prize."

A shadow crept up behind him and waggled her arrow. "Not with this bloody thing."

The second incomer's attire was completely nondescript compared to his companion's: brown jerkin to match his hair covering a black tunic and dark gloves – similar attire to what her father's hunters had worn. Kaianne bit her tongue to keep from cursing. There were two of them and only one of her. The gods had dropped her in a boiling kettle and served her up for a midday meal. It certainly felt that way since the crew's scouts had missed these two. She fingered the outline of the dagger's hilt hidden beneath her loose vest and pressed her heel against another blade in her boot.

"I'm of no interest to you. Just trying my skills with a bow and failing...poorly. If you send me on my way, I'll be sure to avoid crossing your paths and disturbing your hunt again."

"So prim and proper, but ye're a bit far South with that accent. And all on yer lonesome?" Kaianne blanched as the gleam in his eyes turned malicious. "I think not."

Before she screamed a warning, his other palm plastered over her mouth, his fingers digging into her cheeks and muffling every sound she made. His companion grappled at her sleeve while she attempted to maul his palm and pry off his hand.

"Carved," Brock muttered with a hiss as he unsheathed a hunting blade.

Kaianne's eyes widened, one hand slipping beneath her vest for access to her dagger. The first man's hold was so close to her neck. She could practically foretell the snap of it if he jerked her head too hard to one side. Well, Nogo's pits to them because she wasn't going to die complacent. Not like poor Adi, trapped and without a chance to escape his own death. No, she would go like Deacon had, fighting. She freed her dagger, hand shaking, a ringing in her ears building. The hunter raised his knife to her throat.

A gargled yell broke through the woods, and he flinched. His eyes searched over their shoulders. Another muffled holler had him lowering his blade.

"Go. See to Landon and Jirkeg," the guardsman ordered. "I've got this wee one handled."

One moment's hesitation, then the hunter dove into the weave of the wood's shadows. Kaianne squeezed the dagger's hilt tighter and whispered a quick prayer.

"Always in groups ye buggers are. It'll be -" His words fell into a rattled wail as her dagger punctured through his trousers into his inner thigh. Once. Twice. Her hand trembled, so much that she had to wrench it out to pry it free the third time. The ringing in her ears deafened her.

Blood coated her fingers – dripping, flowing, slinking warmth between the seams. He hissed and gasped. She struggled to fill her lungs with fresh air untainted of iron. His hands fell off her, and he tumbled to the moss covered ground, mouthing curses and clutching his thigh. His breaths shallowed. A pool of crimson soaked the greenery and vanished beneath it in mere grainfalls. Too quickly, only the darkened color remained. His pale face drained of color. When his head fell back, the murder in his eyes finally glossed over.

It wasn't until that moment that Kaianne let herself breathe again, and it was hoarse and violent. He was dead. She had caused it, and yet the churning sickness she expected never came. The longer she looked at him – still, harmless, gone – the calmer she felt. Her trembling ebbed. Her breathing slowed, and soon the echo of life in the forest reached her ears once more. There was no pity for him, no sadness, no regret. It just was. It was killed or be killed. He had needed to die, and that certainty settled in her spine. Just like the Bryants needed to. The world didn't need more cruel men like him. It needed less, and she had contributed, perhaps made others safer. It helped ebb the guilt.

She wondered how misled this man had been. Had he ever questioned his task to eliminate Carved and Flawed? How much of his actions were ignorance and loyalty? How much was compliance or worse, willingness? Where did one begin and the other end?

"Biscuit," Ghedi called. "Give us a holler."

Heavy steps trudged through the greenery and dried leaves. A few more sandfalls passed, and Kaianne cocked her head to the side, her gaze unwavering from the corpse. Killing hadn't even been that hard, almost too easy actually. People were so fragile. Her fingers trailed on her vest over the scar that marked her lower abdomen. It was a miracle she had survived that, yet this burly guard who had probably trained to fight since younger than her numbered stretches went down in the span of a few heartbeats.

Her grip on her dagger loosened, but the blade's hilt remained pasted to her palm. The blood had begun to dry, flaky yet shackling, her healthy skin marred in a stiff maroon glove. The warmth had vanished. Oh Pyre spite her, she was coated in someone else. That made the nausea spur up, and she darted to the side as her last meal came up.

Isane and Oidh joined Ghedi's calls as she dragged a sleeve over her mouth and stood. It was bad enough they might smell her vomit, but if Oidh witnessed her moment of weakness… She groaned, already imagining the countless jeers and taunts he would throw, always including something about her youth, size and innocence, that she was only a liability. With movement in her periphery, she crouched beside the dead man and wiped her blade clean on his tunic. So, when the first person appeared on her left, she gave no hint at being bothered in the least.

"There was a hunter with him," she said as a greeting. To avoid meeting eyes, she searched through the guardsman's pockets – a few bronze slags and a handful of copper pars (better coins than nothing), a pocket knife, and some resher grass for smoking. The stuff reeked sickly sweet when burned. She grimaced and tossed the grass aside, knowing full well Oidh enjoyed it.

"Aye, and three others," Oidh said. "Bunch of undergrown milksops they were."

"That your work?" Isane asked, crouching beside Kaianne with a tap to her shoulder. "Impressive. Good on you. Make Oidh eat his words."

A smirk crept up Kaianne's face. Like Kaianne and Oidh, Isane was born and raised in Isyldill, but whereas Oidh held onto his southern brogue and Kaianne's intonations wore heavily on vowels and word endings like most northern Isyldillians, Isane hailed from a tiny village as close to the outpost of Salost near the border with Telfinor as the Order allowed. Her speech was snipped and flatter than most of the realms' folk, and reminded Kaianne of how the Mentees and Greenlings she had crossed at the Bryant's Zesco manor spoke.

Ghedi gripped Kaianne's shoulder and squeezed twice while Isane raided the guardsman's pockets. "Are you hurt?"

She followed his gaze to the blood spray that sullied her clothing and coated her hands. "It's not mine."

"Good." A wary smile lined his face. "You did good."

Warmth filled her at those words, tampered slightly by the lack of conviction in his eyes. Had she disappointed him that much with her poor shot?

"Oidh, Isane, handle the game. The kinder and I will regroup." His tone brokered no argument.

They left without a word, though Oidh did kick the dead man for good measure with nodded approval in her direction. That almost made her feel smug until Ghedi cleared his throat, already a few paces ahead of her.

The silence was tense and heavy between them. The crackle of leaves and twigs and the squelch of mud as they trekked upped the pressure weighing in her ears.

"I'll do better," she vowed. Ghedi finally slowed his pace and faced her. "I swear. Whatever weapon you want, I'll train with it."

His gaze raked over her face for a moment, but he only nodded then pushed onward. Kaianne's heart dropped to her stomach. Before she could think better of it, she reached for his forearm stub and tugged him back. He hated that and had once beat a man in their crew for doing the same. The flesh was extra sensitive – he once explained – and touch often caused phantom pains for sandfalls on end. When his eyes narrowed at the contact, she recoiled and gulped down her worry.

"I will become the best markswoman, if it pleases you."

"Do it for yourself, not me." He sauntered ahead. "Keep up."

She scampered after him, head tucked down. "I said I would do better. That I would be the best."

"I heard." It was all but dismissive.

Kaianne huffed a sigh, not sure what else to add to ease his disappointment. Ghedi wasn't a man of many words, but the silence between them was suffocating. It only grew with each step. Birds frolicked overhead, chattering in tempestuous songs that seemed to mock her. Even the chipmunks were loud in their munching. Papa had thought her a burden to the family, one best kept quiet and demure, then sold off in marriage to the son of his murderer. Little lords, is that what she had become to the Carved crew? Pressure built behind her eyes, and she bit her lip deep enough to draw blood to fight back a sob. Ghedi was realizing she was more trouble than she was worth. And *she* had forced that thought into his mind by arguing about training.

"Someone else could train me. You don't have to."

"No." He had not even slowed his pace.

Her breath caught. He was going to send her away, she just knew it. Just when her nightmares had nearly vanished and she had found her place. Or had she? Maybe this new family of hers was an illusion. There were no other young people her age, no mention of children at all when the others spoke of rejoining other Carved troops. Gods, hope made people foolish.

"Why the tears?"

"What?"

He reached for her face but pulled back when she raised her own hand. Treacherous leaky eyes. Her cheeks were indeed wet. She ducked her head, hair spilling down to hide it while she wiped the show of weakness away. "I'm not crying."

"No stake ever grew old with the bark on." One of his favorite proverbs. Another lesson spoken so casually, as if she didn't suspect he was giving up on her. She had learned enough over the last few cycles to start over on her own. She could fend for herself now if the crew abandoned her. She could figure out a plan on her lonesome to get back at the Bryants. Maybe even see if Mimsee was still in Millian and wanted to join her.

"What does it matter?" she asked. They were not far from camp now, only another hundred paces or so. The wind carried mumbled conversations like whispered secrets. "Do I at least get my dagger back, or are you going to make me steal it?"

This time it was Ghedi that stopped them short by extending his arm against her torso. For long moments, his gaze raked over her before skipping to the woods past her shoulder. "Where is that head of yours carrying you?"

"To the same place yours is."

He raised a brow, and when he gave away nothing else, she bypassed his arm with a huff. A mantelpiece to her family. Abandoned by the princeling. Unworthy of a Craved crew.

"At least have the decency to tell me I'm not good enough. To admit that I've failed your expectations, and you rescind your welcome into your crew. Be honest and say it all to my face. Don't be like everyone else. Don't just treat me like I'm nothing, like I can be abandoned without a care."

The woods turned fuzzy, blotches of green and brown muddled together. Her face prickled with shame. His calloused fingers scraped a tear from her cheeks.

"Biscuit." His gravelly voice seared her. This was it. Even after killing a Marked that might have hurt other Carved, she wasn't good enough. "Whether you care for it or not, you are part of my crew."

She flinched. "What? But I don't...you were going to oust me."

"Nigh."

"Then, why? Why are you…like this? Why have you said nothing? No critiques on my form. On my muscle tremors or my wide shot. How I should have practiced better. That's not like you. And no words of what happened either. I mean, I killed a man. My first. I was defending myself like you said I would be. I stabbed him over and over, watched him bleed to death. I stared at him and felt no guilt. You must have known that. I know you saw it lacking, you see everything. But you said nothing. Not a word on how I could have done better – less bloody, quicker, quieter. No worries about how I felt."

"You had your emotions in check."

"I know I did. That's not what I mean." Kaianne groaned and kicked her frustrations over and over at a moss-ridden rock. "Blockheaded tweeb," she grumbled under her breath, then winced with instant regret, almost expecting a lashing.

Yet Ghedi only snorted, his gaze far off. "You are so much like her. Ag, she would have liked you."

"She?"

"My daughter," was all he added before walking off once more. "Let us regroup before there are any more surprises."

Kaianne hurried after him. "Where is she?"

He didn't glance at her. "With the gods."

"Oh. How long ago?"

He shook his head and with a sigh, leaned his back against a tree. "Understand biscuit, we all make mistakes. It is how we grow from them that defines us. If you turn to regret, the amount of it you shovel down may bury you." His sharp eyes fixed her. "You are strong. You are capable, and I am proud of how well you defended yourself. You should not have needed to so soon. That is on me. On Oidh and Isane too, but I carry more blame."

A trusting smile sparked. "I thought you were mad at me."

"Nigh. It was regret. Regret that tonight you will relive that Marked's death in your nightmares, guilt or not, and I did not prolong your youth longer."

"Only regret? Even when I butchered that shot?"

"You know you can do better, Kay." His gaze grew soft as his shortened name for her dragged between them. He nudged her chin, and she bubbled with pride. "Kay, my crew's little biscuit. Your place with us has been earned every day since you tagged along. Do not doubt that. Once we regroup with the other crews in Lakoldon, no one will be able to contest it. Not even Oidh." He winked, and with that every worry she had went to rest.

Kaianne nearly bounced in place. "How will no one contest it? How many other crews are there?"

"Each seed must wait for its time to be sowed. As should you. In the meantime, perfect your skills. No more lazy shots."

She bound after him. "So, it's a test then?"

"An oath, and no, I'll not tell you more. Come on, off you go. Reach camp, clean yourself and ready your bow. I want five targets hit before midday."

Twenty

*F*or Rau, tomorrow's courage never came. Nor did it make a showing the day after, nor even a quint or bilial later. With each passing moment, Rau found himself more endeared to Eybah. Whether it was her splashing in a tub out of excitement, to her grumbling as he combed down the knots in her hair, or her thrill and joy when dressed in decent girl clothing, Rau could not tamper the feelings. He could not rub them off his chest where they seemed to fester.

She made him laugh over the simplest things, like the scrunch of her face for a food she disliked. She made him smile when she pressed her head to his shoulder as he read to her before bed. She made him burst into a rage when she rolled her eyes and refused to listen. She made his heart ache when she spoke of her life in the cavern, scrounging for food and safety. The point was, she made him feel. The idea of parting with her anchored him down, drowning him far below the Barring Sea's waves. There was no other option: she had to come with him when they left Misthall.

The concept was easier to plan than to fulfill. He hired a permanent stagecoach with a bench cushion that opened for additional storage. A perfect hideout for Eybah or so he thought. Reining her in and convincing her to stay within and keep quiet in the early mornings before a day's ride was more challenging than honing onto a single speck of drynn in a cluster of millions.

Every morning was a test of discipline and will. At first light, the instant the rooster shrieked its song, Rau tucked Eybah into her bench hideout with a graze of his knuckles on her cheek and a heavy heart. Sometimes, when the slightest noise or touch woke her, he plied her with sweet treats if she remained undiscovered and begged the gods she listened. Those mornings were the worst, as his heart crashed against his chest from the lightest sound out of place.

Every moment away from her, his anxiety worsened. Each night, after thanking their new host for the eve's lodgings, Rau hurried to his sleeping quarters where he and Eybah spent the evening before retreating to the carriage in the dead of night like thieves. Getting her to sleep without a fuss was an adventure in and of itself, and what worked best were bedtime stories, particularly those about Schlenkra. Of Nogo, the maker of creatures and Pyre, the death god, and how Aethel and Gaia prevailed against them for their people's right to inhabit Taelgir.

Then, every morning he was forced to sneak back in and make a show of leaving his sleeping quarters before settling in his carriage, curtains drawn. Dawn clawed at his eyes and pried dark circles beneath them. It was exhausting, but worth every moment when Eybah crept out of her hideout and curled up against him.

Each day, he slept off his exhaustion upright as the carriage bounced down the road, waking with her bouts of energy to answer a seemingly endless list of questions from why this carriage had yellow curtains to how long the game of hide-away would last. Somehow, despite the sleepless nights, Eybah displayed even more energy during the day's ride – bounding from one side of the carriage to the other against the carriage's jostling motion – than he had seen from her in the last quint as he finished recovering. She was a true little terror.

She spoke so loudly, Rau cringed. Anyone might hear and dare to check who he was with. It was already an effort to keep her concealed during his numerous calls for the princeling's troop to halt because Eybah's bladder was the size of a pea. It helped that he had primarily kept to himself during their previous travels. As far as he had gathered, his behavior had not been deemed suspicious.

Eybah played with the curtains, peeking out from one side to the other and snorting with laughter. Rau commanded her with firm 'no's' and plopped her back onto her bench. That only incited her as she pried the coverings to the side, glanced at him with a mischievous smile, replaced them, and then repeated the taunt. He tried to ignore his frustrations and worry. He really tried, his hands clammy as he slapped palm to back hand repeatedly. On one particular day when a shadow trotted by, his apprehension reached its crescendo.

"Enough." He forced an accumulation of drynn to slap the curtain shut against the door and dragged Eybah's little form to the bench's center. It had only taken a whiff of his talent now that he was fully recovered and he had not hurt her, but Eybah trembled and hunched her shoulders as she stared at him with wide eyes. That look did things to him. His shoulders twitched uncomfortably and his jaw ticked. He clutched her hand between his own in a desperate attempt to make her understand and softened his tone.

"Enough, flower. They cannot see you. They cannot know you are here. You know this. You are Carved, even if not by your own choices. They will not show you the mercy I have. Please, stay out of sight and mind. For me. For yourself. For your mother who would have wanted you safe."

That last bit he forced out for her sake, because what kind of mother endangered their child by carving out their mark? Something in his speech worked, for at least a few grains of time, until she was restless once more and jumping about as if he had said nothing. Rau spent more drynn control plopping her back onto her seat in those first five days after leaving the Misthallen estate than he had used in the last few centuries.

Every eve he arrived at their night's destination, drynn depleted and ready to crumble into the Mistress of Dream's arms. Every morning he woke bleary eyed and stressed in apprehension of another day battling a young child's energy.

The secret of it and the contradiction of his purpose weighed him down. Something had to give.

*T*hat something came before the end of their first bilial of travel together, in the darkness of eve after the fourteenth day.

Shortly before sundown, they arrived in Alihuerte. The border with Gyldrise – he had not cared to visit his birth realm in ages – was so close he could taste the drynn in it, the vast accumulation of the particles was palpable. Although far enough from the border that no one could stumble on it by accident, the city extended parallel to the border line and spread out in a half-sphere inside Isyldill, with outlying homes jutting in arcs like rays from the sun on the horizon. Unlike the previous cities where the Lord's estates were separate, here the main estate lay in the center.

The residing Lord dressed in jeweled robes did the common presentations, which as usual droned on. After having them escorted to their chambers, the man offered them a tour of the town. It was a welcomed invitation, but the procession through every single street of the city as they discussed certain businesses and the people's prosperity dragged on for far too long. Eybah was waiting for him.

The sun slowly became a distant memory beneath the crescent shape of the Maiesta moon and tampered glow of the Persefin moon. Music thumped and reeded through the night air. The streets had long cleared of traffic, yet Lord Mer insisted they continue to weave through as he held the prince's attention on Alihuerte's trade products and profits. It seemed a town in Gyldrise and Alihuerte had recently developed a trolley and pulley system for the exchange of limited goods. It was ingenious considering the inability to cross borders, but Rau gritted his teeth with impatience through the explanation, even though such topics concerned the Order as well. He clapped his hands against his robe and thighs.

Eybah knew to wait for him before exiting the carriage, but knowing and doing were two separate concepts when it came to that child. If he took too long, there was no telling what she would do or where he would find her. Without line of sight, his ability to control drynn and therefore force the carriage door to remain closed was greatly diminished. Which was why he took the precaution of leaving a tendril of drynn around the door's outline to warn him in case it opened.

When Lord Mer finally escorted their party toward the gates of his estate, Rau blew out a breath full of tension, his fingers fiddling with the air and its drynn. The beat of the music was growing louder along with a cacophony of laughter and chatter. The scents of a feast wafted around him. His stomach growled in approval, but he ignored it because finally, *finally*, he could fetch Eybah and reassure himself that she was -

He stopped short at the sight of the writhing sea of bodies that twisted to the music around the five raging bonfires that filled the Lord's estate's courtyard. The entire city seemed packed within the enclosed grounds – dancing, grinding or laying atop each other in the strangest display of community he had ever witnessed. Decorum went from formal dress to topless or skirts pried up and pants down. To his left, a man was pouring wine between a smiling woman's breasts and licking it up while another couple was in the throes of a pounding while the woman chewed the meat off a pig's leg. Rau cleared his throat with unease and swept a hand over his eyes in case he was seeing things. What in Aethel's good name was this? He must have said it out loud because the Lord of Alihuerte smiled at him.

"A feast of plentitude and pleasure to honor yours and our Princeling's coming." Rau peered at the pudgy Lord Mer in shock, sure he had misheard the Lord's pun. This was utterly depraved, ridiculous, and absolutely demeaning. None of this pleased or honored him.

He opened his mouth to bark such a thing when two women approached him from both sides and leaned on his arms. They groped at his chest and reached into his hood which fell back as their fingers swiped over his jaw and lips. Rau balked backwards, muscles tensed, but they stuck to him like sap.

"You should see your face. Priceless." The princeling burst into laughter as a topless woman pressed against the boy. He wrapped his arm around her with a large grin and traipsed further into the courtyard. His kingsmen followed close behind, mixed looks of shock, disgust and lust plaguing their faces. "You are to be commended my Lord," Andreiyes yelled over the racket. "This might be the best revelry to entertain us so far."

Rau shook his head in revulsion. What happened to old-fashioned dancing and a regular meal at a table? What was the appeal to this lewdness? Not his cup of tea. Not at all. Not now, not even when he had been a young lad. His maha and chichu had taught him better than that.

He shook off the women, but another took their place. After that, a man had the gall to proposition him as well. That was when he forced a barrier of drynn around himself and retreated to a corner wall. The cold stone grounded him against the throes of the bonfires' blazing heat, the press of the drums, the reek of sex and spilled mead and ale and the moans that encroached on his serenity. Any approaching fool bounced off his shield, leaving a ripple effect. Some cursed their upset. Others were so stewed they fell over themselves in fits of laughter. They drank and ate and drank and groped and drank and danced and drank and humped profusely. Bile rose and he swallowed it back best he could. Even if he closed his eyes, he saw the scene still embedded on his eyelids and heard the slap of skin on skin. Never in his five hundred stretches had he witnessed such debauchery.

He crept along the wall, shoulders pried back, eyes fixed ahead on everything and nothing. He thought of escaping into his chambers unseen. Either that or else he considered sleeping in the sanctity of the stables. Horses were better company than most people, and Eybah would probably be thrilled with the idea. Eybah. Oh, Nogo condemn his soul to the pits. How long had she been waiting for him? He had not sensed the particles around her door move. Come to think of it, he was unable to sense much of anything outside his shield. Rau stopped short. Now he was the fool.

He dropped his barrier of drynn and reached out with his senses to the carriage. The particles along the door outline remained. He felt them vibrating to be set free which meant she was still inside. Rau blew out a shaky breath and pressed his head against the wall in relief. He then reached out to feel the particles that made up his little Eybah – because she was *his* now – to see how restless and frustrated she was. It felt...barren. The carriage was made of empty air and unobstructed drynn that floated about seamlessly.

His heart sped, his throat dry like a drunk's the morning after. Impossible. He had felt no disturbance in the door. Shoving through the writhing mob, Rau rushed to the front gates. There was no trap door in the carriage flooring, no roof flap. No one dared to touch his carriage, so she could not have been discovered. Unless she had been spotted gazing out the windows. He stopped short. A window. How had he not considered her overstepping the boundaries he had set? Of course she had chosen to climb out the window. He broke into a running shuffle, his robes restricting the length of his strides as they snapped taut, then loose and taut once more.

With the carriage unhorsed and unmanned with not a straggler in sight, his tension dissipated the closer he got. Until he heard a wail. It pierced the midnight air and the craze of the revelry. Sharp and stringent, full of pain and despair. Fear numbed his fingertips. It nearly brought him to his knees, but Rau forced himself down the street that spanned the length of the Lord's estate's outer wall. He would not lose Eybah like Moira.

The shriek turned to whimpers buried beneath hissed accusations and curses. Rau's legs blurred as he sprinted faster than he had had cause to in centuries. His chest burned. His muscles were aflame. It didn't matter. Unlike his last urgent sprint for Moira up the Temple's Remembrance Tower five centuries before, Eybah had a chance. Her shrieks and begging pleas were his beacon on a low moonlit eve.

Two alleys down, at the tail of a dead end, he found them. Two of the Lord's guardsmen from the talon emblems on the back of their tunics kicked mercilessly at a tiny figure balled on the ground, whose cries grew weaker with each blow. Rau did not grant them the awareness of his presence. All that burning rage that had simmered and festered in his soul for decades and centuries on end burst from him. He wrenched the drynn from their bones and blood until erratic cracks became the percussion tune on the eve's air. Their blood drenched their clothing. It drained between the cobblestones until only puddles of their flesh remained and the reek of iron surrounded him.

Rau panted, a hand supporting his weight against the nearest wall. His reserves of drynn were dwindling. His legs buckled, but he forced them forward. He had to know whether or not his little flower had joined his little greenling's fate. If perhaps he wasn't as much a failure this time around. He had to know, no matter how many more fractures in his soul it might create.

The revelry was a muffled nightmare compared to the horror of Eybah's frailty, and that cracked him wide open as he knelt at her side. Blood soaked his robes and gore stuck to him like paste, but that was not what made him tremble. It was the shallow, gurgled breaths and her flinch from his touch. It was the open wounds and darkened skin from blooming bruises. It was the twisted angle of her right arm and the look of shame on her face when he hauled her into his arms.

"I'm sorry," she burbled, and Rau burst into sobs, cradling her close.

*E*ybah did not die. He refused to let her. With blocks of drynn, he clogged the wounds and stemmed the blood flow. He forced the muck from her lungs, caressing her hair as she wretched it out between mewls, then sealed the organ shut. It wasn't enough and he couldn't hold it forever, but it gave her a chance. She was chilled and shaking, her weak grip bunched on the front of his robes as he lugged her into his arms.

He ran as fast as possible without jostling her, the burn in his body welcome if it saved her. There was only one place to take her where he knew she was in relative safety. Until he found a better solution.

The storage house was just as quiet and forlorn as when he had left it, his stagecoach nestled between a phaeton and a barouche. Perfect place for Eybah to stay while he found help, but leaving her alone proved a trial of its own. Her little fingers tightened their grip on his robes as he settled her into a corner along a bed of hay, and her tiny body tremored.

"No, no," she muttered in panic. Her unswollen eye pleaded with tears.

"I'm here." He stroked her cheek. "But you need help I cannot give. I'll find help. You'll live. I swear it to the gods."

Words didn't lessen the strain on her face. Nor did they give him relief when he pried her grip free, but he didn't have the talent of a Mender, no matter how much he wished for it.

His feet dragged beneath him. His back was bowed from the strain of using his own drynn stores, but he barreled through the gates of the Lord's estate all the same, only to smack into the first group he encountered. He was sent sprawling to hands and knees into dirt soaked in mead, ale and who knows what else. They bawled in laughter, but he ignored them as he scurried back up to his feet. The revel's mob was crowded beyond belief, and he tripped thrice more over the limbs of prostrated individuals that were definitely not pious.

Someone caught his arm and Rau spun around to shove the newcomer. "What in the pits happened to you?" Of all the people, the princeling *had* to be the one to accost him, his laughter grating, his familiarity unwelcome.

Rau shook him off, but his eyes searched the crowd. "Too much drink, I'm not certain."

"Dear Master, you look as though you've seen a ghost."

He searched the crowd. "There's no thrill in this for me."

"Of course not."

Rau ignored the dripping sarcasm, his focus on finding a tuft of curled red and silver hair in the mob, Heaton something-or-other. There, he caught sight of a flash of it. The princeling's personal physician was in an animated discussion with three others, drinks in hand near the buffet tables that blocked the main entrance to the Lord's manor.

"My excuses, princeling. I have some business to attend to." Rau dashed in a weave through the crowd of billowing robes before the princeling could relish further from the sound of his own voice.

⁂

*I*t was far too many grainfalls later before the royal physician arrived at the storage house. He was alone as agreed during their terse discussion at the revel, head-to-boot in black that melted him into the night if not for his shade of hair. Eybah had grown paler in that time, her caramel tone almost ashen in the lantern's glow. Rau had not moved since returning to her side. He clutched her chubby fingers between his own with her head laid on his lap to avoid jabs of the hay against her skull.

"Pardon the wait, your Grace." The man shook his medicine satchel as an excuse. "Had to fetch what you required."

Rau ground his teeth. The physician's nonchalance chafed what remained of his composure. Healers needed their concentration to work their skills. He had observed enough of the Order's Menders over the stretches and this man possessed only a primitive ability to mend wounds, nothing like his Brothers and Sisters.

"No worries." Heaton casually waved off Rau's misgivings. "I was discreet. Now what do we have here?" From appearances alone, the physician would have been considered older than Rau from the creased corners of his eyes and the sunspots littering his skin, but perceived age did not equivocate wisdom. The physician knelt beside them. "A child?"

Case in point. Rau gave a firm nod, his glare daring the man to ask more, yet the healer ignored the warning.

"Where on all Taelgir did you find her? And bludgeoned as she is -"

"You were told to ask no questions."

The physician flinched. "I meant no harm by it. Only wished to know my patient."

"Then know this. She lives, or I will personally claw your soul from your body and watch the life drain from your eyes. Does that settle your curiosity?"

The man's Adam's apple bobbed as he buried his gaze into the contents of his satchel. Rau had meant every word of his threat. It was humbling to realize the power his little flower held over him. In less than a moon cycle, she had dug her roots so deep inside him he might never recover. He gazed down at her. Her jaw was clenched. Sweat beaded around her temple, and streaks of tears ran around the swelling bumps and crusted split skin. Rau pressed a kiss on a patch of unswollen skin on her temple. Her whimper tore at him.

"You're safe with me," he whispered. "I promise."

After the physician pressed a cloth imbued with a sickly-sweet oil to her mouth, his little flower made no further sound. Every tension in her body deadened, and if it weren't for the slight gargle on her inhales or the rise and fall of her chest, Rau might have let his panic loose. He wanted Eybah's perky voice to distract him, her smile to light his own, her energy to rile him up with mixed adrenaline and exhaustion. Instead, there was only the crackle of hay as the man shuffled his weight for the best vantage, Rau's own hissing when the physician made an incision, the snip of scissors or the whispered curses on the man's lips when the internal bleeding kept on. Other than the rugged stitches the healer made on the larger gashes, his work was impressive for someone in need of only their hands and tools to heal. He even went as far as inserting a minuscular hose down her throat and suctioning out pink-tinted fluid. By the end, Eybah's cheeks were filling with color once more.

"She'll live. With a quint or two of rest, she'll be right as rain."

"Good." Rau threw his head back, shaky with relief. "Good."

"Just need to set her arm then I'll be —"

Rau caught the physician's wrist before the scissors cut Eybah's sleeve. "Leave it. I'll handle that."

"Your Grace, if the bone is not properly set, the child will be deformed. I will be quick. The child will feel nothing." The healer reached for her sleeve once more.

"You'll do as you're told." Too late Rau tugged Eybah's arm away.

The cloth was caught between his and the doctor's grip, her upper arm at a jutting angle. The sleeve ripped: at the wrist, past her forearm, to the elbow. The scar and lack of the griffin – the Gyldrit staked finfolk as would have been Eybah's case – bared for the healer's eyes. The man released her and toppled over his satchel onto his rump. The bag's contents clanked and clacked, spilling onto stone and hay. Rau clutched Eybah closer to him. Tension crisped the air.

"You…she…You made me attend a *Carved.*" The last word dragged out of Heaton in a trembling breathiness as he swept his hand over his mouth and caught his index between his teeth. "I…we should have let her pass. It would have been less cruel. All my work. All that time spent. On a Carved. Why would you ask such a thing of me?" The healer's backbone was decomposing to sawdust the more his eyes bounced between Rau, Eybah, and the rest of the storage house.

"I asked for your silence and discretion. You swore. Now keep your word. This was necessary."

"Necessary? You've condemned me." Heaton rose carefully. "If any discover…I'll be branded a traitor. I'm not a traitor, I serve well. I am highly sought after, second only to his Majesty's First Healer. I must tell the princeling."

"You'll do no such thing."

Rau gently lay Eybah on the ground and patted along the stone flooring for the discarded scissors while the healer paced, lost to his ramblings. "He'll understand. He'll know it wasn't my choice. I only need to prove it. Yes, proof. I'll bring him the child. The Carved. Dead. Yes, no wrongdoing after that. Of course, I'll simply do that."

"*No,*" Rau snarled as he jabbed the cold, metal scissors into the healer's chest and released. "You'll do nothing."

No one was going to harm her further. No one was going to take her from him. Not the healer who stumbled to his knees, blood dribbling from his wound, eyes wider than before. Not the princeling. Not Aroawn or even his Brothers and Sisters. Carved or not, Eybah was his. To protect until his last breath.

When the pulsing in his ears simmered down, the extent of what he had just done sunk like a boulder in his stomach. Under Nogo's wrath, he had murdered a man – on his own, no Hefter control required. Rau turned his hands over, a slight tremble to them, eyes fixed on the traces of fresh blood over the dried bits. He gulped with unease. Another dark tally on his soul amongst the sea of weeds it already possessed. This had been…necessary. Such was the same reasoning they used when keeping up the border lines, in exterminating the Flawed, in sentencing the Carved; yet tonight the word had taken on a deeper meaning. This death was *necessary* to him, to Eybah.

The problem, though, was that Heaton was the princeling's personal physician. People were bound to come looking for him come morning, and then the hunt for his killer would begin. That truth was sobering. Rau tapped his hands together and paced. Aethel curse his foolishness, he and Heaton had been seen speaking at the revel. Thank Aethel's good graces they had departed separately, but it might still arouse suspicion. And the two other bodies Rau had left in an unnatural state might tip the scales against him. Who would take care of Eybah and nurse her back to health if they denounced him for murder? A headache was stirring behind his eyes. Only one solution remained, as distasteful as it was. The bodies needed to disappear.

In his carriage, his trunks of Well Water were untouched. For the first time in what felt like entire stretches, he undid the clasp. It thunked against the wood with finality. For so long, he wished to be free of the water's effects. Now, he took one vial, uncorked it, and downed the fluid without lingering on the regret.

☙ ❧ ☙

Drynn swarmed Rau's senses even as he lugged the phaeton concealing Heaton's body through the streets of Alihuerte without the help of a single horse. The ongoing revel drowned out the clop of the wheels between the cobblestones. The clouds masked the moons' already tampered glow as he and his haul tread in the shadows. He made one stop for the corpses of the dead guardsmen – fortunately undiscovered – and then it was a long, straight walk to the border line between the realm of Isyldill and Gyldrit.

His plan was as simple as possible. Alihuerte had been marauded by Carved – long since moved on by Rau's assessment – but it remained plausible for the traitors to have come again and wreaked havoc on a few lives and carriages. They would have then crossed the border with a stolen vehicle. It didn't exactly explain the missing bodies of the men he had killed, but supplied with a basic theory, Rau was counting on the active imagination of the populace to fill in the rest.

The town's edge extended on either side of Rau like a line drawn in the sand between two warring fronts. With the glow of hundreds of torchlights at the Lord's manor and the festivities lingering on the air, it almost seemed like a beacon of hope compared to the shadows sprouted by the woods with their knotted trees and gnarly branches. Rau crossed the town boundary without a misstep. Darkness and he were old friends, stretches of companionable silence between them.

The borders between realms had a distinct smell that reminded Rau of the charged energy that lingered behind a lightning storm. He followed the scent, lugging drynn molded to the carriage to follow his trail until the scent wrapped around him. A switch to his sight of drynn particles confirmed he was in the thick of the barrier. It surrounded him with a wave of stamina and vitality he only ever felt when downing a vial of Well's Water. Its glare threatened to burn through his secondary sight with how condensed the life particles were mixed between golden and purple hues. The amount of drynn was staggering.

The royals did this, whichever one currently sat on each throne. It was a bone-deep reminder of the danger they posed. Of how much the Order was forced to rely on them despite everything. No matter how often the Order sent a Guzzler to suction an unborn royal during a pregnancy, the royal infant's tie to the land could not be severed or reduced. It was a condition imposed by the Creators – Aethel and Gaia Jonah – before they created and ascended to Iltheln. The god couple had left their empire divided between their five sons to become the five ruling lines – Kings Lenierz Jonah of Isyldill, Verdon Jonah of Lakoldon, Ambrosius Jonah of Gyldrise, Croven Jonah of Nimedor, and Duvir Jonah of Telfinor – their first names carried on as each lines' surname.

In those days, the choice had certainly been sensible. History tomes noted the strengths of the five gods-children's talents. Entire records detailed their devotion in nurturing the land, caring for the people, and worshiping the memories left behind by the Creators. They had been great rulers, and perhaps the world of today would have been different had their descendants all held onto the same philosophy. Perhaps Rau would have lived a peaceful life watching his daughter become a formidable young woman and join the Order herself. Perhaps he might have grown old with Tilnee at his side, a few more children to their names, gray hair and wrinkly before they passed peacefully on to Iltheln. Alas, such dreams had long ago vanished.

Somewhere in the centuries between Aethel and Gaia's ascension and the Apostate War, the royals lost sight of their duties. They began thinking the reverence to the gods and the magic in Taelgir was their due. That they were the ones in need of worship. That they were more crucial to the realms than the foundation on which they were based. That they deserved to make decisions solely between themselves without the approval of the Order which Aethel himself had established to balance their power. That's what happened to people when the idea of power was too ingrained in who they were. Blinded by their megalomania, the royals sparked the Apostate War that destroyed thousands upon thousands of lives. They were so wrapped in their vainglory that when they were defeated, they manipulated the treaty negotiations while their partisans attempted to destroy the Order from within.

Rau's breath hitched at the memory as he pried himself out of the border's forcefield. He had been at those negotiations where Crown Princess Shawna of Isyldill had taunted him and

Aroawn with tidbits of the royals' treachery. He had stood there clinging to the hope of peace while Moira and hundreds of Stewards and children were being slaughtered in the Temple.

Rau shook his head. Nothing was going to bring Moira back. At some point in the last bilial, he had finally accepted it. It was now a dull pain in his chest that could be rubbed away gingerly. She was dead, and yet he still had the ability to make a difference in a child's life. Someone still needed him, and he needed her. Rau's lips twitched upward. Eybah was his hope now, his dream of a better future. Her laugh was deeper than Moira's had been, her smile always a little crooked to one side, and her thick hair wilder. The differences between them were what he enjoyed best.

A deep breath centered him. Lingering on these old memories were not going to help Eybah recover from her trauma. It was time to wipe this eve from existence.

He lugged out the royal physician's corpse from the phaeton with a sharp tug of drynn that rippled against his senses. He was reaching his limits. The dead man's arms popped out of their shoulder sockets before the corpse tumbled to the ground in a bundle of tangled limbs.

It was going to be a feat for him to pry both the trio of men and the carriage over the borderline by their drynn. The carriage was concealable amongst the bushes and trees on the edge of Gyldrise, but the act was going to leave him depleted. Better drained and with Eybah than accused of murder. For the first time in centuries, not counting his little flower, he purposefully laid his hands against another person's. Shivers crept up his taut arms. He swallowed back the rise of nausea. His bony fingers dug into the physician's wrists despite the cold rigidity setting into the body.

Back bent, Rau dragged Heaton, and the confirmation that this was the right course of action peaked out from Heaton's retreating sleeve. His griffin head's mark was on full display. With one last pull, the healer's body crossed the border wall and burst into flames. Blue fire greedily engulfed the body, bubbling and melting the skin. Clothes vanished. Muscles crisped, then blackened. Bones popped and cracked. Only a few grainfalls passed before a man weighing ten stones was reduced to a pile of ash. No charred scent lingered. It was as if the man had never been. Wiped from existence, nothing left for his family to mourn. Rau had deprived them of that. He spun around and disgorged the little his stomach contained.

Rau wiped his mouth on a sleeve, his limbs shaky. It was one thing to hear of the effects on a Marked that attempted to cross into another realm. It was another to live it. Nogo damn his body to the pits. There were still two more bodies to submit to this barbaric ruthlessness. Not even ten of the stiffest drinks in all Taelgir were going to wipe the shame of this eve away.

For Eybah, he reminded himself. They had hurt her. Had he not intervened, they would have killed her. They deserved no pity or remorse from him. He dragged the first guardsman across the border and whipped around for the last body before the whoosh of flames broke the steady chirp of insects.

With the carriages carefully ensconced where no Marked Isyldillian could see them and the evidence of his misdeeds unidentifiable, Rau returned to the carriage house, limbs and eyelids heavy, but the night was not over. Not until Eybah lay comfortable in bed, safe from the world.

Yet the threats to Eybah's life did not end there. How long until she was careless again? Until her status was discovered? Until he was too late to save her? Secrecy had not worked. Tonight was evidence of that. He could sooner control a flock of dragons than her rambunctious nature.

He cradled her unconscious form into his arms, careful to avoid her wounds, and kissed her temple. Without hesitation, he shoved her broken arm bone back under the skin until it connected with its other half and wrapped the sinewy tissue shut. Tomorrow he intended to get advice from a healer in town. Until then, a barrier of drynn around the wound was the best he could do. The pounding from the revel was finally dying down. Soon the crowd would dissipate enough for him to sneak her into his quarters.

"You're safe, flower. Always will you be safe with me." He whispered the promise, a plan for her future already half-concocted. Whether the Order and Aroawn approved or not, it did not matter. Rau had made his decision. He caressed the swollen skin of Eybah's cheek with a fingertip. "All you have to do is live. Live and I swear on Moira's grave no one will ever harm you again."

T wenty-one

A mixture of excitement and relief was building amongst the Carved crew the further they trekked into Lakoldon toward 'home'. Kaianne joined in the frenzy. It was a welcomed change to how unfazed the veteran crew members had reacted when crossing the border between Isyldill and Lakoldon a bilial before.

Everyone always spouted warnings about crossing a border, how the gods struck down wayfaring souls to ash. There was even an anthem force fed to every noble child: *I'll not cross and commit treason. If I cross, I deserve consumption by the gods' flames for my everlasting suffering. I would not be mourned. I would not be buried. I swear never to cross.*

Kaianne rolled her eyes, remembering the recitation her tutor had forced from her and her younger brothers every cycle. It was all a tad melodramatic and utterly ridiculous. One moment Kaianne had been in Isyldill, the next she had crossed into Lakoldon. No fire, no ash, not even a tendril of smoke or prickle against her skin. It was a load of crock, but when she said such, rebukes were spewed her way, especially from Maarin who had lost a Marked cousin to an attempted crossing. Either way, that border signified a steppingstone toward this supposed Carved city and the next chapter of her life.

Soon she was to be officially inducted into the Carved as Ghedi had promised. She had passed his tests of loyalty and conviction. He said it made her a promising inductee for the upcoming ceremony. Every night since she dreamed of what that meant and what would happen. All she knew was that the ceremony held a blood oath, and blood oaths were sacred, unbreakable things that when violated stole a renegade's life and banished his soul from ever reaching Iltheln. After everything that had happened, that was far from scary or off-putting. On the contrary, throughout the long days of trekking, she focused on the buzzing thrill of anticipation itching under her skin.

It was either that or fixate on each of the blisters and aches on her feet, the straps of her pack bruising her shoulders, the stickiness of her sweaty skin or the soreness in her thighs from the climb over the last three days. Today it was a never ending steep downhill that increased the burn, loose rocks dislodging beneath the crew's footsteps and tumbling down the Gorge of the Lost.

Where Isyldill was a mass of woodlands, rolling hills and fields, the kingdom of Lakoldon was a medley of lush rivers and lakes, cliffs and canyons. The tallest and widest coniferous trees imaginable blanketed flatlands and the rocky terrain. Its wide palette of colors and tangy air were breathtaking at first. Birds flapped in the wind. Critters crept along the sandstone facades while groups of larger animals clambered up and down the cliff sides to graze. The peacefulness was an illusion, of course. Carved were no safer in Lakoldon than Isyldill, but lately her nightmares had softened to mere dreamy wisps.

Since crossing, it had been days on end marching with little rest, and little lords, exhaustion was wreaking havoc on her muscles. Kaianne was certain to have walked more over the last three quints than in her entire life. For the last sixteen days, hunts were kept minimal. There were no more scavenges, training, and guardsmen to raid or spying – not that she had been privy to more than a little overhearing. It was growing monotonous despite the view.

"Please tell me that we'll settle for the eve soon," she muttered between huffs to no one in particular.

"I'll raise ye one better, little dobber." Oidh's newest term of endearment was not nearly as pacifying as his puckish tone made it out to be, but the older man was strangely cordial since the day Kaianne killed that guardsman. "This'll be the last leg down."

Kaianne eyed this newest gorge that narrowed into a ravine with disdain, the beauty of its mossy gray rocks and bubbly rapids crashing against its cliffside long since snuffed out from pain and sweat.

"We there yet?" she asked intermittently. Grunts were the only responses until finally they reached a cliff that outcropped a few meters above the river.

"Almost," said Isane. A sweeter word had never been spoken, and Kaianne snorted through sobs of relief. "Through there first."

Kaianne followed Isane's pointed finger to the yawning cavern at their backs, shrouded behind a curtain of leafless blood red vines that matched the stone facade. Her face fell. No one had mentioned walking into a bottomless pit. A rough clap on her back and chuckles shook her from her stupor. She groaned and followed behind, taking solace that those chuckling would be the first to fall through any unseen holes.

As anticlimactic as crossing the border between Isyldill and Lakoldon had been, descending into the depths of a cave was an entirely different matter. It was dreary with an oppressive darkness that promised death like the red shroud of vines that had kept it hidden from view. Several strikes of flintstone later, a torch was lit for every five in the crew. Then they plunged further in.

Wind whistled at the entrance, and the deeper they went, the colder the stagnant air grew, seeping into her bones. The walls glistened with the torchlight, trails of humidity in the stone. The crunch of slate underfoot echoed as did her own breath in her ears, but what stuck with her most was the strange unrhythmic humming that lingered around them and seemed so out of place. Every muscle in her body tightened. No one spoke. She dared not whisper the questions 'how much longer' or 'where does this lead' in case the cave's ceiling cracked under the sound and buried them alive. Her legs dragged beneath her, yet she pushed them harder to keep up.

Finally, the group's steps slowed. A current of warm air seeped around her ankles, yet through the throng of bodies, there was no relief of daylight. The humming was loudest here, wrapping around them.

"It's a dead-end," a newer Lakoldesh woman muttered, her inflections rising at the end of each word. "We made a wrong turn somewhere?"

"Patience," Ghedi said.

Metal clanked, the sound grating and harsh, but bit by bit, light flooded every bump and crevice in the cavern walls' shadowed grooves. Warmth rushed through. Kaianne's greasy hair flapped in its tie while dust and the succulent mix of smoked roast meat and the tart of berries stuck in her nose. Voices, dozens of them in the distance, replaced the strange humming that had almost guided the crew here. A splash of water made her beyond curious.

Unable to see over the mass of shoulders and heads, Kaianne crouched. Beyond the legs, the space had opened to reveal a wide chamber. Hints of greenery speckled what she could see with maybe bushes or the trunks of trees. There was movement in the distance, people walking perhaps, but the chamber's end was indiscernible. The stone wall that had blocked their passage now stood at an angle toward them, resting half a meter off the ground while two pairs of legs coming from within the new chamber wedged logs of wood beneath it. Then, like a herd, her crew shifted forward and filed into whatever lay beyond.

Never had she seen or heard of anything like it. This chamber was vast and smooth, almost as if the walls had been carved by hand. Perhaps it had, considering stairs were cut into all four walls from floor to ceiling that led to innumerable dwellings in the stone, decipherable by their holed entrances and windows. From some openings hung curtains or strings of beads. Bushes grew along the base of the walls, and a pair of trees filled the center of the chamber – a shocking sight in a cavern – with benches built around the trunks where strangers sat, read, and conversed with others. Between the two trees, a channeled stream babbled from one end of the chamber to another. People dipped metal cups and pots before setting them to boil over one of the four fire pits spread out near the edges of the space. Their glow gleamed and danced against the cavern's walls, but the smoke did not linger. It careened up the walls to the cave's domed ceiling of threatening stalagmites and dangling roots to a large opening where sunlight bled in.

"Ghedi, old mate." A broad man, followed by a covey of men and women, many one-handed, grappled Ghedi into a hug. His flaxen hair bounced over his eyes with every move of his head, almost glittering beneath the sun. "We were taking bets when you would return. You couldn't wait until tomorrow to save me some beans?"

"Risk what you must, brah." Ghedi tapped him on the shoulder with a wide relaxed smile. "Good to be home."

"Good to have you. Now, to the rest of you, g'day." The newcomer turned to address Ghedi's crew as he wound an arm in a circle in the air. The metal clanking began again, the stone wall behind them slowly descending before thumping shut. "Oidh, Maarin and the rest of you buggers that know my mug by heart, you know what to do."

All of Ghedi's seasoned Carved crew filed out toward the wall's dwellings. Now, only seven remained. Five crew members had joined after her, each one at least four stretches older and nearly a head taller, whether man or woman. Most were missing a hand.

"To those who've never had the delight of knowing me, I am Hogan Matel, councilmember of your new home, Lakoldesh born but like you, my birth realm no longer holds my loyalty. It is my lovely task to welcome you to Credence, one of the four Carved cities in the realms, and the most secure.

"Today you will settle in and find a task that suits us all or one will be assigned to you. Those of you Ghedi has found worthy and steadfast, tomorrow you will be joined to us. If he has not, you will have more than enough time here to prove yourself. Follow our leads, and we will have you settled in quicker than resher grass through a horse."

A shiver of trepidation ran through Kaianne as she stepped forward with the rest of the newer crew members toward the welcoming strangers behind Hogan. Each held a pile of clothing: folded linen tunic, trousers, and a nightshirt. In her current state, she was bound to dirty them quickly, but the thought of fresh linen was too much to pass up.

"Thank you," she said to a one-handed woman from whom she grabbed the clean clothing. It was going to be too large, just like most of the clothing Ghedi's crew had managed to steal over the last cycles, but she was now quite adept at hemming clothing with a little needle and thread. Necessity made previously imposed activities easier to bear learning. With a little work, the hemming was bound to be more flattering.

Lost in her thoughts, the woman's frown skipped her notice until Hogan was towering over her, a tight grip on her arm. He squeezed it almost painfully.

"You are a bit of a cub for this old lot." Hogan raised a brow in question. It made the blue rim around his irises stick out. What did her youth matter?

"Sixteen stretches old," she lied, nose held high, and wrenched her arm free. "So no. I'm simply short, always have been, always will be."

He snorted. "And I'm a Steward. Your true age, girl."

With a glance back at Ghedi, she huffed a sigh. "Thirteen, two cycles past. Don't look at me like that. I'm not useless, far from it. Ask Ghedi. He promised me the oath tomorrow."

"That true?" Hogan asked over her head. Ghedi's face was stretched up in a smirk like he found the whole thing amusing. When he nodded his agreement, Hogan loosened his grasp. "Very well, but she will be your responsibility, no one else's."

"Have a little faith, brah."

With a grunt, Hogan stalked away, his steps bruising and clear despite the constant chatter in the vast chamber.

"What did I do to merit that?" Kaianne asked when Ghedi sidled up next to her as Hogan disappeared through a passageway in the far chamber wall.

"Count the other kinders you see. Sometimes we understand better through our eyes than our ears. Come, you need a meal and rest."

She trailed after him while gazing at the number of people milling about from one task to the other – builders, diggers, bakers, cooks, healers. Everyone had a purpose, but the one thing she did not see were children, nor did she hear the laughter or cries that often followed them. In fact, the youngest she saw – besides herself – had to be no less than sixteen or seventeen stretches old. Odd.

*T*he trill of bells startled Kaianne awake. She jumped from her cot on alert and reached for the dagger she always kept belted around her thigh. There was nothing there. Panic lasted half a grainfall before she got her bearings – the oversized nightshirt, the bed, the privacy of her own quarters regardless of how small. She flopped back down and slipped her hand beneath her pillow of stuffed wool to reach the hilt of her dagger and handle of her hatchet. There they were, easily accessible if needed during sleep. And slept she had.

No pebbles or roots dug into her back. There were no lumps in the dirt to misshape her bedroll, no chill through the night, and no odd sounds except those shrill bells. The bed was solid and uniform. The blankets were scratchy but glorious in their warmth and comfort. Even her nightmares had melted into the night like her tension. This amount of comfort and serenity after all those cycles in the wild was enchanting.

Voices rose from outside her two-by-two-meter den on the highest row of cave dwellings. Feet shuffled. Sandals clacked and boots pounded on the cave's stone steps. People filed by her entryway like shadows. At a glance, it seemed everyone was evacuating their quarters and herding downstairs toward the cave's 'mess hall' they had all dined in the night before. Whatever was happening, she did not want to be left out.

Daylight filtered in from above, but from the darkened clouds and strong hint of humidity, rain was not far from falling.

Thunder crashed. That spurred her to dress faster. If this was a call to reach safety before a flooding, she was not going to be the fool that stayed behind.

Still adjusting her belt, she stumbled out of her chamber and into the steady stream of people on the rickety wooden platform that serviced every dwelling on her level. The wood creaked and moaned from the weight of so many. There would be no surviving a fall from that height if the platform broke. Nerves had her gripping the railing tight as they descended.

"Don't go worrying yourself sick now, girly," a woman whispered behind her, her cane clacking at each stride of her right leg. "We go down every morning and come up every eve."

Kaianne glanced back at the older woman – frizzy hair peppered with white, tired eyes drooping at the edges, and a kind smile on her face – then kept moving.

"And it supports our weight? Always?"

"'Course." The woman's scoff mollified her, a little.

The lanterns that hung every several meters on each platform were being lit, the candlelight flickering, like they had at night's fall the previous eve before most headed for bed. A burst of lightning lit the sky purple before a few droplets of rain plopped onto Kaianne's cheeks. Within sandfalls, the sky was drizzling down a soft downpour. Puddles were already accumulating down below. Thunder roared, and Kaianne slowed her steps down the stairs.

"Move along, girly. Can't stay here all day. And watching the sky hole will not make 'em close it any faster."

"Close it?"

Running footsteps pounded above her, wood creaking and dust sprinkling down, but no dwellings lay above her floor. Those sounds turned into muffled scrapes somewhere above the ceiling wall like the patter of dormice in an attic loft on cold nights. Then the clanking began. Clunk, clunk, clunk – a reminder of the sound of a metal grate lifting. The sky hole was closing as chains tugged a blanket of quilted hides from one edge of the oval toward the other until the sky was blackened out and the metal grinding ceased. All that remained was the murky yellow candlelight from the dozens of lanterns.

"How often do they do that?" Kaianne asked the older woman as she followed the flow of people, careful not to slip on the wet walkways.

"Whenever the weather demands it, or the scouts notice kingsmen too close. We do our best to keep safe and unseen."

Kaianne nodded and followed the advancing line down the steps. The procession of people from each staircase across the walls congregated beneath the smallest of the two trees and single filed from there. She lost track of their flow below the second tree.

"Excuse me," she asked the elderly woman, "Do we…do we all commune for meals like this? Every day?"

The woman barked a harsh laugh and hobbled down the steps with a swing of her heavy, stiff right hip. "No, girly. That would be a dreary wait. Morn and eve meals are replenished over three sandturns, but midday is served only thrice. You miss one of the serving times, you have nothing midday, unless you go make it by your lonesome. But then if you have time to make it, you had time to show for the servings."

"So, why are we all going there now?"

One of the first things she had noticed when eating the night before was how large and chilly the mess hall was. The second was how strongly sound echoed there. Long tables and their benches divided the space in four rows perpendicular to a dais. The dais was a raised section of stone that stretched from one side of the cave to the other and only held two tables with a cold fire pit uncleared of its latest charcoal between them.

"For the Allying Ceremony, o'course. Did Ghedi tell you nothing? I swear, sometimes that man needs a good thumping."

They neared the converging point beneath the trees. The multitude of conversations blended into a cacophony of voices.

"Surely he told you of the ceremony."

"No, aye he did." The precise details remained unclear, blood oath aside, but it had never crossed her mind how public it would be. Then again, she had never imagined so many Carved existed. "How did you know that I was part of Ghedi's crew?"

The old woman gave her a wry look when Kaianne slowed her pace. "You're new. Ghedi's crew was the only one to return in the last quint. 'Twould be a safe assumption."

This woman gestured her forward with a swing of her cane that knocked against Kaianne's calf repeatedly until she did as told. The snippiness of it reminded Kaianne of Mimsee. The touch of familiarity warmed her heart as she pushed aside the lingering regret. Hopefully her old governess was faring well.

"You're a lone child amongst adults, and if you are to be accepted here as you were in that crew, you need to learn the way of things and quick."

"There are no other young people like me?" She had searched long and late for signs of others close to her age the night before with no luck.

"No."

"Why?"

"Children are…complicated. Most are loud, tumultuous, unpredictable and fearful. Or they go looking for trouble for the fun of it. Too many Carved have been found out because a child could not keep quiet or follow directions. And a parent's loyalty lies more with their child than with the good of the Carved as a whole. Before you say it, yes, some are moldable, but many are not. It's easier to forbid them all than deal with the repercussions."

Fists balled at her sides, marching like a good little soldier, Kaianne seethed. "You abandon them."

"We refuse them. If we don't take them in, they cannot be abandoned."

"Semantics. How are they to fare on their own?"

"They most likely will not."

Kaianne's jaw dropped at the woman's cold words, and when the older woman went to caress her arm, she flinched away.

"Understand. You are young and naïve. You think a city such as this is the answer to your prayers, but it's only a haven until discovered. I have lived through every hard stretch you could ever imagine. From losing my children, to near starving, to skirmishes with kingsmen and Carved exterminations.

Sometimes hard choices must be made for the survival of the whole."

"And if any here decide on a family? If a woman becomes with child?"

"She and the man responsible are urged to leave as soon as the discovery is made." There was no hint of emotion in the woman's voice. "A pregnant woman will never be made to leave on her own. If no man steps forth to claim the child, either someone volunteers or two men are judged and chosen by the committee to leave with her. The practice may weaken us a little, but it prevents more seedy behavior. Makes the men more vigilant of those that would take advantage."

Kaianne simply bobbed her head, not exactly clear at what she was getting at, even though she was far less ignorant than eight cycles before. The moans and groans of crew members in the woods had stolen some of her naivety, but it was thoroughly destroyed when she stumbled on a couple rutting like coneys in the wild. It had been horrifying and embarrassing. If only she could scrub her mind like she did her skin.

The line advanced slowly. With so many people ahead of her, she had a difficult time telling how far they still had to go. Everyone's height exceeded hers, from half a head taller to two heads. She ducked around to see the channel of people inching into the next chamber. It was still far away, and impatience riled within her. She counted those before her, and when that was over too quickly, she tallied the number missing an arm: sixty to the total hundred-sixteen. She furrowed her brow and turned to count those behind her which also resulted in a higher proportion of one-handed to bi-handed people. Questions burned on the tip of her tongue, but she hesitated, not wanting to seem impolite.

"Well, spit it out, girly."

Kaianne bristled but leaned into the older woman so that fewer people might overhear. "Why do so many Carved here have only one-hand?"

The matron's eyes widened. "Well, color me surprised. You seem one to know how to speak your mind when you care to.

Why have you not already asked Ghedi, or another of his one-handed crew?"

"It…didn't seem proper."

The woman bellowed her laughter. Heads turned in their direction, and Kaianne's cheeks flamed. "Oh, now that's one for the records. Girly, tell me. Which hand do you see missing?"

Kaianne threw furtive glances at those in line, avoiding any eye contact. "The right one. Only the right one."

"Yes. Now think. What do we all have in common?"

"No mark?"

The matron nodded. "Was your Carving easy?"

Kaianne gulped. No one knew she had never chosen to be Carved, that she had been unconscious when it had happened. She had never even told Ghedi. It seemed shameful, as if it made her somewhat unworthy. So, she shook her head and pretended she understood the response the woman clearly wanted. "No."

"Of course not. It never is, and many bleed out and die or suffer a fever and die. A remedy many have taken to is cutting half the forearm clean off. Yes, you lose a hand, but the chance of living another day is far greater."

For the first time in cycles, she thought of Andreiyes with an edge of wistful gratitude, instead of hurt and anger. Had it been hard for him to keep her alive and with her forearm intact? Had he ever had to consider that drastic measure? As much as she planned to loathe him for all eternity for abandoning her completely, he had saved her from the fire, given her a new chance at this life, and nursed her to health as best as a pompous spoiled princeling could. The gratitude flitted away, the hurt still burning bright as the first day she realized he had broken his promise and was never coming back.

They passed beneath the hollow connecting the mess hall and the main chamber, into a flood of people. The woman clutched Kaianne's wrist and tugged her through the throng of loud and boisterous echoes. The stench of stale sweat and oily soaped bodies lay heavy on the air. They weaved around groups and tables laden with flatware, filled pitchers, and a few loaves of bread.

"Follow me, girly."

"Kaianne. My name. We all have one for a reason."

The matron nodded and smirked at her over her shoulder. "As long as you keep that spirit up, you may call me Seriki. This life is not for the faint of heart."

Seriki led her to the seats closest to the dais where Ghedi, Hogan, and a mix of men and women sat watching the mess hall fill. Benches scratched along the stone and creaked under their new users. Cups were tapped against tables as drinks were poured from pitchers while the crackle of broken bread seemed to come from all sides as Kaianne took her seat. The hairs on her nape prickled from the wary glances those at Ghedi's table gave her. She belonged, she repeated to herself. When Ghedi caught her gaze, he smiled and dipped his head. That little reassurance was calming. After the ceremony, none of them could question her place in Credence. Her knee bounced with impatience.

The night before, the fire pit had been black and cold. Now, an enormous cauldron hung over its licking flames. This close, the fumes of smoked wood, boiled milk and roasted oats with a hint of honey made her stomach groan.

Kaianne leaned over to Seriki. "Why wasn't that pit used last night?"

"Not convenient. No skylights here for the smoke to escape. And those on cooking duties find using the fire pit in the kitchens more to their liking. This one, it's only used for ceremonies, but once lit they put it to good use."

On cue, a line began to form at the fire pit that quickly wrapped around the sides of the mess hall as one by one, people had porridge ladled into their bowls and returned to their places. By the time every person had their serving, the fire lingered on its last flames, embers glowing bright red beneath the orange bursts. Two men unhooked the cauldron, balancing it on a pole between them, and vanished into the kitchen on the far right. Their departure signaled the first clatter of a bowl against a table, then another, and another until a roll of thunder filled the hall. It increased in tempo as Hogan, Ghedi and two women rose from their benches on the dais. This was it. The ceremony.

Kaianne's ears rang with the quickening thump of her heart, outpacing the beat in the hall. She had thought of the ceremony nonstop ever since Ghedi first mentioned it, and finally it was here.

"Settle, settle down," Hogan called to the assembly of Carved. "We're all keen as for the Allying. It's been a long stretch, but our crews are all finally home."

Loud cheers and whistles resounded over the pounding of fists. Kaianne joined in, the coarse wood meeting her palms as she hollered with the crowd with a grin from ear-to-ear. Hogan gestured for quiet once more.

"Twenty-two of us joined the gods over the last thirteen cycles. We mourn their loss and wish them safe travels into Iltheln. But today, twelve join our ranks as true Carved of Credence. And one day soon, with all of us together, we will push back our oppressors and see change across all Taelgir. Once more, the borders will open. Once more, freedom will reign. Because we. Are. United."

"Carved Together," someone yelled from the crowd.

Kaianne startled when nearly everyone in the hall chanted, "Free Forever."

"Yes. Mark my words, we will achieve it." Hogan's gaze swept over the entire hall as the entourage settled down. "Now for the Allying. As the last arrived, Ghedi will start with his selection."

"Selection?" Kaianne whispered to Seriki.

"In order to partake in the Allying, you must have been selected by a crew chief to join their crew permanently. In rare cases, the council will select someone for Credence proper."

"What happens if none of them pick you?"

Ghedi stood and sauntered toward the fire pit.

Seriki bent her head closer to Kaianne. "You spend time in Credence proving you are worthy, but until then you cannot leave. You needn't worry girly. Most find their worth in less than a stretch."

A stretch? Kaianne gulped. But Ghedi would pick her. He had practically implied it, no? "And those who never do?"

"It'll depend."

"On what?"

"My fellow Carved," Ghedi began.

"Their intentions. Now hush, girly." Seriki straightened her posture.

"Before I announce the additions to my crew, I'll share a few words. For stretches, we have assumed that the mark is more than a barrier to crossing the borders, and it would seem true. Since we have put an end to the kidnapping of nobles…"

"Kidnappings?" Kaianne muttered in surprise.

"The number of our deaths has greatly diminished. Our primary tasks are to discover the extent of the mark's reach and how to destroy all border barriers between the realms to reunite Taelgir, as Aethel first intended.

"Until then, know that we must proceed with caution and stealth. The Order has sent a Master to each of the realms, as confirmed by many crews." Whispers spread throughout the hall, reverberating from all angles. "My crew alone lost four men on a reconnaissance party. But we will find a way. We will beat them. They may have the most god talent among them, but that will not stop us. When the time is right, we will fight back. We will bring them down, just as well as those bastard royals. This mountain did not give birth to mice."

Cheers erupted amongst the banging of cups against tables. Kaianne surveyed the crowd, reeling from the knowledge the Carved were targeting both the royals and the Order, unclear as to the why. She had never experienced any hardship with the Mentees and Greenlings she crossed on visits to the Bryant's Zesco manor. Some more than others were quick to display their parlor tricks, but they were always cordial, if distant. Then again, her experiences with royals and the Bryants had been tame until that fateful night. It begged the question: what had the Order done to incite this reaction?

"Now, we all know you are not here for grand speeches," Ghedi continued, his gruff voice seeming to come from all sides of the hall. Though he normally said little, it did not surprise her in the slightest that he knew how to work a crowd. "To the Allying."

"Aye," the crowd shouted with more rumbling tableware.

"Twelve new full-fledged Carved comrades this Stretch of Gain, and I vouch for three. Two from the seven new Carved that accompanied my crew, one from Credence proper." Kaianne held her breath. "The first of which many of you may have noticed this morn as an oddity in our way of life. What she lacks for in age, she makes up for in spirit on the blade's edge of a hatchet. I call forth Kaianne Tilhold of Isyldill."

Kaianne stared up at Ghedi, eyes round, cheeks burning from all the attention at her back as wavering applause sounded behind her. He had given her a surname, one that pleasantly flowed on her tongue, after she was adamant that she had none. The back of her eyes prickled. It was a gift, just as much as being first chosen among dozens of new Carved.

She stood, adjusted and smoothed her tunic, and approached Ghedi with her head held high. When she neared the fire pit, he held out his one hand and she took it. The comfort of the warmth and calluses on his palm blocked out the stares of the crowd that seemed to have gone cold with quiet.

"When my crew first met Kaianne, she did not cower. Nigh, this one held a hatchet to my throat." Kaianne ignored the mutterings and chuckles from the masses, her heart thumping in her ears as Ghedi projected his justifications to the masses. Like her, they hung on every word. "She worked to master every task. And when threatened, she cut down a guardsman that would have slain her first. So, we ask you, Kaianne Tilhold, will you uphold the values of us Carved and defend Credence with your life?"

She nodded. "Yes."

"Will you join my crew and follow my orders?"

"Yes."

"Will you see to the freedom of Taelgir from the tyranny that enslaves it by whatever means necessary?"

She stared into his eyes, past the ring of Nimedorian red around his irises and into the dark brown and smiled. "I will."

"Hold out your right arm over the embers."

Kaianne flinched at his directive, the memory of her burnt skin surfacing, the nerves tingling from shoulder to fingertip. Heat radiated from the glowing embers, the flames all but gone.

She bit her lip and stilled her features. This was what she wanted. This was the next step into her new life and toward revenge. She extended her arm and pulled up her sleeve.

Ghedi leaned in and whispered, "You are stronger than you know. Keep your arm locked and in place. Do not let them see your fear. And do not flinch."

At her nod, he unsheathed a dagger from his belt, and she turned her head to survey the crowd. The blade carved into her skin twice, quickly yet still too slow, and she bit her cheek hard to avoid crying out and widened her eyes to stop rising tears from shedding. The trail of blood around her forearm tickled, a stark contrast from the radiating pain. It wasn't until Ghedi grabbed her wrist and joggled it that she looked at the wound. And just in time to watch droplets of her blood drop to the embers with hiss after hiss that sizzled into a tendril of smoke.

"Carved Forever," Ghedi yelled, raising her bleeding arm high above their heads.

"Free from Embers we Rise," the entire hall boomed in return.

"The Carved clan of Credence welcomes you, Kaianne Tilhold."

The grin of pride on Ghedi's face made her pain dull. He handed her a soaked cloth to wipe away the blood from the tiny '<' cut halfway up her forearm. It was worth it. *All* of this had been worth it.

As she returned to her seat while Ghedi called his next initiate, even those that had looked at her with wariness or distrust congratulated her with a pat or a smile. Joy flared inside her. Here she had a future. Here she had a knit of people as tight as family.

"Welcome home." Seriki smiled at her.

A lone tear escaped Kaianne's eye as the old woman patted her cheek and swiped it away. Yes, finally, she was home.

Twenty-two

*I*t was the first sunny morning in Alihuerte in days, and the warm rays outdid the wind's chill. Stamped and sealed parchment in hand, Rau strode confidently down the sunken stone steps of the rundown Huertan Orphanage he had just had the pleasure of doing business with. For the right price, everyone was bribable. He pushed open its rickety gate, a slight tremor in his fingers lingering from Well Water's withdrawals. By this time next stretch, if the headmaster put the silver blitz and gold mig coins Rau had 'donated' to good use and tended to the windows, roof and cracks in the wall, the orphans inside would be kept snug and well-fed for several stretches, if not throughout the Stretch of Blight's most frigid cycles.

As he made his way through Alihuerte's busy streets, vendors barked advertisements and bargains. The tart scents of fresh cut fruits and yeastiness of warm bread filled the street with a comfort and lightheartedness he had not felt in ages. Families weaved between merchants: the women in their long dresses casually hung from the arms of their spouses and peeked through windows for interesting wares while their children trailed behind. It was such a stark contrast to his first night in Alihuerte just over a bilial before that he shook his head with a titter.

A child's sapphire dress with its matching muff coat in the display glass of one store caught his eye. He stopped short, imagining the awe and delight on Eybah's chubby face if he brought it back to her. She was healing nicely from her ordeal, but with a leg and arm still in splints and no assurances in place, she had yet to step a foot out of his chambers in Lord Mer's manor. Unfortunately for Rau, that had meant dealing with numerous tantrums cured only by cradling embraces and sweet pastries. Today though was set to be different, and this outfit combined with a box of pastries and some eye colorant from the alchemist two alleys down would perfectly announce his surprise.

*T*heir carriage bounced down the cobblestone road, the wheels groaning to the rhythm of hooves clopping, as Alihuerte disappeared from the horizon like a bad dream. Stress and tension drained from Rau's shoulders once only fields, trees and hills surrounded them. On the bench across from him, Eybah visibly relaxed as well, her posture almost slouching.

They were four days behind the princeling and his retinue whom he and Eybah would meet up with in Hallore, their last eastern stop before heading inland to Millian and Zesckar. For once, Rau was thankful for the princeling's impatience as his tardiness was unlikely to change much. Warnings of Carved sightings were growing more and more scarce as the cold season approached, almost as if a Master on tour had them scurrying back to their holes.

After the healer's absence had been noted, the princeling had called on a bone-weary Rau for the search, which of course came up fruitless aside from the planned misplaced transport. Somehow, not only were his two other victims added to the search, but another three were reported missing. The remains of one were found mauled and dismembered, the disarrayed, wide bite marks a clear sign of a pack of shadow wolves. After that, the rest were declared dead, whether as a drunken promenade gone wrong or by more nefarious means was still up for debate. Considering the numbers, Rau was amazed how quickly the affair was put to rest. Then again, the last murder in this town committed by a Carved had left its mark.

After assuring himself no other discoveries were made, Rau holed himself in his chambers in Lord Mer's estate to tend to Eybah while proclaiming an illness related to his head injury from over a cycle before. At first the princeling showed signs of compassion when he proffered his aid to Rau. When Rau continued denying the princeling entry or any healer he sent, those signs quickly turned to frustration the longer the illness endured. Four days earlier, the princeling proclaimed his exasperation by announcing in the corridor through Rau's chamber doors that his party could not delay their departure any longer and Rau was welcome to rendezvous with them in Hallore once recovered. That had suited Rau just fine. Eybah needed more time.

For two quints, only the maids entered his chambers to clean or to drop off his meals and water. Even then, it was only when the curtains around the bed were drawn. Rau handled Eybah's needs day and night. He sacrificed sleep to track her breathing and force fluid from her lungs when her inhales gurgled, and when the fatigue threatened to drag him down, he sipped Well's Water from a vial and refocused his energy. He changed linens and compresses, bathed her in hot or cold temperatures relative to her fever, fed her, calmed her tempers and told her tales of his youth and his initiation into the Order. They were stories from happier times, before the war and the tragedy that had burned its mark on his soul, and he lost track of time recounting memories he had long thought forgotten.

It was all time well spent. The swelling in her broken leg had nearly vanished. The abscess beneath the bone puncture wound above her elbow no longer oozed, and the inflammation was reducing. Now, Eybah sat on the bench across from him and swayed with the carriage's rocking, a little smile on her face. Only a few bruises around her eyes and chin lingered. She fanned out the silk of her blue dress demurely and flattened the lace at its hems.

"You like it?" he asked. The mannequin in the vitrine had not done it justice.

"So pretty," she said whimsically, and because they had been working on basic etiquette, she added, "thank you."

With a shy grin on her face, she pulled a pastry from the box beside her. Powdered sugar flaked off at each bite down to her dress, which she flicked off with much less grace than the garment implied. She adjusted the material once more, traced the embroidery lines of the bench cushions, tapped her good heel to her own beat, counted the number of ridiculous tassels that hung against the sides of the carriage, and when she got bored, she ate another pastry. One thing Rau noticed she did not do was gaze out the window. If ever her newly golden-ringed eyes – the alchemist's colorant was effective at replacing the Gyldrit purple around her irises – flickered over the window, a quiver of fear raked over her sweet face instead of the bursting excitement he had come to know.

"Do you see those birds?" Rau pointed to a pair of golden-winged tuffs headed toward a dimple tree, its branches bare of the leaves pooled on the ground. Eybah followed the stretch of his finger. "Those tuffs are going to peck their way through that dimple tree to shore up through the Blight in the softness of its bark. They will fend off any dangers together, gather food and take care of one another until the harsh season has passed as I will do that for you, flower. I will protect you. I will take care of you, and nothing out there will harm you ever again."

Her lips quivered. "I don't like getting hurt."

"No one does." He stretched out his skeletal hand and clasped her fleshy one in it. "You no longer have to fear it."

"If someone does, will you hurt them like you hurt those bad men?"

"If I must." A shiver ran down her arm to the hand he held. "Does that frighten you?"

At first, she slowly turned her head side to side, then seeming to think better of it, she nodded repeatedly. Rau sighed and released her hand.

"I protect what I care for, Eybah, but I wish you had not seen that. It will not happen again." Rau fetched the parchment from that morning's excursion from within his robes. "Do you know what this is?"

There was no point in breaking the seal and unraveling the calligraphed words penned by the orphanage's headmaster. Eybah needed to be assigned a tutor when they returned to Castle Ravensten before the words and letters became more than nondescript symbols to her. Her big eyes jumped from the rolled vellum to his face. Apparently his mirth was contagious. In no time, the girl was bouncing in place as best she could with splinted limbs. Her good hand grasped air in silent calls to hand it over.

"This gives you my surname. It terms you as my daughter." His eyes turned soft, his vision glassing at the power of the word. "You are now Eybah Hirai."

"You'll be my chichu?"

With the Gyldrit moniker for father between them, Rau smiled wistfully and nodded. Not even Moira had ever called him Chichu. It would be his and Eybah's alone.

"Yes, flower. No more sneaking in and out of carriages. You will always be presented as my child with a warm bed, food, and clothing at your disposal. But there are a few unbendable conditions."

She nodded fervidly.

"This is serious, Eybah. Disregard this and it'll be both of our undoings." Her little head bobs continued. Rau scratched the back of one hand. From her reaction, this conversation would require reinforcing over time. "You are not a Carved. You never were."

She tilted her head in question.

"Only traitors are Carved, and they show their hatred and disloyalty to the realms, the Order, and the gods by taking out the marks bestowed on them at birth. Do you understand?" Her nod was weak, but he went on. "As such, you cannot be my daughter and be Carved, and after this conversation, we will never discuss you as a Carved again. To everyone, you will be a Marked. To them, yourself, and me, you have the Isyldillian griffin's head on your forearm. You must believe it."

She gently pried up the sleeve of her healing arm, her forearm's skin concave in a long scar. "But I…don't have it."

He adjusted her sleeve. "I know. You know, but no one else must ever know. You are never to discuss it, not even to me. You are never to show your right arm. Even if in the zenith of the Stretch of Fervor's heat you are drowning in sweat, you will stay covered and endure. If anyone learns the truth, you will bring the matter to me. Immediately. I cannot keep you safe otherwise."

Her excited smile completely vanished.

"You will add droplets of the colorant to your eyes every morning."

"No, it stings."

"Yes, but you must."

She slouched against her backrest with a huff, her bottom lip rolled out in a pout.

"Eybah, this is just as important." Rau grabbed her good hand once more to focus her attention, despite her glower. Yes, this would absolutely need to be repeated over and over for good measure. "You have *never* been outside Isyldill. Your home was always Alihuerte, from the streets to the Huertan Orphanage to now my care. We met only this morning. You know nothing of Gyldrit. You have never seen the sea, and today was your first carriage ride ever. Is my that clear?"

Her glare was fierce for such a young face.

"Then repeat my meaning."

She groaned. "I am Marked with a stupid animal's face. I can never show my arm. I am not me, and I have to pretend forever."

"It will become your truth, flower. Repeat it enough and you'll believe it."

"I want my maha. I want to go back to before." Tears poured over her cheeks. "I miss her."

"I know." Rau squeezed her hand and buried down his turmoil, the memory of his life before with Tilnee and Moira was painful. "We keep our loved ones in our hearts forever. She will never leave you, but the world goes on whether we want it to or not."

"Why did it happen?"

"If only I knew." Rau gazed out the window as the scenery crept by. Compared to that morning, humidity lay heavy on air, weighing him down like the lump in his chest. "The gods have a plan for us all. We each play our part to the end as your maha did. Everything is how it should be."

"You think?"

"I have to." The alternative was unthinkable.

Cawing drew his attention to the sky that had slowly filled with dark clouds, threatening a heavy downpour. A flash of lightning burst in over the horizon on a cloud tower that seemed to drift in a whimsy curtain toward the ground. No thunder roared in response, the center of the storm too far.

"What is it?" Eybah leaned toward the window.

A dot of movement lowered from the skyline, wide wings snapping on approach. The bird circled above their moving transport before diving grotesquely, clawing its way through the carriage window and flapping its too large wings about as it landed at their feet. Eybah screeched and jumped to Rau's bench, burrowing herself behind him despite her injuries. It took restraint to bury his chuckle.

Beakwhiffers were harmless birds. Purblind, they lacked subtlety and grace in their approaches or landings, but their heightened sense of smell courtesy of their long, rounded beaks made them particularly adept in tracing smells over long distances. It made them quite desirable as messenger birds among noble's that maintained aviaries, since the sender needed only to present the bird with the receiver's scent instead of training the animal for a location. This one, as it nudged Rau's thigh, seemed to have been tasked with his scent.

He retrieved the rolled scroll strapped to the bird's belly and unfurled it. Eybah perched her head over his shoulder, her chin burrowing uncomfortably into the muscle.

"What does it want?"

There were two parchments. The first was wrapped loosely around the second, darker in coloring, the paper coarser than the second. He recognized the princeling's large, looped scrawl.

'*Hallore is three days' ride east from this village. You are closest. You handle this. My men will join you there should your talent prove insufficient.*'

Rau raised a brow. It was clear the princeling needed some pointers on subtlety and on how to address his betters.

The second vellum unrolled on its own with a crinkle, unrestrained by the leather straps. The ink wafted off the scroll, the script heavy yet pointed.

Princeling Andreiyes Xander of Royal House Lenierz,
Your Royal Highness,
At two sandturns past the Rising hour on the 6th day in the Noven moon of the 236th Stretch of Gain, a Flawed ripple appeared on the edge of the village Mekworth, three days' ride southwest from Hallore, a day northwest from Alihuerte. As the closest in those parts, I defer to your good judgment and stature, as ever your faithful servant, to follow his Majesty's Flawed Edict enacted on the 23rd day in the Alpha moon of the 236th Stretch of Gain.
Yours devoted,
Lord Aiofe Hectin of House Sertrios,
Southern Commander of His Majesty, King Triunn Uther of Isyldill

Rau almost mockingly applauded the princeling for his delegation. Distaste for the deaths to come roiled in his stomach. This gave the princeling plausible deniability while pinning Rau with a task neither wanted. He had witnessed the princeling's reticence against this form of duty at Castle Ravensten before their long trek across the realm. Yet oddly, despite their several Carved encounters, it had not hindered his response to the traitors. This displayed Andreiyes' obvious dislike of an obligation required for the safety and sanctity of the realms and the Order. And yet if Rau did not handle the Flawed and its family – as the princeling had so eloquently stated – it would be his failure. The conniving, arrogant, gilded weasel. Rau tapped his hands, a smirk playing on his lips. Well played, princeling.

"Well, what does it say…Chichu?" The term was hesitantly tacked on, but it softened his cynicism all the same.

He sighed and scratched uncomfortably along his jaw line. "It seems you will need to remain in the carriage a little longer."

"You said—"

"I know. I have business to attend that I cannot do if I need to worry for you. I will be quick, I swear it." For both their sakes. Executions were better quick, simple, and from a distance. A vial of Well's Waters was going to help with that, because he was not about to leave Eybah vulnerable while his drynn stores were diminished. He would down ten vials a day if it kept her safe, but it was better if she did not witness this part of his life. He propelled the beakwhiffer out the window and it took flight with an unpleasant squawk, wobbling with the wind. "And then, it will be as promised."

Rau knocked his fist against the carriage roof, then stuck his head out the window. The breeze had turned to gusts that slapped against his cheeks as he yelled the new directions to the coachman. The reply was lost in the wind, but the coach veered left at the next crossroads. Eybah was chewing her lips and keeping oddly quiet.

"Swear you will keep hidden and quiet while I am away. What happened in Alihuerte…"

"Teach me."

He balked at her hopeful gaze. "Teach you what?"

"That thing?"

"What thing?"

She twisted the grip on her dress, head bowed. "That thing you did to make them stop when they…when they were hurting me."

He sunk back into his seat and winced. "It's not something that can be taught if you don't have the talent for it."

"I don't?"

Pained, he examined the flow of drynn in her body. It was whimsical at best, perhaps a little heavier than other children her age, but not overly active. Any talent she ever might develop was bound to be subdued, nothing higher than a Mentee, and that was an overreaching estimation.

"It depends on your heritage, flower. On your Maha and your birth Chichu. But we cannot know for certain until your twenty-fifth name-day. Any talent you may have will only manifest then."

"So maybe." Her new smile radiated with excitement, and she bounced in place pushing off one leg.

"Yes. Maybe. When the time comes, if you do, I will personally handle your training."

She hugged him tight, whispering her thanks over and over. For someone who had avoided touch for centuries, he sunk easily into the embrace of her little broken form as he whispered prayers to the gods. He prayed she was a god's descendant. He begged that she be given a talent even if she was not from their line. This was something he wanted to share with her, something he would have shared with Moira had she lived to see her twenty-fifth. He would get Eybah across that fateful number no matter what it took. Right now, what barred his way was a Flawed and its family. After that, only time could tell.

Twenty-three

"Well look at this. Didn't know our princeling had a talent for finding abandoned camps." Jereown strutted forward, a mischievous grin on his face. Beds of leaves crinkled, trampled in his wake. "There a reason ye've been glaring at it?"

Andreiyes' lips hitched up in a smile he did not feel. Concern tickled his spine. This camp near the charred remains of Millau Estate was long abandoned. Dead leaves covered the floor with varying degrees of thickness, a few seedlings sprouting from within. He had pried out soaked and torn furs that reeked of mold and unearthed rusty dulled blades. The fire pit had been dug through by wild animals, dirt sprinkled throughout, but a couple of pans and skewers remained. By the looks of it, Kaianne had long ago left this place behind. The question was if she had done so willingly.

It bothered him, more than it probably should. He had done right by Grayson and her. He had kept his promise and returned, albeit nearly seven and a half cycles later, yet it niggled at him that perhaps his late return was a cause of her disappearance. Which was why he was still standing here a sandturn later, staring at the empty woods like a dullard.

"Right." Andreiyes cricked his neck. "There is nothing to be found here. Whoever lived here is long gone."

Jereown kicked at a bucket sloshed full of rainwater. "Seems they left in a hurry."

Andreiyes nodded absently. Alive, dead or wounded, there was nothing he could do for Kaianne now. She was on her own, and no longer a concern he wanted prickling the back of his mind. He wished her freedom, wherever she was among the living or in Iltheln.

"Fancy yourself a last bout before we head on to Lityoll?" he asked the lordling that had quickly become a close friend.

Jereown furrowed his brow. "We not staying with the Northern Commander?"

Andreiyes forced a laugh. "So you may spend our time comparing him to your Lord father in a game of 'who is Isyldill's better commander'? No, I would rather not."

"No need. We Sertrios know we're the better choice. No contest. Same for any southerner against a northerner."

"I shall have you challenged on that."

With a snort, Jereown drew his sword. "Did none ever advise ye 'tis dangerous to play with fire?"

Andreiyes mirrored his actions, grateful for the reprieve from his thoughts. "They did. It never took."

He lunged and their swords met with a pleasing clang. Parry after parry, thrust after thrust, their skirmish went on for what felt like sandturns. Everything else melted away into the thrill of the game, the anticipation of the next move, the weight of his weapon and strength of the blows blocked. This was what freedom felt like, and he reveled in it until the sting of Jereown's blade against his arm forced Andreiyes to drop his weapon.

"Bloody pits." He grinned despite the trail of blood blooming on his sleeve. Another loss, but this time it had taken far longer.

"Better." Jereown swiped sweat from his brow. "Ye'll be a swordsman yet."

Pride lit him up. That was one mighty compliment from Isyldill's most talented rising swordsman, but Andreiyes inclined his head as calmly as his racing pulse allowed.

Appearances were everything, and he had seen the respect in his kingmen's eyes grow for him since he had begun joining them in the practice yards.

Jereown and he were both panting hard as they sheathed their swords. Andreiyes leaned against a tree trunk. This bout had been exactly what he needed. Strain from the exercise heated his shoulders and back, but the tension from earlier was gone. His friendship with Jereown was a far cry from the solidarity he and Grayson had shared. Nevertheless, it was an easy camaraderie. Jereown was playful but straightforward. His meanings and intentions were always clear. It was calming to be able to enjoy the presence of another without wondering if an unknown hand was being played. Unlike Rau, who always looked at him with suspicion, and now suddenly had a daughter - a stark surprise that had been when Rau announced he had adopted an orphaned child that he had found abused and injured.

"Ye certain there's nothing to know between ye and the Bryants? Anything untoward perhaps?"

Andreiyes chuckled at the implication and shook his head. If only Jereown knew he had once propositioned his sister. That might not go over so well. "If you mean Ladyling Itsne. No. Never. Nice lass, very pleasant on the eyes, but very betrothed and very happy for it."

"Then 'tis the letter from yer sister that has gotten ye in a right twist."

Andreiyes glanced at the abandoned camp once more. Admitting the unease he felt around the Northern Commander since House Lyssandre's demise would leave him open to too many questions. The memories of Lord Pascual and Lordling Willik's faces when Andreiyes raced to Millau that fateful day were things he cared to block out entirely. To the point that he had avoided all eye contact with the Bryants since arriving the previous eve. It was better if Jereown believed his concern lay with his sister.

He sighed a huff to convey a touch of exasperation. "Women. What else is there to say?"

"'Tis more than enough."

"But…she is family. And future queen after Father. It would not do well to ignore her plea for comfort."

"No, certainly not."

Edmira's letter had been short and concise, but her emotions had bled off the page along with teardrops staining the ink. Her husband-by-proxy, Arkov of House Dresden, had annulled their current marriage, but conceded to a contract binding him to her within the next three stretches under the pretext that his House needed to prepare his brother to take over as heir. It was obviously a tactic to avoid conflict with the royal family by replacing the rejection with a counter proposal, but Edmira had seen the truth of the insult, just as he had. Arkov hoped the delay would compel Edmira to turn her gaze to another, and she was grieving his dismissal. It was probably best if Andreiyes returned quickly before she did something she might regret. Then he required a chat with Arkov to set him straight. No one disgraced his sister.

"Will you stay long in Ravensten once we arrive?" Andreiyes asked.

"Aye. The national tournaments are still a ways away, but I've a mind to join the ranks of kingsmen and earn my Pa's Commander title from under my brother, Alrik. Bah, the blind rage on their faces. I can see it now."

Andreiyes chuckled at Jereown's antics. "Well then, we best return and prepare. Only time will tell what becomes of us all."

He meant the words for Jereown, for Edmira, for Kaianne wherever she may be, and for himself and his family's dealing with the Order. Time did not heal all, nor did it fix the problems at hand, but sometimes it offered opportunities to seize. He planned to be ready to grab them with both hands however they were presented.

With a last sweep over the Weldolf woods and a muttered prayer to the gods, Andreiyes followed Jereown back to their horses. Given time, he would force all of his enemies to their knees.

Twenty-four

Five stretches later…

Adec cycle of Stretch 952
237th Stretch of Blight

Edmira clucked her tongue. "Father only wants what is best for you."

She clutched Andreiyes' arm as her boots skidded on another icy puddle slicking the contours of Castle Ravensten. Her weight bore onto his shoulders as she adjusted herself, and he caught the stare over her frame of one of her two ever-present parasitic zealots in blue robes and cloaks. The Masters – associates of Master Rau's apparently – stalked behind her and only her like constant shadows. It was disconcerting. Their attention rarely wavered. Worse, Edmira seemed to have grown so accustomed to their company since their arrival from the Order's temple three cycles earlier that she sometimes spoke as if they were not present. "You need to find a purpose other than training with the men."

"I enjoy it." More than she would ever know. "Besides, I have no desire to wed, nor have any interest in anything long-term."

A gaggle of young women curtsied as Andreiyes and Edmira ambled past, their warm colored dresses contrasting the snow blanketing the grounds. One caught his eye. She was a new courtier to court, daughter of a wealthy merchant from Tehial if he remembered correctly. Brown-haired, fresh faced with smooth contours and lips made for ravaging. Andreiyes winked at her, and she reciprocated with a seductive smile. Already he was picturing what lay beneath her furs and woolen dress, eager to make time in his schedule to visit her chambers. With a grin, he continued onward, his eldest sister leeched to his arm.

"You need to watch that wandering eye of yours." Edmira reveled in spreading her wisdom as the eldest, but that did not pull his gaze from the brunette. He was looking for new flavors to visit his bed, and she looked quite promising. "One day, it will do you more harm than good."

Andreiyes snapped his head around. "Do not compare me to Arkov."

"Never." Vulnerability bled into her voice as she cradled an arm beneath her pregnant belly, caressing the bump over her dress.

Andreiyes cursed himself a righteous arse. Edmira and Arkov had been wedlocked by blood oath two stretches before, but the man had adamantly refused to stay in the castle. For the first stretch and three quarters of their union, she had stayed at his father's estate in Welburn and endured three miscarriages alone without family at her side. Her letters home were always concise and bare of emotion, yet Andreiyes had deciphered the strain in her life from the few words. After news spread that Arkov had slandered the princess by impregnating another, Andreiyes had gone to visit his also newly pregnant sister only to discover the emotional wreck she had become and spurred her home. It had taken every measure of restraint in his body not to run the man through. If the blood oath from wedlock joining a royal had not made Arkov untouchable under Aethel's bloodline curse, Andreiyes would have done far worse than only toss the man into his own father's dungeons.

"I know you would be better than him," Edmira said. "And the gods know I had a hand in the blame."

"Ed, he had no right." His fists clenched.

"No, true, but I tried to force love. I was young and foolish and believed my right as princess superseded his right to reject my advances. Now…" Edmira slowed her steps under the tunnel that led around to the castle's rear training yard. She caressed the velour over her belly with a wistful expression. "My child will pay the price and never know a loving father. I just do not want you to one day look back and regret what could have been."

"My time is far too occupied for regrets." A bitter gust of wind whistled through the archway and slapped against their faces. The crunch of snow and gravel behind them was an uncomfortable reminder of the two Masters' presence. Whereas Master Rau was a Hefter – having the ability to displace drynn – he had overheard these two called Guzzlers. By the definition in the books of old, they held the talent to suction the drynn life force out of another. It unsettled Andreiyes that those two only followed Edmira around, and he found their talent to be much worse than that of the permanently disgruntled Rau's. How Eybah managed to wrangle smiles out of Rau was difficult for Andreiyes to glean. "You need not worry. I never want for company. My bed is rarely cold."

"Not what a sister wants to hear."

He shoved her hip with his own and grinned at her outrage as she teetered off balance.

"Pregnant or not, I can still whip you." She lunged for his collar, and he darted out of reach, scuttling backwards. Again she tried and failed, and he twirled in a victory circle.

Her face burst into a rare, bright smile. "You are ridiculous."

"Yet you would not have it any other way." He scooped her beneath his arm, her head pressed to his shoulder, and they continued their walk through the hedges to the training yard.

She patted him on the chest. "Aye, brother. Whatever would I do without you?"

"Probably wallow all day."

With a roll of her eyes, she swatted his arm. "Never."

Swords clashed throughout the training courtyard. Men huffed and roared in their exertion. Spears thumped into wooden targets. Arrows whooshed in volleys into hay scarecrows. A few engaged in hand-to-hand combat over muddy ground that had been cleared of snow that morning while new flakes fluttered down from the sky.

Edmira turned to her stalkers with intent. "Leave us, I will return shortly."

No bow, no curtsy, only a quick jerk of a nod from each before they slithered around the barracks through the hedges toward the castle. As much as Andreiyes had grown used to Master Rau's presence, such was not the case with these new Masters. They stalked Edmira's movements with unending fervor. Wherever she went, they followed. Grandfather had approved of it with not a word of explanation and no room for debate. It pricked at his senses.

Andreiyes watched them leave, their clothing sashaying with their steps. The crunch of snow dissipated beneath the commotion from the training yard long before they turned a corner and disappeared.

"An." Edmira's tone turned wry, her eyes focused on where the two Masters had vanished. She still held her belly. "I have not found anything that might make my child safe from them. What if…what if nothing can be found?"

"Never fret. I have a plan, and it will rid us of their influence before Father even takes the throne." He squeezed her hand. "My niece or nephew will never know their touch. I swear it to you as your brother and as a princeling who will one day be your subject."

Ed relaxed in his arms. "You deserve a good woman."

"Ack, not you too."

"I know no one more deserving of happiness than you. You are the best of men, and you work so hard for your family. Whoever you choose will be the most fortunate of women."

"I could not have made it clearer to both you and Father today. I have no wish to take a wife."

"And yet, it is time. You are nearing your twenty-first nameday. Would it be so terrible to find someone to cheer you through your darkest moments, keep your secrets, bring you the greatest joys? Someone to hold you in moments of need, to love you for you and not your title? Never mind the torrid love affairs it creates behind closed doors." She waggled her eyebrows at him, and he snickered. "Granted, I may not be your best reference, but I admit to my mistake. Arkov is…well, he is not my match, obviously. If I were in your boots, I would jump at this chance. Do not waste it."

"And that, dear sister, is what makes you a woman. My boots are well off as they are."

She laughed at him and patted his arm before excusing herself from his embrace. "Think on it, An. Battle strategies and a good toss in bed do not have to be the only pleasures in your life."

"They certainly bring the most amusement."

She shook her head at him in sardonic mirth, then kissed his cheek. With a curtsy, she left him in the training courtyard to drink his fill on the sweat, effort and bone thrilling strain of a good training session.

"Your Highness, come an' join us," Jereown called from the outside of a combat ring as he sheathed his sword and clipped his shoulder fur around his neck. With a huff of insouciance, Jereown gamboled his way over, his braided bun bouncing at each step on top of his head, his grin large and careless, which made it difficult to take him seriously if not for his skill and commanding presence. "Ye missed a brawny fine display there."

"And yet it seems your adversary got too close for comfort." Andreiyes tapped his own cheek.

Jereown wiped at the small slash on his cheek and spread the trail of blood down to his square jawline. "Eh, 'tis nothing. I let him close, then gave the healers more to manage in retribution."

Andreiyes chortled. "I would expect nothing less, my friend."

"Something the matter then?" Jereown mirrored his stance, gaze fixed on the men training.

"If war came to our door, would we be prepared?"

"War in Isyldill? Ye taking the piss?"

"No." Andreiyes clenched his jaw. "Just answer the bloody question."

"What sort of war are we prattling about? Limited to a village? City? Region?"

Andreiyes shook his head.

"A trench between North and South. Oh, the gore in that one. Vultures would be picking flesh for bilials."

"More," Andreiyes answered dismissively in an attempt at nonchalance. Jereown's whistle of surprise said he had failed, and the raking gaze his friend gave made him reluctant to say more. Mayhap it was too much already. No one could know, not yet. Andreiyes squeezed his fists closed for reassurance as he schooled his features.

A few more tense moments passed between them until a sudden grin broke out on Jereown's face before the man fell into a fit of laughter. He clutched his belly and slapped his thighs, sucking in air between guffaws.

"Ye near had me." Jereown caught his breath, pretending to wipe a tear from his eye. "Twas pure dead brilliant. Was already forming logistics on recruiting ten times the men, wondering what the pits ye might need that for, before I saw the twitch of yer eye. Ye've a feral twist in ye to match my own heart."

He patted Andreiyes' back while Andreiyes swept a hand down his face. Ten times the men. That was if Jereown's estimate was not low. He wanted to pull his hair out. How was he to manage that inconspicuously? And he had just sworn success to Edmira. Nogo swallow him whole. His fingers scraped into the skin where his jawline met his neck. He needed a new strategy to train more people. Perhaps sending out master-at-arms to large cities with funding to train the plebs. As for a probable argument to present to Grandfather for him to authorize it, he could tell him such measures could protect the people from Carved attacks and retain the realms' resources.

Jereown slapped him on the shoulder. "Oye, I lost ye there. Ye need to relax. Cheer up. The news from yer Pa cannot be that bad."

"Oh, that...that is a dreaded issue indeed." Andreiyes sighed. "I am to find a bride."

Jereown stared at him for a few grainfalls before his features tugged into a tight-lipped grin. His restrained chortles released in bursts, and Andreiyes rolled his eyes. "I'm still waiting for something a wee bit more dramatic."

"I am to visit several Lords over the next cycles and grow acquainted with their daughters."

"Aye, we calling it growing acquainted now, are we?" Jereown thrust his hips forward, his hands placed on an imagery woman before him, with a wink in his direction.

"Bedding any one of those women would have ramifications." Not to mention the animosity it might brew between the crown and the woman's father, and the difficulty that might befall Andreiyes' attempts to recruit more kingsmen.

"Poor princeling, the worst that'll happen is that ye'll catch yerself a wife."

Andreiyes huffed with annoyance.

"Oh, come on now. Meet with the lasses," Jereown said. "Can do ye no harm, and it'll appease the old prince."

"You sound like Ed."

"Oh, compared to a woman." Jereown fawned a cry of pain, clutching his chest. "Ye strike my heart."

Andreiyes chortled and shook his head. "You cockeyed oaf."

"When are we leaving then?"

"You are not. I need you here to train four potential kingsmen with the master-at-arms and get them up to par with the others."

Isyldill's kingsmen were a fearsome lot now. Seasons before, they had been a ragtag group given respect only because of their title. To think he had looked to them for approval. Their skill was lacking, and their coordination was pitiful. But what they lacked in talent, they made up for with droves of courage and determination when given the right leader. And the right leader Andreiyes was.

Andreiyes had convinced Grandfather to let him have control over the kingsmen's handling for his nineteenth name-day. With Jereown at the helm of training the men whilst aiding the castle's master-at-arms and with their princeling to look up to as he trained beside them, there was pride in the kingsmen's movements now, loyalty in their actions, and a bond between Isyldill's guard as a whole.

"What new men?"

"His Majesty has received a missive from Commander Bryant detailing his and his retinue's arrival in around two quints." Andreiyes nodded his approval at a sergeant after a rather impressive hand-to-hand takedown. He smirked. How long would that sergeant stand against him in a practice row? Andreiyes strode to the nearest weapon rack and unfastened his cloak while Jereown stalked behind him.

"Ye going to take off before those men will see ye?"

"I intend to depart long before there are any chances to cross Bryant on the road. Knowing the man, he may attempt to cajole his way on my travels, and if it so happens, I may have to strangle him."

"Ye'll not be able to avoid him forever."

"I have done well enough so far."

"So you have." Face drawn, Jereown watched Andreiyes hang his cloak over the rack so that none of the fur touched the snow. "Next time ye go, I'm coming with ye. 'Tis in my blood to defend king and realm against dangers, be it Carved, Flawed, or common criminals. I cannot do so if ye keep me locked within Ravensten's walls, only training those ye see fit to battle at yer side."

A shiver bristled over Andreiyes' spine and shoulders. Jereown was more than worthy of riding at his side. If he had the choice of it, Jereown would already hold his father's Southern Commander title, but there was a vast difference between dreaming of skirmishes and being in one.

"'Tis not all glory," Andreiyes said as he unstrapped his belt and scabbard. Exposed to the elements, he was ready for the heat of a sparring session. "The weight of a death on your hands, especially the first…It makes you question who you are, what you have done, what it meant. Then you spend time wondering if it was truly deserved. If you are like me, every kill shall haunt you every spare moment you have."

Every night, the faces of the lives he had ended returned to haunt him, and he did not wish it on his worst enemy. From his first kill – a Carved woman in the caves on the cliffs of the Fist, near Misthall. The anger and fear clear in her eyes, the salty mist from the sea stuck in his nose. To the first Flawed family he led a raid against – their strangled cries and pleas for aid still waking him in the night four stretches later. Master Rau had made sure he could not escape that soul-wrenching duty for long after having avoided the Flawed from Mekworth. One day, his retribution against the Order was bound to make up for it. He clung to that hope.

"Train the men, Sertrios. And see to it we are able to add these fledglings to our count by the time I return next cycle."

Andreiyes tread through the snow toward the ring where two fighters exchanged blows, more than ready to serve and receive a few bruises. Not once did he look back. One day, Jereown would understand the courtesy Andreiyes was giving him. It was a common truth that battle no matter how small found all men, but those who went looking for it often unearthed a new home in Iltheln. Those that came home returned with blackened souls difficult to cleanse.

Twenty-five

*K*aianne crouched behind a boulder on the incline that oversaw the snow-muddied road. It showed no sign of her men or the waiting ambush. The plan was coming together perfectly. Little snow sprites were camouflaging her crew members' brown leathers and gray wools, but she knew where each of them was and detected their slightest movements. That tactic had been one of her most brilliant ideas: soak clothes in mead and after dried, let the sprites mass to them to binge on the honeyed wine and appease their sweet tooth.

Ignoring the buzz of snow sprites that flocked to her, she inhaled deeply imagining all the goods and coins today's raid would bring to the crew and ultimately to Credence. That was only the immediate profits. The true treasure was the opportunity this raid was going to forge them, the chance to change the tide. Knowledge was power, and soon the Carved were going to hoard it like the currency it was.

The biting cold stone numbed her uncovered fingertips in fingerless gloves. The wind nipped at her eyes and forehead that were exposed above the kerchief tied around the lower half of her face, but the excitement kept her alert and warm. The naysayers in Ghedi's crew were about to be squashed and sent to the pits. She could do this. She would. Dare or not, young or old, woman or man, she was made to lead a crew, and today would prove it.

Horses neighed. Packed snow squelched beneath the stomp of hooves. Muffled conversations and laughter made the caravan's position unmistakable. Kaianne grinned. It was almost too easy. Soon the convoy would be right below her, ripe for the picking. She whistled a bird call to the crew members hidden among the landscape and gestured to hold.

The first of the caravan came into view from the cover of trees to her far right: a guardsman on horseback. Next came the first covered wagon, with a driver and his spare up front bundled in furs, trailed by two more mounted guardsmen casually drinking from flasks and working to outdo each other in bawdy japes. The drunker, the merrier. It would make the crew's job easier. The second covered wagon followed with four more guards pulling up the rear instead of the two Kaianne had expected. That was a slight snag, but nothing the crew could not handle.

Yet the caravan did not end there. A third unplanned wagon made its appearance on the road below. No, not a wagon. A red post-chaise carriage, towed by two horses with golden trappings. Adorned luggage was fitted to its front, the view inside concealed with curtains. Someone of wealth or importance traveled with the merchants. Kaianne's heart sank with the complication. She had not planned that sort of kidnapping. Worse, three more guardsmen followed behind. One gestured to his companions, whose movement pushed aside his cloak and revealed the spread-winged griffin atop the leather cuirass. Kingsmen.

Kaianne slumped behind her boulder. She cursed silently and kicked at the snow. Gods stricken and buggered she was, they all were. The god Pyre was probably egging her on to receive her on his bark toward Iltheln with this much opposition.

A bird call to her left pulled her gaze. Oidh, as annoying as ever, was already signaling to her the retreat. She shook her head. This was her call, her mission, her plan, and she had been working on the particulars for too many cycles to simply give up without a fight.

Oidh glared at her, his hand signals lacking the colorful words he loved to spout while nomadic spots of white crept back and forth over the shaggy black of his beard. The sprites feasting on his beard made him far less fearsome and far more grody than usual. She gestured firmly forward, laying out a new formation in hand signals. Eyebrows furrowed, face scrunched, he nodded in obvious aggravation. Well, he could take his frustration up the rear for all she cared. Her plan, her rules, success for all as long as nothing else botched it all up.

He spread the new strategy to the crew members on their left, the ruffle of his clothing the sole audible indicator. She did the same on the right, then let loose a harsh squawk to beckon those posted on the opposite hillside along the road to mirror their movements. Her fellow Carved shuffled downhill behind new trees and boulders, most congregating to her position, the rest to Oidh's. Still the convoy continued on, no more aware of them than a spider was aware of an ant, but these ants had claws.

The crew awaited her orders. Hunkered into a ball and nearest to the road, Kaianne reined in her frenzy and watched her heavy breaths leave like puffs of smoke on the cold air. This was it. Her chance to impress Ghedi and the elders of the crew and move the Carved ahead of the royals and Order's game. Most alongside her had volunteered to follow her plan, but it said something that Ghedi had requested others like Oidh do so as well – all drynn talented Carved notwithstanding because they were too few in numbers and too valuable to endanger on such missions.

The first horse trampled through the snow, its snorts just as heavy. It passed with no hint of slowing. Next came the crush of packed snow beneath thick wheels that magnified to a crescendo as it crawled past. The two jeering guardsmen followed, too slowly for Kaianne to absorb all their drollery, their horses huffing in tandem with Kaianne's eye roll. Men could be such irritants. They were about to be Ghedi's problem soon. Time for the second wagon – the snow rasped beneath the pressure of its passage. More stomping trailed on the approach. Kaianne counted grainfalls for their passage as she pried free the two hatchets secured to her back.

She edged herself around her hideout – the line of four guardsmen with their backs to her – and took aim. A toss later, one guard was down, her hatchet deep in his back as he tumbled from his horse. Within grainfalls, it was as though the pits had spit out the death god, Pyre himself.

The crew descended upon the caravan with battle roars while flurries of escaping snow sprites buzzed and fogged the onslaught. Screams and cries of pain filled the air with a coppery tang. No further communication was needed, everyone knew their tasks. At least two guardsmen needed to survive, the rest were fair game, and none of the kingsmen were going to live to tell the tale with her at the helm of the crew today.

Kaianne jumped atop her boulder and leapt to the road, landing with a roll. The dead guard's back cracked and his flesh squelched as she pried her hatchet free before turning on her knees to block a strike from another guardsman's sword. One downside to being a woman with a small stature, no matter how hard she trained, her strength rarely equaled a man's. Her arms were already trembling with the strain of the force of the guard's weapon against her own. Thankfully, she didn't mind preying on men's fragility.

With a growl, she headbutted the long leather cuirass shielding his groin. The man jumped in shock, the cuirass having protected his 'asset', but it gave Kaianne the relief needed to drop a hatchet and throw an uppercut behind the cuirass' defense. This time he tumbled to the snow, cradling himself and struggling for air. Men, she rolled her eyes. She slashed his calves to avoid any further participation and kicked away his sword before racing toward the fray.

A horse galloped by, blood smeared on its coat as it dragged a dead or unconscious kingsman whose foot was trapped in the stirrup. His head smacked into a rock. There was little chance of recovering after that. A yelp pulled her back to the skirmish. Another kingsman had just impaled one of the crew, while the third battled three other Carved at once. The second kicked his victim off his sword and made to help his compatriot. Not on her watch, not with Carved blood on his hands. She balanced a hatchet in her throwing hand and released. The kingsman's head snapped back with the force of the impact. It distracted the last kingsman long enough for the Carved to deal a pommel blow to his head and disarm him.

Kaianne grinned wickedly as she approached. The battle was dying down behind her. The morning was won. The plan had worked. Dead kingsmen were an added bonus, and she refused to think of her side's casualties just yet. There was still one last kingsman to finish, and the beating he was taking to his face and arms was not nearly satisfying enough. And yet the royalist laughed through the crunch of his nose.

"Go right on ahead."

That voice…

He coughed after a blow to his stomach.

"Kill me and see where it brings you."

The kingsman hollered as a crew member at his side twisted his hand at an odd angle. "That was for me sister."

Marlin, the arrogant little dweeb. Kaianne groaned. He knew none of the crew were meant to speak a single word.

The kingsman spit over his shoulder at Marlin, and Kaianne froze at the sight of his battered face, eyes widened. "May Pyre piss on your grave."

Oh, shite on a stick. This whole ordeal had officially been dragged through dung. So much for impressing Ghedi. He might as well come out and bury her now.

"Not before you," Chidinni said from in front of her victim. Well, apparently those two cared nothing for the plan. Chidinni – a woman ten stretches Kaianne's senior who had joined Credence after the slaughter of her brother's family – raised her short sword to drive through his throat.

Kaianne's eyes widened. There were grainfalls left to stop this and too many paces between them. She threw her second hatchet, praying no limbs came up before its target. Metal clanged, knocking Chidinni's short sword away.

"What're you doing?" Chidinni asked as Kaianne raced over.

Kaianne shook her head and gestured for the three Carved to look at the kingsman's eyes, but they were too far gone in their bloodlust to understand. Marlin made to grab her coat. She batted his hand away, drew her dagger – the one that nearly never left her hip since Ghedi had returned it to her – and slipped the tip beneath the fake kingsman's chin.

If she looked past the swelling, the sharp angles of his jawline or the heavier ridge above his eyes, and the scowl forming a one-sided dimple despite the facial hair, the boy she once knew was right there. He who had saved her, forced her into a life she knew nothing of, and then abandoned her. How many times had she thought of pummeling his face for it? His dark skin was already discolored from the thrashing he had received without her contributions. She gritted her teeth behind the kerchief, set on clinging to the old anger. So, what if his abandonment had led her to a true home where she had grown into more than some simpering, little bride-prize?

Eyebrows furrowed, the man's gaze was focused on her dagger for every single grainfall it took her three Carved crewmates to notice and curse the amber of his eyes. When his eyes flicked up to Kaianne's, it was not fear or anger that lined his features. It was confusion.

"Kaianne?" he whispered the name, and her chest seized. Her kerchief tickled her chin; it was still in place. It had to have been the dagger.

To the pits with them all. How after all these stretches had he remembered? One glance at a family heirloom and he knew. Shite on a stick, and of course the god-blessing on his family line meant that she could not silence him forever with a slash along his throat. With a hiss, Kaianne twirled the hilt of her dagger until the blade faced inward.

"Hello, Yierd."

With a jerk, she socked him against the head with the pommel, and he crumpled into oblivion. That would give him one splintering headache when he woke up. It should have satisfied her, at least a little. Instead she sighed with a tinge of regret.

Chidinni tugged on her shoulder. "You acquainted with a royal?"

Kaianne clasped her hand over the woman's mouth. This was most definitely *not* the time for those remarks. Everything here was about silence and stealth. Chidinni's unruly eyebrows pinched, frown lines bunched in clear aggravation despite the following silence. Already Kaianne imagined the report the woman planned to give Ghedi. The whole thing was turning into a bloody disaster.

Now, somehow, she needed to work Andreiyes, a very Marked and very blue-blooded royalist, into her plans. Gaia was forsaking her. This had been her one chance. She wanted to yell loud enough for the dead to hear and swipe her hatchets against a trunk until her frustration melted away, but leaders did not do that. Leaders sucked up their pride and anger for the betterment of the crew. That's what she had to do.

With a shaky exhale or two later, Kaianne motioned to the third Carved that had not spoken to tie the princeling up and restrain him in the post-chaise to take with them. It was pointless to further dwell on the new player on the board.

The fighting had died down to whimpers and a few curses from the conscious and tied guards. Sweat and blood sickened the air. She glanced over the wagons where the merchants and their aides were peeking out their heads from the safety of their wooden shelters. The merchants and cargo appeared untouched. Good. At least that part had been successful. And they had managed to capture a few guardsmen. Alright, not a complete waste.

A few injuries had been sustained, and one crew member had fallen to his death. His dead eyes stared at her in blame. Kaianne tugged at the corner of her eyes with a heavy sigh. He had been one of the newest of their crew, about her age, full of ideas and hope for better days and change. Poor lad, but such was life. Carved came and went, but as long as their lives made an impact, it was worth it. When her plan came to fruition, his sacrifice would be worth it. Oidh hauled up his body and settled the lad over a guardsman's horse, not a word spoken between them as agreed. Tonight, after they reached the others, they would honor his death with a proper burial to send him safely onto Iltheln to meet his loved ones.

Kaianne whistled a nasal bird trill, circling her finger in the air. Time to barricade the road with pre-cut tree trunks and get moving. The longer they lingered, the higher the chance of discovery was. Hopefully a snowstorm in the next quint would cover the blood, bodies and tracks. With still another cycle and a half before the Stretch of Blight's end, there was a high chance of that.

Twenty-six

Few Isyldillians ever left the comforts of their towns. Even less took refuge in nature and within the darkness of caves – which was laughable to Kaianne after having lived half a stretch in the kingdom of Nimedor, where its residents dug and shaped their abodes into cliff sides and beneath hills instead of erecting buildings in the middle of nature. Hunters or drifters rarely went further than the delimitation of light offered through the grotto's mouth. Therefore, the subterranean chambers that littered western Isyldill's underground were the perfect shelter for a Carved crew. As a bonus, many were interconnected. Often, they led to underwater springs. Some were warm and inviting, if one overlooked the reek of rotten egg, while others were chilled and refreshing to the taste.

When Kaianne and those she had led on their mission returned to the cave where Ghedi and the remainder of the crew awaited, it quickly became clear that no amount of foliage was going to camouflage the gaudy red and gold carriage or its oversized wheels. The wagons, yes, as planned. The oversized eyesore, no. Another headache to manage, which probably meant traveling through the caves was futile.

Never mind the burn of Ghedi's disapproving glower behind his kerchief. It only got worse when Oidh dragged a half-conscious Andreiyes to Ghedi's feet and pinched their prisoner's face upward until the meaning behind his amber eyes sunk in. That was when Ghedi's face morphed into disgust, then murderous rage aimed at her, and Kaianne shrunk into herself. Never before had she given him reason to scowl at her that way, and it made her feel raw like the little girl that had once begged for his approval. Shite on a stick, she had to fix this.

Their three guardsmen prisoners were chained in a far chamber to the wall and to each other. The sound of rushing water babbled through the walls and blocked any potential conversations from being overheard. The merchants were fed and huddled into a separate chamber with cots, no exceptions were made for the Carved's informants compared to the other merchants. Andreiyes was not placed with either group. Instead, Ghedi ordered for a chain to be bolted to ground in a chamber with a heated spring. There, the condensation had water dripping from stalactites into the pool constantly.

When the princeling had been secured, his features marred in pain with one eye swollen shut and clutching the arm of his broken wrist, Ghedi hauled Kaianne to the cave's forefront with a bruising grip on her arm. In the woods, they passed two crew members digging a grave for their fallen comrade, only a grunt of acknowledgement between them. It was not until they were far enough from prying ears that Ghedi spun her to face him.

"Do you realize what you've done?"

"I had no choice." The excuse sounded weak even to her, and she cringed.

"You have more sense than this. A royal?" He buried his fingers into the hood of his cloak. "Eish, you're miffing us upright with this."

"I can fix it. I can."

"How?" He bellowed, no trace of his sunny disposition. "No crew has managed to ransom a higher noble. Not in a single kingdom. They'll find us here."

"So, we keep moving as planned. It's not over yet. We can still do this. We head for Ollin. Slowing the pace, it'll take a good bilial to arrive. Add a few days more before the Lord Welnit sends a search party."

Ghedi grunted, then shook his head. "Ag, the issue remains. Why not leave the royal behind? No horse, no food, no true form of your concept and half frozen by the time he woke. Now, he is a burden bound to break us."

"He…," Kaianne bit her cheek, "recognized me."

"You unfurled your own plan?"

"What? No, never. Not a word was spoken. No face covers dropped." There was no need to mention Marlin or Chidinni now. Just as Ghedi had said, she should have left him behind unconscious, but the idea of it had not even struck her. "T'was my dagger, he recognized it. He called me by name."

He eyed the sheathed heirloom tied around her hip. "He knows you."

She sucked in a breath. Too many stretches had passed without her revealing the truth behind her carving, of who she had been before. She had settled on half-truths for fear of being shamed. Now it was chewing her raw. "He knew my brother. They were close before I became Carved."

"Then we abandon the plan."

"No." She gripped her arm. "I can fix this. I swear it."

"You are not a young biscuit anymore. You cannot leap without knowing the particulars."

"Sometimes we must have faith. We are *this* close to having someone on the inside. Imagine how much easier the infiltration might be if it were the princeling himself who let us in."

Ghedi raised a brow. "You believe you can convince the man of this?"

The truth was no. She and Andreiyes had never had the relationship for it, so instead she shrugged. "Worth an attempt. I have a few tricks up my sleeve. Last resort, we can always bash him over the head and abandon him in the middle of nowhere."

*K*aianne steeled her nerves and cracked her neck before entering the chamber where Andreiyes was being held. The steam from the spring settled in her lungs despite the kerchief tied over her lower face while cocooning the rest of her in a bubble warmth. It was a shock to her system; only grainfalls before she had been shivering after having shed her furs. The spring was inviting, a constant trickle of water rippling through its multi-colored pool that glittered in the reflection of the two burning sconces that lit the space. If not for the stench wafting from it or the forced company, she might have reveled in this place.

Andreiyes sat in the far corner stripped of his leathers, his undamaged wrist chained to the floor and his opposite leg restrained in the same manner. His features were settled, despite the puffy bruises along his jaw, the mangled curve of his nose and the black eye that had swollen an eyelid shut. No one had come to tend to his injuries, and it showed. Blood crusted his face from his nostrils to his chin, with dried drops speckled across his tunic. He did not glance at her as she approached. Nor did he turn his head when she set nuts and a thin stretch of meat before him along with a full cup.

"I want to speak to the Carved called Kaianne."

"You're not in the right place to make demands."

He scoffed, but kept his gaze averted. "How long do you think you can keep me? Kingsmen will come looking. They will find me, and they shall tear you all down like the swine you are."

"How poetic. They may come, *Yierd*, but you won't be here for them to find."

"So, it is you." His head slowly turned to face her, facial muscles twitching, the movement clearly agonizing him. "Grayson would be ashamed that this is what you have chosen to become."

She barked a laugh. "I would not hold my breath on that one. Let's not forget which side betrayed my family first. But maybe you mean Grayson would be ashamed that I as a woman am far more proficient with a weapon than he ever could've been. That one, yes, he would've held against me. He's probably cursing me from Iltheln over it while Deacon socks him over the head for the lack of decorum toward his sister."

With a chuckle she kneeled before him, placing the short tree branches cinched beneath her armpit to the ground, and pulled wrapping cloth from the pouch at her waist. It had been several cycles since she had let herself dwell on old memories. That she survived when they had not. She had grown to live with the guilt, but thinking on it was the blow that kept on coming. Almost six stretches had passed, and she still hadn't avenged her family. That was the only thing that shamed her, so much so that she could no longer bring herself to visit their ash grave.

"What happened to you?" Andreiyes croaked.

"I survived. It's what you wanted, no? It's why you abandoned a young girl to a fate worse than death."

"I should have put you out of your misery that day."

She nodded. "Perhaps. Would've made my life easier. But you didn't, so the point is moot. Now let me see your arm."

He didn't oblige. "Why do you hide your face?"

"You may recognize my dagger, but you no longer know my face. That's a privilege you don't get."

"Why? Are you hideous now? Do pockmarks and scars line your features?"

"With that tongue of compliments, I'm surprised at the number of successful conquests you've had."

"Oh, they never complain about my tongue."

"Poor you, you thought those moans were real?" With a snicker, she shook her head. Now hand over your arm if you ever want to wield a sword with it again."

Still he kept it at his side, even slipping his bad wrist further between the cave wall and himself. "You a healer now as well as a bandit?"

"I would never have the patience to tend moaners all day."

"Why does that not surprise me?"

"Because I was never that patient to begin with."

"No, you never were." He was frowning as his unswollen eye bounced between hers. For a few tense moments, she thought she was going to have to use force to pry his arm out until finally, he shakingly offered it, teeth gritted. "Did you ever…" He sucked in air as she prodded gently around the jutting bone. "…manage to light…a fire on your first try?"

She smiled softly, recalling those first few attempts with a flint stone. "My younger self would be giddy with joy if she could see me now."

Kaianne set down his arm, satisfied that no large bone shards lingered beneath the unpunctured skin.

"You should eat and drink now because once I start setting the bones you won't want to."

Eye fixed on hers, he picked at the nuts. His chains clanked and scratched against the floor, the sound echoing amongst the constant drips from the ceiling into the springs.

"How do I know you will do it right?" He sipped at the tonic in the cup, not seeming to taste the bitterness over the blood coating his teeth and the nuts' slightly acrid savor.

"You don't. You'll just have to trust me. Only a little. Not nearly as much as I once trusted you."

He downed the rest of his drink with a wince and tore into the slice of meat. Quickly his eyes began to droop. His head fell back against the wall.

He groaned. "I wanted to go back and check on you."

Kaianne scoffed and looked down over his slumped form, his unblemished eye struggling to stay open. "Want or not, you didn't. That's all that matters. Now stop fighting it. Take this lack of pain as a kindness you don't deserve."

*T*he rocking of the post-chaise carriage was far more unsettling than Kaianne remembered from her youth. Her stomach rolled with the motion, and she forced the edge of her nausea back down again. The many unpleasant sandfalls in this box that nobles somehow felt privileged to be tucked into were passing by far too slowly.

Andreiyes moaned at her feet, his lower body sprawled along the carriage flooring, his upper half resting against the door, head slumped against the seat cushion's edge. He was finally waking after a whole day of sleep. The bruising on his face had flourished with another splotch of red after she had shoved his nose's cartilage back into shape. Bloody cloth was rolled into both nostrils to stem the flow. His wrist was immobilized in a splint while his forearm hung in a wrap that stretched around his neck and bound his arm around his torso.

As stubborn as he was, Kaianne did not trust him not to move and aggravate the injuries. The resetting had not been easy, but after having done similar tasks over the past stretches, the feel of moving muscular tissue and bone and the pressure needed no longer bothered her. All Carved in a crew learned to set bones, relocate a joint and bandage a wound because no crew could depend on just one healer to survive.

Andreiyes' good eye fluttered open and shut again, his body fighting off the lulling dregs of the tonic. He groaned and huffed and whimpered from the shift of positions. Oh yes, all that pain the tonic had dulled was coming back to haunt him. For his benefit, she lounged her body along the cushion, one arm resting nonchalantly on the windowsill.

"Well good morrow to you too, Highness." The contempt dripped from her tone.

"What did you do to me?" he grumbled and licked his dry lips.

"A favor. Keep your wrist steady for a cycle and you might just recover your full range. Your nose, unfortunately, might forever have a little kink in it. Your pretty image might suffer, but you cannot say I didn't give my all."

"Why help me?"

She frowned and shrugged off his question. True, other Carved might not have been so giving, but the idea of torturing information out of Andreiyes was distasteful. There was nothing to gain in pure cruelty – not if the goal was to gain his trust – and those sorts of screams gave her shivers. She looked into his unswollen, amber eye. Would she have treated him differently if it had been any other royal in his place? She pressed her fist to her mouth, unsettled by her doubts.

"Where are we?" he asked. She welcomed the change of topics.

"On the road. I told you if your kingsmen came to the caves, you would no longer be there."

He groaned, jaw clenched, most certainly from the pain. "If we are not headed to Ollin, they will know, and they will come for all of you."

"And how would they know?" Kaianne sat up. He seemed so certain of this, and his good eye hardened before rolling to stare at the flooring. This confirmed as some had suspected that royals were tracked somehow, perhaps even all Marked were. It explained how no one had successfully ransomed or kidnapped a noble.

"I went back," he said.

"What?"

"To our camp in the Weldolf woods. Not until the end of the Noven cycle in that stretch, but I did return."

"Eight cycles after? I was long gone by then. You had promised three."

"I know, but I did what I could." He lay his head back, the bounce of the carriage lulling it from side to side. "There were too many guards in Millian at the time, a Master too, and I had no means of tracking you. I still visit their grave every stretch. I guess now there is no need to ask their forgiveness every time for not aiding you further."

"Do as you like. I never visit them anymore."

"Aye, understandable, they would be ashamed. Oh, come now, not even you are naïve enough not to know what these Carved do to the realm and its people."

"If it were truly that simple. I will never regret joining this crew. Since the realm murdered my family without so much as a second thought, I highly doubt even my father scorns my actions from his place in Iltheln."

"Then why not visit their gravesite?"

Right then, the gaudy curtains held more appeal than his battered face, but not answering made her feel weak, subordinate, everything she had determined not to be.

"I made them a promise," she finally said. Vengeance – a simple concept, but difficult to accomplish. She twisted her sheathed dagger between both hands, her gaze fixed solely on it. Andreiyes' legs were tied together, and his good arm was secured beneath his broken wrist, the rope wrapped twice around his waist. He was no threat. "Every time I return with it unaccomplished, I feel a failure."

"Then fulfill it."

"Aye, I plan to. Problem is, the scope of my promise gets larger as the truth of the problem gets revealed."

"And what is your truth? What do you need to achieve?"

She waggled her dagger at him. "You're handsome when your face is intact, but not that handsome. Besides, I'm almost certain you have an idea yourself. I'm not sure you really see us Carved as the enemy."

"All Carved are traitors."

"Sounds like spitless fodder to me, Highness. You have a brain beneath all those lumps. Use it."

He shook his head. "You have changed."

That made her cackle. "What did you expect to happen? I couldn't remain that helpless child forever. Not in this kill or be killed world. And don't pretend to be innocent yourself. We all know your hands are far from clean. I may have killed guardsmen and kingsmen to ensure the wellbeing of other Carved, but you…you have murdered entire families of Flawed and strung up Carved to die for only missing a mark that you yourself once carved out of a dying girl's arm. You may have saved me, but those actions make you no better than the worst of men."

He said no more and kept his gaze averted for sandfalls on end. When the caravan stopped to break bread, he chewed his meager ration without enthusiasm before slumping against the door at his back. He was hooded and dragged without protest by another crew member to relieve himself behind a bush and collapsed back onto the carriage flooring without so much as a grunt or groan as the metal cuffs were clanked shut around his ankle and functioning wrist. Kaianne rubbed absently at the scars of her right arm. It was disheartening to watch, and yet it put her on edge. Resignation was not at all what she expected of the man rumored to be the first warrior-trained royal in ages.

"What are you planning?" she asked when the silence became insufferable as the carriage rocked them.

"I am permitted silence."

294 | M . T . F o n t a i n e

"Well, this is disappointing. I was looking forward to wrestling your submission at each escape attempt."

He snorted. "I am chained. My sword arm is broken. I can hardly see out of one eye. My head pounds at every motion of my jaw. I have no idea if any of my men are alive. And unless I slept for far longer than I presume, we remain on the road to Ollin. I doubt your party would head back toward Lityoll as that would arouse far too much suspicion. We were originally a three day's ride from the nearest town along the road. I suspect you will circumvent it, but as you continue toward where I had planned to go, escape hardly seems practical at this time. Not until I know your plans for me. What are your plans?"

"That depends entirely on you."

He huffed in what was most likely annoyance, but it was the truth. His presence was going to make or break her plan. So far, she was making no progress with him at all. Despite him being arrogance and ignorance personified, it was up to her to somehow attempt to appeal to his better nature, if he had one. The Lords above were laughing at her as she scrambled to find some topic that might not spark further ire between them. Gods below it was hard, and nothing seemed worthy or sensical enough to mention.

"Is something wrong with you?" he asked.

Her first reaction was to snap at him and cut off any delusions that she was meek and inept, but she reined it in. Actually, a demure attitude might appeal to his views of women. His company was not awful, she had to remind herself. Sure the stench of his sweat embedded in his attire was beginning to tickle her nose, but the habit of traveling with others meant the smell was familiar. None of his words had been cruel. Most in fact had been her doing, which was flustering her good sense even worse.

"No," she sighed. "I'm simply tired of arguing with you. Finding a topic of discussion not to avoid is proving difficult." She settled her back and head along the seat cushion, her legs riding up the side panel. "Perhaps in a way I should thank you."

"What?"

"Think on it. I had no purpose as a ladyling except to breed the next set of lordlings and to raise any daughters to be the same. I am more now. I can fell a man in a skirmish. I can survive in the wild with no hardship, and I have seen so much of our world and its wonders that most will never get to experience. And the world is wondrous."

His chains clanged and the flooring creaked as he straightened his posture. "Will you tell me of it?"

She smirked at her little success and closed her eyes to seek the memories. She told him of the waterfalls across Lakoldon that spanned hundreds of meters and pounded into the rivers below them so loud one could not speak above their constant roar. Of Lakoldon's royal castle that seemed to float on the very edge of one such waterfall. Of the gorges and ridges that made up the landscapes with forests filled with poisonous fruits and terrifying snakes wide and long enough to swallow a man whole. Of the barnacled megalodon and dragon skeletons washed along the edge of the Barring Sea's far shore.

Next she spoke of Gyldrise. The mainland's south was covered in swamps and grasslands with little to no hills. Bamboo flourished there, as well as fruit trees that reached no higher than her neck. In general, most trees there were rarely taller than a home's roof, and the grasslands were covered in fields of edible flowers spotted with bushes of berries. She could still recall the soothing perfumes of each flower. Gyldrise's islands were connected by rope ladders from their closest edges and through a series of subterranean tunnels dug through the islands' cores and beneath the sea floor. It relaxed her as she recalled her adventures from the time the crew had dove off a cliff in Gyldrise to escape a swarm of imperiums – the Gyldrit equivalent to kingsmen – to how they had once gotten lost in the maze below seawater while trying to map the tunnels. She even swore she had seen the head of a finfolk before its humanoid body slipped into the water and its tail slapped at the surface.

Andreiyes gobbled every description up, never interrupting. He adjusted his position with a slight wince when she mentioned the dragon's shadow that had circled above them near Onlooker's Peak in Nimedor, how its roar had echoed straight to her core, and how the red tips of the Agorethney Mountains where the dragons and griffins still resided to this day had seemed a mirage in the distance. She described how dry the land in Nimedor was no matter what Stretch the season fell in, and yet the plants were bursting with juice when cut open. Whilst Nimedorians dug their homes instead of building them, she and her crewmates had taken shelter in long-abandoned wyrm holes during their stays, since the populace remained superstitious of the long-dead beasts from before the era of Schlenkra. Kaianne croaked near the end of her tale, her throat dry and overused, and yet the wonder on Andreiyes' face made every word worth it. It was relaxing for once to talk about something other than the crew's objectives and strategic planning.

When the moons began to rise and the sun hung a hand's width above the horizon, the caravan reached a hunting cabin's equivalent in size to a small mansion. Usually noble households or royalty sojourned in these hunting cabins with an entire array of servants that arrived well ahead to prepare for their masters' stay. Tonight, the princeling was about to understand how much those beneath him polished his cushioned arse. There would be no decadent meals or warm bed waiting for him.

Inside, sheets covered every inch of furniture. A thick layer of dust blanketed the flooring while mites floated in the stale air. The occasional footprints made it easy to see where previous squatters had stayed, but there were no lingering smells of anything left in their wake. Kept separate from his guards, her crewmates led Andreiyes into an opulent bedroom with a four-poster bed, rugs, and a fireplace, but the mattress was for them, not him. She helped the others restrain him to a bedpost.

"Thank you," he said as she handed him a blanket, amber eyes locked on hers. His fingers grazed her hand.

At first she stumbled over how to reply to the misplaced gratitude. It was so unlike the royal she once knew, yet not once had he fought against her while in captivity, or even raised his voice. That in and of itself had her questioning her sanity. And it hit her. He was playing her as much as she was him. Clever, clever Yierd.

"It wouldn't serve for you to catch a fever when we've not yet decided what to do with you. Enjoy your night."

With that, she strode away and out of the bedchamber where her male comrades could better watch him. Not once did she look back until she was in the hallway and the creaking at her back signaled someone was shutting the door.

"Hope ye know what ye're doing," Oidh whispered behind her.

She simply nodded. So did she.

The days continued much the same: pack, travel, rest, repeat. No one took her place with Andreiyes in the post-carriage, so it was just the two of them from dawn to dusk. With each day he healed more from his exterior wounds, but he started complaining of stomach pains and burns.

"The fault of that slop you feed me," he complained one morning after retching. It was a close guess, but not quite right.

Rather than be bored or dwell on the nauseating sway of the carriage, it became a habit for them to spend the time in conversation. Sometimes it was clear he was attempting to gain more knowledge on the Carved population. Bloody good it would do him since they were spread across all Taelgir and he was forever restrained within his borders. She provided insight into other realms, and he spoke of his recent achievements with the kingsmen and gossip on nobles. He subtly complimented her grace, her voice, and what he had seen of her in the skirmish a little each day. He plied her with honeyed words about how he understood the essence of the Carved's plight thanks to their time together.

In truth, she enjoyed his company now more so than in those last days before he abandoned her in the Weldolf woods. The laughter they shared was genuine, at least on her part. It was like airing out loneliness she had not known she held and having someone fill the void. Which was frightening because if she wasn't careful, she might trust him too much. In another life, perchance they might have been friends or even more, but here they were: each playing the demure Carved or princeling to win over the other with pleasantries. More the fool Andreiyes as he had yet to see that she was no simpleton to be seduced by a title and rich airs. That was put further to the test when Andreiyes began to insert a few touches in his snare. Over days, he started with a press of his foot, to several grazes of the knee and evolved to innocent caresses of his fingertips along her arms. They were few and infrequent, but how she craved them: the contact, the sensation, the illusion. So, she distracted herself with further conversation.

"People become Carved because they either believe in our cause or have nothing left. We find a family and a community with each other, but it's rare for any of us to go looking to make a family."

"Why?"

"Two Carved will only ever make a Marked. So far, none that I've heard have ever borne a Flawed. A Marked is always found, somehow, and carving an infant always results in death. So no, being a Carved means giving up on the idea of family life."

"Do you not want children?" His question surprised her. Did she? Stretches ago the answer had been a clear no. Now, though... In truth it did not matter.

She traced the scar that lay along her pelvis beneath her clothing. "Do you remember this wound? You secured it with brooches." She sneered at the memory. "I cannot have children because of it, but perhaps it's a blessing. What could someone like me ever bring of worth to a child?"

"Love."

"Don't you sound the romantic fool. Love cannot fill empty bellies or stop the swing of a blade. It's pointless. It's a wasted emotion that hinders at the worst possible moment."

"No wonder there are so few of you."

"It's entertaining how little you know. We're over two thousand strong. I reckon we'd give you a good toss for your coins if we ever assembled together at once."

The swelling around his eye had reduced, the blemishing green looking pungent on his dark skin, and both of his eyes widened sizably. "So why do you not?"

"Rebelling against one realm would not be the end of the hardships in the others. Carved and Flawed will be hunted as long as marks bear as much weight as they do. Isyldillians may be born with a griffin's head, but it's no different than a Lakoldesh with its basilisk or a Nimedorian with a wyrm's mark. In truth, I find it odd that each kingdom hunts the same traitors, though none of you correspond with the other. Or do you have contact with the royals of other kingdoms that we have not heard of?"

"Not that I would tell you," he deadpanned.

"Of course not." She smirked. "Did you know the same royal decree against Flawed and their families that condemned the Lyssandres was enacted in every single realm on the same day? Strange, no? As if someone or something *other* dispersed their will?"

She watched him gulp with unease, but he kept his thoughts to himself for the remainder of the day's ride.

After that day, every once in a while, a mention of the Order and its Masters came up. Each time there was a moment of deep contempt that shined in Andreiyes' eyes before he masked it once more. It was not until over two quints had passed that she was certain she had made progress with him.

"The borders are enacted for a reason," he said defensively, as he wiggled the fingers of his mending hand.

"That's not the question. I'm asking for what reason? Do you even know?"

"Is that your objective? To discover the king's motives?"

She shrugged and plopped a handful of dried berries into her mouth. "Want some?" At his refusal, she swallowed the rest. "The borders have been there for centuries. Seems hardly only a king's motives. Which means more than the royal family is at play."

His eyes narrowed. Barely a hint remained of his facial wounds except for a slight curve on the bridge of his nose.

"Besides," she continued, emboldened by his reaction, "if it were only the royals, why can none of you cross? Not the Lenierz of Isyldill or the Verdons of Lakoldon or even the Ambrosius of Gyldrise. If it were solely the Kings and Queens at the helm, I find it difficult to believe they would limit themselves."

For a while, Andreiyes focused on his wrist. The bones were far from fused, but he still stubbornly tried to work his hand and fingers open and closed.

"What is the border like?

"It feels like nothing, at least not to me. Everyone always spoke of it with such fear, but to all Carved it's as if it's not even there. We only realize we've crossed a border by the change in landscape or humidity, or if you're reading a map. Being a Carved is freedom." She locked onto his eyes from where she sat against the window. "It's only the Marked such as yourself that are prisoners within your own lands. Even the Stewards are free to wander, and that begs the question why. Don't you think it strange they're not named traitors as well?"

"You know nothing."

She grinned and shook her head. "No, I know different. We know the Order has something over you royals. The what eludes us, but I think *you* despise them as much as my crew and I."

"And what would you all ever have against the Order?"

"Those who seek power always seek more zealots to fill their ranks. The Order is no different. They take what they have no right to." His confusion spurred her on. "They take people with talents. And when they do not come willingly, they steal their lives instead."

"What do you mean they take people?"

"Exactly that. They demand they serve their temple and stuff them into wagons headed toward Telfinor. They often stop in Salost before crossing the border the next morn. It's still not clear what they do to allow them to pass through the borders, but they do it all the same. No blue fire, no wrenching agony. As if they were not Marked at all."

"Why?"

"To maintain control, I suppose."

"Of course." Andreiyes knocked his head against the carriage door and whispered to himself. "If any and all talented individuals are controlled by the Order, then the realms remain at a disadvantage."

Kaianne nodded. It was what had happened to Ghedi's daughter. On the woman's twenty-fifth name-day, she had developed a basic Hefter's talent and levitated bundles of hay after a heated argument with one of her children. Ghedi, as mayor of their village, reported the sight as a blessing from the gods. The news spread and soon a pair of Foremen trailed by kingsmen came with an offer of employment in the name of the Order. The caveats were clear: she needed to leave her family behind and travel to the Nimedorian outpost of Mnatundo, along the Telfinorian border immediately. Her refusal sparked a melee which ended in the deaths of most involved. That was when Ghedi chose to carve out his mark.

He had told Kaianne the story a stretch after she had found him butchering a female Foreman in fern-green robes and her retinue to pulp. The state the crew chief had been in, the rage and fear in his eyes. It still sent a shiver down her spine whenever she thought of the lack of warmth in his gaze. The worst part though, the kills had done nothing to settle his vengeance against those that had taken his daughter and grandchildren's lives. What did that mean for her vengeance against the Bryants?

Her voice was shaky when she used it again. "I want better for the world, Andreiyes. I know you do too. And I don't mean just for Isyldill. Can you imagine what Carved and Marked could do together, side by side without the hate mixed in? I want that. So much."

He reached out his hand, the loose chains dragging along the flooring, and cupped her cheek over the kerchief. She leaned into it, the warmth both hopeful and distant. When he pried the cloth down and exposed her features, she did nothing to stop him. For what seemed like sandfalls, his gaze swept over every inch of her face. Perhaps he did it to memorize her features, or perhaps it was in search of something he needed. Whatever it was, nothing else mattered right then. His actions had sealed the path they would follow whether he wanted it or not, and yet she found herself wishing life between them could be simpler. When his eyes fell to her lips, her breath hitched.

"Gods, you have changed."

She barked a fit of laughter, thrilled for the break in tension. "I would certainly hope so. Twelve was not my most flattering stretch."

He tucked a strand of hair behind her ear, and she fell into the mesmerizing gaze of his amber eyes. "Come to Ollin with me. Leave these bandits behind, and I will take care of you. I swear it."

His face angled further in. Oh, if only it were not all an act. It took some reminding that royals only cared for their own objectives. Worse, men like Andreiyes only saw women as whimpering subservients.

"But I'm Carved," she pleaded, head turned. If only she could blush on demand. "There's nowhere safe for me now."

"With me, you are. And no one need ever know."

"You make it sound like you've done this before."

"No." His breath fawned her cheek. "Only you."

She arched a brow, eyes fixed on the window. Was he mocking her or did he truly think that all women believed such adulation?

"What would I do in Ollin?"

"I will give you shelter while together we plan for a better world. One for all of us, Marked and Carved alike."

Kaianne wanted to snort – as if she were a poor damsel – but reined it in. No need to spoil the moment.

"Do you remember Mistress Omga Harleston?"

"Mimsee, you mean?" Where was he going with this?

"She meant much to you, yes?" She nodded with reticence, eyes vacillating between his. "She is in my employ at Ravensten. Come with me, and I shall reunite you. She still speaks of you often."

Gods, Mimsee. It had been a long while since Kaianne's thoughts had rested on the old governess, longer still since she had asked Oidh news of her wellbeing. Andreiyes' fingers trailed down her cheek to her throat and rested on her coat's collar. It was the touch of a lover, sweet and coaxing, and gods curse him for how she melted into the ghosting tingles it left behind. But if he switched tactics and went for suffocation, her handy boot dagger might leave him with a few extra holes in some non-lethal parts. She fingered the hilt for support as she gazed into his eyes.

"When would we leave?"

"As soon as we can manage to free what remains of my guard." At her arched brow, he continued, "I am not fool enough to ignore the hushed conversations of the Carved sequestered with me every eve."

The guardsmen had always been part of the plan, hence why her crew members had worked so very hard not to kill them all in the melee. Now she wondered if Andreiyes might use their presence against the crew and then her, honeyed words be damned, but this was the best she could get from him with only another two day's ride until they reached Ollin's outskirts.

"How would I ever manage that?"

"Free me and leave it to me."

"And you'll swear not to harm any of them?"

His hand swept along her face. "For your tender heart, I swear it."

Lies, but she restrained the outburst. She settled on a teasing eyeroll and a tap on his chest for him to settle back on the floor.

"Tomorrow you'll be a princeling again. Today, I'm still in charge."

"Of that I have no doubt," he mocked, and it took every bit of her strength to ignore his sarcasm. "You shall aid me then?"

She pretended to mull it over until Andreiyes' foot began to bounce and he was nibbling his lower lip. "Aye, very well, this eve. Once they're all asleep. I'll need to slip them a brew."

He kissed her wrist as though she were still part of the gentry and not caked in several days' worth of sweat. It was an effort not to grimace at how thick he was laying it all on. Little did he know his water had already been laced with something extra the past ten days. She turned to the window and grinned. Everything was falling into place quite nicely.

Twenty-seven

The Lords of the privy council deafened Rau with their ceaseless bickering and contestations. Their cacophony built to a crescendo echoing against the wooden walls of the Hall of Accords as Rau buried his head between his sleeve-covered hands to massage his temples. For the first time he pitied the royal family with how often they dealt with these curs. Nothing was ever good enough for them. No negotiation settled their greed. No words appeased their tempers. They just refused to be quiet, and he was at his wit's end. Aethel keep him, why could no one else have been chosen to cover for crown prince Balliol during his illness?

Compared to the Temple's vast Chamber of Concords with its delicate white marble walls, the Hall of Accords was a morose and narrow room furnished with chairs and benches that circled around to a thin passageway. The heavy fumes of floral oils were nauseating. Wooden planks lined the bottom half of the wall while golden fabric with black designs of the gods, Eidenhail trees and griffins lined the top.

The King sat comfortably on his raised throne behind Rau – snoring quite loudly at times – while Rau occupied the middle seat of the three laid out for the royal brood. With Balliol quarantined while suffering from erysolio, Andreiyes vagabonding to find a wife and Edmira resting with a recent

cough after her Steward shadows had guzzled far too much
drynn from her the previous day, Rau presided over this band
of peacocks that refused to agree on anything. At this rate, it
was no wonder the royals took all decision making power from
them. Gods below, he hated politics in Isyldill, at the Temple,
wherever. It made decent people turn into pariahs.

"Enough," he bellowed as he slammed a hand atop the
balustrade of the dais that separated the royals from the Lords.
The drynn in every paperweight along the rectangle table
between him and the Lords responded to his frustration by
raising each object a finger-width before plummeting back
down. The outburst bounced through the hall to be met with
wondrously stunned silence. Sadly, the King startling awake
downplayed the effect. "I call this meeting of the privy council
to an end."

They stared at him listlessly as though he had muttered a
string of incoherent words.

"Now," he roared as he tugged the particles in the door for
them to open.

They rose with stark huffs of indignation and murmured
protests. Benches creaked with the shifting weight. Chair legs
scratched against the tile. The first Lord made his exit, boots
clacking extra hard on the way out, before the stampede of
petulant men followed.

King Triunn's chuckle behind him had Rau grinding his
fingers into his temples. That council session had been ten times
more stressful than Eybah's worst tantrum.

"That," Rau punctuated, "was not what I expected when
you requested my assistance."

Triunn guffawed, the deep cadence of it filling the hall. The
King's voice was more baritone yet less gravelly than Aroawn's.
If Rau turned and focused on the swarming drynn within
Triunn, he was certain Aroawn's silver form would be shaking
with mirth at his expense.

"Must the King sleep throughout?"

"Old age is fickle, old friend." Rau cringed at the moniker
Triunn used. Even after several stretches away from the
Temple, Rau never grew used to Aroawn's words coming from

306 | M . T . F o n t a i n e

Triunn's mouth. "As much as I try to level his health with my own, fighting his body's fatigue will only wear me down and leave me unable to attend the other realms."

"May Balliol recover quickly. I don't have the patience to deal with these Lords. For the life of me, I never thought grown men could squabble over the meaning of one's scowl as if it meant war."

"They are fat and bored," Triunn mumbled. "We close their borders and remove any chance of battle, so the wealthy look between themselves to brew a little excitement. This is nothing compared to the worst I have witnessed."

"Don't tell me, I don't want to know. Their troubles are not worth the time it would take to listen." Rau rose from his seat, his muscles locked and joints aching from the half day spent immobilized. He cracked his neck and sighed with relief. "Now, if you'll excuse me Archchancellor, I intend to fill my belly, enjoy some time with my daughter and give in to a few sandfalls of rest."

He made it to the main floor – which served as the Hall of Accord's stage for those presenting their case – before Aroawn called his name. It was a challenge to rein in the sigh of disappointment that caught in his throat. Gods, he was tired. He could feel the corner of his eyes drooping as he tapped the back of a hand with the palm of another within his sleeves for comfort.

"Rau," Triunn's voice repeated at his back. "I believe it's time for you to come home. I will send another-"

"No." Rau cleared his throat and turned to face a panel of chairs the privy council had occupied so that Aroawn was not presented with the disrespect of his back. It was a sign of deference, but their once friendship still had yet to recover from his forced exile from the Temple. "Send another, as is your will, but I will stay put."

"You will follow my directives."

"I have always respected that you work for the betterment of the Order and chosen to follow you for it, but I will never leave my daughter behind. She cannot leave Isyldill. As such, neither may I."

"You are weakening, old friend. I see the poor state you are in. You are not the same as you once were, and you require the support of your Brothers and Sisters to set it right."

Rau kept his features bland. True, his strength was waning, but it had little to do with his distance from other disciples and much more to do with a lack of Well's Waters in his system. Wrinkles had already begun to line the creases of his eyes and forehead. The skin on his hands was not as firm as it once had been. His joints were beginning to ache from centuries of overuse. All because he drank down only one vial of Well's Waters a quint instead of every day. That took restraint, so much so that it withered him down to the core, because one vial never seemed to be enough. The Waters called to him to drink more, and every few days after taking his dose, the nausea, fatigue and headaches kept him bedridden for a few sandturns. It would have been better to cut off the supply completely if not for Eybah. She needed him, and he planned to see her through her growth in adolescence, adulthood, and finally old age.

"The girl will be safe in the charge of another. No harm will come to her if you leave her side. Come home. Come back where you belong."

This time Rau turned to face Triunn but gazed through him to fix instead on Aroawn's ethereal figure within. "After what happened at the Temple's massacre, how can you ask such a thing of me? She has only seen her tenth stretch, and I will not leave her side until she has seen at least her twentieth."

"I am ordering you to return. She is not even yours."

The Hall of Accords filled with the slaps of Rau's hands. "With all due respect, Aroawn, she may not share my blood, but she is as much my daughter as Moira was. Send as many of my Brothers and Sisters here as you wish, but you will need to drag me away. Even then, I will endeavor to return. I will not leave her. You sent me here for a change of perspective. This is who I am now, who you made me become, and there is no changing it back."

Physical distance between Aroawn's corporal form and himself made the words flow easily. Thoughts were easy to voice when there was little chance of repercussions. Three stretches ago, Aroawn had voyaged from Telfinor to Isyldill and back to establish a mental bond with Balliol for when Triunn died. Now even as Archchancellor, he would not waste the resources of sending other Masters to retrieve Rau simply for refusing to return to the Temple. No treason had been committed, it was merely a little clash of priorities.

"Good day, Aroawn." Rau bowed his head, and when the silver flecks of drynn turned amber, he repeated the nod. "Your Majesty."

Then he left.

When the door to Rau's chambers clicked shut behind him, he took a moment to breathe through his clamoring heartbeat. The way he had spoken to Aroawn, his defiance. Gods below. He swiped a hand down his face, stunned at how adamant he had felt. When it came to Eybah, his allegiance had shifted. He was no longer a simple pawn for the Order with a single focus where everything else came second. He had done that and lost everything for it. Never again.

Humming came from the suite's common room, a dreamy lilt to it. Tension relaxed from his shoulders as a smile crept up his face. He followed the sound through the doors that joined his rooms to Eybah's shared suite. Whereas his bedchambers were minimalized and with walls lined in dark fabrics, the common room was in stark contrast with its cream-colored sofas with golden accents against plush purple rugs. The walls were painted in pastel tones to reflect different landscapes on each panel. Marble columns framed windows that lit the room with a type of ephemeral transcendence only paintings seemed to capture. The blaze in the fireplace further added to the room's comfort with its warmth, cracking wood and wisps of smoke unable to exit the chimney. Much of the room was of Eybah's design, as young as she still was. The light of his life.

Bent over her davenport, she hummed a tune while scribbling her quill on parchment. Rau watched in admiration.

"Is it a new tale?" He peeked over her shoulder at the pages.

Eybah startled and clutched her chest. "Chichu. You frightened me." She rose, kissed his cheeks and clung to his neck. "You took so long. Did they bore you to tears? Did they complain as much as they do in the halls? I bet they did."

"It was…tedious but necessary." He glanced at her attire. "Why are you still wearing that?"

Her horse riding lessons had taken place earlier in the day, yet she still wore high boots and riding breeches beneath the shortened dress skirts that reached halfway down the knee. Not a fibrous hair lay loose along her nape, all of it tied tight like a noose around the top of her head, despite the preferred half-up half-down style most young ladies wore these days. The only thing out of place was a purple Gaian rose resting over her ear, its stem buried in her hair. They did not normally grow during the Stretch of Blight except in indoor gardens. Gods, he hoped she had not stolen one. He sighed with exhaustion.

She still held the figure of a child, thank the gods. He loathed the day any gentlemen came calling or preyed on her wild nature. It made his head spin and the roof of his mouth go dry just to think of it. Finding trouble was as easy for Eybah as arrogance was to a royal.

"I like them." She patted her thighs unceremoniously. "At least my legs don't get stuck when I climb trees. And I can run and jump however I want. Dresses are so heavy and full of fluff."

"They are not the fashion of this court."

"Just because every highborn does something does not make it comfortable. Actually, I think too many enjoy torture." She rolled her eyes which made him smirk before cleaning off her quill on a cloth and capping the bottle. "I tried to wear the same shoes as Princess Katheryn, you know, the stick thin ones everyone is in love with since they *graced* her feet. I wanted to hack my feet off after one sandfall. That's how much they hurt. If that pain is what makes me a woman, I *never* want to be one."

Rau huffed a small laugh, pride warming his heart at the firm set of her posture – shoulders back, arms crossed. He had never hidden his disdain of royals or nobles from her, and now his contempt seemed to have embedded itself in her personality. She was his daughter, through and through. To the pits with blood relations. The upturn of her scarred chin exuded independence and strength while her naturally hooded eyes held constant mischief that often overpowered the innocence of her young stretches.

He frowned and grabbed her chin. The rims of her irises were far too purple compared to the amber they should be to avoid suspicion. The shape of her eyes was already unique enough in Isyldill to have raised unwelcome attention. This color was bound to bring Rau's carefully lain backstory crashing down. His breath quickened. If anyone saw, if anyone went digging, then Aroawn would have reason to come down and fetch Rau himself. What might happen to Eybah, what others might do to her…His stomach churned from the nauseating possibilities.

"You need new drops," he said with urgency.

She tore her chin away. "No, I hate them. They burn every time. I don't want them anymore."

"You have no choice." When she tried to turn from him, Rau clutched her shoulders and gave a little shake. "This is not something for you to toy with."

"I'm sick of lying. I want to be me. What's wrong with me? Why can't people accept me for me? I want to be seen."

He tore the Gaian rose from her hair, its purple similar in shade to the true Gyldrit color around her eyes. His fear turned ugly with the realization. "Is that what this is? Your attempt for everyone to see the truth?"

"Give it back." She grappled at the air, stretching to reach the flower. "It's mine. He gave it to me."

"Who?"

"I'm not telling you."

He threw the blossom down and clasped down her arms. "Whoever he is, if anyone discovers what you are, they will kill you. They will hurt you, and your life will end. For nothing. I will not let that happen. Being different is foolish. Blend in. Follow the masses. Survive."

Tears brimmed her eyes and blurred away the sight of her irises.

"I don't want to be like everyone. I'm not like them."

"You have to be," he shouted, squeezing her shoulders tighter.

His heartbeat thrummed in his ears. From fingertips to his toes, his body burned with the urge to toss every speck of drynn in the common room into a chaotic maelstrom. He already imagined her captured in chains headed for the executioner's block or in the midst of fleeing with ten arrows buried in her back or a sword buried deep in her gut. It would not happen. He would not let it. She would be safe. He would keep her safe. Not even if he had to lock her in these chambers for stretches on end. His breaths turned ragged, his muscles aching from how tense he held himself.

"Chichu. You're hurting me."

He loosened his grasp as rivulets of tears wracked the guilelessness of her features. Her shoulders trembled. Her lower lip shook. That sight turned his fear into rage, and his focus tunneled onto the rose blossom at his feet. He stomped on it, crushed it, and dug his heel into it until its secretions smeared into the rug.

"I hate you," she said scathingly between sobs. She fell to her knees to pick up the remains of petals and then scampered away from him, her soles smacking the room's flooring. Within grainfalls the door to her chambers slammed shut, hard enough for him to feel the vibrations in his ribcage. Its lock clicked secure.

That was when the shame hit, when her words broke off a shard from his heart. She did not mean it. She couldn't. He clenched a bundle of his robes in his fist over the beating organ and exhaled through the ache. He was not going to regret his words. He refused to. A parent did what they had to, to ensure the life of their child even if it meant going against their wishes. Everything he did was for her. Absolutely all of it. One day, Eybah would understand.

Twenty-eight

*T*hat evening, the Carved settled into yet another
hunting lodge. Andreiyes was appalled at how easily
these criminals used such manors as shelters. Despite the hood
placed over his head – not his problem that his captors never
checked the cloth for newly made holes – Andreiyes recognized
this lodge with its black, white-veined marble, thin columns that
lined each doorway, and portraits of royals and Lord Welnit's
family spaced in a one-by-one pattern that assumed affiliation.
It was farcical, considering the Welnits had as much royal blood
in their veins as the Bryants – even a drop was an exaggeration.

Mounted animal heads adorned the hallways, and the walls
were as dark as the floors in a dreary attempt at coziness that
suffocated instead. The furnishings were full of mite holes and
out of fashion in their gothic ornamental decorations from a
time long past. The entire place smelled stale and closed in.
Combine that with breathing through his stifling hood on which
acrid residue from his most recent stomach purge remained and
he was rightfully lightheaded.

A Carved ripped his hood off and stuffed him into a
bedchamber – unceremoniously as always – with today's
rotation of four guards, two missing their right hands and half
a forearm. Like overeager trollops, they bickered over whose

turn it was to share the bed or take the chaise lounge. Limbs weak and stomach aching from frequent heaving, Andreiyes rolled his eyes and ground his jaw at their quibbling. He settled in against the bed's footboard as he had done every night for the last bilial and waited for the dinner slop to be brought in. He had learned to keep comments to himself, shackled as he was; spoken words only brought out their hatred for him by use of fists, whereas cursing them in his thoughts was just as cathartic and far less painful. At least on the floor, the pungent waft off his guards' unwashed bodies was minimal.

With the incessant clamor of their arguing, his thoughts turned to Kaianne. His thoughts had often turned to her over the stretches. She had grown into a fine young woman with a pleasant face. Why she kept it hidden, why any of these Carved did, remained an unpleasant mystery. How he loathed being kept in the dark. The plump cheeks of her girlhood had melted to define a squared jawline and strong cheekbones – a little too concave for his taste. She really should eat more. Whereas the dark eyes that everyone sported other than the royal family tended to blend everyone together in a sea of commonality, hers stood out with the wit and confidence she projected.

It was a shame that once she helped him escape, he would have to send her to hang. A shame, not for her looks – although that would be a loss for men everywhere – but for her mind. Their conversations were stimulating and riveted his attention like few rarely could. There was an alluring quality to her voice, so unlike the regular soft seductive voices of the women at court. Her company and prickly jabs had become one of the things he looked forward to most throughout this voyage, most likely because there was nothing else to enjoy.

The comforts were appalling. The care was mediocre to lacking. And the food, his tongue would never forgive him. No one in their sane mind would call the slop they fed him food. With how much his guards grumbled each time it was served, Andreiyes gathered that this treat was reserved just for him and those keeping watch. What a delight.

He shut his eyes as the simpletons continued to argue out their sleeping arrangements. Yes, it was a pity Kaianne had to die. To have once saved her only to kill her, but she had chosen this path. He may have carved her, but that was all. The rest were her choices, and the pits could swallow him whole before he lingered on how her path may have been different if he had ignored the summons home. Gods below, is this truly what he needed to do? She was gullible to a fault, always had been, but Aethel keep him, she had done him no harm. She had even treated his injuries and kept him good company. Then again, she had murdered several guardsmen. Lords, this was muddling his mind.

A knock rapped at the floor-to-ceiling doors. The room went quiet. Another knock and while one man made to head for the door, another held him back with a sly smile.

"Help anytime would be welcome," Kaianne called from behind the door. Andreiyes sat up straighter. Never had she delivered his meals before.

The men snickered. "And what will you give us for it? A nice tumble perhaps?" a squirrely voice asked.

"Sure, we'll have a tumble…with my knee. That'll also mean you'll have my blade in your arse while licking your meal off the ground because that's where I'm bound to spill it if you don't tuck yourself back into your trousers, Marlow, and open this pitting door." And they did, with a bounce to their step.

Andreiyes' eyes widened. That did not sound like the gullible woman he had seduced earlier that morning. The one she had threatened cupped his groin while another of his captors bit into his fist to suppress the peals of laughter that shook his shoulders. There were no further disrespectful mutterings. When she stepped into the bedchamber, hands full with a tray of bowls and a lone cup, one side of her mouth curled into a vicious smirk before she schooled her features into the willful but earnest woman he had grown to know. Gods below, he had fallen for her act. How had he not seen it before?

"What is this?" Andreiyes snarled.

Kaianne rolled her eyes. "Yes, I do believe the game is up. Leave us, will you?"

His watchdogs filed out, one slapping a hand over Kaianne's shoulder in camaraderie as the two whispered a few words back and forth. When she shook her head, the Carved man glanced back at Andreiyes, dark eyes fixed on his with a certain strain to them. Whatever Kaianne muttered next had the man acquiescing and shutting the door behind him.

"He worried? You alone, here, with me."

She clucked her tongue. "Hardly anything new with our travels."

"Ah, but my injuries lessen every day. Nor did we have as much room. For entertainment."

"I am very good at repelling unwanted advances." She cocked her head. "But I'm not certain that's the type of entertainment you meant."

At his silence, she sashayed further into the room, the heels of her boots thumping along the hardwood in beat with his frustrations. There was a certain elegance to her demeanor, not as graceful as a courtier or a true Lady of the court, but her posture held a strength of mind hidden during their carriage rides. She placed the tray atop a dusty serving trolley, chose a bowl, and set it before him.

"Eat up. You're growing weaker by the day."

He huffed. "Why is that?"

Her shrug only fed his annoyance. The tendrils of steam and whiffs of herbs from the bowl taunted him, despite his foresight of the porridge's horrible taste. His stomach growled, half-starved from quints ingesting these rations.

"Drugged?"

"No."

He eyed the other bowls. "Are any of them?"

"No."

"It was all a ruse then. You were never going to sedate them."

"Not the way you hoped." She sat across from him, shoulders relaxed, armed only with her family dagger. "Truthfully, I never told you a lie. Not once. I never particularly misled you either. You saw my gender as a vulnerability, as if it gave me a simple mind, and that was your downfall. But women are much more than our smaller muscles and a sleek warmth for you to satisfy yourself with. I'd wager we can strategize and manipulate far better than any man. For example, right now I know my lack of worry is causing you disquiet."

He ignored her and hefted the bowl to his lips, hoping the churning in his gut would end.

"Do you want to know why I could never fear you?" she asked.

Andreiyes gulped the slop down despite the rising nausea. Food was nutrition, no matter how bad it tasted, and his body needed that if he hoped to overcome whatever illness currently possessed him.

"Because I have you right where I want you," she stated.

"And where is that?"

"We are a day's ride from Ollin. Tonight, my crew is going to stage a mock skirmish that will free your remaining guardsmen, yourself, and the merchants. You will then take on at least four of us, including myself, with you to Ollineol Manor as thanks for valiantly saving your life."

"This is your plan? To infiltrate Lord Welnit's manor?"

"That is only the beginning."

He snickered and shook his head. "If you think that I will aid a traitor, you have one smarting thick head."

Her responding smirk was distressing. "My plan was good before. Your presence made it better." She rested her head back on a table leg and stared up at the ceiling decor. "Did you know there's a frog called the Necrose that lives in the wraith swamps of Gyldrise whose skin is deadly to the touch? It gets better. You see, the secretion that covers its skin can be diluted in fluids. It loses much of its potency. Instead of killing quickly, it desiccates the body inside and out, *extremely* slowly."

Andreiyes' face tingled with a sudden loss of blood. His fingertips grew numb, and his breath hitched at her implications.

"Have you not wondered what that extra bitterness was at the end of every drink you gulped in the last bilial?"

"You would not."

"I did."

"But Aethel's curse…"

"You think I care about dying when I have no future in this world? I have my missions. Nothing else. I'm not the girl you once knew, so do not presume to know my limits."

Andreiyes' eyes bounced between hers, jaw dropped, choking on words that never reached her ears. She could not be this cruel. Yet desperation twisted even the best of people, and their world was filled with desperate people searching for hope within their shadowed lives.

He licked his lips. "You would not tell me this if you had not the means to change my fate."

"Very good." She patted his leg condescendingly and smirked. "There is a remedy. No cure though. So, if you wish to delay the poison's grasp on your innards, you'll need to take a special tonic every morn and eve that I alone will supply you with. You and I shall become the closest of accomplices."

So, he was not fated to die. Whatever remedy she provided, his healers could concoct their own version.

"No, I'll stop you right there. No need to deliberate on whether your royal healers will be able to replicate it. You see. I made it clear this frog exists solely in Gyldrise. No one in Isyldill has access to it, no Marked, anyhow. And the remedy, it's made from a cactus flower that grows in Nimedor's Desert of Omens. Do you grasp my meaning?"

"I am not a dullard."

"I know you're not, so don't act like one. This is how we will play it. Tonight we stage your rescue. I'll be dressed as a lad—"

"You are too thin-framed to be a lad."

"A lad," she snapped. Her irritation made his lips twitch. "We'll be peasants that have come to your aid and will escort you and your men back to Ollin with the kindness of our good hearts. Most of us will leave you there, except for me and one other."

"Why?"

"Because as the gracious royal you are, you're going to reward our valor and loyalty by taking me on as your personal manservant." The mocking lilt of her voice stoked his rage.

"I want you nowhere near my chambers."

"And that is where you have no choice if you want the tonic only I can provide you."

Several grainfalls passed while he absorbed that information. As if on cue, nausea twirled up his throat, burned through his chest and radiated up his neck. He winced from the pain, inhaled deeply and hit his skull against the bedpost. Why had the gods cursed him with misfortune and placed him at the mercy of this woman? He needed to live to bring his plans against the Order to fruition. This was yet another complication in a long string of them.

"The second Carved will serve as a liaison to my crew. He will obtain your remedies at my behest and only mine. I will communicate with him whenever I please without your interference. Do not think for a moment that eliminating me will provide you better access to it. If he doesn't hear from me, none will be delivered. If I don't hear from him, none will be given. Are we clear?"

"And how long…" Gods, it felt like his insides were being ravaged by flames. An acrid taste built in the back of his throat, "will this charade last?"

"Until my crew has the information it needs."

He massaged his chest. "What happens to me then?"

"That depends solely on you."

His nod was automatic. "And the cost to assure my survival?"

"Lodging, food, clothing and decent treatment are all I ask for. The rest I will handle on my own."

"For what? What is it you are searching for?"

"Nope. Good try, my dear Yierd, but trust is built. And the little we had has just crumbled."

He huffed in agreement, the annoyance of that moniker a marked truth to her point. "I do this, and you will give me the tonics?"

"Aye."

"How do I know you are telling the truth about the poison?"

She fetched the cup off her tray, then crouched beside him, cup extended. "You've been vomiting. Nausea, heartburn, and it feels like your arse is on fire, yes? Drink this, and in less than a sandturn the symptoms will have abated."

The murky, green-tinted liquid in the glass was taunting him with a certain sweetness that was not altogether unpleasant. His stomach took that moment to cramp. "How do I know this is not another ruse?"

"You don't. But do you want to risk it?"

He challenged her with a glare. All of the softness and innocence he had taken note of in her features had been replaced by the hardness and determination of her cunning. Gods, he had been a fool to believe her the same gullible child she had been stretches before. That girl never would have survived all this time.

Maintaining his stare, she dipped the cup to her lips. She gulped with a wince, and her throat bobbed. The volume of liquid had lowered when she held the cup out to him once more.

"See? Harmless, but not the best taste. Nothing to be done about that, unfortunately."

He took the tonic and guzzled it down. It was overly sweet to the point of revulsion and so thick that it clung to his mouth and throat like a glove. Even the slop tasted better. He wished there was some left in his bowl to rinse down the tonic as he shoved the cup back into her hands.

"Now what?" he asked, his palate still grimy.

"You wait. See how you feel shortly. Then decide if you would rather forgo my aid and die a long painful death, or if you would rather provide me the help I need." She sighed, almost ruefully if that could be believed. "We are doing this for the betterment of Taelgir, Andreiyes. This is not self-indulgence or arrogance or a misconstrued idea of grandeur. Carved are not the traitors you think we are."

"Everyone will know you are not Marked by your lack of it."

"Don't you fret about that. We're a canny lot with tricks up our sleeves." She winked at him, and he recoiled, feeling as though she was a Master pulling his strings.

"And my men? Once you get what you desire, what of their lives?"

"If they do not attack me or any Carved, they have nothing to worry about. A dead Marked is one less potential Carved. But if you gamble with their lives and babble the truth, their deaths will be solely on you. Are we clear?"

He clenched his jaw. Beguiled by a woman, worse by a Carved. The situation had completely escaped him, and now he was but a player on someone else's board. "We are."

"Good, until a few sandturns then." She made to stand, but he snatched her arm in one last attempt to regain control.

"Kaianne," he murmured. There had to be a way to turn the situation around. Something, anything. Something to appeal to her feminine sensibilities. "I would have provided for you and kept you safe if you had only just freed me."

She chuckled and gave him another patronizing pat on the leg. "Let's not start off this collaboration with lies. We both know you would have seen me hang. What can I say? Not every woman falls for your predictable charm." She picked up his cup and bowl and made for the door. "Be ready for the sound of a horn. Until later, your Highness."

Barely had she exited before two of his four watchdogs – the ones with two hands – filed back into the room, except this time their faces were uncovered. By the lean, fit stature and short cut of one man's hair, Andreiyes recognized the Carved that had held Kaianne back earlier. While the second Carved gobbled down two bowls of slop before sprawling on the bed, this one stood before Andreiyes with his arms crossed, glaring at him as though Andreiyes had done him grave harm. He held the man's gaze, unwilling to shrivel or show any measure of vulnerability, despite the chains that restrained him or his healing wrist.

This man was around his age or a couple stretches older from the firm features of his face and the maturity of his posture. A deep scar disfigured his pointed chin, but the rest of his features were rather mundane. In a crowd, Andreiyes might have had difficulty singling him out.

"I'm to be the Carved you will choose to accompany Mistress Tilhold," the man said in an equally banal voice. The only quality Andreiyes could decipher was the slight influence of Isyldill's southern brogue in his accent. The name Tilhold though did not ring any bells.

"I will not be told what to do."

The man's jaw twitched. "I'll be your worst nightmare if any harm comes to her."

"Are you lovers then?" Andreiyes could use that against her, though the concept that she would degrade herself for someone so coarse and commonplace was distasteful.

"Of course your mind would go there." The fellow sounded affronted. "What I have for her is a respect a man like you could only dream of."

Now that caught his attention. Rare was it in his world that a woman gained the respect of men of equal or higher statuses, yet Kaianne seemed to have garnered that with at least this Carved brute. How many others held the same for her? That tidbit warranted more probing. How much influence did she truly have for her age and stature? More pressing, what did she plan to do with it? It made her almost admirable in his eyes. But he spoke no more, letting the man assume he had won.

Twenty-nine

$\mathcal{A}$ ndreiyes had to hand it to the Carved, they were surprisingly good actors. From his spot tied to the bedpost, he had not seen the fake brawl that ensued, but he gods well heard it. The yells, the clang of weapons, the cheers from a successful encounter, the pounding feet through the lodge, and the cries to 'Find him. Find the princeling'. It was all a tad overdramatic for his tastes, and he rolled his eyes several times throughout.

The door to his chambers slammed open – the words 'he's here' nearly screamed in his ears. Andreiyes was quite literally dragged out, coddled in furs and surrounded by able-bodied men. He wretched himself from their grip. Plan or not, no one carried him about like a fragile youth.

That done, he followed their lead. They raced through the lodge accompanied by the witchling herself dressed in a young man's leathers. Kaianne's long hair was left to air beneath a cap, her facial features more prominent with shadowed streaks. Her face remained smooth. Despite her efforts, as he had told her, she could not be mistaken for older than a young lad.

The merchants, their apprentices and two of his guardsmen – the third had sacrificed himself in a failed attempt for his comrades to flee days before – among Carved infiltrators and unknowns raced to the horses. They hurdled over the few bodies strewn about. All the while some Carved raced away and others continued their sword fighting engagements. This was a surprisingly well conceived scheme.

Indecision warred on Kaianne's face as he caught her glancing at the fights and blood around them, but when she returned his stare, her eyes narrowed in determination. She gestured for him to move. Andreiyes snorted at her audacity but mounted his horse and rode in the middle of their small group, careful not to jostle his wrist.

No one spoke until the horses began to slow in their gallops. Dawn broke through the trees. The hard ride had his muscles aching, but there was nobody on their trail. He was free, as unfettered as his ball and chain to Kaianne allowed. With his stomach at ease for the first time in days, cold air stung pleasantly on its way into his lungs. He welcomed it. That was when one of his guardsmen stole a sword from their 'saviors' and addressed those unknown with the blade tip one by one.

"Show me your arms. All of you."

This was bound to be interesting. Andreiyes stood back, interested to see how this might play out, yet his pulse increased all the same. If she was caught, he was doomed to a slow death. When he flicked a glance Kaianne's way, she winked at him before schooling her features to play the part once more. He could not help the scoff that escaped.

"We are but tavern folk, come to our princeling's aid," one said.

"How did you come to know of his need?" the second guardsman asked as he took charge of their weapons as well.

One by one, their rescuers lifted the sleeves of their tunics to show the griffin head marks. Each had one, even Kaianne's chosen associate, despite the scar tissue. Andreiyes raised a brow but said nothing. When the guard attempted to wipe it clean or poured water on it, not a single mark smudged.

"Ol' Tavirig there did no' visit his nephew as planned three days past," said another as he tossed his head toward one merchant. "Lad thought something amiss and followed the tracks. Spied on 'em, heard of their prisoner and came to our town for aid."

"Where is this lad?"

"'Tis I," Kaianne said, her accent thicker, voice deeper. He found the sound a little forced, but passable for a young fellow attempting to make himself sound more important than he was. The answer was shocking though. These merchant travelers were not unknown in the trade of transported goods. He knew with certainty they were not Carved. The question begged: how deep did Carved influence reach?

"Can you not speak for yourself, boy? You need keepers? Show me your arm."

She thrust her arm out for the guardsman but kept her eyes averted. "I speak for m'self when given permission, sir. For good prospects, I hold me tongue in front of m'betters such as yourself."

Andreiyes held back a snicker. This young woman was more surprising at every turn, her flattery was dauntingly aimed with a purposely uncultured turn of words, but her luck was about to run out and his along with it. He rushed forward as his guard lifted her sleeve.

"Telrin, no need. I can vouch…" The words died on his lips as he caught sight of the dark outline on her arm. The griffin head was as disfigured as her scarred skin, but it was there. Even the steely golden eye, though misshappen. Impossible. That moment, the first time his blade had ever cut through skin and muscle was scarred into his memory. The sinewy yet giving texture of raw flesh, the wet sticky feel of blood, the fear of digging too far.

"What happened there?" the guard asked, his tone a blend of suspicion and curiosity.

"M'home burned, sir, while m'family slept, a few stretches past." She pulled her sleeve past her elbow. Goosebumps riddled the scarred flesh that remained bubbled and uneven compared to her Carved comrades. The damage extended far past the joint, her bare arm toned and defined for a woman, but no embarrassment crossed her features. "M'father pulled me out at his own loss."

The guard huffed but dropped her arm. That was the end of their tests, for how did one test a mark embedded so deep into the skin that the outline was perfectly aligned like an extension of the body itself? Andreiyes seized her forearm before she had time to hide it beneath her sleeve and passed his finger atop the mark. Impossible. The dark lines felt grainy. Somehow, these Carved had managed to reproduce the look and texture. His throat went dry. This was terrifying on its own. How many had already accomplished to do what Kaianne was attempting?

"How did you manage that ruse?" he hissed when he finally managed to corner her without prying ears as she closed her saddlebag. Their reprieve had been short, no more than a sandturn for the horses' benefit, lest the Carved catch up to them.

"Oh Andreiyes, you don't really think I'll tell you that, do you?" she smirked over her shoulder at him as though he was no threat at all.

"Do not turn your back on me."

She ignored him and mounted her horse. A wicked gleam burned in her eyes as she whispered, "Are you asking out of curiosity, or fear? Because neither look very good on you." The wink she gave him was just as conniving as she was because when she straightened atop her horse, her next words were loud and clear for the audience around them. "It was m'duty, yer Highness. An honor. M'sword and purpose are yers."

⁕↓⁕

They rode all day with only the briefest of breaks between jaunts until Ollin came into view. The town was unchanged from Andreiyes' visit from over five stretches before, still built with more stone and mortar than wood. But unlike Lord Welnit's manor, the mosaic of stone colors brought charm to an otherwise olden architectural style.

Announcements of their arrival trumpeted through the streets, gossip bouncing from home to home like a plague, faster than their horses could trot to Ollineol manor. Andreiyes' heart quickened with trepidation as the open manor gates came into sight and the Lord's personal guard came to greet them on horseback, dressed in the finest of chainmail and leather, polished enough to shine, and not a scratch on it.

This was it, the moment he willingly admitted two Carved into a manor, the moment he placed the value of his own life over other Marked. It was the right choice. It had to be. The realm had no one else ready to fight for it against the Order.

He eyed Kaianne, completely at ease straddling her saddle, her features entirely too feminine by his standards. What exactly was she intending to discover or do? He needed to pry it out of her and delay or thwart her efforts. He might have willingly admitted a viper into his life, but Nogo would swallow him whole before he betrayed his realm to her plotting.

"Yer Highness, welcome to Ollin." The lead guardsman slowed and bowed his head. "I am Lord Welnit's captain of the guard. Are ye well?"

"I am now that we are in your care."

"Lord Welnit has not heard from ye since yer departure. He feared ye'd been called back. This yer escort?" Welnit's man eyed those accompanying him.

"Aye, we do make quite the odd company, but with our circumstances it could not be helped." He straightened his shoulders to hide his shame at the state of himself. A bilial's worth of sweat and grime plastered his hair to his face and molded his tunic and trousers into every crease. "We came upon a swarm of Carved bandits a bilial past. My two guards, these merchants and I are all that remain our original procession. Your Lord will forgive our lack of correspondence."

"Of course. And these others?"

Andreiyes licked his lips a moment and caught Kaianne's narrowed gaze. "Our liberators." The word stuck to his tongue like that syrupy remedy of hers, and he sighed. "Lead us to Ollineol manor, if you would be so kind. My patience for a bath, fresh attire and hot food has run far too thin."

"Very well, yer Highness."

They slowly trotted down the cobblestone street, the captain and his men flanking Andreiyes while the rest took up the rear. Anticipation thrummed down his spine the closer Ollineol manor drew. True rest in a soft bed. Food, still simmering hot from the kitchens. Fresh air unbound by chains. And a true physician to care for his mangled wrist. He swept his good hand down his face, ignoring the remaining sting of his nose. Soon.

"I have a task for you, dear captain. Our coin was lost in the melee. May I count on you to relay a message to Lord Welnit?" He did not check to see if the man nodded. "I require these good tavern folk be compensated for their hard efforts on my behalf, and a room be given to the youngest there and that good man with the blank face. I intend to take on the lad as my manservant for his efforts."

"Such generosity, yer Highness."

"I simply pay my dues."

The captain may have grunted his acknowledgement, but the silence was solemn and deferential. With a few simple words, Andreiyes knew he had garnered the captain's respect, not for the title he bore but for himself, and that would carry him a long way into the future if he ever had need to call on this captain. The true currencies in life were trust, hope, and adoration. Receiving them was very fulfilling indeed.

※↓※

*O*llineol Manor was the same relic he remembered from five and a half stretches before: outsized, tired and overbearing, just like the Lord who manned it. Andreiyes' little troop had barely crossed the courtyard's threshold before he was set upon by a volley of servants – Welnik's band of spies. There was no privacy to enjoy the warmth and comfort of a bath as they scrubbed him raw, or take a much-needed nap, or visit the healer without prying ears. They followed him like tethered adornments, and it was further taxing after the last bilial's cumbersome adventure. What advantage Welnik planned to gain from this was unclear because within a sandturn, Andreiyes was ready to set on the road once more, propriety and comfort be damned.

Dinner took a turn for the worse in the dreariest sense. He almost wished he were still a Carved prisoner. Andreiyes' stomach growled at each new dish served, of meats and greens and broth and rice – his own personal torture. The aromas were enough to set his head spinning with delight after weeks of slop, but he sampled only a spoons' worth of each lest it all come back up as had become habit. He downed wine unreservedly if only to drown out Welnik's never ceasing ramblings on Ollin's prestige, and how a royal union to his daughter was bound to benefit them all.

If Andreiyes had cared to fit a word in, it would have been with difficulty. And Welnik's daughter, she was as lifeless as her father was boisterous. She spoke at most in three-word sentences, her voice almost shrill in its high pitch, and chuckled like a simpleton at every poor joke made around the table. She was decent to look at but lacked any wit whatsoever. Demure, simple and boring. Any conversation she attempted with him were led by yes or no questions followed by stifling lulls of silence.

If he were to marry, he would not avoid his bride at every turn like his father did with Pearle. No, if he was forced to share his life, he wanted a partner. Someone to rely on. Someone strong-willed and opinionated. Someone who held her head high and gave as good as she got.

Lord Welnik's daughter was not the prize for him, especially considering his eye quickly wandered to her maidservant standing tall behind the ladyling's chair. The maid threw him furtive glances through her long eyelashes. Her cheeks flushed red whenever his gaze met hers, and mischievous grins twisted her lips. Pretty little thing she was, nice firm holds to her hips. It had been too long since he had released the building tension in his body, and now that he was clean, fed and in reasonably good health, a good knobbing was in order. This maidservant was bound to be the perfect distraction from the headache that had become his life, at least for the night.

A sandturn later, the conversation at the table had not moved forward. The cheese plate and dessert were yet to be served, and Andreiyes' impatience to leave had reached a crescendo. He scrunched his napkin onto the table and stood, the chair screeching over the tile. Every head turned to stare at him.

"I am afraid the day's events have caught up with me."

"Oh, but you must stay," Lord Welnik insisted. "We have yet to consider my daughter's dowry."

"Let us leave the topic for the morrow."

Welnik's acceptance came unwillingly with a slight inclination of his head, but it was all that mattered. Decorum was upheld. Andreiyes turned to Welnik's daughter whose face brightened.

"My dear ladyling, I thank you for the stimulating company. If you would be so kind as to lend me your maidservant, I would be forever grateful. You see, in my current state, I do think it well advised to request assistance in getting situated in my chambers. Should I get turned around in your good home, of course."

Her mouth opened in a soundless retort, eyes dropped in dismay before she nodded and

gently waved the servant forward.

"May the Mistress of Dreams greet you well this eve," Andreiyes said to those assembled before he turned to his new guide. "Lead the way."

✳↓✳

*T*he maidservant slipped a key into a door's lock as Andreiyes trailed his mouth down her neck, the cloth of her bonnet tickling his cheek as the fingers of his good hand tightened against her waist. He pressed himself against her, her moans pushing him onward. He groaned when her rear rubbed his trousers just right. Yes, this would be the perfect tension relief.

She managed to jiggle the key to flick the lock, and the door opened with the force of their two bodies against it to smack against the wall and rebound. He did not care about the rugs or furnishings or warmth from the fireplace as he kicked the door shut behind him. He was simply intent on loosening the laces of her bodice as quickly as possible. Her breath quickened as his lips found the back of her neck.

"Oh, m'princeling. Yes," she muttered.

"Well, you certainly waste no time," another voice said with clear amusement.

Andreiyes jerked back from the maidservant, his heart thundering as his eyes immediately searched for the source of the intruder. Kaianne, still dressed in a tavern boy's attire, was hunched over his fireplace and staring intently at the flames.

"Oh, for pit's sake. Get out," he snarled.

The maidservant recoiled, squeaking an indignant mousy noise, and clutched her slackened bodice to her chest as she raced out the door.

"Not you," he called after her, but the door had already slammed shut.

He scraped his fingers down his face. One decent bloody night, that was all he wanted before dealing with Kaianne again, but no, the gods had to have another go at him.

"Now that you have lost me my night's entertainment, what further torture are you bound to saddle me with?"

"Oh, you poor, arrogant arse. Bored already with the Lord's daughter? That cannot be healthy for the wedding."

He ignored her sneer to locate the liquor cabinet and poured himself a measure of too-young kerchdy, the harsh grainy taste burning on the way down. Anything was good enough to drown her out.

"You are like a curse, easy enough to tack on, a pain to be rid of." He pointed a finger at her. "Like an insect. Always crawling where you are not supposed to be."

"Yes, I do seem to crawl into your life at the most inopportune times." She tossed him a vial, which he caught one-handed. "Your dose for the eve. Your curse I may be, but I will uphold my end of our bargain."

She pushed off the marble decor overhanging the fireplace and made to leave, but he caught her by the elbow and twisted her to face him. The orange glow from the fire rippled over her features with its movement. It amplified the sharp contours of her face, the pout of her lips, the crease of her eyes. So entirely feminine, so intriguingly stubborn. Her dark eyes locked with his, and it shocked him to find a softness there beneath all her fierceness and defiance.

"I hold doubts you poisoned me so thoroughly," he whispered more to himself than to her.

"Right, of course, you would." She tore her arm away. "You've been cushioned your entire life, Andreiyes, so you cannot understand the extent of what people will go through to achieve what they need. I don't actually want to hurt you, but I will if you force my hand." She patted his chest and sighed. "Let us work together. And take that tonic before your innards punish you."

The tone she took, it was a command, and yet it did not grate his nerves. Instead it was invigorating, a challenge that he wanted to parry. That confused him. He watched her slip out of his room and close the door with no sound to her steps, no creak to the door, no click of the handle. He downed the rest of his glass, wincing from the burn, his mind turning over each and every one of their conversations. What was it about her that left him so intrigued?

A knock resounded, and he smirked. Back so soon, was she?

"Yer Highness?" an unknown voice called. Andreiyes' grin twisted with frustration. Could no one leave him in peace? "There is a letter for ye. Arrived by beakwhiffer from Lityoll."

"Enter," Andreiyes said with a groan, turning to the fireplace to rest the forearm of his healing wrist against the overhang. The warmth soothed his irritation, the fire playful in its curves and flickers. He tucked the vial of green tonic into his doublet pocket. There it would remain until the morrow. He had a theory to test.

The butler entered without further hesitation, dressed in all the pompery Lord Welkin seemed to deem fashionable, from the pointed boots to the wig curled in ringlets. The man, though older, never met his eyes and only extended toward him a serving tray with a letter on top. As Andreiyes grabbed the letter, his mind wandered for an excuse to minimize his stay on this farcical bride hunt without offending Lord Welnit.

Politics were a game of flattery and leverage – a delicate balance of pleasing to be pleased, but one could not negotiate without a level of deference. He needed more kingsmen to train. As much as Andreiyes had no interest in Lord Welnit's daughter, he certainly wanted his men.

Andreiyes yawned and pulled at the corner of an eye with a palm. The hour was late, and his mind was weary and overworked with stress. He could not think in these conditions. He set the letter down amongst the bottles within the liquor cabinet, barely paying notice to the manservant's exit.

Whatever the letter said could wait. The glorious, cushioned four-poster bed in his personal chambers called his name and took precedence. Besides, nothing urgent ever came by beakwhiffer this far south from the castle. With a last swig of another pour of underripe liquor, he ignored the twinge in his abdomen and undressed.

Thirty

Kaianne steeled herself with a deep inhale. Her hand pushed down the balcony's door handle to Andreiyes' chambers. There was a new development – a blistering twister of a dilemma – but he needed to know sooner rather than later. Pits, if he was anything like her, the news was going to pommel him. No one deserved to hear these sorts of tidings. She scrunched her eyes and mouth shut and pulled open the door.

Earlier, he had refused her admittance to his chambers when she had politely knocked, and his suite's door had been locked. That had been a simple hindrance. If the princeling was not going to be civil, she had to enter by less savory means, which had involved sneaking into his Lordship's study and scaling down from one balcony arch to the next. Thank the Lords for the wall climbing challenges in Credence. She had never been the best of cragswomen, but it had been instructive.

The first thing that hit her once in his sitting room was the stench – acrid and pungent – which did not fit with the opulent dark marble and imperiously ornate accents. Next was the chill, the fire in the hearth on its final sputters. And last it was the loud belching preceding wet heaves that came from the doorway to her right.

"Idiot," she muttered. Her legs carried her in that direction as she massaged her temples. Andreiyes was on his knees, hunched over his chamberpot. "You were supposed to take the forsaken tonic. I'm not wasting it on you for nothing."

"I would have no need…" He heaved again, then tapped a cloth to his lips and rested his head against the wall. He looked so forlorn and wretched, legs sprawled carelessly on the hardwood floor at his bedside and head lolling to one side. "For your bloody tonic, if you had not poisoned me."

"And what sort of fun would that be for me?" She crouched in front of him and dragged the cloth over his stubbled chin where a drop remained. "You reek, Yierd."

"Glad to know my misfortune amuses you."

"Always." She forced a smirk and dug out the morning's dose from within her coat. One stashed vial was not going to make or break her plan if he kept it. "Now take it you fool, or are we not through with these tests? Do I need to force feed this rubbish down your throat every morn and eve?"

He snorted before downing the vial in one gulp. "So comforting to know you care."

Lords, he was exasperating. "Is it so hard to believe that perhaps I take no pleasure in your pain?" Kaianne dropped her head with a sigh and stood. "I don't have to be your enemy. We could get along. Work together. We almost did once, those days before you left me."

"You still hold *that* against me. And I shall always hold *this* against you."

"Tell me, was there ever a chance that you would have let me and the Carved crew go free, or even remotely accepted our plan?" His silence said it all and yet nothing. It stretched the chasm between them, between Carved and Marked. "Then you know I did what I had to."

"Much as I appreciate the questioning of my morals and your custom delivery, why are you here? In my chambers. The door is…was locked."

"A simple door could never keep me out." Kaianne pinched a smile as she straightened her spine, hoping an edge of humor might lessen the blow. There was no easy way to deliver such news. Hunched and weak as he was, this was bound to only hurt him further. "Listen, you need to return to Castle Ravensten. Now."

His laugh was wry. "You seem to forget I am on tour for a bride. This was only my first option, and I will not be hastening whatever your plans are."

"No, Andreiyes. You don't understand. You can choose to continue your search. I won't stop you, and a few more cycles won't change anything for me. This is for your sake. I know how it feels to wish for one last moment with family." Her vision was turning glassy. "If you don't steer your horse toward Lityoll today, it will be too late. It might already be. Trust me on this or you will forever regret it."

"What in the Aethel's good name are you...the letter."

He shoved her aside to scramble to his feet, his legs shaky beneath his weight. He burst into his sitting chamber like a man possessed, headed for the liquor cabinet. The bottles clinked as he moved them about with one hand.

"I doubt drinking is the solution." She peered around his shoulder.

Crystal tumblers refracted light in the middle of the cabinet while bottles of liquor lined the sides, but it was not a bottle he removed from within. It was an envelope with an unbroken seal of Royal House Lenierz stamped into the wax.

With an elbow on the envelope, he cracked the seal with his good hand and tore the letter free. His eyes swam across the vellum, the crease in his brow deepening. Kaianne wrapped her arms around her waist, lost between the chill of the room and the heart wrenching cold that came from knowing the pain he was going through.

The further down the page his gaze skimmed, the larger his eyes widened. His jaw was clenched as he flipped the letter around, clearly distraught by the back's blankness. He read the letter once more. With a rumbling groan, he tossed the parchment away then dug his fingers into his cheeks. The letter floated down to the hardwood like a taunt.

"Andy, I know what you must be feeling." She pressed a hand to his shoulder to offer support. He jerked it off.

"You did this," he accused. He shoved her away, and she tumbled backward, tripping over a footstool onto her backside. Hate and hurt flared in his eyes. "How weaselly and conniving can you be? She is with child."

"I didn't do anything." She rubbed her backside. "Lords, you can be a dimwitted arse,"

That was apparently the worst thing to say, because he was quickly swiping his hands across the top of the liquor cabinet, the bottle and tumblers left there smashing to the ground. Next, it was a sweeping across the chimney overhang where small marble and porcelain statuettes and figurines crashed into the ground in large chunks. One nicked her in the calf, and that forced her into action.

"Andreiyes, stop. This isn't helping anything." She tried to reach his shoulders to shake some sense into that primitive male brain of his, but he gripped her throat with intent, the sudden pressure cutting off her airway. Surprise froze her. A few moments, that was all she allowed. Then she was kneeing him in the groin and watching him crumble to his knees before her, coughing and red in the face.

"Don't ever do that again," she hissed. For good measure, she unsheathed her dagger. She crouched to his level, ignoring the sting in her calf and the sticky feel of bloody. "I would never hurt a pregnant woman. Especially because I can never have that myself."

His jaw still ticking, his gaze swimming over the room, the broken mess, the furniture, anywhere but her, but he sat back on his calves. She tried not to take offense.

"I have no idea what has even happened to her. I swear. Whatever it is, I have no blame in it."

"Then how can you know this?"

"I don't. Not the how, at least. Only what will happen." Gods below, this conversation required strong alcohol. It meant divulging information the princeling might not believe while exposing Carved assets. She gulped directly from the nearest intact bottle and winced as it scorched her throat.

"Bloody pits and all that's sacred. Lords, that's terrible." She gulped down another draught in the hopes it got better after the first sip and cringed again. "Are you rational enough now? Can we try to trust each other?"

No, probably not, but this was going to be a long partnership between them, lasting however long it took until she discovered a way to sever the connection between borders, the Stewards' repression on the people with gifts and stop the massacres of Carved and Flawed alike. Someone had to take the first step. Right now, it had to be her.

When he didn't answer, she sighed – her eyes never leaving his – and bent to retrieve the parchment from the floor. When her gaze finally tore from his to the calligraphed words on the vellum, her throat bobbed on the swallow.

27th day of the Adec cycle, Stretch 952

An,

I worry for you. Your captain of the guard says there has been no word for over two quints. If you were not so stubborn, I might have worried over your silence earlier, yet it seems to be a trait we both carry so I will not hold it against you. I only hope your ire over the matter will lessen quite quickly.

I write the following with the knowledge you will be preening over my confession. Go well on ahead and gloat like I know you care to. I give my full permission while all the same covertly rolling my eyes at you, brother dearest.

The truth of the matter is I may have been overzealous in my wishes to see you well-matched. There, I admit it. I only desired the very best for you as your older sister and dearest friend, but now I need you to return.

In my greatest time of need, I require your unwavering support and the close bond we share. You see, I seem to have gone and contracted a severe case of erysolio.

As you have surely already heard, Father fell ill shortly after the Bryants took their leave and only as of yesterday he remained quarantined. He has recovered, gods bless him, but unfortunately the healers do not feel as optimistic toward my health, which as of this morning seems to have taken a turn for the worse.

Do not be angry at others for this late news. It was by my decision that you remain uninformed lest it tear you from your duties, but now I beg you overlook them and come to my aid. Selfish, I know, but it is my privilege as princess, do you not think? Please, I need you at my bedside to help pull me through, for me and for your niece or nephew. You know how I hate to beg.

I pray to the gods this letter finds you this eve in good spirits and good health.

All my love, brother dearest,
Your sister,
Ed

Her eyes closed. She knew the words for what they were. Last words from a loved one to another, whether Edmira realized it or not. It was such a precious thing that Andreiyes could not afford to lose, something Kaianne herself wished she had to fall back on in dark moments. With this letter, he carried her voice and spirit for stretches to come.

For a grainfall, she let herself envy him. The legacy of her family relied on a dagger that none of her loved ones had taught her to use. One with which she had made still unfulfilled promises on their grave. How lucky he was to have a final piece of Edmira, even if he could not see it yet. She folded it preciously and slipped it into her coat pocket. For his own good. So he would not do something foolish such as feed it to the fire or leave it behind in his anger and grief.

"You need to go home, Andy."

"Do not call me that."

She licked her lips and pressed on. "In a cycle's time, Edmira will no longer be your father's heir. You will."

"No." He slammed a bottle atop the cabinet. "No. You cannot know that."

"I do, because it has been seen by an Augur." His confusion was palpable. "Before the Flawed Edict, some family members of murdered Flawed made themselves Carved. A few developed talents when they reached drynn maturity. One of those is the ability to visualize scenes of the future. We have a person like that in our crew. The talent is arbitrary in what she sees, but she sent word of this."

"And you shared this with me." Not a question, it was a statement filled with resentment.

Kaianne nodded.

"No. Edmira will be fine," he whispered, voice broken and unsure.

Isane's visions had been wrong before: about decisions made, about the chosen outcome when there were multiple options, but never about a person's fate. Edmira's fate and that of her unborn child were written. Only a Mender could save her from the future erysolio reserved for her, but Isane's missive made it seem Edmira's future was set.

Credence had a Mender but only one, and his talent was meager. It took him days to recover from healing mortal wounds, so he stayed within the city's caves as often as possible. Even if he had wanted to provide aid to a royal, the travel distance was too far. He would never make it in time to save Edmira or her child.

"Could the Order not send a Mender to cure her?"

His laugh was cold and dry. It died as quickly as it came with a shake of his head. "The Stewards…"

Kaianne debated what he needed: a squeeze of a hand, a hug, a silent companion? In the end, she settled for a pat to his shoulder that felt as awkward to her as his flinch made it seem for him. Silence consumed them, the right words escaping her. "For what it's worth–"

He shrugged off her hand. "Get out. Leave."

"I'm sorry. Truly."

"I cannot deal with you right now." He stared at the wall. "Please leave. Please."

It was the supplication that did her in, the chink in his armor. He had been captured, injured, manipulated and poisoned, yet not once had he sounded as broken as he did now. She left the same way she had come, but not before hearing the creak of a door and the princeling's request to the guards at his door to ready his entourage and the horses.

Thirty-one

*I*t was a minimum of twenty-three days of hard travel between Ollin and Lityoll, four quints save a day before Andreiyes could reach Castle Ravensten and see to Edmira's good health for himself. She would recover. She had to, strong headed and stubborn as she was. Not even Arkov had kept her spirits down for long. Erysolio stood no chance. She was the strongest of the two of them, about to be a mother for pit's sake, and he...he was never meant to rule.

Gods below, if it fell to him, if ever the Order took control of his mind, the entirety of what he had built and developed would all be for naught. This was simply another manipulation on Kaianne's part, a tactic in her grand scheme. It had to be. It absolutely was.

They took to the road by midday with a troop of fifteen guardsmen and several welcomed servants including his two original men, Kaianne in her squire attire, and her boorish Carved companion named Yannic. Lord Welnit's protests against Andreiyes had fallen on deaf ears – a Lord without empathy for his future sovereign's health was not one Andreiyes was willing to stomach for any longer.

For an entire bilial on the return trip, Andreiyes avoided any communication with Kaianne despite the glances she threw at him every so often. He did not care for her placid words, and he certainly did not want a single grain of her pity. She handed him his tonic morning and evening, but he cut off every attempt at an exchange between them. At first she had taken the dismissals with grace which had soon turned to muttered curses, then insults and as of the eve before, a downpour from a canteen atop his head in the frigid weather.

"What was said in Ollin was no game," she had told him as his hair dripped water down his tunic. "Think of it what you like, but stop playing the arse. Petulant men are too low on my bar for more effort than I've already exhausted on you."

He watched her storm off to her tent with a frown and had rubbed a dull itch building in his chest. Fortunately for her, this act was committed in the privacy of his tent, and as much as he loathed not punishing her for it, she held his life in her hands. Not once had his stomach revolted since he had adhered to taking the routine remedies. That did not mean he owed her anything.

Unfortunately, those fifteen days of silence did not abate a curiosity their last discussion had sparked. There were drynn talented among the Carved, if Kaianne was to be believed. She spoke of Augurs and Menders as if they were commonplace. How many were Carved? How many of Isyldill's talented had turned to the Carved over the Order? Most importantly, were there drynn talented Marked waiting to be discovered? His thoughts bounced between those questions for sandturns on end, haunting his sleep like the brightness of the two moons above that lit the woods as luminously as cloudy day tapered of color.

The Maiesta moon was halfway full and glowing pure white. It announced the approaching middle of the Cusp cycle. In comparison, the Persefin moon on the other side of the night sky was at its roundest, its golden glow mesmerizing – a clear sign that the stretch was nearing its end. In the next half cycle, the Stretch of Rebirth was going to replace the Blight, but no rebirth going to tame the scars from this stretch if Kaianne's rumors were true.

It was on the sixteenth day that his curiosity bested him. He signaled his men ahead, but pulled back until his horse's gait matched Kaianne's and they were trekking the path side by side. "Is it true then? There are Carved drynn-talented?"

"Oh, so you're speaking to me now?"

He gritted his jaw. "Obviously."

"And I should grace you with an answer because…"

The fact that she believed herself free of wrongdoing only irked him further. But damn her, he wanted an answer. He needed to know if there was such a possibility, if such a thing existed for Marked as well. It could change everything. He sucked his pride in and chewed out words that had eaten at him since they had left Ollin. "I should not have acted as I did that last morning in Ollin."

Her head snapped in his direction, a knit in her brows. "No, you shouldn't have."

Her stern eyes glared into his soul. He returned it with one of his own, willing her to accept his peace offering.

"Yes," she finally said. "There are talented, along with many more untalented."

"Kay," Yannic growled between his teeth from the horse walking behind them.

Kaianne waved his warning off. "What's it to you?"

"Could they…are they talented enough to challenge a Master?"

She cocked her head at him, her lips teasing into a smirk. "Why does a royal wish to challenge a Master?"

That response had him bristling and clenching his jaw. He urged his horse forward just in time to hear her chuckle. Why he had thought it possible to get an honest answer from her was beyond him.

⁜

It was over the following three days that Andreiyes wondered what benefit lying about his sister's health gave to Kaianne and the Carved. He avoided sending a beakwhiffer for news to the castle – though it squawked unpleasantly in its cage during the entire day. He had informed Jereown and Father of his hasty return the day of their departure from Ollin. He had included a note to Edmira for reassurance: 'Recover promptly. Stay safe. Much love, An'. He was certain that by the time he arrived, his family was all bound to have a laugh at him over his nonsensical worries.

It was whatever Kaianne hoped to gain from announcing Edmira's supposed impending death that troubled him. Who would have thought he would ever have to worry about little Ynnea's behavior? If only Grayson could see them now. He would laugh himself raw over it.

Andreiyes' thoughts were so preoccupied by the end of their eighteenth day of travel that he did not hear the pounding approach of horses and the drivel of extra voices until a band of five – one with flaming red hair – had crested the horizon of trees on a narrow trail that intersected the Western Highland Road. His entourage unsheathed their blades despite the griffin insignia painted on the cuirasses of those approaching. Who was to say that the Carved were not shrewd enough to approach wearing the realms' colors? Especially now that he had glimpsed their ingenuity with that false mark on Kaianne and Yannic's arms. He still needed to gather how they had accomplished such a feat.

"Your Highness," an intruder called out.

Nogo's wrath, he recognized that grating voice. He stifled a wince and held up his hand as a signal to his men that there was no danger. Well, at least no risk of bodily harm. His eyes immediately searched out Kaianne as he surveyed the team at his back. By the tick in her jaw, it seemed she too had recognized the voice's owner. Her horse's reins were twisted in her tight grip. Her posture was painfully straight and alert. Willik of House Bryant was obviously a weakness of hers. One he could manipulate, but gods below it was Willik. Andreiyes could hardly tolerate him on the best of days.

Willik's hair was a marked contrast against the snow patched ground and trees. It was detectable from hundreds of paces away. The fact he did nothing to limit its visibility spoke volumes of his arrogance and ignorance. In fact, he sported it like a badge of honor – slicked back with the oiled strands bobbing in the air with each gait of his horse, his beard trimmed to mirror a spear's edge – as though it were an identifiable marker of a man to be feared. Andreiyes cracked his jaw with annoyance as he urged his horse onward with no intention of halting to greet the man with more than a passing nod.

"Greetings, princeling." Willik wormed his horse beside Andreiyes'.

Andreiyes in turn provided no response. He was far too busy wrangling in the need to sneeze from the overabundance of cinnamon in the lordling's cologne.

"So fortunate for us to join you on your return."

Andreiyes restrained himself from rolling his eyes. More than likely the lordling had planned this. His motives were transparent. Most certainly Lord Bryant had gotten a whiff of his early return and planned for this ambushed escort. Lord Pascual was all too aware of the tension that had long festered between them. It was something Andreiyes held no intent to reconcile, and certainly not with a flippant arse such as Willik.

"I confess my surprise at your early return," Willik continued. The man did love to hear himself talk. "No ladylings to your taste in the South? Ah, it's not too astonishing if they are all as undisciplined and wanton as Sertrios' daughter. The shame. Did you know he only managed to marry her off to a merchant? Bah, Lorelai Sertrios, daughter of the great Southern Commander, demoted to peasantry. Bryants are far better matches. Istne married well. Now, Teisha is of marrying age."

Willik nudged Andreiyes' elbow with his own as though they could possibly have that sort of camaraderie. He leveled Willik with a glare that at least had the lordling clearing his throat.

"I seem to recall you were matched with a Lyssandre." Andreiyes' tone urged the man to have the decency to cut off his gabber. A lost hope.

"And the gods intervened. Further proof of Bryant worth. I know Teisha will make a fantastic match for you, Andreiyes." Again, with the familiarity. It had Andreiyes grinding his teeth. "Very pleasant on the eyes, soft spoken and obedient. You could not do better."

"I am certain whomever *I* choose will be *my* best match."
Aethel, give him strength against this dunce. Nogo was certainly
egging him on to give this lordling a good beating.

"None would be more supportive as your queen than
Teisha."

Andreiyes started as though he had been dealt a physical
blow. "What did you just say?"

"You are to be heir soon. Congratulations."

"*Congratulations…*" he repeated in a whisper. His gulp
reverberated in his ears. It was a poor coincidence. It had to be.
"I fear you have been misinformed, lordling." His voice
sounded shaky, even to him.

"You've not heard?" There was a mischievous glint to
Willik's gaze, almost a giddiness to it that made Andreiyes'
stomach churn. "The princess lost the child two days past, and
her fever has worsened since. I wager by the time we reach
Lityoll, you will be the heir."

There was a sandfall of shock before Andreiyes reacted to
the sickening burning weight that was building in his limbs and
head. He clutched Willik by his beard and tugged. It forced the
lordling to lose his balance and tumble from his horse into a
heap of a man, limbs over his head. All around them, guffaws
of laughter rose as the entire entourage paused to watch Willik's
struggles to right himself.

"Real men do not fall so easily or take pride in the misery of
others." Andreiyes glared down at the poor excuse for a noble.
"If I am to be heir, take this to heart. A Bryant will never be
part of royalty, and you will not follow in your Lord father's
legacy as Northern Commander."

"You cannot do that."

"Why is that, lordling?" Andreiyes kept his words terse, loud
enough for Willik to hear but soft enough they were drowned
by the peals of laughter around them. There was satisfaction in
watching Willik's pale skin draining further of color. "What
power do you think you hold? Not even your men come to your
aid against me."

Willik had barely saddled back onto his horse with a
satisfying groan of pain before Andreiyes bellowed, "We ride."

He kicked his horse into a quick canter. The quicker they returned to the castle, the sooner the growing twist in his gut could unravel. Edmira loved her unborn child. He had seen it in every caress she made to her belly, in every lullaby sung, every word whispered to the child. He had seen the worry in her eyes when she had spoken of the Order maintaining their control on royals. If the child had passed on, he feared the grief that would follow. He dreaded the truth behind Kaianne's prediction and the taunt of Willik's words. He needed to be there for her.

⁜↓⁜

*T*hey rode through the day, the night and the morrow until the horses became unruly and their pace slowed despite their riders' demands. Other than short breaks for water and food, there had been no true rest for any of them. Andreiyes had pointedly ignored everyone's grumbling and frustration up until that moment, and yet the moment his belly was filled and his head hit the cushion of his bedroll within his tent, sleep overtook him.

It was a haunted sleep that skipped between his best memories to his worst, a scorned blend of reveries and fits of heartache. He woke in a pool of sweat, his heart thumping in his ears, his fingers tingling with a ghostly sensation. Sleep would not find him again that night – he refused to close his eyes for fear it would – as he counted the beams and lines that held up his tent. The nightmare of Edmira's cold flesh against his own as he dragged her body into a grave near the desecrated Lyssandre ash grave replayed over and over in his mind. Skulls on five skeletons had creaked as they turned to watch him pass, and it racked a chill down his spine to remember their eyeless sockets and snapping jaws.

A crack sounded outside his tent, followed by the crunch of snow in slow measured steps. Each one grew more distant amongst the snores reigning in the camp and the hooting owls. Four guardsmen were posted as sentries to roam the outskirts of the camp in two rotation watches, but as Andreiyes' tent was erected dead center of their camp, they would have no reason to come near enough for him to hear. The rising hour was still a few sandturns away considering the moonslight shining through the trees and the flaps of his tent. His curiosity was officially piqued, and it loosened the nightmare's hold on his mind.

Boots laced, trousers fastened and his fur coat wrapped around his bare shoulders, he slipped out of his tent into the crisp pine-freshened air and hurried in the direction he had heard the footsteps go. Twenty paces later, he halted at the sight of a shadow stalled before the flaps of Willik's tent. It did not have Willik's build, but the person's identity was impossible to tell beneath the cover of their hooded cloak. There was clear hesitation in this person's posture, gloved fingers flexing and closing.

In one swift motion, the hooded figure unsheathed a dagger. It gleamed in a streak of moonslight, the detail on the blade and golden cross guards immediately recognizable. Oh, Andreiyes certainly would not miss the lordling, but how likely was it for her not to get caught in such a small entourage with guards on patrol? Kaianne took a small step forward and shook out her shoulders, the cloak rippling.

"Kay," he whispered. Her flinch and whirl of her head only confirmed his guess. Andreiyes stepped from the shadows.

"What do you want?" she hissed between her teeth.

"You do not have it in you." He gestured toward her weapon.

"You don't know what I'm capable of."

The sound of crisping leather pulled his gaze down to her dagger.

"You misunderstand. I know you are a murderous little thing, but cold-blooded, I doubt that."

"There's more than enough justification for his death." She made to invade Willik's tent, but Andreiyes clamped a hand on her wrist and tugged her against him into a shadowed nook between a copse of trees.

"Do not be foolish."

"Let me go," she growled. Any louder and she might rouse the camp, but with the way she writhed against him he was hard pressed to care. Her dagger tip pressed to his throat, and he stilled. "Let go, now."

"For you to muster up the courage to murder a defenseless pit of a man? I watched your hesitation. You know there is no honor in this."

"Where was honor when my family was slaughtered? Where was his honor when he left my brother to scream and burn to death? Or when he spat in my face as I lay dying, telling me it was my place? He deserves no better than a faceless death."

With two fingers under her chin, he pried her face upward. "What then? How quickly do you think you can run before my men catch you with blood on your hands? After all the trouble you went through to infiltrate my ranks. You would give that up so easily?" Her dark eyes were piercing in contrast to the whites of her eyes, and it stirred something in him. Something uncomfortable. He gulped and released her chin before glancing over her shoulders at the camp's checkered shapes in the lattice of moonlight. "Who would provide my tonic then?"

"That's what this is about?" She shoved him away. "You called Willik here as penance for my misdeeds against you. Are you really so petty?"

"I would never willingly spend a lick of time with that reeking heap of turd. Nor would I wish him on my worst foe. You want his death? I will gladly look the other way, but not here. Not now."

She huffed with aggravation and rolled her bottom lip with her teeth. In the cold air, their breaths mingled in puffs of fog that fanned each other's cheeks. His eyes latched onto the moisture glistening off her bottom lip as he imagined the feel of her lips on his, the graze of her teeth, the flick of her tongue. What was wrong with him? She must have gleaned the direction of his thoughts because a wicked smirk was growing on her face.

"I need you to live because I cannot afford to die yet."

"Yet?" When had her voice become so sultry?

"I have goals to accomplish. I need those tonics." He bent his head down, her lips only a finger-width from his own.

"Yes, the tonics. Because it would be a mistake for you to care about my well-being otherwise. Am I right, your Highness?" Her whispered words had him clearing his throat.

He stepped back, but she followed. "That is what it means to use another merely for your own benefit."

"I agree. We all use each other to obtain what we desire. That's all relationships are. A means for closeness, for business, for…intimacy." She leaned in. Andreiyes stood at his full height, yet when she bobbed onto the tips of her toes, there was little to no distance remaining between them. When her mouth brushed against his chin and his bottom lip, his breath quickened, and his blood rushed downward. "Do you fear intimacy, Andy?"

The sound of her murmurings was so alluring, it made all the rest disappear. He wanted to close the distance between them. This strong, resourceful woman before him who took charge in unforeseen circumstances. This woman who did not shy or soften to his demands. Who gave as good as she got and preened over it. Whose fervor smelt of nightfall and thrills. He was due for a good tumble. After all, she had interrupted his last attempt at Ollineol Manor.

"Perchance you're right," she continued. "Perchance this isn't the eve to enjoy Willik's death with other such delectable offerings available."

He forced her back against the nearest trunk, one hand pressed against the flaky bark beside her head, the fingers of his bandaged hand digging into the clothing over her hip. "I am not the offering here, woman." To emphasize his point, he pressed his hard body against hers to give her a feel of all of him. The hitch in her breath was exactly what he was looking for.

"But you forget, I'm not a woman here."

Andreiyes stilled as reality crashed down. This was a troop of solely men. A woman's moans in the throes of a romp were bound to arouse unwanted attention. And she was an enemy. A Carved for Aethel's sake. One that had poisoned him. One that had manipulated him and continued to do so. What in the blazes had he been thinking? He pushed away from her, groaned at the sudden loss of warmth and ran his good hand through his hair.

"Do not go near Willik tonight."

"Are you serious?" She hissed between her teeth. Gone was the sensuous edge to her words, but he refused to be further beguiled by the supposed confusion, downturning her features into anger. "You unbelievable pompous arrogant numbskull. I may be your new shadow, but never deign to think I am yours to command." Then she was stomping away.

And that was the problem. This woman danced to her own tune. Carved or not, by his hand or her own, her agenda would never match his own.

Thirty-two

*L*ityoll was in full preparation for the Festival of Life's change of season celebration when Kaianne, the rest of the princeling's entourage and Pyre-cursed Willik reached the city. Ten days from then would mark the beginning of the two hundred thirty-eighth Stretch of Rebirth, the nine-hundred fifty-third stretch since Aethel and Gaia won the rights to terraform and settle Taelgir after Schlenkra.

Banners in pastel colors spanned from one lamppost to another. Posters were glued to the walls announcing the festivities and events to come. Fresh flowers and streamers decorated windowsills. They twirled in the chilled wind promising fun and excitement, yet the city lacked any of the joviality the decorations promised.

Few people wandered the streets, but the reek of the place still matched her memories. The tunes sung by passing bards were morose and tinged with grief. What Kaianne missed most was the promise of children's laughter.

Children had no place among the Carved. As recently as half a stretch earlier, another dear friend with a belly on the verge of rounding and her spouse had taken their leave from Credence in the hopes of starting a family. At their goodbyes, there had been unfiltered hope and happiness on her friend's face, despite the dangers she and her spouse would face on their own with a Marked child. What was it about children that sparked such a fervent desire? Long ago, she had vowed never to have children. Now with the option forever stolen from her, Kaianne could not help but wonder. This had been her chance to experience their joy and to understand the pull others felt, but there was very little of it.

The entire city seemed blanketed in a dreary layer of loss despite the vibrant colors on the ramshackle buildings. Kaianne caught sight of the spread-winged griffin banner flying at half-mast atop the crenellation of Castle Ravensten's two watchtowers. A black flag clung to it. With disquiet, she pressed a hand to her mouth. The signal was clear. A member of the Royal House was dead. Lords, they were too late.

Her gaze found Andreiyes' back as their group trotted through Lityoll's streets. This was going to be the final nail in the coffin after the rumors that had followed them through villages the last several days. There was nothing in his posture to indicate he had yet noticed, but then again, perhaps he was masking his grief.

They had not spoken since the night of their almost-tryst. If it weren't for the exchanges of tonics and for his constant need of a manservant, they might have avoided each other completely: him for mistrust, her because he was supposed to be a means to an end. Yet, somewhere along the line she had grown fond of his company and their banter, had found his brooding arrogant nature almost charming, and looked forward to the battle of wills each side presented. That was problematic. Distracting. Awkward.

Too often in the last quint, she had considered having Yannic deliver the tonics, but that would leave precedence for Andreiyes to bypass her altogether. She would not be shut out. It didn't help that as they neared Lityoll, he became more distant. And today those Gaia forsaken flags were going to darken their tenuous relationship further. He had been there in the beginning of her grief stretches ago. It was only natural for her to want to return the favor. At least, that's what she told herself.

"Your Highness," she called, urging her horse forward to keep up with his. "The banner..."

It took a long while for his head to lift enough to catch sight of it as though he knew what to expect and was dreading it. His head fell to his chest and shook. His shoulders slumped. There was no fight in his posture, no denial left in him after twenty-three days on the road.

"I'm sorry." His sorrow ridden eyes met hers as she spoke, all traces of anger and disbelief gone. Her heart ached at the pain she saw there, at the thousands of words left unspoken to a sibling, never to be shared. "For what it's worth, whenever you need someone to talk to, I'll keep you company."

He nodded, his gaze now fixed ahead on the march up the butte's switchback road to Castle Ravensten. "This will be my first return to the castle without her to greet me. I already dread her absence."

He sounded defeated, but the grief which was so obvious a few grainfalls before cleared away. His features hardened to indifference. His posture straightened and solidified. He held his head high like the heir to the throne he now was, his anguish buried deep, no visible weakness for others to extort. It made him appear strong, but Kaianne knew the weight of it. How it ate at the mind, how the body bore the brunt of the denial and was desiccated from inside out, how it burrowed its way into nightmares that haunted the soul.

With all Andreiyes' entourage around and the townspeople watching them pass, Kaianne — disguised as a young lad — did not dare lay a hand on the princeling, but her foot in the stirrup knocked his, then grazed it back forth as a small act of comfort.

"We are all but passing shadows in the grand forest of life, searching for a light to carry us through. Hide your darkness from everyone you need to, Andy, but I will pry it out of you to force you to find your light once more. We might not agree on much, but you have a bright soul. Edmira wouldn't want you to bury it."

His jaw clenched. "If I recall, that was never your purpose here."

"It doesn't have to be for me to help someone in need."

"There is no *need*." He urged his horse into a canter, and Kaianne coughed out the dust from his wake.

"Always an arse," she muttered between dry coughs. Most of the entourage sped past her, only Yannic remaining behind, patting her back.

"Might be healthy for our sakes if you try not to anger the royal so much, no?"

"Where's the fun in that?" She forced a grin before nudging her horse to catch up.

*K*aianne's memories of the castle were of grand rooms, ladies and their lords in fine dresses, and elegant banquets. Childhood visits to Castle Ravensten were moments to explore the adult world and be seen by others. Now, the stone walls and excessive fripperies were stifling in their stark reminder of the difference between the nobles and the poor. It was a world apart with customs in decorum and staidness that made her want to roll her eyes and shudder.

Andreiyes' youngest sister welcomed him home, dressed in amber and black from her slippers all the way to her lace veil – Isyldill's colors of mourning to match the shade bestowed upon the Royal House by their godly ancestors. Katheryn was a young woman now, yet she appeared more frail than ever. Her arms were no wider than ice picks, and her waist was the width of Kaianne's thigh. The princess' eyes stayed lowered, even when Andreiyes' much larger form consumed her in an embrace. If ever the title of heir passed to her, the crown would eat her alive.

Since Andreiyes had made it quite clear to their entourage that Kaianne's male persona was to be his manservant, when the others were excused, she patiently lingered through the familial embrace. Waiting on Andreiyes was a breath of fresh air after the last eight days suffocating in Willik's presence.

It was a betrayal to her family's memory to allow his heart to keep beating. It would have been so easy to slit his throat that first night or any others since, but what Andreiyes had said rang true. Death had been calling his name for six stretches. A few more days were not about to change his fate.

Instead, she people-watched and analyzed the scene before her. She noted how delicately Andreiyes treated Katheryn, as though she might wilt at the slightest improper word. Someone like her required structure and balance, which seemed to have toppled with Edmira's passing and left her teetering on the edge of a cliff. Andreiyes cupped her face, the grief previously on his features set aside, and whispered words of hope and encouragement. It was sweet, gentle and loving – a side of the princeling Kaianne had never seen. She couldn't help the soft smile that crept up her face.

Once the siblings went their separate ways, it was as though the exchange had never happened. Somber and solemn Andreiyes returned as he weaved through the corridors and hallways. He gave only brief nods to those who greeted him. When he entered his chambers, he nearly swung the door back into her face, her quick reflexes just barely saving her nose.

The rooms were as she remembered them from the few glimpses she had stolen when spying on Grayson and Andreiyes to see what lads did for fun. They always guffawed behind closed doors while other girls her age fussed over the ribbons in their hair and their dresses. Often it had been Grayson's raspy laugh that sounded the loudest. The memories tingled through her skin with a pleasant warmth.

Andreiyes' furnishings were ornately simplistic in that they demonstrated wealth and taste without being overly ostentatious. The craftsmanship was exquisite and unique, from the carved edgings in the wood to the cornices and inlaid motifs. As a boy, the furniture had been oversized and ill adapted to Andreiyes' rambunctious nature. Now it molded to him and seemed to breathe with his aura.

A relaxing scent of pine and sea-brine drifted from burning candles around the space. Golden-threaded cloth covered the walls in the sitting room – trinkets and paintings of coasts and landscapes pinned about it. Exposed stone and brick decorated his bedchamber and timber wainscoted the bottom half of his study's walls. It was like glimpsing into completely different homes with each one, but his bedchamber remained the room she cared most to explore. She had once spied Grayson and Andreiyes disappearing into a hidden tunnel there.

She followed him to his bedchamber where he slumped – head buried in his hands – on the edge of his dark elkwood four-post bed, a myriad of colorful balloon-draped curtains overhead.

"So, this is where royalty sleeps."

He jerked upright, his hand reaching for his hilt, before his tension sunk at the sight of her. "Bloody pits, woman."

"You startle easily."

"I am not in the habit of entertaining when I have not propositioned."

She waved him off. "No, not here for that."

"Shame." He grunted, with an edge of amusement or perhaps irritation. "What are you doing in my private chambers?" His tone was almost playful as he strutted toward her. "Do you miss my presence so terribly after so little time apart?"

She clenched her jaw as his finger grazed her cheek while tucking a strand of hair behind her ear. "If I'm to be your manservant, it seems only natural that I be here."

"You know quite well stalking me is not a part of that duty." She shrugged innocently. "Note my manservants are rarely seen and never heard."

"Oh, you'll be seeing plenty of me." She smiled wickedly. "And I imagine quite soon my voice will follow you into your sleep with how often you'll hear it."

"Delightful." His voice dripped with sarcasm. Kaianne wiggled her eyebrows with a satisfied smirk until he returned hers with a mischievous one of his own. He eyed the room divider in the far corner of his bedchambers that probably hid a tub. "If you are to take to the task so adamantly, then you must bathe me. A good manservant will always assure his royal charge is presentable and well taken care of."

He unbuckled his cuirass and let it clatter to the floor. Instead of falling prey to his games and shying away as she supposed he expected, she leaned into him, clasped a handful of his tunic and bent toward his ear. "A real man would ask me to bathe with him."

The words were worth the heat in his eyes. "Is that what you Carved do? Tell me, how many men have you *bathed* with?"

She snickered and let her eyes crawl over his features. "Wouldn't you like to know."

He was a good looking man, with a strong jaw and dark hair that offset his unique royal eyes. His broad shoulders and toned form were appealing. Combined with the scruff of his beard in need of trimming and shaving, there was a sure promise of a good time. Plus those thick fingers, she could imagine quite a bit of fun with them. But he was grieving, looking for any way to ignore his pain. This would be nothing more than a one-off between them. It meant agreeing to be used and discarded as nothing more than an insignificant plaything. That was something Kaianne refused to tolerate in any aspect of her life.

"Unfortunately for you, if you ask, I'll say no. I won't be the distraction you need right now, Andreiyes."

"Is that so?" His lips grazed her cheek, gliding down closer to her throat at every hitch of her breath. "I could convince you otherwise."

Kaianne shoved him off and ignored the shock on his face that quickly hardened. "I highly doubt that. Not everyone is subject to your charms, at least not the pitiful ones you just attempted. Now, how about you bathe on your own, tell me where I'll be staying, and I'll be on my way."

"We do not give rooms to vipers." His sneer said it all.

She harrumphed. "How quickly you turn from seduction to insults. Your bedmates must get exhausted from keeping it straight."

"Even the servant quarters would be too pleasant for you."

"Very well then." She hopped onto his bed's comforter, still dressed in her riding clothes coated in mud and grime and the reek of a horse. She spread her arms and legs out. "Yes, very comfortable."

"What are you doing?"

She feigned ignorance and batted her eyes. "What does it look like? I suppose we'll have to share."

"Oh, for pit's sake." His eyes were smiling despite his supposed frustration. "Woman, get your sullied rump off my bed."

She chortled. "You're so easy to rile up. It's too exciting to stop now."

As if on cue, a knock sounded with a tentative call.

"Sire?"

Whatever amusement had shown on Andreiyes' face vanished, the somber solemn look returning in full force.

"You *have* been distracting me," he accused.

"Is that such a bad thing? You've finally smiled after quints. Edmira wouldn't want her death to lead you into misery."

"You have no idea what she would want."

Kaianne ignored the venom in his tone. "I may not know her, but I know siblings. If she was anything like Deacon, she wouldn't wish this burden on you. It'll only weigh you down the longer you deny her loss. At least, you had no part in it."

"She died yesterday. If I had read her letter when I received it, if I had sacrificed some rest and ridden through that first night, I might have been here when..."

"Living on what never happened will not change what did. You'll always remember her as vibrant and strong. She would've preferred that, yes? I'm certain she forgives you for not returning for a last goodbye."

"How can you be so certain?"

"Because she loved you. In the end, it's all that matters."

He shook his head with a sigh. Another knock and call for his attention came from the sitting room.

"Does the pain ever leave?" he whispered.

She tightened her lips into a thin line. "Not truly, but you'll get used to it, and it'll grow dull. You learn to accept it and live with the weight of it on your chest." More knocking cut through the emotional undertones of their conversation. "Now go open that door before your men ram it down."

"You dare command a prince?" His lips twitched upward despite the rebuke, and she rolled her eyes in response.

"I wouldn't dream of it. Now go. Have them fetch water for your bath while you're at it."

He shot her an unamused glance over his shoulder. "Do not move from this room."

As if he could stop her. She winked at him and reveled in the momentary confusion riling his face. He was going to quickly understand that she made her own rules.

Kaianne tiptoed to the revival wardrobe she remembered from her childhood. It stood in the same place, smaller than she remembered and yet massive, the oak lacquer and painted decorations on each door panel slightly faded. At its conjunction with the stone wall, a draft brushed along her fingers.

"*What is it?*" Andreiyes asked from the next room over.

She opened one of the wardrobe's doors, cringing when it creaked, to find an array of men's clothing all neatly arranged tightly together. It was hefty work shoving half to each side to arrange enough space for her to slip through – death by attack of cloth, that was not something she had ever felt threatened by before.

"*Your father requests your presence, your Highness, in your sister's chambers.*"

"*Very well.*" Andreiyes cleared his throat.

Kaianne hesitated, imagining the pained expression on Andreiyes' face. Confronting Edmira's death was going to be a difficult moment for him, but until he accepted it, her support would only be a crutch.

She shut the door panels behind her and pushed through to the back of the wardrobe with hands outstretched. She and darkness were dear friends, and if it were not for the ruffling and scratching of cloth around her or the overwhelming scent of cloves to keep moths away, she might have taken a moment to relax and settle her mind.

Once at the rear, her fingers patted and ran down cracks and seams, running along the edges and zigzagging from left to right. It wasn't long before she found a juncture in the wood panel that spanned from top to bottom. It did not budge with nudges. It did not even jostle a little when she shoved her full weight against it. If force wasn't the answer, she needed to find a lever, a button, or something. Something that young boys of ten could find or handle. She needed to do so quickly before Andreiyes discovered her and delayed her efforts in ways only he could devise.

"Kaianne?" his muffled voice called. Just her luck.

If she were a young lad, what would she do? She crouched and passed her hands where a child would instinctively reach.

"Where the blazes are you, woman?"

Her finger pressed into a deep indentation. With a click, the back panel gave way under slight pressure, snapping onto a rail. Then it was solely a matter of sliding it to the side to reveal the wall's stone veneer. The moment the panel reached the end of its railing, another click exposed cracks in the stone to shape a hidden door. A gust of musty air assailed her. The cough was involuntary, but it came out in a burst. No sooner had she placed a hand on the cold, smooth stone than tampered light from behind swamped the wardrobe with an aggravating creak.

She glanced over her shoulder. "You really should oil that door. It's a dead giveaway."

"Kaianne, get away from that passage. Do not force me to call the guards on you."

"We both know neither of those things are about to happen."

He forced his clothing apart, pyramiding them from their hangers to mold around his form, his handsome face downturned with aggravation. Before he could come closer, she dove forward, the force of the shove enough to thrust the hidden door open an ample sliver for her to slip through. Quickly, she made to close it shut to stop his advance.

"Leave it open," he said. "'Tis one of the rare few that cannot be opened from inside the tunnel. So you may return once you have expunged your invasive needs."

"How gentlemanly," she purred. "And yet, no need to fret for my safety. I'm quite capable."

"'Tis not your safety I worry for."

"I do love a good compliment." With a sly smile, she bowed for flourish. "Until this eve, Andy."

With a giggle, she left him and his wardrobe behind to gallivant and explore whatever opportunities the tunnel might offer. It was solely lit in dotted beams from peepholes. Its chilled, mildewy air was oddly comforting. Scouting the caverns near Credence had had a similar ambiance – the darkness, humidity, and whistling chill a pleasant reminder. Best of all, there was no one here to cut her personal time short.

Thirty-three

The archives chamber was her goal – a room she had never set foot in as a child. She held not the faintest idea of where it was, and not a single peephole she spied through gave any indication she was any closer to finding it. No matter how many turns she took, stairs she climbed or tight spaces and spiderwebs she crept through, the darn place was elusive.

She saw and heard plenty, nevertheless. Noblewomen were tedious in their gossip. Who was the most favored in court, how much suffering the princeling must be experiencing with his sister's passing, who would he turn to for frolicking. Kaianne noted very few mentioned their own grief at Edmira's death. And tired tidbits such as: 'Oh, did you see how rumpled her gown was?' It was worth the eye rolls if that was the least of their worries. Lords, she was grateful not to have grown up with that lot.

Some people weren't too careful on how privately they carried out their clandestine rendezvouses. Kaianne spied two, and one couple was far from discreet. Other dark corners revealed exchanges of markweed, a reef plant found only on the ridges of the Barring Sea that induced euphoric hallucinations when eaten or boiled in tea. It was worth a hefty sum on the black market, and the drug of choice among the wealthy and bored. She had even heard that the Carved city Paradise in southern Gyldrise's Wraith Swamps harvested and sold markweed to fund themselves when other resources were low.

Through one peephole, she witnessed Andreiyes sitting at a bedside where Edmira lay, wrapped and ready for cremation. Poor Andreiyes, it pained her that this was now the memory of his sister that would stick with him. His face was reddened through strain, eyes puffy. Candles speckled the space with their glow. Their smoky sweet scent of myrrh and an aromatic touch of roasted chicory root wafted through the peephole. It effectively masked the unpreventable reek of death.

At Andreiyes' back stood Crown Prince Balliol, a hand resting on his son's shoulder. The crown prince looked far worse than Andreiyes. Time had obviously not been kind to him with the number of wrinkles dug into his forehead and around his eyes. Never mind the grief that he seemed to carry like a second skin. When a tear escaped Andreiyes' eyes and trailed down his cheek to his chin, Kaianne retreated. It was far too tender a moment for her to disrespect his privacy. She walked on.

Further down, there were spy reports being given on Carved movements and mentions of unrest in a northeastern town after the recent execution of a Flawed-born family – it certainly wasn't a popular edict, and caused fear and anger more than anything else. Where she would have imagined such things reported to the King or Prince Balliol, they were instead relayed to a Steward in what looked like a woman's sitting room from the golden accents and purple rugs.

Kaianne stood there completely immersed in their conversation, rubbing a little warmth into her arms with her hands. She had never seen a Master before, but their sapphire hooded robes were legendary. This man looked to be in his mid-forties, his face obscured in the shadows of his hood, his hands as gaunt as those of a skeleton laying one atop the other on his lap. His voice was severe and baritone, his words clipped and to the point. One of his spies mumbled their response.

Kaianne shuffled her weight and leaned closer to the peephole to hear better. A few pebbles of the wall's stone lining fragmented off and clinked against the uneven dusty stone at her feet. The sound echoed around her. Bloody shite on a stick. She cringed. But the worst of it was when that hooded head jerked in her direction.

The edge of his chin jutted from the shadows, and she swore he was seeing her, as if there were no wall, no peephole needed. She felt the man examining her, because with that stately posture there was no doubt this was a male Master.

There was an eerie tug in her body. It sent every nerve ending inside her on edge. Her entire body went rigid, a shiver racking her from head to toe. Then the pain started, and she gritted her teeth to keep from crying out. It was as if pieces of herself were being ripped out and sucked away.

She had no control. Her hand reached for her dagger of its own accord. She ground her jaw, trying her damndest to stop its movement, to force her arm back. She forced it back a finger-width only for it to shove past her will three times harder. Her fingers felt numb and tingly as they gripped the dagger and pried it out of its scabbard. The tip of the blade clanged against the sheath's rim. Her heart thumped in her ears. She chuffed air for courage as her hand raised and the blade was pressed to her chest. This was not how she was supposed to die. This sort of death deserved to be mocked by Oidh and all the other doubters from her crew.

"Chichu?" a soft voice called.

The spell broke. Her arm dropped. With a shaky hand, Kaianne sheathed her dagger and slumped in relief, panting. A respite she allowed for only an instant. Then, she ran.

She ran despite not seeing every step ahead. She misjudged turns and slammed into walls, her cheeks and knees taking the brunt of it. She tripped on the uneven floor and jutting stones, the fall scraping her hands and legs. It didn't matter. She jumped steps on dust-covered stairways. She slid down steep, slick corridors. She ran to put distance between herself and that Master. For the first time, she understood the fear and hatred Carved held against the Order.

It wasn't until the fear had dissipated and her heart was drubbing in her chest solely because of the exercise that she finally stopped. Her legs wobbled, and she collapsed to her rear against the nearest wall. Every part of her ached, her knees and hands more than the rest. There was a dark sheen to them. She must have cut them open, but she didn't care. That Master had almost impaled her on her own dagger without laying a hand on her, without even knowing who she was. Granted she had been spying on him, but that reaction was a tad extreme.

Gods below, what had she gotten herself into? If he was staying at the castle, she was bound to see him again. It was a small comfort that he would never know it was her. The slimy feel of his talent clung to the skin. She shuddered, feeling an urgent need to wash growing.

The problem was, she had no idea where she was. At this point, it was going to take sandturns for her to find her way back to Andreiyes' chambers. Not to mention there was always a risk of passing that Master's chambers once more, and that she adamantly refused to do.

She concentrated on the need to find an unoccupied room accessible from the tunnel to clean up in. Goal in mind, she forced her legs to carry her weight and dragged one shaky foot in front of the other. It wasn't long until she found her quarry. From the small visual the peephole displayed, the room was lavish in its furnishings and in recent use by the fire crackling in its hearth and the trunks placed at the foot of the bed. That meant there was a higher chance of a tub, hopefully filled, and some attire for her to dress into. No sound emanated from the bedchamber. Perfect.

There was a lever in the wall a few paces away which disengaged the lock on this room's hidden door that lay behind an enormous tapestry. As she navigated beneath the entire thing, it attempted to swaddle her in its scratchy wool. It then spat her out into the bedchamber even more disheveled, hair standing on end yet plagued with a little less dust.

Lo and behold, behind the cloth partition in one corner was a wooden tub. Steam and the brine of jasmine salts wafted from it. A tray of cheeses, cold cuts of meat and a cup of spiced wine rested on an end of the tub.

Kaianne stuffed a few pieces of the fare in her mouth, hoping it might lessen one ache in her body. Flavors exploded on her tongue. Lords, she had forgotten how sublime the food of the wealthy tasted. Everything was spiced and aged to perfection. She eyed the rest of it with envy, but taking any more was reckless and enticing danger. Already this arrangement meant either the room's occupant was expected shortly or had recently taken his or her leave. By the lack of wet footprints or used linens and the decently filled tray, Kaianne guessed the former. That was a problem waiting to happen.

Before she could make a move to return to the tunnel, the door to the guest's sitting room slammed open. Orders were barked. Heavy items clanged and clattered to the floor.

"Useless," a voice bellowed. "Surrounded by imbeciles."

Footsteps pounded toward the bedchamber.

"Pardon my carelessness, m'Lordling." There was a slight shake to the second man's voice, and it did not grow closer despite the footsteps.

"I could have your head for that. Those swords are worth more than every copper par your ridiculous family could ever touch in fifty stretches."

Lords, that irksome voice, she both knew and hated it. Her mind had to be playing tricks. To run blindly through the tunnels only to land in the Bryant suite, more specifically his room, out of all of them? But how many lordlings was Castle Ravensten currently entertaining? She had unwillingly traveled here with the worst one, but there was also the youngest Sertrios that had a permanent suite. Either the gods were cursing her with the worst luck or blessing her with the best.

Curiosity had her peeking through the cloth ties spaced along the poles holding the partition up. The lordling's red hair was a dead giveaway. Kaianne clamped a hand over her mouth to stifle a laugh. It was him. She glanced again at the pale, freckled face. It really was Willik Bryant.

"Get this off me. Must I detail everything I require?"

A male attendant scuttled close to remove Willik's cloak and coat. It was not quick enough by the lordling's standards because within grainfalls he was already grumbling more complaints about his attendants' inefficiencies.

"I want those washed and brushed. Worthy of royalty. Am I clear?"

"Yes, m'Lordling." The young man left in a flurry of footsteps.

"Lordling," a timid girl stuttered. The girl stood outside of Kaianne's limited viewpoint. "Would you care for some tea before your bath?"

"Did I address you?" Lords, this disgusting nitwit loved the sound of his own voice far too much. "Women are to be seen, not heard."

A clap and a gasp sounded. Sobs filled the room, and Kaianne bit her lip and clenched her fists to keep from acting.

"See that you remember your place. Now get out."

Rushed footfalls clamored out the bedchamber. A door clicked shut, gently. It contrasted with the tension in the room, so thick that breaths fought their way into Kaianne's lungs. And what was Willik doing while the maid scampered out in fear and submission? Snickering. A cruel smirk consumed his face. Lords, the man was reveling in this.

He deserved the faceless death she had spoken of to Andreiyes, but she wanted to see the disgust and horror on his face when he realized death was coming for him in the shape of a woman. To be murdered by his once-betrothed. It had a certain poetry to it. To think, had Thad not been born Flawed, she might have already been Willik's wife per her father's schemes. That bit still stung after all these stretches.

She stepped out from behind the cloth partition, hands on her hips, her dagger resting behind her hip but still within reach. "I see you're still the same despicable man."

His jerk made her chuckle. Even the way he drew his sword was pontifical. "You're not to be in here."

"Do you know who I am?" She took a step closer to him. It was bold and maybe foolish, but never did she want Willik to presume her weak again.

The question made him pause as his gaze searched her face and fell to her attire. "Yes, the princeling's servant lad. Though I thought he took better care of what belonged to him."

She chuckled hoarsely to keep her laughter contained. As if Andreiyes could own her.

"So, tell me boy, what's the princeling's message?"

"What?"

"That is why you're here, no? Despite your ragged look and weathered drabs. So, tell me of his summons. The answer better be pleasing, boy, or I'll have no qualms running you through."

"Oh, I'm not here on royal business. I'm here for my own purpose."

Willik barked a laugh and sheathed his sword. Still laughing, he settled his rear on his bed and unlaced his boots. Clearly the lordling didn't realize the threat that shared his chambers. "Your sister, whomever she is, is not worth your pitiful life, no matter the fleeting amusement she gave me."

Bile reached up her throat. "Pits, you disgust me. I should definitely send a prayer of thanks that our fate to marry was so brutally ended."

He furrowed his brow with confusion. "I don't bed lads."

"This is quite anticlimactic." Kaianne stepped closer, the edge of his bed brushing her knees. "I didn't think I had to be so forward for you to recognize me."

She undid the leathered tie on her hair and let it cascade down her back and shoulders.

"A woman. I'm intrigued. Explains your voice and soft features. Is this how Andreiyes sneaks women into his chambers? Ingenious."

"I haven't the time to drag on your idiocy." She crossed the remaining distance between them, grabbed a handful of his tunic and pressed the tip of her dagger to his throat. "Maybe this will jog your memory."

Now alarm was bouncing in his eyes. "Get your hands off me, woman." His attempts to knock off her grip were weak and untrained, his male strength of little asset as she maneuvered around them.

"You once told me I was a lamb. That you looked forward to my slaughter, but it's I that will get that joy. Tell me lordling, are you frightened?"

His nose flared and jaw clenched. "A woman is never frightening."

Kaianne dug the blade into his neck until he hissed and a rivulet of blood ran down to the collar of his tunic. "You don't believe that. Not right now. Not when you're looking death in the eye. I wasn't strong enough six stretches ago to save my brothers, but now I will make certain you never harm another again."

She dragged the heirloom blade across the lordling's neck. The pour of blood was immediate. The hot spray of it speckled her face. Her limbs felt heavy and cold as she glared into Willik's shocked eyes. He gasped for air. He gripped his throat, blood cascading down his front. He clutched her neck, and she let him, his strength waning with each passing grainfall.

"How many will mourn your death, do you think?" The man collapsed to his knees. "When you reach Iltheln and you are condemned there for your actions, remember Ynnea of House Lyssandre was your end."

A spark of recognition lit his face, but it was meager and that made her frown. His eyes were shaking with fright as he grappled at her clothes while crumbling to the hardwood floor, but she could not shake the unsettling feeling that her family's deaths had been insignificant to him. To her, they had been everything.

There was less satisfaction to his collapse or the lifeless gleam to his eyes than she expected. A monster was dead, one that had chased her in too many nightmares, but his death did not unravel the knot that had formed in her chest stretches ago. She rubbed her breastbone absently and glared at the body. A sandfall passed, then another before tears tracked down her face. Adi and how many others died because this man had no heart, no soul, and now no blood in his veins.

It wasn't enough. Kaianne kicked his stomach. The body twitched. Again and again she pummeled into it, a soundless scream bursting from her sobs until she slipped in the pool of blood. It drenched through trousers and flooded her nose with its sticky, coppery stench. He was dead, but it wasn't enough.

Time passed as her emotions drained. Changes were made by those who acted, not those who waited and pitied themselves. Enough wallowing. She picked herself up. Someone was sure to check on the lordling within the next sandturn, and she needed to disappear without leaving a trail. As it was, her boots were tacked with nearly as much blood as her clothing.

She stripped to her underdrawers, the thin cloth shorts dry and untainted. They served her far better than the tighter and shorter delicates generally made of lace that women wore beneath their dresses. Everything else went into the fire, which hissed and smoked as it pierced through the clothing's wet spots and purged the room of the coppery reek.

Now that Willik was dead, there was no point in letting a decadent bath go to waste. She sunk into it. The hot stones warmed the soles of her feet, the back of her calves and her rear. It should have been perfect, but dissatisfaction cloyed at her emotions. She sighed and ate. The food filled her belly, but the remarkable flavors fell dull. Somewhere in Iltheln, her family was looking to her. She hoped Willik's death satisfied a little of their pain because it certainly had done nothing for hers. He was one man in a colossal scheming empire. One death did not topple the whole. Her vengeance remained unsatisfied, but she had more purpose than avenging her family. The murders of all Flawed and Carved alike needed to end.

Lord Pascual still needed to pay his dues. Not today. Perhaps not for cycles to come. She had been patient thus far. A few more bilials, cycles, or even a stretch or two would not void the blood debt she had sworn on her family's graves. Until then, the priority fell to the Carved's objectives. Find a weakness and exploit it. Rid the realms of Steward influence. Destroy the border barriers. Who would have thought infiltrating the castle would have been the easy part?

It helped that toying with Andreiyes was such a fun pastime. He was so easy to tease and prod, so passionate and headstrong. He was a challenge to decipher and twist, and he had so far been an asset in this little project. Warmth filled her at the memories of the last cycle. A smile stretched over her face, and her fingertips grazed the creases it formed before her hand fell away. She had only smiled because it was rare to find a worthy conversationalist, she told herself. There was no other reason.

With the water mucked with a mixture of brown and pink and the dust having settled at the bottom of the tub, Kaianne exited the bath. Clothes were easy to find. The wardrobe was filled with fine ensembles for both genders. This bedchamber must have been available to whichever Bryant was visiting Castle Ravensten at the time.

Unfortunately, Willik's clothes were too big. Never mind how wearing anything that had given him comfort made her stomach clench with unease. Women's clothing it was then. Lords, just looking at the dresses dangling from the hangers made her remember the discomfort of wearing such things: the long, weight-laden skirts, sashes, tight chest-sucking corsets, frilly undershirts that would tickle her relentlessly, and brazen necklines. Whoever decided that torture and beauty went hand-in-hand deserved to be suffocated in the tightest of corsets and stabbed in the arches of their feet with heel tips.

She picked the simplest of dresses and used a nightgown as an under-ensemble to avoid the ridiculous frou-frou of the others. The gown was made of a green satiny cloth with brown accents and loose sleeves that hung off her shoulders and enlarged at the wrists to dangle uselessly. She cinched a leather braided belt around her waist, which reduced the entitled priss demeanor a touch. Jewelry, she avoided – each golden and gemmed piece was too recognizable. Her hair, she braided – simple yet elegant. Her dagger, she strapped to her thigh, invisible beneath her skirts. The entire point was to melt unseen into the plethora of young women that roamed the castle and its garden. To be noticed and forgotten an instant later. With the finishing touch of a fur shawl, she left as she had come, though this time she bundled her skirt hems to her abdomen. She snickered as she imagined the horror a speck of mud or Gaia forbid a tear on a woman of high birth's attire would cause among the over privileged. It was almost worth being careless.

Thirty-four

*M*idday had come and gone. Little headway had been made while Kaianne ate biscuits and drank tea in the gardens among all the nobles and courtiers under the veranda in the lower courtyard. With the snow about to melt with the start of a new season, the air was crisp with the smell of wet dirt like that after a good day of rain.

Gossip had been poor and unhelpful. The only interesting tidbit she had picked up was regarding two Masters that had been trailing Edmira everywhere before her death, and were now set to return to their Temple on the morrow. Two Masters for a royal that was neither the King nor the direct heir – that was odd. Kaianne's first assumption: Edmira had been conspiring with them. Yet the deceased princess' ladies-in-waiting seemed to find the Masters' behavior contrary to the royal's wishes for privacy. They griped how only one of them at a time had been permitted to keep the princess company on her deathbed while both Masters had been always present. It was interesting, but not mind boggling.

Before she could snoop anything more relevant, bells sounded. Calls to arms followed and kingsmen assembled, most vacating their posts around the garden to gather at the castle. That could only mean one thing. Willik's body had been discovered. That was her cue to leave before anyone questioned her presence.

All attention was riveted on the soldiers filing into the castle grounds and surrounding the entrances and exits. The chatter rose amid gasps. A garden table was upturned as a lady rose suddenly, porcelain crashing in the pebbled section of the veranda. Many sashayed closer for a better view, exchanging muttered suppositions on what had occurred. Kaianne followed the last cluttered group as close as she dared, avoiding eye contact when anyone glanced her way.

It wasn't until they made it to the steps leading to the upper courtyard that Kaianne slipped away behind the marble pedestal that held up a statue of King Triunn in his youth. There she withdrew from the mass of courtiers that had nothing better to do than prattle and watch their peers. Then it was a matter of pretending to belong. She kept her head high, her stance relaxed but proper, and her gaze fixed on the guards with hopefully what looked like troubled curiosity while she walked away from the scene. To anyone else, she hoped she seemed like a delicate courtier in need of respite and a stroll.

A bird's trill was whistled, the same type Carved often used for signals. Kaianne glanced innocently over her shoulder, seeking the origin.

In the shadows of a passage between the tall hedges that divided the garden into sections, Yannic signaled with his head for her to join him. It meant backtracking behind the swarm of courtiers – a sure way to be noticed. Nor was it a good idea for Yannic, dressed as a gardener, to abandon his post to come meet her. Instead, she gestured down the length of hedges on her side of the garden, the implication clear that they meet at the fountain where both hedges ended.

The fountain was a sculpted masterpiece with the coiled form of a dragon along its exterior. Its maw spouted water toward the centerpiece – a griffin posed to strike, wings extended, at the base of an Eidenhail tree. While the rest was made of granite, the white marble used for the tree had blue veins, similar to the rumored color of an Eidenhail's leaves.

"Kay," Yannic whispered, still holding garden shears, with a frown on his face. "Have they found you out?"

The irritation she had at being summoned lessened. "No, never. You know I'm too clever."

The creased lines between his brow however did not ease. "You put an awful lot of trust in that royal."

"Just enough. He reckons his life hangs in the balance. He'll not harm the hand that feeds him."

Yannic's grunt gave away his opinions on the situation, but they didn't matter. She knew Andreiyes, better now than she ever had. The man had no intention of harming her, at least not while she was the key to his survival.

A shrill trumpet sounded and pulled her gaze back to the castle.

"Any idea as to what has all the guards riled?"

"I suspect a body has been found," she said, not missing the questioning rise of his brow.

"Your work?"

"And long overdue."

"Who?"

"A pig of a lordling no woman in Isyldill will miss."

"Bloody pits, Kay. You'll attract the wrong attention to us. Enough to make your plan go tits up."

"Relax, Yannic. I know what I'm doing."

His gaze swept around them, but no one was close enough to spy. Yannic was a cautious man a few stretches her senior who always took every precaution. His nondescript features, especially with his hair hidden beneath a linen biggins – the scar on his chin hardly counted against that – were perfect for undercover work. For anyone that did not know him personally, his face and voice were unmemorable.

When they had first met, they hadn't seen eye-to-eye – namely because of her darker skin that hinted at her noble heritage – but after tying his shoelaces together one too many times to teach him a few lessons and saving his life once or twice, they'd grown to be thick as thieves. Now, if she had an idea, Yannic was the first to offer his support in front of the crew. Yet, for the first time in stretches, doubt creased his eyes.

"You have to trust me."

"I do, but you've never been one to serve your own agenda before. People put their lives on the line for your plan. What of those that already passed on to Iltheln? How does your self-serving vendetta honor their sacrifice?"

She flinched at the intensity of his words, gaze fixed on the fountain's rippling water. "You don't understand. I swore a blood oath to my family. I had to get revenge. For them."

"No, I do. I understand as much as most Carved will. Do you think it easy for me to be here with the people whose name was signed on the order to hang my brothers?" He closed the distance between them. "It's torture, but I abstain from action for the good of us all."

His body heat melded with her own. It should have been a comfort in the cold weather, but instead it was overbearing and unwelcome. She kept her gaze averted, unwilling to see admonishment in his eyes. His words were already digging uncomfortably beneath her skin.

"For the first time, Carved have infiltrated the griffin's lair. We have a real possibility of uncovering a way to change the fate of Taelgir's people. We cannot throw that away."

"I know," she whispered just loud enough for him to hear.

"It was your actions and leadership that have led us this far. I've trusted you with my life, Kay. Don't give me reason to doubt that."

"I understand," she gritted through her teeth. "I get it. I know what's at stake."

"Good, see that you do. The sooner we gather usable intel, the sooner we leave this pit of gilded wretches and return to Credence."

He shoveled a hand beneath his cloak, between his laced-up jerkin and tunic to remove four of the vials full of Andreiyes' green tonic. The vials clanked against the fountain's granite edge when Yannic slammed them down. As he left, he said over his shoulder, "Oh, and Oidh extends his well wishes."

That made her snort. Kaianne shoved the vials along the belt at her waist and scrubbed at her forehead with irritation as she ducked around a row of hedges. She could already hear the reprimands Oidh would ferret her way. No matter how close she and Yannic had become, the man was not about to keep secrets from Ghedi's second-in-command. If this mission did fail, never would Oidh let her forget it, nor would she forgive herself.

She glanced back at the castle. The courtiers were only beginning to scatter while kingsmen were seemingly patrolling the grounds. Others stood vigilant around the entrances and archways that conjoined the gardens and rear patio to the front courtyard. In her green gown and dark furs, she stuck out against the snowy ground patched with spots of dirt and sprouting grass. Unless she scaled down the fortified stone walls that curtained the castle grounds over the entire length of Gaia's butte to reach that hidden door down below, there were no other passageways at the rear of the castle grounds that she knew of.

Yannic was right. This headache was of her own making. Now, her options were to wait out the storm or risk discovery. It was one thing to pretend to be Andreiyes' manservant to which the princeling's story would lend credence. It was another thing entirely to dress as a courtier affiliated to no particular House or wealthy merchant.

A fool, that's what she was. Her dagger chafed against her thigh, the griffin crossguards digging into her skin as she wandered further from the castle. It was a stark reminder of how true Yannic's words were. Idiot, oaf, she was a hog of a woman. People were counting on her while she succumbed to the hungers of her appetite. Lords, she wanted to kill something. Again. The irony of that in this situation was not lost on her, and she kicked snow, ice and mud across the walkway. Not that it released even a tidbit of her frustration.

"What are you doing?"

Kaianne startled at the sound of the gentle voice. She craned her neck to see a child sitting on a bench dressed in a maroon gown with beige undertones. The girl's dress might have been the picture of wealth, but her demeanor didn't match. Her black stringy hair fluttered freely in the light breeze. Her shoes were muddied, dirt caked on the tights covering her ankles. She leaned backward on her palms, a book pressed face down beneath one. The smirk on her round face was mischievous, and the child swung her legs about as though she had no care who saw her mannerisms.

"Wandering. And you?"

"Hiding."

"What has a child like you have to hide from?"

The girl's eyebrows raised. "You do not know my chichu then?"

Kaianne frowned at the use of a moniker solely used in Gyldrise and took a closer look at the child. The girl's crescent eyes were atypical of Isyldill's habitants, but then again stranger things had been seen. Her face was smoother than many her age, her bone structure less angular. Kaianne had interacted with enough Gyldrit Carved in the last stretch to find the similarities between them and this girl disconcerting. The girl was a Carved. That was Kaianne's first assumption, but the blunder of hinting at it caught in her throat as she caught sight of Isyldill amber rimming the child's eyes. Odd.

"What?" the girl asked.

"Sorry, you remind me of someone I once knew." Kaianne schooled her features into mild curiosity. "Who is your chichu, then?"

"An overprotective bore that lets me do nothing." The girl rolled her eyes dramatically. "If he had his way, I would never experience much of anything."

"Saying such things to a stranger? Aren't you worried I'll take your sad tale to your father?"

"Please do. It will be fun to watch him spend his anger on you. Small as you are, he will throw you across the castle grounds a good dozen times before tiring out. Do it, it will get his mind off me, if just a little."

"You're an odd thing."

The girl shrugged.

"You know your father means well."

Another shrug.

"Right. Well, enjoy your book."

Kaianne traipsed off in her original meaningless direction, attempting to put extra elegance into her steps. Her back tingled with awareness, the feeling of eyes on her. There had been so much visible in eyes so young – pain, hurt, wariness. Could the girl tell she did not belong? Would she relay her suspicions to someone else?

The crunch of snow underfoot made it difficult to hear the girl's movements. Trailing her hand along the hedge's millions of tiny leaves, the remains of loose snow tumbled and dripped from the top edge. The ice-cold frost numbed Kaianne's fingers. She glanced over her shoulder as inconspicuously as possible, but the girl was gone. Kaianne's heart sunk, the thoughts of the dooming accusations the child could spread weighing it down.

"Are you headed to the training grounds?"

Kaianne spun about and held a hand to her chest as if to suppress the fright. The child stood behind her, head reaching Kaianne's shoulders in height.

"Lords, you're a quiet one."

"Sneaking is one of my best qualities." The girl gave a saccharine smile.

"Of that I have no doubt." Kaianne turned and took a few steps toward her undecided destination. Annoyingly, the girl followed, and Kaianne chewed on her upper lip to contain the irritation. "Are you following me now?"

She took a few more steps. The girl mirrored them. "I have nothing better to do, and you have me curious."

"About?"

"Well, what is a lady of your stature doing with a weapon under her dress?" Kaianne stopped short as the girl continued, "I was under the impression that we ladies were to be kept from violent conducts."

Strapping her dagger to her thigh had been a risk, the shape momentarily outlined by the cloth at each step with that leg, but few would have assumed it a weapon. Isyldillians, compared to Gyldrits or Nimedorians, were positively bigoted when it came to women wielding anything more dangerous than needles.

She inhaled deeply and faced the defiant child. This little thing with an innocent face was far more observant than most people that were trained to be, skills people developed when need demanded it. There was more to this child than the pampered, sheltered demeanor her father probably imposed on her, but Kaianne kept her suspicions blank on her face.

"Is that what you believe, or what you've been told?"

"Does it matter?"

"Always." Kaianne trudged forward, knowing the girl intended to follow. "Women should not rely on men. We have everything men have that counts. Two arms, legs, eyes. The swinging appendage between their legs makes them far too moronic half the time, yet they seem to think it adds weight to their worth. The day I see one use it as more than a means to gratify themselves will be the day the world ends.

"We can smell and see as well as them. We might not have their brute strength, but we move swifter and can handle more than one task simultaneously. So, tell me, why is it that ladies are not worthy of fighting? Why are we reneged to the sidelines and treated as weak?"

The girl huffed a breath. "Because we are frivolous beings meant solely to bare and caretake children."

"Lords, please tell me your father is not the one filling your head with such nonsense."

"No." The girl broke a dead branch off a tree that lined the hedge and dragged it along the snow. "It is what everyone believes, so I have to follow. Almost half the Stewards are women, and yet that doesn't matter to Chichu since he believes I will never be one of them. I have to prove him wrong."

"And you believe there's glory in becoming a Steward?" It was difficult for Kaianne to hide the incredulity in her tone.

"If I can achieve half of what my chichu can do, I will be happy. Plus, Stewards are free. Their mark does not limit them to one kingdom or to stupid rules."

Kaianne raised a brow at the insight. Never before had she considered the Stewards to bare marks. They traversed the borders unrestrained yet were not hunted like a Carved or slaughtered like Flawed. Of course, it made sense for them to be marked, and yet it didn't. They forced talented individuals from their homes to towns and outposts near Telfinor's borders. There were reports of many of those people crossing. Perhaps their marks were changed instead of removed. But how was that even done, and what kingdom brand allowed them to travel freely?

"You've seen this mark?"

The girl stopped her playful etchings in the snow and cocked her head. "You truly do not know who I am."

The awe in the girl's voice was followed by a bright smile that scrunched her eyes nearly shut.

"Difficult to know who you are when I don't even know your name."

"No, no. I would rather we continue with anonymity." The child skipped to catch up with Kaianne. "I like this. No one else acts so open with me. And I want to see what you can do at the training yard."

"What makes you think I intend to go there?"

"Why would you not? I reckon there is not a single guard there at the moment. Just you and me, two women." Kaianne scoffed at how easily the child described herself as an adult. "Doing what the boorish men here think us too fragile and delicate-minded to handle."

Kaianne bit her lower lip to contain the smile that tugged at her features. This child was certainly a handful, more than she had ever been, for sure. "Very well. Lead the way."

It wasn't far. They cut through a few paths in the hedges to arrive at a large field, curtailed by a short fence that served as a poor deterrent. It was the diametric opposite of the elegant garden maze. The area was sparse of plant life regardless of the snow. Reddish-pink stains marred the patchy ground, where kingsmen had probably earned new wounds and scars. Delimitations with stones marked sections for archery, target practice, sword fighting and tumbling, she presumed by the size and length of each. The castle's curtain wall, darkened with erosion and moss, defined the outer limits of the training yard. Racks and stands for weapons stood beneath awnings and wooden canopies, but no weapons lay in sight. The trainees probably brought their own weapons to the yard. Kaianne's shoulders slouched on an exhale. Understandable, yet disappointing.

"It'll be hard to do much of anything without something to train with," she murmured. It placed a damper on the thrill that had built at the prospect of exercising some tension out of her muscles.

"Over here, silly." With an old shed at her back, the girl couldn't have looked more out of place in her courtly gown, hair batting in the wind. Its stone structure was as weathered as the curtain walls compared to its relatively new door and roof. "Is a little lock about to keep you out?"

Kaianne shook her head. "I can see why your chichu wants to rein you in. You have Nogo's blood in you."

"I wish. Can you imagine soaring like a griffin or a dragon? To be free in the wind to choose your lot in life?"

Kaianne grabbed the lock and twisted a hairpin within the keyhole. "Sequestered in the Agorethney Mountains, are they truly free? Or is the word 'free' just an illusion of limitations and expectations we set ourselves? Is anyone free? Or do each of us bear the weight of our life's contingencies?"

"Should you not be trying to excite my young self to the joys my future has to bring?"

"No, I'm a realist. I don't spout fairytales."

"Well, aren't you lovely."

The lock clicked open under a last forceful push. With a glance over her shoulder for any onlookers, Kaianne pried the lock off. Rust tinged the hinges and the door creaked open, but the sound was lost in the wide-open space.

"Pyre stricken earth." Kaianne frowned at the girl's odd curse. "What is that smell?"

It was impossible to hold back the burst of laughter at the child's obvious disgust. Lords, it was refreshing to witness her innocence. The stench of sweat and gore assaulted them before their first step within. The shed was bathed in it, but the odor was as familiar to Kaianne as the handling of a weapon. A swirl of air twirled in, a layer of dust spiraling upward from the floor.

Thick gambesons hung on either side of the door, salt stains making it clear they needed washing. One shelf held bandages and ointments, the rest of the room was filled to the brim with weaponry – wooden or metal. There was one tiny window at the shed's rear from which light leaked in and cast shadows on the organized rows of bows, arrows, swords ranging from cutlasses to broadswords, daggers and her favorite – axes. Otherwise, it was only what the open doorway had to offer, which bathed one side with light and left the other in darkness.

Kaianne perused the selection, humming a tune as she inspected the blades. Most were blunted, the sharp edges overworn or damaged. Some spear and arrow tips were dulled or chipped from overuse. She held true to her initial presumption. Trainees more than likely brought their own weaponry. These were the spares.

The girl followed her in. She trailed a finger along the weapons, then rubbed the dust off.

"Are you any good with these?"

"I'd say so."

"Then, I would care for a lesson. I am a good study, I swear."

The eagerness in the noble girl's face was hard to deny. It reminded Kaianne of times in her youth when any opportunity to shed the docile feminine lifestyle was an excuse in and of itself. How many times in her childhood had she wished that someone had treated her as more than a delicate flower to sell? Had included her and made her feel important for more than the rearing of children? This girl wanted more, and the pits could swallow Kaianne whole before she dampened the little one's hopes. Never mind that it would help pass the time.

"We'll start with these." She plucked several throwing knives from the stands and handed two to her pupil. Each knife was made from the same stretch of metal from blade to hilt. It balanced easily on her fingertip despite its nicks. "Before we start, I'll make this clear once and for all. You listen to what I say. You follow my motions, and you don't get hurt. The moment you ignore my lessons, we're done here. We clear?"

"Very." The girl was bouncing in place with a grin as wide as her face.

They neared a target constructed of old wood, stacked tall and wide for this purpose, with a bullseye painted lower center.

"Grab the grip like you would a hammer. No, like this." Kaianne demonstrated her hold, and when her pupil overcorrected, Kaianne adjusted the girl's fingers. There was something to be said about imparting knowledge on to another. It was a powerful feeling, a warmth of pride that began in the chest and spread to her face. "You've never held a hammer, have you?"

"And you have?"

The question had Kaianne clearing her throat with unease. She turned from the girl, continuing with the instructions on aim and follow through.

One knife was lost to the girl's poor aim far beyond the target. A few others clonked and bounced off the wood every which way, as though it were a repellent. A lucky few thunked into the target, all off-center.

"This is hopeless." The child stomped her boot and chucked a lump of snow.

"Careful, your spoiled nature is showing."

"Then you do it. I bet you're all talk. No better than another simpering courtier tossing lies like birdfeed."

Kaianne smirked. Her pulse quickened, warming her fingertips. This would be fun. She flipped a knife in one hand, blade to grip to blade over and over as she picked up the others. The child did not speak while Kaianne readied herself on her marker. Even the birds seemed to quiet as she focused on that chunk of trunk. Nothing else existed.

One after another, the five knives were thrown like pointed extensions of her arms. Every single one thumped into the wood. Better yet, they lined the circle of the bullseye in near-perfectly spaced increments.

With her hand on her hips, Kaianne turned to the girl. "Practice. No one is perfect the first time."

"An absolute truth," a man said behind them, accent heavy with the southern brogue. "Though I think we can rightly agree, some have more talent than others."

Kaianne stiffened. She cursed the sky, trees, ground, even the air, anything to not turn around and let the stranger take note of her tension and angst. Just her luck some wanderer would chance time at the training grounds as well. And she had been careless, demonstrating skills few achieved without rigorous practice.

"Lady Hirai," the stranger said with reverence.

The name had Kaianne whirling to face the girl with surprise. There was only one family with the name Hirai, and it belonged to the Master and his daughter that had lived in Isyldill for nearly as long as she had been Carved. Eybah was her name, per the reports. This child was a lady, not a ladyling – because there was no elder figure that already held the title – and the Master was no Lord. Shite on a stick and stab her through with it. With the memory of her encounter with the Master in the tunnels still fresh, Kaianne's stomach churned on itself, threatening to consume her innards.

"Lordling Sertrios," Eybah responded with an inclination of the head. "A pleasant day, is it not?"

Well, this was just pitting fantastic. Not only had she been fraternizing with the child of a man that could apparently suffocate her through a wall without touch. Now she had gone and gotten herself noticed dressed as a courtier by none other than Jereown Sertrios, the princeling's close friend and confidant, captain of the kingsmen and the realm's best swordsman. Lords, Yannic and Oidh were never going to let her hear the end of this if they ever found out. If she escaped this man's scrutiny alive.

"Ye know very well this area is not open to ye."

"Oh yes, we women are too fragile to lay a foot on such a faraway yard," Kaianne countered with a roll of her eyes.

"Perfectly said." Eybah's grin was saccharine while Sertrios' glower might have made lesser people wither and cringe.

This lording held his head high. His stance was domineering with authority. His broad shoulders and strong arms made it clear the two-handed sword hanging from his belt was no ornament. The sides of his head were shaved while his blond hair was braided up top into a bun. It amplified the hard-set features of his angular face.

"And who keeps yer company, m'Lady?"

"A friend." Eybah's tone brokered no argument. Kaianne snickered at the child's lack of fear when faced with such a foe. It was a reminder that these snakes fed on fear, and she had better swallow every bit of hers down. "What is it we can do for you?"

"'Tis not safe out here on yer own."

"I am not on my own."

"Yes, well, no matter how you flick a knife, ye're no match for an assassin. Ye should not be here after Lordling Bryant was found with his throat slashed through." The man nodded at Eybah's gasp of alarm while Kaianne widened her eyes and raised a hand to her chest, as if to stifle off her shock.

"How dreadful," she said.

"Aye." The lordling seemed unimpressed by her display, going as far as frowning before snapping his attention back to Eybah. "Yer father worries. Sent me on a grand merry search for ye. So get yer wayward legs and mind back to where it needs t'be before the man brings down the walls to find ye."

"Oh. Right, that sounds like him." Eybah sighed dejectedly, before peering up to Kaianne. "More lessons another day, then?"

"As you wish, Lady Hirai."

With a pointed glare, the girl huffed. "I swear names hold too much power."

With Eybah's departure, awkward tension hung between Kaianne and the lordling. His eyes raked over her. Silence spread in the growing chasm. Under his scrutiny, she felt self-conscious of her posture, voice, and appearance. It wasn't just her life that depended on her role here. Yannic in the gardens, Oidh in the city, and every Carved hoping for a solution to the situation.

The number of times her path and Jereown's had crossed in her childhood could be counted on one hand. What in the world

386 | M.T. Fontaine

could she say to him to not raise his hackles further? Kaianne rolled her shoulders and cleared her throat to dispel the strain holding her prisoner. When that did not work, she set to plucking the knives out of the target.

The crunch of snow underfoot signaled his approach. "'Tis rare to find such a skilled noblewoman." He had broken the silence first, and she sighed in relief.

"Rarer than you think since I'm not noble." The lie fell like silk from her tongue after so many stretches of repetition. She unloaded the five knives into his waiting hand.

"Yer skin says otherwise."

"Tragedy of my life. I'm a bastard, you see. A noble thought it his right to force himself on a young woman too handsome for her own good, and I was the consequence."

"Ye speak so freely of it?"

"Why not? The only one it should shame is him. My mother and I deserve none of it."

He harrumphed. "Then what's a bastard doing in m'yard, with Lady Hirai of all people?"

"Training."

The lordling raised one brow, clearly unimpressed. With a shrug, she strolled right past him to the shed door and tugged it open without flourish. The smell assaulted her immediately, but that was not what made her bite her cheek. That was all his frown's doing that turned his round eyes to slits.

"Ye raided the outer armory?"

"You can hardly say those weapons are more than child fodder with the state they're in. No raiding was done once you kindly return those knives in your hands." She winked in the hopes a little charm might loosen his posture.

"What of the blade beneath her skirts?"

Kaianne's smile dropped as she fought the sudden panic clamping her muscles. "My own. You can hardly expect a young woman such as myself to walk around unprotected after my mother's hardship."

"And do ye?" He closed the space between them. His staggering height might have been intimidating if she had not grown surrounded by taller men. A Carved woman only strived if she did not cower beneath men, and that was what Kaianne was, through and through. She met his glare with her own.

"Do I what?"

"Protect yerself with it. Specifically, today."

"You're not very subtle in your interrogation."

"Answer the bloody question."

She shook her head at his upset. "No, dear captain. I did not thrust my blade into the Bryant lordling." Which was true, there had been no thrusting. "However, if it's the Bryant I've had the inconvenience of meeting before, I'll not shed a tear for his death. The man deserved the title of bastard far more than I do."

"Something tells me ye've trickery further up yer sleeves than is natural."

"Call that feminine guile."

He snorted. Clearly she was beguiling him. "The question remains. How was a bastard permitted on castle grounds dressed as a courtier with a weapon strapped to her body?"

There was only one person of importance that could identify her. She had to hope he corroborated with her story because clearly the captain had no intention of loosening his obstinate personality anytime soon. "Andy requested my presence, so I came. I could hardly leave such a friend alone in his time of need."

She cringed inwardly at the use of Andreiyes' pain to protect herself.

"Andy?"

"Yes, Andy. Andreiyes. The princeling. The crown prince's heir."

"The princeling and ye?"

"Aye, it's what I said. No need to be all skeptical about it. You'll make me self-conscious." For emphasis, she tugged on her gown and adjusted her hair.

"He's never made mention of ye."

"That sounds like a you problem."

"Ye're handsome enough, but that tongue on ye is too wicked for his tastes."

"Why thank you."

"There was no praise in it. Where did ye meet him? Show me his correspondence requesting yer presence."

"You can hardly ask me to own up to all my secrets, or show you such sensitive material."

"Oh, I can." With one quick lunge her arm was fully in his grip, and it took considerable control not to drop to her rear to get free. Instead, she scowled and tugged at it weakly. "And I do. Come along, lass. Ye've a tale to prove."

"Are all captains of his Majesty's kingsmen such overgrown, bullheaded oafs? Or does that title solely fall to you?" she asked as he dragged her back through the garden hedges.

"Careful, or I'll know ye're too brutish for the princeling's liking."

"We shall see."

"Which village did ye say ye were from?"

"I didn't."

"There's a bit of an odd twang to yer words I've not heard before."

Any further protests to his treatment died on her tongue. This was something she had not considered, had not even fathomed. But why would her accent not have changed? After stretches spent in the company of Nimedorians, Lakoldesh and Gyldrit Carved, it was only natural for her speech to evolve. Why had Andreiyes not mentioned it? If he had been waiting solely for this sort of opportunity to oust her, the future was looking rather grim.

At the first sign of people, servants and courtiers alike, he wrestled his arm through hers as though they were gallivanting young folk returning from a pleasurable stroll. She let him with a thin-lipped smile, if only to continue the ruse, because never would she escape the castle with so many kingsmen eyes on her. But she didn't miss the flash of worry on Yannic's face as they crossed by him.

The captain leaned toward her until his breath skimmed her ear. "If the princeling cannot confirm yer person, ye'll be hanging from the gallows by morn."

"Is it my charming personality that irritates you so, or the fact a woman can throw knives better than you? If it's the latter, you'll be shamed when you see my skill with a hatchet."

"Is that so? And how does a lass such as yourself come to learn such a trade?"

"As like most things in life. Necessity."

"Whatever would a lass with noble skin have to fear?"

She scoffed. "You've no true experience outside of what wealth and privilege brings. I may have had a noble father, but my life was far from pleasant."

"That furthers the oddity of yer acquaintance with the princeling."

He forced her through the castle's threshold, then tugged her down the corridors at a hurried pace while passersby flattened themselves along the wall, mostly soldiers and servants. One such servant caught Kaianne's eye the moment the woman turned into their corridor. She held a bouquet while a coterie of maids trailed behind her, their arms brimming with bedding, decorative pillows and candlesticks. Whereas the three young servants kept their heads ducked on their approach, Mimsee held no such compunction.

Kaianne's old governess watched them behind stern eyes. They were further creased than Kaianne remembered. Strands of gray wove through the braid weaved over her head. Her visage had plumped up to hide its heart shape, but those thin lips, wide cheekbones and her signature high-neck dress trims gave her away.

With watery eyes, Kaianne smiled at the woman. It had been so long. Oidh had kept Kaianne apprised of Mimsee's wellbeing. Seeing her in person and well-cared for made her warm and thankful inside and out. A weight had cleared from her conscience.

"I've missed you, Mimsee," she mouthed as the lordling hauled her past them.

Mimsee frowned, the look turning contemplative before her eyes widened in shock and she whispered, "*Ynnea?*"

Kaianne nodded discreetly to not attract the lordling's attention. Her breath quivered as she suppressed happy tears from trekking down her face. If only she could embrace her old governess.

"Later?" Kaianne mouthed, but Jereown led her around another bend before Mimsee could respond. Still, her heart swelled. A piece of her old self was here, someone she could trust, someone who didn't care what she was.

Sandfalls dragged before they reached Andreiyes' door where two guardsmen stood sentry. One of whom had been a Carved captive along with the princeling, and that bull of a man with hair that reminded her of Willik's was frowning at her. All the flurries of lightness she had felt at Mimsee's passing vanished.

"Is he within, Uslan?" Sertrios asked the familiar guard.

Lords, if this Uslan recognized her, made the connection to the young lad who had saved them all… Shites, another problem to handle, but she buried her anguish and whirled on the lordling with flourish.

"I'll expect a full apology after this." Head held high, she knocked hard on the door without waiting for his response.

The door was hauled open from within.

"What?" Andreiyes' tone was harsh and unforgiving.

His eyes found his captain's. The puffy edge to them had darkened into droopy shadows. His tunic lay half-in half-out of his unlaced trousers. There were no boots or slippers on his feet, and his hair was arched to one side as though he had spent far too long tugging at it. He looked unstable and completely sloshed if his unsteady movements and the tumbler of spirits clutched in his fingers were anything to go by. When his head and eyes rolled about and met hers, his expression softened. Relief – she hoped that's what it was – smoothed his features.

"Kaianne. You brought me Kaianne." His breath reeked. Yes, he was absolutely drowning in liquor if he was that thrilled to see her. "My best mate, you rightly are, Jereown."

Whereas the lordling's grip had been bruising, Andreiyes' clutch was clumsy but direct. He tugged her into his chambers – she was getting rather sick of men manhandling her today – and waved his men off with his tumbler.

"That will be all."

A laugh bubbled from her at the stunned look on Sertrios' face. Just before the door closed in his face, she mouthed '*apology*'. She had rarely felt such satisfaction at receiving a narrowed glare.

"Where did you go?" Andreiyes asked. She craned her neck to look into his turbulent, amber eyes. "You left me."

He still held onto her arm, but she didn't feel the need to fight him off. "I didn't think you cared what I went on about."

"My tonic." His throat bobbed. "You might not have returned in time to give it."

"No. That's not your reason."

He grunted and swirled the molten liquor before downing it in one gulp. "Willik Bryant is dead. The guards arrested someone. A groundskeeper."

Yannic. Panic hit her like a blow to the chest, her fingers twitching with the need to aid her comrade. Lords, this was her fault. If anything happened to him…

"How long ago?" she pressed.

"A sandturn, maybe more." Not Yannic then. Her body sagged with a sigh of relief. "I thought-"

His eyes trailed over her face to pause on her lips before cutting off to stare at his blazing hearth as brusquely as his words had.

"Aw, were you worried about me?" she teased.

He flinched, cleared his throat and raked a hand through his hair. There was almost a jittery quality to his movements, but instead of answering he poured himself another glass of liquor while still holding onto her firmly. Well, that would not do. If he was going to ignore her, then she was going to rid him of his alcoholic distraction. It was a cinch lifting his glass from his fingers. Even better, it burned deliciously down her throat with an earthy edge.

"Exquisite." She licked her lips of the last drops, but it didn't loosen his. He simply stared at her. She rolled her eyes, taping her heels in irritation. Men were so dull when inebriated, their minds turning into empty pits. She ducked beneath his arm to twist from his grasp, but he resisted and pulled her back into his chest instead.

"Yes," he whispered, laying his forehead against her head. "Gods below, yes I was. A tormented mess."

His lips tickled her ear. They pressed against her skin, soft and passionate. They trailed to her neck, and she arched her head to give better access. This was not at all how she had expected this to go, but it had been so many cycles since she had last been touched.

"What you do to me..." He tugged on the collar of her coat. Another kiss, this time to her collarbone. Each press of his lips turned more demanding than the last. Her breath hitched at every touch. His fingers dug into her skin. "You buried yourself beneath my skin. You hold my life in your hands, and I find myself unable to hate you for it."

They were sweet words, words that made her heart race, but that's all they were. "Andreiyes, you're drunk."

"Yes. Yes, I very well am."

"You'll regret this proposition tomorrow."

His hand wandered to her stomach, edging a little higher at every decadent kiss. Every single one warmed her and threatened to turn her into a puddle for him to slip through and soak in. Perhaps if he were not in this state and she was not feeding him tonics, a momentary lapse in judgment would not be so ill-advised. But here, now, it was wrong. This heat, this passion, these sensations couldn't happen.

"Andy..."

"I wish you were not Carved."

That chopped through the fervor like a butcher's knife through bone. She stopped his roving hand at the underside of her breasts and faced him.

"If I wasn't Carved, I'd be dead. Even if I weren't, I wouldn't be the same woman before you. This life made me who I am. I wouldn't choose another one. This *is* who I am."

He leaned in, seemingly unfazed by her declaration. His lips grazed hers to place a kiss at their corner.

"I care for you as you are."

"No, no you don't. This is the liquor talking. You're grieving."

He nodded. "Yes, yes I am. Help me grieve, Kaianne. Be better to me than I was to you."

That did it. That ended the momentary delusion of whatever this was. "Wouldn't be hard since you left a girl of twelve to fend for herself." She pushed him back and he stumbled to his rear with a thump. "I told you once, I won't be a distraction for you. Company, yes, but I'm no courtier for you to use and discard."

She extended her hand to him. With a resigned look on his face, he grabbed it and let her pull him up. "Tonight we talk of Edmira for however long you wish. Tomorrow, you face the world head-on with the truth of what you now are, your father's heir."

His head fell to her shoulder, but just as she was about to push him off, his body trembled. Her neckline's shoulder moistened. He sniffled.

"She did not deserve this. The babe did not."

Kaianne patted and caressed his back. "Very few do."

His sniffles turned to sobs and then to blubbering. It was awkward. Where did one place their hands when trying to comfort someone without being too familiar? She let him grip her cloak and dress in firm handfuls while he unleashed his pain in the crook of her neck. She crept her hands up and down his spine like Mimsee had done to her as a little girl. Even grown men with kingdoms at their feet needed soothing. He was being vulnerable with her, no masks, no etiquette, no recriminations. Right then, she forgave him his absence in her young life. It had led them to right now where he shared his pain to her in a way she imagined few would ever see again.

When he calmed, they spoke for sandturns on end. Near the hearth, on the lounge chairs, on his bed. Every tale featured Edmira as the main character through the pranks he played on her, their conversations, her hopes, her wedding. He detailed every bit of it, laughed through some of it, raged through other bits, but overall he relaxed while his rock of a head crushed her thighs. The day's bright gleam faded slowly through the windows and sprayed the eve's pink and purples through sheer curtains.

They ordered meals brought into his chambers, which she forced him to eat. Never mind that his stomach rebelled against the liquor in his system and sent the lot of it spewing back into his chamberpot. She held his hair if only because she hoped someone would do the same for her. But she made him change himself, unwilling to let any spark of what she had so abruptly put an end to earlier reappear.

After tucking him into bed – Lords, he was dependent when drunk – she readied his vial of tonic. He was still muttering through the hopes he had held for Edmira as queen when the uncorked container met his lips.

"You'll have to be the one to achieve all those goals now. For her."

Quick as lightning, he caught her wrist before she tipped the vial's gunky contents down his throat. His eyes were wild and shaky. "You do not understand. I was supposed to save her from the Stewards. Who will save me?"

She gave him a soft smile and smoothed his locks from his forehead. This vulnerable side to Andreiyes was worth basking in, and it warmed her inside and out that he was willing to show it to her. "I will. We will. Together. Everything will be alright. Drink and sleep. More can be discussed on the morrow."

A glass of water followed the fluid down his throat. All the while he held her gaze. A range of emotions twisted his face from one to the next too quickly for her to grasp. Soon his eyes were fluttering closed. Her breaths evened out. His soft snores filled the bedchamber with a rhythmic presence. She laid her head upon the pillow beside his, his profile the epitome of peacefulness. The comforting scents of pine and sea-brine remained despite all the candles having gone cold. She closed her eyes, feeling calmer and more relaxed than she had been in a long while.

Right here, right then, there was no one to attack her. It was just her, the princeling and their hopes for a better future. The more time she spent with this man, the more she convinced herself he did not condone the systematic slaughter of Carved and Flawed. By his side, even the memory of the Master's talent squeezing the life out of her did not hold her captive.

Perhaps there was a chance they had a common enemy. Already she imagined how strong the realms could be if Marked and Carved banded together against the Stewards. It was a good dream - a vision of the people united and a world where nobody cared what brand stained their arms. Before that could happen, she needed to tell him the truth and hope he did not hold it against her.

Thirty-five

When Andreiyes stretched his limbs and opened his eyes the next morning, he startled at the sight of Kaianne's face so close to his own. For a moment, he considered sending her tumbling out of his bed, but there was no panic to her presence, no disgust, no wariness. Only a twinge of embarrassment at yesterday's behavior.

For the first night in nearly a cycle, he had slept with a measure of peace. The pain and shock at Ed's death persisted, but today instead of a throbbing burn, it was steady and settled like a paperweight on his chest. It hurt, but this was bearable. And this stubborn, maddening woman beside him had helped.

He relaxed his head back on his cushion, taking in the resting features of her face, her ash hair splayed around her head. Peaceful like this, she resembled an offering from the gods instead of the conniving woman she was. Not a speck of grime marred her skin, and her scent reminded him of the freshness brought by a new day.

His fingers itched to caress her hair from her face. He longed to see her dark eyes flutter open to show their constant strength and defiance. It was so much more gratifying than the reverence and awe his past bedmates gave him. And those lips, gods he wanted to devour them, but she had already given him two rejections to his advances. No matter his title, his ego would not handle a third dismissal well.

As he denied himself, an unpleasant sensation gnawed at his chest. He trailed a finger along her face while he imagined palming her cheek and caressing her neck, her breasts, the dips in her waist and further still until he was buried completely within her. He bent in toward her only to restrain himself a hair's width away. Her soft breath warmed the skin beneath his morning stubble. He groaned. The unintended consequence of his desire for her was now firmly pressed against her thigh. This was wrong, and not just because of what she was. He wanted to possess her as much as she was pushing him toward insanity, but he was not the drunken knob he had been the night before.

A peck to his lips made him flinch. Worse, her giggle had him wanting to take it further, to consume her, to show he was worth more than a peck.

"Good morn to you too, handsome."

"Aye," was all he could manage. Gods, she stole his reasoning away.

"You look better." Her fingertips grazed his chin's stubble in a comforting tickle.

They each stared at the other, the amber ring around her dark eyes pulling him in despite the fact the color was no different from that of any other Isyldillian-born.

"Do you always attempt to steal kisses from sleeping women?"

He settled back along the bed, an arm supporting his head and a knee propped up – a carefree portrait, or so he hoped.

"This is new territory. Never before has a woman sampled the comforts of my bed without my thorough perusal first."

His attempt at nonchalance had her features bunching before she swept the emotion off her face. He even wondered if he had imagined it. Then she rose with a sigh to sit on the edge of his bed, her back to him. His throat bobbed from the sight of her back outlined in a simple nightgown. From this vantage point, he could make out the curve of one breast. Thoughts of that breast in his hands, its nipple in his mouth jumped to the forefront of his mind Oh, how he wanted to tease her to the brink and back before pushing her to her limits again for making him feel this way.

"Do you…" she began, her voice uneasy. "When is Edmira's pyre being set?"

He blinked. All erotic thoughts were doused. He had not expected that topic to come up, not after just waking up in bed together. "Not until the Festival of Life's eve."

"Another nine days?"

"Aye." A shaky breath escaped Andreiyes. Edmira's body had been treated, oiled, salted, and today would be wrapped. The cremation could wait. He only hoped her soul and that of the little babe had already reached Iltheln, and that they were enjoying the splendors and peace of the afterlife. She deserved it. "We mourn. Our people too. Together we shall all send her off with the start of a new stretch. Father believes it will be a better omen."

"Of course," Kaianne whispered with a nod. "And what does your resident Master think?"

Those words sent a chill down his spine. "What does it matter? It would have been best if the Master had long since returned to his temple."

Her brow creased. "Does that mean you meant what you said yesterday?"

"A great deal was said."

"I meant about you needing help against the Stewards." It was his turn to balk. Gods below, he wanted to impale himself. "You implied requiring a knight to rescue you."

The teasing lilt to her voice had him recoiling. "I never took you to trust the words of a roaring souse."

"What lovely words to describe yourself."

"If it irks you, I might press the advantage."

She raised her head, her long hair reaching closer to the sheets as she whispered mutterings to the ceiling.

"I'd like a chance to help you, Andy." She peered over her shoulder at him with a hallowed look.

"Yesterday's events are elusive."

"You seem to remember enough," she spat.

Now he sat upright, fists bunched in the sheets, jaw clenched. "This is not something I will share with you. 'Tis not your concern."

"What a surprise. The great princeling is unable to acknowledge he needs help." She flung herself off the bed. "It doesn't make you a greater man. It makes you weak. Do you think you're the only one with secrets?"

"It only takes one misguided individual to topple a kingdom. Too easily can secrets slip from the shadows. How long until everyone is aware of mine?"

"The difference between the two of us is that given the chance, I would choose to trust you. I would choose to work together."

"Is that what they call an exchange of poison and tonic these days?" he sneered.

Her face tightened in anger. "Now you're just making excuses. How long are you going to hold that over me?"

"'Tis my life, how long do you expect?" He stood, his nightwear brushing his knees.

She bit her lip, mauling it between her front teeth.

"Do you know why I'm here? Why this ruse was put on?" Her eyes were burning, despite their dark color. She clutched his hand. "Carved and Marked are at each other's throats, and for what? At least Carved fight for our lives. What do Marked gain except an enemy? The royals all across the realms are turning their people against them. Do you realize how many more Carved have joined since the Flawed Edicts of 947? How long until there is no one left on either side?

"This needs to end. A Marked is no better than a Carved. A Flawed is no worse than a Marked. If you could just try to see the logic behind this. If you could as third-in-line address it with your father. Have him address it with the King. Work to change the laws. Work to unite the people. Unconfine the border."

"Nothing is ever that simple."

"Then explain it to me. Make me understand. Help make our world better. Isn't that your duty as Isyldill's princeling?" She crushed his palm between her fingers, her eyes pleading.

"I *cannot*."

"Is it saving from yourself that you need then?"

"Do not turn this around on me." She made him want to tug out his own hair. "What of the other realms? Are you going to plead them as well?"

"Change has to start somewhere before others can join."

"Why Isyldill first?"

"Why not?"

They stared at each other coldly. All the warmth Andreiyes had felt at her presence upon waking had vanished. Finally, she broke their stare and shook her head.

"Unbelievable. You would rather hide and do nothing. Lords, I thought better of you." Her words were clipped. "Well then, I'll not trouble you further. Just tell me where I can find some appropriate attire and I'll leave you be."

"Who will you impersonate today? A soldier? A jester? Or for once in your life, a Lady?"

"I'll never be one of those. Your Northern Commander and kingsmen made sure of that, but now that your captain has noticed me, the games have begun. Unless you plan on telling him you're sympathetic to a Carved. No? Then I'll have to pretend to be the same courtier, won't I?"

Irritation thrummed through him at the mention of Jereown. Despite his drunken stupor, Andreiyes had caught the disapproval on his friend's face, and yet what bothered him most was that the man had spent time with her. It was unseemly, ridiculous, but his skin itched with unease.

"Courtiers are usually more discreet when they spend the night."

She scoffed. "I highly doubt that."

"And they always leave before daylight sets in."

"What are you saying?"

"Leaving my chambers at this hour will spread rumors. I cannot have that."

"Rumors? You think I give a spitting fire pit about your rumors?" Her nose flared. Her eyes burned as hard as the red tinge creeping over her caramel skin. "I'm not one of your playthings you half-witted, bedswerver, tawdry ninny of a wanker."

It was hard to bury his surprised chortle. She collected yesterday's attire and slipped it on without a care to his proximity or his stares. Gods below, whatever was he to do with this woman?

"I expect to be given clothes and a guest chamber of my own as your part in this ruse."

The request was terse and demanding as it fell from her clenched teeth, and yet he was nodding despite himself. Once her belt was cinched around her waist and the fur shawl was wrapped around her shoulders, her gaze met his again. Her prior anger was replaced with an emotion that sunk into his chest and too closely resembled disappointment for his liking.

"We cannot keep going as we have been, Andreiyes. Something has to change for us all to have a chance at freedom."

"Marked are already free."

"Are you? From what I've seen and lived, no one is." She made her way through his sitting room and to the main door. "Carved and Marked together against the Stewards. Think on it."

Once she had left, he slumped onto a chaise, buried his fingers into his hair and tugged in frustration. Thinking was always the easiest part. It was the doing that took effort. The enacting that revealed the challenges. The enforcing that changed lives for better or worse. Nothing consequential ever happened with the snap of one's fingers.

Thirty-six

*F*or days he avoided Kaianne, and she returned the favor. Every morning when he awoke and every eve before he retired, he found his tonics on his davenport along with a letter.

The first time, he crumpled the parchment in his hand. He needed time to deliberate over their conversation and decide the best course of action. More words from her would not hurry his thoughts, but the crumpled ball of paper taunted him from inside his wastebin. In the end, frustration and curiosity bested his restraint and had him unfurling the note. What farfetched notions would Kaianne spout now?

Will you please, dear princeling, have me directed to the archives chamber? It seems your castle is too large and this mysterious chamber too elusive.

The Snake in your Pit, K.

He scoffed, stunned at the banter and the request without a hint made to their argument. What was she playing at now? His initial response was a terse 'No', but the curled N with the singular 'o' were so forlorn on the long strip of vellum that his quill scratched out more.

*No, dear snake, it would be too simple a thing to award you what you
wish. I very much desire to prolong your frustrations.*
The Wrangler to your Notions, the Princeling

With a smirk, he handed the letter off to be delivered to the
chambers he had arranged for her on the opposite wing of the
castle to avoid too much gossip. Courtiers and nobles alike did
enjoy far too much of it.

The rest of that first day he spent attempting to avoid
contact with much of anyone. Unsuccessfully, much to his
regret. Unlike Kaianne who showed him no pity, others were
quick to offer their condolences and smother him with their
expectations of his woeful state and how heartsick he must be.
Mothers attacked with presentations of their daughters as
though they might soothe his loss. When it was not those types
of nobles he escaped from, it was his stepmother.

It was disturbing how satisfied the woman was that her son
was one person closer to the throne. Had Aethel's curse not
protected the royal line, Andreiyes held no doubt the woman
would have poisoned them all to assure her son's succession –
Nergail, the eleven-stretched old boy who still threw such loud
tantrums. Just that afternoon, the boy had gashed a cook's back
with a butcher's knife after the man refused the boy a fourth
cake. Andreiyes witnessed the tail end of it and had been forced
to lock his half-brother in the larder while waiting for the guards
to subdue the boy.

Then it was Master Rau offering sympathies that came out
as stiff and formal as the man himself. The Steward lectured
him detachedly how the royals could lean on Stewards if need
be, how their collaboration was as strong as ever, and that
Andreiyes' new future duty would bring them closer than ever.
The way the Master droned, it was clear the monologue was
costing him as much to say it as it was for Andreiyes to hear it.

It was a blinding relief when Andreiyes locked himself in his
chambers that evening. His head fell back against the door with
a thump, the silence among the crackle of flames in the hearth
the best of sounds. Gods forgive him the need for peace. Yet,

when his eyes caught on the vial and the note beneath it on his davenport, he smirked.

Wrangler,
I see you deem me unworthy of your name despite having memorized it in my early age. No matter, two can play this game. You were always up for those, weren't you?
What outstretches your existence, spoken or penned, and known as fact or fiction? Can you guess it? I do hope so, otherwise I might presume my estimation of your worth an oversight.
The Pit Viper in your Thoughts

With a chuckle, he set himself to writing a response. The candlelight from the candelabrum on his davenport flickered as shadows from his hands and quill splayed over the parchment.

Dearest Viper,
The name suits. I do so enjoy knowing you hold me in such high esteem. I would not dream of failing it with an answer so simple as history. Perhaps try harder next time, or it is my esteem for you that might falter.
Is history what you seek, then? What will you do with it if I grant you access to the archives chamber?
The Wrangler of your Intentions

Andreiyes read over his response once more with a curved smile. There was a lightness in his chest at how easy these exchanges were, at how calm he felt after such a tumultuous day. He had been hoping to find another letter from her. That last realization almost had him tearing the paper and throwing it in the bin. Instead, he downed the vial of green gunk and placed the empty container over his response.

That night, sleep evaded him. He lay wide awake, staring at the darkness, unable to wrestle away his thoughts into oblivion. Normally, no matter the events of the day, the Mistress of Dreams pried him into a deep sleep the instant his head hit his pillow. That night, he felt the sandturns pass as the moonslight dappled through his curtains only to be conquered by the rays of sunrise creeping in.

That was when he heard the click of a lock and the creak of an entry. Andreiyes held perfectly still, waiting. He noticed the slight dip in temperature and the patter of footsteps. The armoire tunnel passage, that was where she was coming from. Clever woman. At least he hoped it was her. That was confirmed when parchment was ruffled, a woman chortled, and glass clanked softly. He closed his eyes, imagining her shaking her head.

A tap against a jar and the scratch of a quill in use in the next room were soothing. A yawn crept from him, and fatigue pulled him under before the quill had finished rendering its message.

※⬇※

M y Honored Wrangler,
I only need to be shown the way before I grant myself access. And that will be to read a tome or a few, of course. From there, relevancy will need to be discerned before any expectations are made. For now, this viper coils hope tightly while the hunger grows for a morsel to sink her fangs into.

I hope to not misplace my words when I say my esteem for you has recently grown. Much more than I had ever thought possible. That said, I know our reacquaintance has done little to build yours for me. Our last encounter has made me realize our intentions will forever differ. I should not have involved you, but I cannot regret my actions if the ends justify the means. Help me, Wrangler, to justify those means. Help me and this viper will slither away from your life to give you the peace you deserve.
The Viper who Plagues you

Andreiyes squeezed the vellum in his fist, the parchment crackling. He had rushed from the warmth of his bed for this? Begging words of regret and an implied farewell. It left a sour taste in his mouth.

Outside, dark clouds blocked the sun graying the sprawling view from his windows of Lityoll and the forest surrounding the butte and city. What peace was she referring to, because he was feeling none of it. Did she think another Carved giving him murky dosages of tonic might lessen her guilt? That sort of

406 | M. T. Fontaine

peace sounded one-sided. Or was her thrill in this twisted game of hers over and she was willing to withhold his tonics to end both their lives?

His hair was disheveled by constant tugs by the time he ordered his servants bathe and dress him. He commanded his breakfast be brought to his sitting room, and he ate in silence, anger simmering under his skin. Always, his gaze returned to his davenport. Peace, that word haunted him. There was no peace in his life as it was, and this – what she was offering – was doing the exact opposite. Finally, he hastily scratched a few words on a parchment.

My Toxic Viper,
And if I do not let you go? If I want no peace from you? If I want the plague? What then?
These circumstances were initiated by you. Only I have the right to end them.
The Wrangler that Overrides you

Before he could give his words a once-over, a knock at his suite's entrance stole his focus. He folded the note and placed the empty vial atop it. Without a glance back, he stomped from his chambers.

It was a new day. Today, instead of confronting feigned platitudes of pity, he needed to meet with the Seer of Events for Edmira's funeral and to finish the planning for the Festival of Life his sister had begun on her deathbed. Gods below, he was not made for this, but the gods had never given the royals a choice. The line of succession had to be respected, no matter the dread swishing in his gut.

❊↓❊

Several times throughout his morning meeting with the Seer of Events, Andreiyes considered sprinting to his chambers to destroy the ridiculous note written to Kaianne, but for propriety's sake he stayed the course, trotted through the grounds and city and performed his duty as heir to the crown prince to plan revelry for the people. Gods above, below and in between, what had possessed him to write such words?

When he returned to his chambers after midday meal, a full vial lay ready for him for that eve, but there was no parchment beneath it. The dread that had been with him all morning grew heavier, but he tampered it down. It was only midday after all.

The afternoon was no better as Andreiyes was left to deal with Edmira's abandoned correspondences and to choose the arrangements for her funeral as his father played the statue with a face of frozen grief. Andreiyes could not fault him for it. Not after Balliol had already lost the love of his life, an unborn child, and now his eldest child and first grandchild.

His stomach churned when the Seer of Events had him choose a burial gown for his sister's cremation. The discomfort in his gut turned putrid and ready to burn through flesh and bone when he found in Edmira's secretary a letter dated only a quint ago from his brother-in-law demanding his wife send him more funds to help manage his estates. While his wife had been dying, after the child had already been lost. That piss sucker.

They had not heard a word from the man since her death. His father, Lord of House Dresden, had sent notice of his impending arrival to Castle Ravensten in a cycle's time to pay his respects to his departed daughter-in-law and grandchild. If Arkov was not with him, if that foul soul had remained behind, well then, not even Balliol could keep Andreiyes from skewering the man up his arse until his sword jutted out of Arkov's throat. By the gods, he swore he would do it now that Aethel's curse no longer protected the lordling since Edmira's passing.

It was with that rotten mood that he returned to his chambers. And there it only worsened, for still no new parchment awaited atop his davenport. Worse, the vial for the eve was gone. He froze at the sight. First, confusion blanked his thoughts. Then, a rage he had never felt before took over.

Andreiyes swept his davenport clean of everything. Ink bottles clanged to the floor and spilled their contents. Quills littered the black pools of ink. The feathers quickly drenched in its color. Papers did the same. A vase crashed and shattered.

Flowers were scattered among the dark puddles. The liquid crept along the crevices in the hardwood blackening everything in its wake.

He tugged at his hair, then dug his palms into his eyes. That gods blighted woman was at her machinations again. All those words, all those moments when he thought her more than what she was, those few moments when he thought of trusting her. That had dread cramping the storm in his gut. Something seized at his chest and threatened to crush it. It had to be the panic, had to be, and yet it ached like a loss. He was a fool, a shortsighted one for having written that letter and so much more. If this was her version of peace, he wanted none of it.

And yet, he could not find in it himself to send the guards to fetch her and demand she give him his tonic. The gods knew he wanted to inflict pain on her, but not tonight. Not until he devised the perfect plan. Instead, he drank his weight in kerchdy, willing the liquor to dissolve his misery of the day.

⌖⌖⌖

*H*e woke the next morning seated in a chaise, squinting at the painful sunlight beaming through his sitting room's curtains. A cold compress was pressed to his head. He winced and wiped the wet cloth over his eyes. Someone tugged it back up and stuck a glass of orange liquid that reeked of fermentation with a fruity but vinegary tang.

"Drink up," Mimsee commanded.

With those two words, he knew there would be no point in arguing. Despite their difference in rank, Mistress Harleston took her duty to her chosen charges quite seriously. If she wanted him to swallow the thing, he would find it down his throat one way or another. The question was why she was in his chambers imposing her care on him instead of waiting on his sister, Katheryn. He did as bid but hacked at his throat. The concoction tasted as vile as it smelled.

"There, there, we'll be having ye feel as fresh as an egg in no time."

He groaned at the headache her overly loud voice caused. "Whisper, Mimsee. Your voice carries."

"Aye, perhaps then ye'll reconsider burying yer head in the bottle."

"Not that I do not appreciate your help, but why are you here?"

"Ye have m'lady in a worry. As her tongue is more clipped than ever, I thought it best to hear the cause from the horse's mouth. And here I find ye drunker than a maiden on her wedding day."

"Did you just compare me to a horse and a maiden?" He shifted to standing and gripped the back of the chaise as the room spun. "What has Katheryn so worried?"

"Not the princess, dear boy." Andreiyes grunted at the term. "I mean, m'lady of the House I've sworn m'self to."

"Oh. That woman. I think the term 'lady' is too loosely applied. She poisoned me, you know. Has set herself to ruining my life."

"Quit yer wallowing. Ye do that all by yer lonesome carrying on as ye do."

"I do not wallow." He clutched his gurgling stomach as he bent to grab some bread off his breakfast platter. It seemed the least likely thing to make him heave. Even the smells of eggs drizzled with lard had him gagging.

"Could ye fault her to get yer stubborn self to give her time o' day? Just give m'lady a chance. Try and see through her eyes."

"I would much rather fall into an eternal sleep and never cross into Iltheln."

Despite his back being to her as he gulped down a pitcher full of water, he could almost hear the roll of her eyes that accompanied her sighs. The water washed down his powdery palate, but his head still ached something fierce.

"That might be my best idea to date." He lumbered toward his bedchamber, the plush of pillows and the mattress a high motivator despite the uncomfortable churning in his belly. "Have my meetings rearranged for tomorrow and lock my door on your way out."

With that, he tumbled face first into his bedsheets and dragged himself without ceremony up to his pillow.

"Stiff-necked ye are, as always. And yet M'Lady still cares for ye."

He groaned in dismay at her lack of departure but did not protest when she tucked him in. "If she told you that, 'tis just another one of her ploys."

"She needn't say the words for them to be written on her face. Sleep, Andreiyes, and may the Mistress of Dreams soothe yer soul."

Words, they were just words, and yet they weighed on his mind as much as this gods-blighted headache. Andreiyes watched Mistress Harleston retreat, listened for the click of the door and lock, and relaxed when muffled and distant conversation reached his ear. He glanced around his room for unknown threats before settling into his pillow and reached to grab the one beside him. Paper crackled with the ruffling of sheets. Without rising, his hand fumbled for the origin until a parchment rubbed between the crook of two fingers.

He choked back an inhale. How long had this been here? His fingers shook as he unfolded the vellum and recognized the familiar scroll.

Wrangler to my affections,
These letters make me bold.

If I were to take a chance on you, what would you do? If you were to discover there was no lethal poison, that the tonic only settles your stomach from a toxic resin applied to your clothes? That none of it had been given to you for two quints? What then? If I gave up my leverage, would you seek my end or my gain?

I want trust between us. I've taken the first step. Will you take the second?

> *The Viper that Preys on your good Heart*

That did it. His stomach finally revolted. Andreiyes barely reached his chamberpot in time to catch the sick that launched out of him.

Thirty-seven

During the day after Andreiyes had read her final note, he caught sight of her only once. Within grainfalls, she averted her gaze and ducked into a throng of courtiers he had no desire to throw himself into.

It built his turmoil further. Their discussion, argument, squabble, whatever it was, played on repeat in his head. Compiled with her deviousness, her admissions in their notes and how she refused to confront him directly, it was driving him steadily insane. He despised uncertainty, yet it lingered with him for over a day.

In the training yard, he watched his men spar and breathed in the grunts, the pounding and the clanging of weapons. Their footwork skidded through puddles of melted snow and squelched in mud. He did not partake, keeping his thoughts on his choices, plans, and men. The ones whose numbers were bound to prove insufficient against the Stewards' talents. But to ally with Carved traitors...

Andreiyes rubbed a thumb over the griffin head mark on his forearm. A symbol of Isyldill and a binding to it as well. Carved chose to renege their homelands. Removing this brand was a denial of their allegiance to their kingdom. A decision to deny their loyalty and refuse to contribute to their country. Could he overlook that treachery?

He swiped a hand over his eyes and down his jaw. He too had committed such treason stretches ago. The carving of Kaianne's mark still haunted him, but the truth was worse. If he had correctly interpreted his glimpse of the realm's floating golden-dotted map, it had saved her life. How many others made that choice, not to abandon their kingdom but to save their lives? Was it truly a choice if death was the only other option?

There were stark differences between the dusty historical tomes buried deep in the archives chamber and the history taught by more recent elaborations. Edmira and him had often compared notes on the divergences on topics dating even before the Apostate War. How much of what they knew of the Marked, Carved and Flawed was truth and what was misconception or downright lies? There were entire prophecies written about the bleak future a Carved and Flawed uprising would cause. They were set to destroy the realms. But where did the Order stand in all this? After spending so many stretches with Master Rau, it was hard to imagine anyone overpowering them.

"Andreiyes."

The princeling whipped his head around, shocked he had been so absentminded to miss Jereown's approach.

"Are ye well?" Jereown asked, a crease in his brow.

"Aye."

The last of his kingsmen was retiring for the day as the sun set over the horizon. The sky melted into reds and purples while clouds approached from the north. The air had gone heavy, weighted with the humidity promising rain on the morrow. Andreiyes rubbed at his temples, suddenly aware of the tinge in his legs. He had stood there for sandfalls, lost in thought and with nothing to show for it.

"Ye've not been the same since that lass barged into yer life."

"I have had much to consider since Edmira's passing."

"Oh feck all. True, ye're mourning, but this…" Jereown gestured at Andreiyes' face. "'Tis not the face for it. Ye're a brooding mess, and if ye were not one of the ten in line for the throne, I'd slit yer throat just to put ye out of yer misery."

"What a good friend you are."

"Aye, the best." Jereown tapped him on the back before he leaned and rested his elbows on the wooden fence that designated the edge of the training yard. "And this friend'll tell ye that that lass is the worst trouble there is. She'll drag ye through more muck than ye need."

Andreiyes snorted. How right he was. "'Tis the circumstances not the woman that trouble me."

"If ye believe that, ye're further gone than I thought." For a while, they stood side-by-side as the sun crept further below the horizon and pulled the sky's color along with it. "I know there's much ye've not made me privy to, but don't let that beating kernel in yer chest drive what spouts from yer mouth."

"You make me sound like a halfwit."

"Aren't we all with women? No shame in being led by yer todger. Happens to us all, I'd wager."

Andreiyes sighed. "I have been avoiding her."

"I know. If ye want to keep on that path, ye need to leave. She'll be coming around to train shortly. Does so every morn, midday and eve, if the yard is clear."

"And you let her? I would not think you prone to letting just anyone in your yard."

"Aye, but she's not just anyone, is she? And if it were only that..." Andreiyes waited patiently for Jereown to continue, knowing the man was baiting him. "For such a wee thing, her range of skill is quite impressive. Her footwork too. Better than some of the men. No balking under pressure, either."

"You sparred with her?" Bitterness gnawed at him.

"Oh, aye. And she's got quite a handle on polearms." Jereown rubbed his arm. "Got m'self nicked with one of her vicious thrusts."

"That must have satisfied her taste for blood."

"If her grin was anything to judge by. I've rarely seen one that bloodthirsty. Wherever did you find her?"

"You almost sound admiring, considering your earlier admonishment."

"Perhaps I meant the lass is not good enough for ye."

Andreiyes raised a brow at his friend. "But she is good enough for you, is that it?"

His captain slapped his back and chuckled. "Ye worried 'bout a little competition? Should we try to see who can gather the lass' attention first?"

Andreiyes gripped the fence and squeezed. The leather of his gloves squeaked in the creases of his hand as he ground his teeth. His fool of a friend was grinning like a ninny, probably mocking him for the restraint it took to keep his fists locked tight around the wood instead of pummeling Jereown's blond face.

"Teasing aside, have yer fun but keep alert. None are that proficient, especially a lass, unless they made themselves be."

This conversation had quickly turned from unpleasant to unnerving. Andreiyes cleared his throat and relaxed his hold on the fence with a shaky breath. "Have you found the Bryant lordling's murderer?"

"No." Even without facing Jereown, Andreiyes felt the prickle of his gaze. "Any reason ye mention it now?"

"So that you drop any mention of Kaianne."

"Such familiarity. If she's yer mistress already, why the misery?"

"Not my mistress."

Jereown grunted beside him. "Ah, then that explains it."

A breeze drifted past, ruffling their fur cloaks. With every day that passed, more brown patches were unearthed beneath the layers of white the realm had been buried in for nearly a stretch. Soon the weather would only require a simple overcoat.

The crunch of snow and voices signaled others approaching. Excitement filled a jumpy high-pitched voice while a more-mature woman's voice attempted to calm her. Andreiyes glanced over his shoulder. A girl wearing riding pants bounced with giddiness beside a woman dressed in men's trousers.

"There's yer lass now," Jereown whispered.

Andreiyes' eyes widened. He raked a hand down the lower part of his face as he followed their approach, but she had yet to notice them standing on the far end. The idea of facing her with an audience was daunting. What would start a conversation?

Those trousers hugged her figure and were far more appealing than he would have thought possible. The sway of her hips was downright sinful, yet her walk was measured and calm. A soft smile played at her lips but did not quite reach her eyes. Her laughter at the girl's antics was real yet mellow. This restraint was a contradiction to the Kaianne he had grown to know over the past cycles. Oddly, that irked him. Where was her fire? Her passion? It was not until they arrived at the first empty rack of weapons that Andreiyes realized who her young companion was.

"The Master's child?" he asked Jereown.

"Aye. Seems the girl has taken a liking to yer woman. Follows her everywhere like a boil on an arse. And if yer lass has her way, soon we'll be having two lasses trained in weapons 'stead of one too many."

"And here I thought you were admiring her skill."

"Oh, I was. I simply worry what raging, sword-savvy women can do. Threats against my manhood I laugh off just fine. 'Tis them followed by a blade that I worry on."

Andreiyes slapped Jereown on the shoulder. "Then you best not give a woman reason to use it." His eyes remained fixed on Kaianne and the Hirai girl as the two slipped into the weaponry shed. "You gave them a key?"

Jereown barked a laugh. "Yer lass has no need for those. Better chain and weld shut the treasury doors or ye'll be finding her in there too."

Andreiyes did not think he could stop Kaianne if she set her mind to that. Hardheaded woman as she was, he had to admire her stubbornness. She knew what she wanted and went for it. Too many people gave in at the first sign of trouble, yet she persevered. She pushed and prodded until a weakness was found and her goals were accomplished. But was he solely a mark in her plan? Did that matter?

She was dedicated to the Carved, and they were bent on ridding the realms of the Stewards. It was what he wished for, what his family and people needed. There was no reason to stand in the way. The question begged, could he join a people he did not trust? Could he trust her?

"Mistress Tilhold," he called. Her startled gasp had his lips twitching.

"Your Highness." Kaianne and the girl curtsied, which was far less elegant a display when dressed in trousers.

"A word, if you will." He stepped off to the side, far enough he hoped neither Jereown nor the girl were able to overhear. This woman, the cause of his recent frustrations, held her head high despite the way her eyes scoped their surroundings. He could almost hear the wheels in her head turning, her next machinations being assembled. "I see you have made friends."

Kaianne peered over her shoulder at the Hirai child. "She's a sweet girl. Reminds me of myself."

"You do realize who her father is?"

"The poor girl can't help that."

"And you would work against him? Aim at making the girl fatherless?"

"I have a hope that won't be an issue." Andreiyes furrowed his brow. "But if it comes to it, I won't sacrifice the good of all for one man. Master or Royal."

He stepped closer and hissed through his teeth. "Is that a threat?"

She ducked her head and replied in a whisper. "No. I'm not interested in hurting you, Andy. And I'm sorry I have, truly."

Her words were a balm to his troubled nerves, yet the way her focus kept slipping toward Jereown and Lady Hirai, he wondered if they were not simple platitudes for him and their audience. She could not manage to keep his gaze for more than a few instants as he stared her down. It was disconcerting and set his heart beating hard with unease. It was not until her features and shoulders slumped as she turned away that he realized she was as troubled as he was.

He caught her arm, his grip gentle, and traced circles over her sleeves. Her widened eyes caught his then fell to his lips. They were only a pace apart, bordering on indecency.

"Just tell me," he whispered, "your last letter, was any of it true?"

"Every word." Her exhale tickled his chin.

He closed his eyes for a beat. "Then meet me this eve. My chambers. There's much we need to discuss. Together."

When she nodded, he released her and hurried off before reason could return to him once more.

Thirty-eight

*K*aianne lifted her fist to knock on the door to Andreiyes' suite. She blew out a shaky breath and rolled her shoulders, too aware of Uslan's glare on the side of her face.

The burly guard had done nothing but act like she was Pyre's spawn come to burn the realm down since she had approached and declared the princeling's invitation.

Instead of announcing her, the man had simply stepped aside and allowed her the honors. She was never one to shy away from a difficult situation, whether or not the next sequence of events resulted in her neck being bereft of a head or with a noose about it. She knocked, the thud ominous and pressing.

Earlier that day, Kaianne mentioned to Yannic that she might have botched the whole plan only four days after arriving. Her comrade had not been pleased, rightfully so, and she had pleaded he fall back into Lityoll in case her gamble left her swinging by the neck. A gamble was exactly what she was calling it because she was truly coming to think Andreiyes did not see her any differently now than he had a cycle and a half before. It had taken the princeling so long to seek her out. When he had, it had been abrupt and distant.

With the weight of the stress that was currently suffocating her chest, her prediction of how this eve was going to play out made her eyes prickle, but she needed to know the truth of it. She needed to see that she had been wrong to trust him. She had to learn from this experience even if it broke her. Yannic had called her a fool, and perhaps in this she was.

"Tis Kaianne, Andy," she said when her knock went unanswered.

"Come in," his muffled voice replied.

With a deep breath, Kaianne pressed the latch down and walked inside the princeling's suite.

Andreiyes stood near a window in his sitting room. His back was to her as he gazed at the unimpeded view of Lityoll and Isyldill's forests and fields. Dressed in a tunic and fitted trousers, he was the depiction of a man in his prime – elegant, chiseled, strong.

The back of his head was a taunt. He did not turn to face her when the door creaked shut, nor when her heels clacked against the hardwood. Kaianne looked to the ceiling in dismay, the remainder of her hopes crumbling. The vial in the lining of the shawl tied around her waist weighed on her, but if it came down to it, she wasn't even sure how she would get him to ingest the sleeping draft. Long moments of nothing stalled their meeting. She shifted her weight and rubbed her hands, the silence burrowing a hole in her.

"Will you not even look at me when you order my execution?" she spat out.

He huffed. "Your brother must be laughing at me from Iltheln."

"What?"

"The viper that preys on my good heart," he whispered. "He would have had a good laugh at that, I imagine. At us."

"I don't understand."

"Tis what you wrote, is it not?" He turned to face her with his hands clasped at his back. She nodded, dumbfounded at where he was going with this. "Did you not mean it then? That you prey on my heart?"

"Are you…are you trying to bait me?"

"I would not dream of it." The hint of a crooked smile on his lips had her frowning in confusion. "How long was your scheme to last?"

She sighed heavily. "As long as it needed to." When he only grunted, Kaianne crossed a few more steps into the room. "This is more important than you, me or anyone. I'm tired of looking over my shoulder just because of a scar. I want Carved to not be hunted. I want Marked to roam freely. I want our talented not to be prize targets for the Stewards. And I want to see Flawed live. You know what I mean. Something about the Stewards weighs you down as well. Don't you also want to be free of it?"

He stared at her with those golden pits for eyes that were devouring her soul.

"Say something," she demanded, but he remained still and quiet. "I'm driven, alright? I wanted more and faster, so…I might've gotten ahead of myself."

"Might have?"

"I should've found another way to enlist your help. The poison…" She shook her head and wrapped her arms around herself. "It was the first idea that came to mind. I never told anyone you carved out my mark, and that was not the time for it. Perhaps I went about it the wrong way, but this was a chance I could not pass up. I cannot regret taking an opportunity to further the greater good, but I do regret the hurt I caused you. I truly do. So if you want to send me to my death, then give it a whirl. I'll even make your first attempt easy on you."

"Attempt?" he harrumphed.

Her head was ducked into her chest, yet she heard his approach from the soft tap of his boots. She prepared to lunge to one side or the other if he struck, but he was painfully sedate as he stood before her. The round of his boots poked out from beneath the hem of his trousers. His fingers gently pried her chin upward. Their featherlight touch left a pleasant chill over her skin. His amber eyes fixed hers, soft and gentle, not a hint of the hatred and anger she expected. The tension in her jaw loosened. His palm cupped her cheek, and she leaned into it, breath quivering.

"I should be offended that you used me for your own means. That you poisoned me, deadly or not."

She smirked at his playful tone. "Dear wrangler, I should be insulted at how easily you believed me capable of such cruelty, or that I was willing to die simply to poison you."

His deep chuckle had her gaze fixing on his lips. "Then we forgive each other?"

Instead of a worded reply, Kaianne raised her mouth to his. It was a gentle kiss, full of hope and kindness, what should have been if there had never been animosity between them. It was a caress, a promise of more if he wanted. And he did, if his groan was any hint. She massaged his lips with hers, coaxed them gently, warmed them as it was warming her blood. She was just about to pull back when he responded. Where her approach had been a soft crawl, he lunged. He gripped her hip and tugged her against him as she wrapped an arm around his shoulders. Their mouths tangled in a deepening abyss that had her desperate for more, and when she opened for him, he dove in.

His hands moved just as forcefully, one burying into her hair while the other cinched around her waist, tugging her closer and forcing the fabric of her dress higher and higher. The press of his fingers on her skin tightened. Her fingers dug into his hair as he tore his lips away to nip down her neck. His forehead pressed against her shoulders, his pants warming her skin through her gown. Her heart thumped in her ears.

"Am I a fool for this feeling?" he asked with a shake of his head. "For missing your presence? For wanting you coiled in my life?"

"No, Lords, no." Her fingers stroked his cheeks. "I'm right there with you. We're the jokers to each other's foolishness. No matter how horrible of an idea, no matter how long this lasts, right here and now, you're mine and I'm yours."

That seemed to snap the last tether of his control, because his lips crashed into hers once more and wrangled them into submission. There was nothing sweet about this kiss. It was punishing and demanding. His hands slipped beneath the skirt of her dress as she sunk into his chest, his defined muscles teasing her through their clothing. She wanted to feel every firm edge, every smooth expanse of skin. She needed all of him, even if only for this moment. When his hand reached the apex of her thigh, she moaned through his chuckle.

"I will have you making that sound again." He squeezed her rear then trailed his fingers around the crest of where she wanted him. But gods below, he did everything but touch there. Yet she obeyed, she couldn't help it. She whimpered for more. "Again." His other hand teased one breast through her dress while his mouth suckled the other, but it wasn't enough.

Too many clothes. Too slow. More. It had been too long since her last romp, and lords she needed this. The next time they could go slow. Right now, her craving was urgent.

She tugged his tunic out of his trousers with hurried movements. When it caught on his elbows, she let him finish and set to work on his trousers. Her kisses trailed down his throat and over his shoulders before she pulled away. Eyes fixed on him, she untied the laces of her gown and pried it over her head. Her underdrawers came next until she was bare on display for him.

This was far from her first time, yet she felt oddly vulnerable despite not being a blushing virgin. Her body was a map of her life since her carving with the mottled scars all lighter than the rest of her skin. The cut-out griffin mark, the disfigured skin past her right elbow, the nicks along her back and legs from close calls, and the several stab wounds, especially the one to her lower abdomen he had tended to were on full display. In contrast, his broad shoulders and chiseled chest had not a single mark on them. She fought the urge to cover herself as his gaze raked over her, a hand rubbing his chin. Was that excitement in his eyes or shock? Lust or disillusionment? She couldn't tell. Never before had she been ashamed of her history and she wasn't about to be now, but she had never been with a man that was not as damaged as she. His unending traveling stare was not helping her disquiet. Not until his eyes finally met hers, the desire and heat in them were enough to make her shiver.

"Beautiful, you are beautiful." He circled an arm around her waist and nuzzled her earlobe, his voice deeper, thicker. "I envy every well-earned adventure on your body. I might despise every weapon that has cut your skin, but I relish in every perfect imperfection. You once said this life made you who you are. You were right, and right here, right now, you are who I want." Then he was kissing her again. He pulled her into his arms and carried her into his bedchamber.

There was no time for ceremony once he lay her down because in mere moments, he had rid himself of clothing. And he was as impressive as she had imagined. There might not have been a nick on him, but he was a mass of long, lean muscle. He might not have been a fighter, but she had witnessed his training regimen in the yard. Her eyes trailed over him, and she bit her lip at the delectable sight of what awaited her.

"A little viper indeed," he said, and she responded with a wicked smile.

With a laugh, he pounced. Their hands explored each other as his mouth went down the valley of her breasts, her navel with a flick of his tongue over her stab wound that sent an aching jolt between her legs, to even lower and exactly where she wanted him. He licked and suckled as her back arched and her hips pressed for more. He gave and gave until her pleasure peaked as her body writhed and spasmed. Then she was crab crawling further into the bed to force him to follow because the emptiness was too much, and she needed him to fill it now. He followed willingly. By the aroused length of him, he needed it as much as she did. So when she pushed him to his back, he did not protest. And when she straddled his thighs and gripped his length to aim him where it belonged, his groan was encouraging.

"A dream, that is what you are," he said as his hands settled on her hips.

"We should make sure it's a good dream." She sunk down on him.

He met every roll of her hips with a thrust of his own. Filled her to the brim. Perfectly, so much better than any before him. The tension, Lords, it was glorious as it built to heights only he could satisfy. His hands roamed over her body. They squeezed her rear, her breasts and hips, yet it was his eyes that made the feel of them sensual. Awe, tenderness, trust. All of it burned through her chest matching the heat of his thrusts, his rumbling groans, the shared loss of their control.

More. She needed to possess more of him. It was primitive and overwhelming. She moaned his name, the storm inside her cresting. When she bent to devour his lips again, he flipped them over and took control.

"My viper." His hips never stopped slamming into her, forcing her into submission. Right then, she didn't care.

His eyes never left hers. She was captured by them. It was like that that her body crested and shattered around him, molten and writhing. With a shuddered groan, he followed her over. She watched the pleasure tighten his features.

When a smile crested his face, it unshackled a knot of worry in her chest. He didn't regret it. She saw it plainly in that smile, and she returned it with a fierce one of her own. He tumbled into her arms, speckling kisses down her cheek and nuzzling her neck. When he fell to his side, he pulled her into the crook of his arm. His breath cooled her damp skin as his fingers teased caresses along her back.

"Stay the night, will you?"

His words were so simple, yet they said so much. She basked in the warmth that cocooned her, that almost made a hardened woman like her giddy. They were a balm to feelings she shouldn't and couldn't feel. A Carved and a Marked princeling. It made no sense. It had no future. None of this was what she expected, but lords, here and now, it was perfect. She buried down the ache that itched over her breastbone. Right now, she was going to relish in what there was and take it for as long as she could. There was going to be no wallowing in self-pity, definitely not when his fingers kept gliding over her skin, nor when he whispered sweet nothings into her ear.

"My wondrous, little viper. Who knew you would take charge?"

A laugh burst from her as she gazed at him over her shoulder. "Oh, you knew. You never had any doubt of that."

"Aye, 'tis true." The look in his eye had her melting. "Wrangle me all you desire."

"Who would've thought your poor attempt at seduction as my prisoner would lead to this?"

"Nothing poor about it. I was biding my time. You simply never realized the truth of my strategy."

She laughed and playfully smacked his chest as he kissed her forehead. "Can you imagine if you had not rejected my father's promise contract to marry me all those stretches ago?

"That would have been an arrangement. This, whatever this is, is much more."

Her heart thumped hard at that. "Real, is that what you mean?"

"Aye." He rested his cheek on her head.

"What about tomorrow? What happens then?"

"I fully intend to ravish you again and again," he said simply, as though there was no other option. She didn't know how not to be amused by that.

"No, you ridiculous man. About this. Us."

"One day at a time. We shall enjoy and be merry while we can because trouble will come on its own. We need not force it, and I would far rather enjoy your company without it."

"Then you'll help me? A sort of alliance?"

"Is that all you can think of, woman?" He sighed, but his lips tugged upward. "Aye, I will escort you to the archives chamber in the morning. We shall see if you can find something to save your precious Carved."

"And you." She pressed his arm tighter around her. Tethered, secured, it was so much more comforting than being afloat. "There will be something there for your problem too, whatever it is."

His grunt was not an acknowledgement, yet warmth tingled over her face as she snuggled into his embrace and closed her eyes to the world.

Thirty-nine

*F*unerals were always somber affairs. Rau understood the pain from them all too well. Whereas the Order buried their dead and planted a grieving tree in commemoration, Isyldillians burned them to ash. Flesh, hair, bone – all reduced to but a shovel's worth of what a person once was, while the smell of a charcoaled boar clung to their mourners like a second skin. There was no honorable return to the dirt to feed that which had fed their bodies throughout their lives. It was selfish and so very *royal*.

The heat from the blaze of the princess' pyre dried all tears that might have trekked down cheeks. The flames lit up grim faces of onlookers with an orange intensity. It superseded the glow of the moons that would be at their roundest and brightest tonight and the next. Tonight, they burned a body. Tomorrow, the two-hundred thirty-eighth Stretch of Rebirth would begin with the Festival of Life to celebrate it.

Rau stood on the dais – level with the top of the funeral pyre – upon which the King and Prince Balliol sat, an arm around Eybah's shoulders. For once, it was King Triunn himself that was present, not a twitch of Aroawn's silver drynn about him.

Back bowed and features drawn in sorrow, the man seemed older than his sixty-six stretches. The crown prince beside him was little better, his mouth agape and amber eyes nearly dehydrated from how wide he kept them, as if he were still shocked eleven days later that his eldest child was dead. Rau could not even chide him for it because, Nogo take him, he understood it. Almost five-hundred nineteen stretches later and sometimes he still felt the aftershocks of Moira's death.

At least now Rau had Eybah. He squeezed her tighter into his frame. When she glanced up at him in question, he smiled and kissed her forehead. Her responding hug filled him to the brim with purpose and satisfaction. She was all he needed in the world to know the gods required him living. For her he would do anything, because losing a child was the worst pain imaginable. It was with that reasoning that he offered a few words of solace to the crown prince whose pain racked face mirrored that fissure in his heart that was scabbing over, but would never fully heal.

"She might walk the halls of Iltheln and be separated from you in this life, but she will never leave your heart. No matter how long."

"Kind words, Master, but there is no need." The crown prince never turned to face him. "I grieve. I will continue to do so until 'tis my turn for the crown to shackle me. Perhaps it will be a reprieve."

"Not how it works," Triunn's gravelly voice said flatly. The King massaged his temples before slumping in his seat. "An invasion. No reins. Lonesome without. Monotonous."

Rau raised an eye at the king. The royal's mannerisms and speech without Aroawn's assistance were growing more and more jarring with every stretch. Gently, he unwrapped his arm from Eybah.

"Flower." In case the royals said more on the subject, it was best if she made herself scarce. "Go express your sympathies to Princess Katheryn."

His stern glare cut off the retort he saw building on her face. With a roll of her eyes and a grunt that shook her shoulders, she tread down the steps.

"You will regret such an act if ever something were to take her away from you," Balliol said.

"Is that a threat?"

"Emptiness before death. Set sail and hope. Amber and silver to work together. Griffin and wyverns, a promise, a goal, their achievement. A new world," the King whispered.

Balliol slowly pulled his gaze from the pyre, eyes narrowed on Rau. "Why would I threaten another man with losing what I have just lost myself?"

Rau grunted. It was a conclusion he agreed with, to an extent.

Half his face warmed by fire, the other half chilled by the night air, he watched the glazed expression on the King's face. The man stared at the blazing pyre without blinking, and that set him on edge. Tapping into his second sight, Rau clasped his hand in the other and squeezed to tamper any other reaction at the shock of the sight before him. Golden drynn pulsed in the King, not dramatically but more than it should have, more than what was safe inside a royal. It was clear from the pulses that the King would have been an Augur if they had permitted it, but royals were no longer meant to have any talent whatsoever, not with the precautions the Order took during each pregnancy's gestation. Aroawn needed to know about this. More cautionary steps needed to be taken. It would only take one slip for them to return to the precipice of doom the royals had thrust upon them centuries before.

Rau blinked his vision back to what was conventional and searched out Eybah in the crowd. She was whispering in the ear of a young, unknown-to-him courtier around ten stretches his daughter's senior. This woman was simply dressed, the elegance of the gown's material meeting the standards of the court, but the style was relaxed and simplified with no corset integrated and no bustle or crinoline to influence the shape of the skirt. It was a style he could wholeheartedly see Eybah desiring with all her complaints over the court's uncomfortable fashion. It alone was enough to set the woman apart. By the glances of others assembled, he was not the only one whose attention she had unwittingly gathered.

Whereas he was watching the woman because she had managed to befriend his daughter – the one that found most too boring, conceited or senseless to even speak to – the huddled whispers from other nobles and courtiers were more concerned with the man that stood beside her. Princeling Andreiyes' fingers were fiddling with hers and caressing her sleeve-covered arms without a care for those watching. His attention remained on the pyre, but his demand for comfort from the mystery woman did not waver.

"Does your son have himself a new lover, your Highness?" The title held less of a rebuking edge every time he used it.

"Does that matter? My eldest is gone." Balliol released a shaky sigh. "I want him content, I do not care who with."

"A message. A child of both," Triunn muttered deliriously.

Rau's facial scar itched with the pull from the knit in his brows. There was something about the woman that felt familiar, something that had him tensing and wishing to strike. As a precaution, he switched to his sight of drynn once more.

His breath caught, and he ground his teeth at the familiar drynn signature that greeted him. There had been a spying rat in his walls ten days before. It had been a danger to Eybah and to him, but it had scampered away before he ended its life. Who knew how long that person had stood there before Rau had noticed?

A lordling had died shortly thereafter. The death of the noble was irrelevant. It was the fact that that murderer might have been the same person spying on his suite, and this mysterious woman had the same drynn signature as that rat. Now his daughter seemed captivated by her, and the princeling clung to her.

"If she were the Bryant lordling's murderer?"

Balliol snickered. "That woman? Unlikely. My son is no fool."

Lord Bryant had yet to arrive for the cremation of his son, but his letter to the King had simply requested the execution of the poor groundskeeper named as the culprit. No other requests for retributions or reprisals were requested. No explanations either.

"Now, if you would, let me grieve my fill and leave your tedious questions for tomorrow."

Balliol did not wave him away or glare him down until Rau ceded, not that either of those would have influenced his actions. Instead, the crown prince simply disconnected from the world around them and stared at the diminishing flames head-on with an expression so harrowing that it left Rau feeling the intruder. It sent him treading down the dais' steps toward the mysterious woman it was imperative he meet.

The closer he drew, the stronger the overwhelming stench of burnt meat and wood assaulted him. His eyes stung, and he pressed a sleeved hand to his nose.

"Kaianne." Eybah slipped her hand into the mystery woman's and pulled. "Come. Let me introduce you to my chichu."

"Oh, that's not necessary," the woman, Kaianne, said with a widened gaze his way. Rau's lips thinned. She attempted to pry free from his daughter's grip, but when Eybah applied both hands to get her moving, the woman gave in with a grunt. "Honestly, I would rather not bother the Master."

"You have nothing to worry over, I swear. He's going to love you." Rau highly doubted that. "Because you mean a lot to me."

Eybah was absolutely overestimating his affections. Neutral was his preferred position, unless anyone intended Eybah physical or emotional harm. And he had no doubt that this woman, hiding in walls as she had, was a danger.

As Eybah pried Kaianne toward him, the woman glanced behind her at the princeling who returned whatever emotion she had displayed with unease. Still, the royal met Rau's gaze and placed his hand on his weapon's hilt – a clear indication that the woman was under his protection. Interesting.

"Chichu." Eybah raised herself onto her tiptoes to kiss his cheek. He met her halfway. "I want to introduce Mistress Kaianne Tilhold. She's been my close friend and confidant these last quints."

"Your Grace," Kaianne curtsied, then held her head high. Despite her protests to meet him, she held his gaze with a stern commanding one of her own. Rau grunted and turned his attention back to his daughter.

"Eybah, sweetheart, would you bring me a chalice of water?"

For a moment Eybah frowned, looking between the two of them before she murmured a simple, "Of course." Then she was leaning in for another kiss to his cheek and whispered, "Don't scare her off, please. Please, please be nice."

He waited until she was more than a dozen paces away before his attention fixed on the wall rat.

"Mistress Tilhold, was it?" She inclined her head. "And how did you meet my daughter?"

"In the gardens."

"The gardens?" he asked in disbelief. "And she took a liking to you because what? You happened upon her? Why were you following her? I am not a Master to be bought, and my daughter is not a pawn. This…acquaintanceship will not curry you favor, but if I find you intend to hurt her-"

"Never. I didn't even know who she was until her name was revealed to me by another. Your daughter is quite stubborn when she wishes to be, and she-"

"Don't presume to tell me what my daughter is or isn't. Is this acquaintance with my daughter an attempt to get closer to me? Is this why you spied on us?"

Her breath caught. "I…"

"Stay away from my Eybah."

The Tilhold woman gritted her teeth. "You can't control her that way. She's not an object. Do this and she'll resent you for it."

In his periphery, Eybah was approaching, chalice in hand, consternation clear on her young face. "Heed my warning. I'll be watching you, Mistress Tilhold. Count on that. Next time you step out of line, nothing will save you from me."

Even for Eybah's sake, he could not manage a cursory nod. It took him a few taps one hand over the other for him to calm the boiling rage that begged to tip over.

Logs crumbled from the pyre and crashed against others. Sparks and embers went flying. A few of the obliged or privy to attend yelped and reared back. The water in the chalice Eybah carried sloshed some liquid over the edge, but she kept onward.

He smiled, proud of the trust she felt in him. Never would he have let that pyre tumble near her, and she knew it.

"Well?" Eybah asked as she handed him his glass. "She's wonderful, isn't she? You should see how well she throws a hatchet."

"Tilhold is proficient with weapons?" He vaulted around, ready to tear the drynn out from the woman's spine to deal with the threat immediately, but Eybah stilled him with a hand to his arm. There was so much misplaced excitement on her face, it turned his stomach.

"She is teaching me. I am learning to defend myself. This way you won't have to worry over me so much."

"I would rather worry over you than have you spend another grainfall with that woman. I forbid it, Eybah. I forbid you from speaking to Mistress Tilhold again."

"You never like anyone I spend time with or anything I do." She pulled back from him, her features pinching, eyes going glossy, face reddening. "No one is good enough if it's not you. Why do you get to decide everything? Why can I not have anything for myself? It's my life."

She was backing away from him, amidst the gazes of onlookers. Tears ran down Eybah's face. She sniffled and wiped her face. It tore at him, but at the tender age of ten there was still so much she had yet to understand. Hidden dangers being one of them. He dragged her into his arms and held her tight.

"Flower, I'll be more lenient. I will try."

"You, lenient?" She dried snot off with her sleeve. "Really?"

"Yes, but you have to promise you'll stay away from that woman."

"Chichu, I like her. I really, really trust her."

"She's dangerous, Eybah. You are not to see her again."

She shoved her palms against his stomach. "Always the same thing. Why can't you be more understanding? Why do you hate me so much? Why couldn't you pick someone else as your daughter? I just want someone to understand me. She does. You don't."

She wrenched herself free and ran from him into the darkness of the gardens. He groaned with exhaustion. Always the same fights. So much dramatization, and it was growing worse with every stretch. One moment everything was fine and he was her hero, the next he was the spawn of Nogo sent to torment her. Whoever thought that raising a child by oneself was simple either didn't have children nor wasn't doing the raising. With a sigh he set off after her, trailing her drynn signature through the hedges.

Forty

With a huff of disappointment, Kaianne slammed the tome she had been reading shut. Dust billowed in a puff. She swatted the air and cleared her throat of it. With a groan, she rested her head against her palms.

"I told you that one would have your eyes crossing," Andreiyes mocked from his seat beside her. A page crackled as he turned it.

"You would think '*Schlenkra: A Recounting*' would be far more stimulating. It's as if the scribe chose to bore his readers into abandoning the reading of it."

"I still find it amazing that you read old Syldian."

"Well…" She rose from her seat and traversed the archive chamber's rows of stacks full of old tomes, returning hers to a tier hidden behind a first row of newer books. The Steward Greenling that managed the library had left for the midday meal a little earlier, so she made no effort to keep her voice down. "I wasn't naïve enough to believe the old tomes here were all going to be in Elginich. So, I stole a few from the Hallore Lord's estate a while back for a refresher course."

"Only a refresher? You read it better than I do."

"When I was young, learning to read the old language was preferable to stitching and sewing and learning to play an instrument like all the other ladylings. It allowed me to hide in the Bryants' library whenever we visited. That way I avoided you, my brothers, even Willik."

"Is this your attempt at preying on my sympathies?"

With a shake of her head, she leaned against the back of his wooden chair and bent to his ear. "No worries. I know you have none."

With a twist of his abdomen and a grip around her waist, he wrestled her to stand between his legs. "Now, that is just cruel."

"No, what's cruel is the number of stretches it will take me to make even a dent in all of these," she grumbled. There were hundreds of old tomes within the thousands that might contain even a sentence worth of information the Carved could use.

His thumbs massaged her hips over her dress. "I could think of more entertaining ways to pass our time."

She rolled her eyes. Obviously their romp earlier that morning had not been enough. "You're insatiable."

"With you as my muse, 'tis far from a hardship." He kissed her navel through the silky cotton of her dress and nuzzled her belly, which had heat exciting her most elicit parts. "And 'tis a blessing I need not think of any consequences coming from our fun."

Kaianne reared back as if he had slapped her. For a moment, she said nothing and stared into the flame flickering in the lantern on the table, collecting herself. She had to be misreading his words. He must have felt her flinch because he looked up.

"By consequences…you mean…unwanted pregnancies?"

"Well aye, would not want any of the little bastards crawling about, now would we? I for one have no intention of being a father. For that, this is perfect."

She rubbed a sudden ache in her chest and furrowed her brow to keep the sting in her eyes from building. Here she was, letting him have a piece of her she had never imagined being able to give to anyone when in turn she was simply a convenience to him. A willing woman with no complications attached. It surprisingly hurt. Never mind that she was unable to have children. It made her feel small and insignificant. She was, in the grand scheme of Carved, Marked and Flawed, but she had foolishly begun to believe that maybe she meant more to him than that.

"Lords, I've been blind." She stepped back from his warmth and wrapped her fur shawl tighter around her shoulders. "I need a rest. Excuse me."

"Kaianne, wait." Andreiyes' chair skidded against the stone flooring as he rose. "That is not what I meant."

"We both know it was. No, it's better this way. At least now I can be honest with myself about what this is and what it isn't."

He gripped the back of his chair. "Then what is it? Explain to me what this is, between us."

She scoffed. The audacity of him, placing this all on her shoulders.

"Fun, amusement, entertainment. Since, after all, that's all I'm worth." Tears welled in her eyes, and she blinked them away quickly. The pity she saw in his face had shame creeping up her skin at how easily she had fooled herself into believing this was more than that. "I have to go."

She turned and strode out, head held high. Those few words had flayed her, but Nogo would burn her alive before Andreiyes would see the full effect of them. He called her name, once, twice. She ignored the desire to look back and see whether or not he felt the slightest dismay at her leaving. It didn't matter in the end. There was no clapping of boots behind her to indicate he was following and wished her to understand differently.

She was a meaningless distraction to him. That was all it was, and she had fallen headfirst into that trap. Novice, dimwit, simpleton – descriptors she had thought no longer applied to her came back full force. She scampered out through the archive chamber's heavy oak door. When the feeling of his gaze at her back vanished, she slumped against the nearest wall and let the tears flow without restraint for a few moments. Then her resolve to overcome this tightened.

This vulnerability wasn't like her. She was no whimpering, self-conscious lass. She might have been an amusing way for him to pass the time, but he had been the wrong type of distraction for her. This needed to end, now rather than later. Her Carved brethren needed her, and whatever this was with

Andreiyes was only diverting her attention. Perhaps this was a blessing in disguise, even if she had to force that viewpoint on herself.

†

*K*aianne traipsed through the gardens, a gloved hand trailing over the hedges that sprinkled droplets behind her. More and more patches of snow were melting and exposing the cobblestone passageways between the dirt flowerbeds that lined the hedges. Sunlight dappled through the canopy of white clouds overhead. Birds were beginning to chirp and sing more regularly. Only seven days into the new Stretch of Rebirth and the climate was already warming. The wind was not as biting, and yet it made her feel no better.

The sleeve of her dress dropped slightly, revealing the misshapen feathers of the fading counterfeit mark. She slipped her sleeve down further. The ink lines had thinned, with some sections missing, and the golden eye had vanished altogether. If anyone checked on the ruse again, it would not stand through any scrutiny. Another headache.

Normally Taelgian skin scarred but was unable to be further decorated than by the mark, which made this fake mark a godsend. The eye had been a drop of gold poked through the skin. Somehow the skin still managed to eat through the metal to dissolve it to nothing. Money spent and gone. The inked pattern was another matter altogether.

Another crew in Credence had happened upon a beached cephallusc – a deep sea creature created by Nogo and Pyre with twelve arms, three tentacles and two distinct pointy heads each the length of two men – in a cove where Lakoldon meets the Barring Sea. The creature was being feasted on by a pack of fossas that attacked the crew to keep their prize. What was surprising and led to the discovery was that a mauled crew member had a black stain around the puncture mark that remained for nearly two cycles.

It was a boon, one she and her Carved brethren took advantage of when the need arose, but it was the touch of color in the mark specific to each realm that caused the most problems. Isyldill's golden griffin eye had been simple in comparison to Gyldrise's purple finfolk eyes. All of it she had explained to Andreiyes the day before until his curiosity was satisfied. Now, she wondered if she shouldn't have.

"Bloody gods, Kay." She vaulted around to find Yannic behind her. "You're alive. You're well."

He wrapped her in an embrace so snug that she almost lost her emotions to it. Something that no Carved had seen from her for stretches, something that Yannic of all people might be shocked or even repulsed by. She sucked in a deep breath, patted his back in reassurance and pulled away. Just as well, because then he was clenching her arms in a firm grip and tugging her out of sight into a small passage between hedges.

"You had us worried. Where the pits have you been? I've been checking for word on the stocks, gallows and executioner's block like a madman. To find you here, in a lady's garb. What the bloody pits is going on?"

"It's going. Everything's fine. I've been working, all right?"

"Working?"

"There's so much information to go through, it's just taking time, but I'll find something. Soon. We all knew this wouldn't be quick. It might take cycles, a stretch even before anything of value is discovered."

"You know right well that's not what I'm referring to."

Kaianne rubbed her forehead and sighed. "I'm sorry I scared you. I overreacted."

"Overreacted?" His voice raised. What was with men berating her today? "You made me think I was leaving you to your death."

"Keep your voice down." She glanced around in case someone was trailing them. "I was wrong, all right? Is that what you want to hear? Is that what you're going to tell Oidh? I judged Andreiyes' reaction poorly. That's all."

"Gods, you've shared his bed."

"I don't see how that's any of your concern."

"He's a royal. They use and they discard. You're worth more than that."

She tried to ignore the pang his words caused. "It's mindsets like that that make change difficult to accomplish. Marked see Carved the same way you see royals. If you want the world to be different, set the example. Until then, get your head out of your arse and off of whom I choose to bed."

She turned her back to him and plucked a leaf from the hedge. It rustled back into place with a rush of droplets pattering the ground. Between the crush of her fingernails, the thick leaf split and released its woodsy aroma blended with minty earth. She let the scent settle in her nose, a reminder of home and freedom.

"If I'm more tolerant, what then? You're family to me." Kaianne sighed because they were, in every way that counted except blood. "I cannot see you hurt, and he will do so. What happens when he grows tired of you? He can find twenty more warm bodies without your baggage."

"Lovely, you certainly know how to charm a lass."

"Honesty is rarely delightful."

"Well, keep your yapper shut. I don't need your–"

"Mistress Tilhold," the gruff voice of none other than Jereown Sertrios called. Kaianne raised her head to the blue sky and pinched her eyes shut. Was she to deal with all the tiresome men in her life today? "I thought I heard yer voice amongst raised ones. This peasant lad bothering ye?"

Jereown strutted toward them, his entire form a gradient of color from light to dark starting from his blond hair to his black boots with no cloak over his coat jacket. His swagger was arrogance personified, even if the man meant well in his own way.

Kaianne did not restrain her eyeroll. "You know very well, dear lordling, there'd be little contest were he to attempt any further pestering."

"And has he attempted any such thing?" Jereown's tone turned dark and heavy with the implication. His sword hand fell to his hilt.

Yannic might have stood impassively in place so as not to startle the noble, but Kaianne caught the twitch beneath his eye that conveyed his need to defend himself. She stepped between them.

"You think I would let him? You're giving me far too little credit. He's a gardener, Jereown, and we are in a garden after all. I happened upon the young man and asked for the name of this hedge I have grown quite fond of. And then we seem to have evolved the discussion into how to grow and maintain it in the cold season. It was a pleasant conversation, if a little heated."

That had Jereown snorting, his posture relaxing. "Only ye, Mistress Tilhold, would school a man on his life's work."

"We cannot all be well versed in so many matters."

"Yes." Amused, the lordling shook his head, which had his bun of braids rebounding from side to side. "I can almost see what he sees in ye."

Poor Yannic looked positively perplexed, and it would be comical if Jereown had not just referenced the princeling. Kaianne cleared her throat and forced a smile.

"What may I help you with, captain? Surely we've passed the days where you spy on my every move. Or is it a sparring match you're after? I'm not dressed for the latter, but I do need the exercise. Give me a good sandturn to ready myself, and I'll even let you have your choice of weapon."

"Ye know the right words to tempt me, Mistress, but 'tis Andreiyes that seeks ye." Jereown must have caught the momentary pursing of her lips, because he sported a goading grin. "Ye make the poor princeling wretched."

"He does that all on his own." Aware that normal ladies were not prone to expose their problems to the help, she inclined her head to Yannic and took Jereown's arm. "Until another day, sir. I suspect there will be more lessons in the future."

Jereown led her away, the mixing crunch of snow and gravel a silent companion.

"Dare I ask why Andy dearest sent you to retrieve me and not himself?"

"He assigned me the gardens while he searched the castle grounds. I pride m'self in knowing I accomplished what he couldn't."

"Finding me is an accomplishment?"

"I've spent more time in the last bilial running after Lady Hirai and ye than I've spent sharpening my blades. I'll take pride in the little things or I'll start thinking I have none at all."

She slapped his arm and laughed. "Oh, you poor unappreciated lordling. Whatever is to become of you?"

With a glance over her shoulder, she winked at Yannic who stared at them in bewilderment. By the look on her friend's face, he was only now beginning to realize that she truly did have everything under control.

She and Jereown sauntered through the rows of hedges, exchanging short snippets and teasing words. His presence was a comforting distraction to her doubts, even though very little was actually said. The lordling shared little to nothing about himself that she didn't already know, preferring to joke. In return, he asked little of her, which was convenient since in turn she felt no need to lie.

They crossed a great many nobles and courtiers strolling the gardens, the women in their elegant gowns and their male escorts in fine vests and coats. It made Jereown stand out even further as the military man he was. They inclined their heads to them both before whispering whatever nonsensical gossip they could invent. Probably more rumors centered around her, the woman warming the princeling's bed. Kaianne rolled her eyes. Lords, these people were far too bored in their wealthy, Marked lives.

"What news of Lord Bryant?" she asked Jereown between nods and fake smiles, even to those who refused to meet her gaze or looked down their nose at her. "I've heard his son's body has yet to rest on a pyre."

"No, but the body has been sent down to Zesco manor per his request. They shall cleanse his body there."

"So, Lord Bryant will not be traveling to Lityoll?" Well, that was an inconvenience. She had hoped to have fulfilled her blood oath sooner rather than later. Jereown must have noticed her frustrations because he paused their walk and frowned.

"Is he yer noble father?"

Shocked, it took her a moment to recall her lie. Then she burst out laughing. "Lord Pascual Bryant? Are we thinking of the same Lord? The one that smiles for anything and everything? Sweet tempered as he is. In which part of me do you see even a hint of a Bryant?"

"Never seen the man crack a smile. Don't think his face could twist one." Now Kaianne wondered if there was a miscommunication. "But aye, as flat and weary as the Lord might be, I cannot for the life of me see the man forcing himself on another."

"I'm dreadfully confused. Lord Pascual Bryant? That Lord? He smiles far too easily for his own good."

"Ye have him confused. I've not seen a flicker of a smile on that man's face since I first met him near six stretches ago. How do ye even know the Northern Commander?"

Kaianne had to force her hand not to fidget. "Oh, he stopped by my village a few times in my youth is all."

"Ye never did say where ye're from."

"It's not –" A girl's cry cut short Kaianne's brush off.

Two small figures darted from one side of the upper courtyard to the other within the narrow limits their hedge rows afforded. A young boy by his trousers was giving chase to a girl per her dress, and the distant yells made it seem like less than amiable play.

Right before they fell out of sight, the boy tackled the girl. Her yelp had Kaianne spurring into a run, skirts bunched to free her heeled boots. It wasn't until she had halved the distance between her and the wrestling duo that she recognized the girl's fibrous head of hair and those scrunched, angry eyes.

"Eybah," Kaianne shouted, but it didn't distract the pair in the slightest. More than a hundred paces to go. Gravel crunched behind her. Jereown was giving chase as well.

"Give it to me," the boy snarled.

"It's mine." Eybah struggled to keep her grip on a sheathed dagger that flashed in the sun. "Get off me. Help."

"I want it." With a grunt, the boy threw a punch to Eybah's side that had her mewling. It was a cacophony of grinding gravel and snow, the ruffling of clothing and the tussle. "I am your princeling. Do what I say."

Kaianne barely let that register before Eybah was screeching and an arc of red sprayed into the air. Fifteen paces now. Nergail lifted his head at them, frowning his royal amber eyes at Kaianne – no remorse there, only twisted confusion. As if the boy could not fathom why she was rushing to meet them while Eybah sobbed and clutched her arm, her little legs making tracks in the gravel below her.

"Tis mine," Nergail said, as if that justified his actions. He turned and sprinted into the castle, blood-muddied dagger in hand, the sheath abandoned beside Eybah's head.

Kaianne landed next to Eybah, her knees skidding to a stop. The ground's lingering wet coldness seeped into her dress and chilled her bruised joints. A coppery tang mixed with her young friend's flowery perfume.

"That was the young princeling," Surprise stained Jereown's voice, but she ignored him, too focused on the child before her.

"It was mine. You have to believe me," Eybah whimpered. Tears drained from her. "My chichu gave it to me. It's mine."

"I believe you." Kaianne wiped away the girl's tears and shushed her gently. A red stain on the girl's sleeve was growing darker and wider. "Let's worry about the dagger later. Right now, I'm going to check your arm."

She didn't wait for the girl's approval before prying Eybah's arm from her white-knuckled grip. With how bloodstained the sleeve was, the two halves needed to be peeled away. A deep laceration split the skin. Warm blood oozed from it and over Kaianne's fingers. Already, Eybah was trembling despite her coat.

"I want my chichu. I need him." The poor child was sobbing.

A shadow fell over her, and Kaianne's heart quickened. Jereown. Quickly, she replaced the sheared sleeve over the wound. A gash on Eybah's arm would be the least of the girl's worries if he spied the scars Kaianne's fingers had felt around the wound. Scars on a right forearm only left behind by a successful brand carving.

"What do you need?" he asked as Kaianne tore a strip of her dress to create a tourniquet below the girl's elbow. Quickly, the blood flow seeped to a trickle.

"Cut me another few strips to quench the blood." Anything to keep him busy.

Kaianne pulled Eybah's face between her bloodied hands as Jereown busied himself between his dagger, coat jacket, and tunic. "Eybah," she whispered, jostling the girl gently. The girl's droopy eyes fixed hers, despite the fatigue her body must have felt from the loss of blood. "Does your father *know*?"

In silent indication, Kaianne darted her gaze to the girl's arm then back at her face. It took two more attempts before her message registered. Eybah's eyes went wide with panic, her lips quivering. The tears that had slowed returned with a vengeance. Kaianne understood the fear of such a secret and tried to imbue some comfort in her thumb's caress along the girl's cheekbones.

"I don't care. I won't harm you. Just tell me, is the Master aware?"

"Yes," she whispered and choked on a sob. "He will be so angry."

"No, he won't. He loves you." With a shake of her head, Kaianne focused her attention on Jereown. "Help me get her to her rooms. You'll need to fetch Master Rau."

"No. No, do not get him." Eybah clutched Kaianne with her unharmed hand.

"She's going into shock," Kaianne interjected. "Get him. It'll probably calm her."

"She needs a healer. We should take her to the galley. There might be one there that-"

"No. I will treat her, and I'll do it *only* in her own chambers. Help me or get out of my way." When Jereown only scowled at her surly demanding tone and made no move to help, Kaianne dug her hands beneath Eybah's back and knees and hefted her into her arms with a grunt.

"Stubborn woman. I'll take her."

For that, Kaianne's back was thankful. As small as she was, Eybah weighed far more than a feather.

They had amassed a watchful crowd whose murmurs and gossip had escaped her until the moment she was on her feet and moving toward the castle's glass parlor doors. Now, it was noisy and overwhelming. So many onlookers, yet no one had intervened. No one had dared stop a capricious boy from harming another all because of his royal status. Kaianne shook her head in disgust. As if status was worth more than dignity and respect.

With the state of her dress befitting a bloodbath, she glared at the closest nobles that approached only to feed their curiosity. After confirming Eybah's Carved status, perhaps it was for the best the selfish turds had not stepped in to help. Still, she vaulted around to face them before following Jereown inside.

"You all should be ashamed."

Forty-one

*E*ybah hissed as the needle punctured her skin once more, and Kaianne pressed her forearm harder against the girl's elbow at the edge of the settee to stop her from thrashing. At least the girl flailed less than when the wound had been doused with liquor to reduce risk of infection. Anyone might have thought Kaianne was slaughtering the poor girl from all the howling.

In the wild, she and her Carved compatriots carried melken salve to numb pain, but Kaianne had nothing at her disposal in Master Rau's sitting room. Eybah had been quite adamant that no one else was to treat her before Jereown had bustled from the suite to find the Master. So, the girl endured the pain like a seasoned crew member.

"How much longer?" Eybah gritted out.

"Another four. Just four." Kaianne tied off the stitch.

"Then what? Are you going to turn me in?"

Kaianne gave her a stern look. "You think I would stitch you up if that was my intention?" She dug the needle in again. "As far as I'm concerned, until these separatist condemnations are done away with, no one needs ever know. Your secrets are safe. I promise."

It felt odd not to share her own truth with the girl, but Kaianne didn't trust Eybah's relationship with Master Rau, especially considering his warning at their last encounter. It was rather confusing to know he was aware of Eybah's status. Did it mean Stewards were more tolerant than previously assumed? That didn't fit with stories like Ghedi's.

"You cannot be here when my chichu returns."

Kaianne had no wish to be. "Don't worry, I'll be done soon. Then I'll leave."

"No, I mean you cannot be here, in this castle. If he finds you…" Eybah's eyes turned wide and panicky. "Stop now, go, please go."

"I'm not leaving you unpatched. This wound is getting closed and then I'll go, alright?"

It took long moments for Eybah to nod haltingly. This was the girl who seemed to grab the world in her hands and shake it until it fit her mold, yet now that enthusiasm was nowhere to be found.

Kaianne hurried through the next stitch. She wasn't fool enough to ignore Eybah's warning, especially with how the girl's eyes kept darting toward the suite's door at every tap of a boot, every whisper, every creak. It set Kaianne on edge, the room's rugs and decorations far too cheerful for the mood.

"No one is ever supposed to know. It's our secret," Eybah murmured. She stared at the needle between Kaianne's fingers and winced when it pierced her flesh. Her muscles strained beneath Kaianne's hold.

"Don't stop. Talk, Eybah. It'll reduce the strain."

A tear slipped down the girl's cheek. Oddly, the rings around her eyes now looked far darker than the normal amber of Isyldill. Dye, the girl had to have been using eye colorant every day to modify her birth color.

Kaianne had worn it once in Nimedor when infiltrating a cliff-carved keep as a maid. The sight of the Nimedorian red bands around her irises had been shocking, but the burning when the colorant was applied and constant itch thereafter had made her dread undercover work outside of Isyldill.

"Why does he keep you hidden? Wouldn't it be simpler for him to simply say you're under his protection?"

"He can't."

"Why?"

"I...I don't know." Eybah clutched the settee's cushion when Kaianne accidentally pulled the stitch too tight. "But no one can know. Carved are evil. If anyone knew–"

"Carved are far from evil."

"But chichu says –"

"What do you think of Nergail?"

"I don't understand."

"The youngest princeling. Give me one word that describes him."

"Demented."

Kaianne chortled with a nod. "Aye, very well. Demented. Now his brother, Andreiyes. Would you use the same term for him?" Eybah shook her head, too distracted to notice Kaianne readying the needle for another stitch. "How about the lordling Sertrios that carried you inside?"

"No."

"So, you see, three boys, all three Marked, yet only one you would categorize as evil. Same goes for Carved. There might be a few bad seeds in the lot, but most are no worse than any Marked. It's prejudice, nothing else."

"The last person who discovered that I'm...the way I am, tried to kill me."

"But they didn't," Kaianne reminded her.

"Only because chichu tore his head from his neck before he could."

Kaianne's fingers faltered before she could tie the last stitch.

Hurried pounding footsteps sounded in the corridor leading to the Master and Eybah's shared suite. The deep voice barking commands had fear prickling over her skin. The hair on her arms stood on edge. Kaianne would never forget the cold, hard edge of the Master's voice before he had nearly killed her, nor his warning during Edmira's cremation ceremony. She steeled her spine and rushed to finish her work.

"Go, please, you have to go now. Please," Eybah urged, practically forcing her off the settee with more strength than her bucking from the pain had.

The alarm on Eybah's face had Kaianne fighting the distance and clutching the girl's plump cheeks. If the Master was a danger to Eybah, Kaianne was going to take her away from here. There was only one way out of the suite aside from the doors that led directly to the corridor. The thought of the passageway in the walls chilled her to the bone. The memory of that day had given her nightmares, and she had avoided this area of the tunnels since then. She eyed the framed canvas built into the veneered wall between the Master's chambers and the sitting room with trepidation.

"What will he do to you?"

"To me, nothing. Go, hurry."

Kaianne hesitated a moment longer, debating whether or not to force Eybah with her. And it cost her.

Master Rau burst into the room, the door slamming into the wall with a crack before rebounding shut. Kaianne jolted away from the settee. His blue robes billowed as he stormed toward Eybah. His hood fell back, the scar along his face as vicious as the thunderous expression on his face.

"Who?" His stare never left his daughter, but Kaianne knew he was aware of her. There was no unnatural tug in her body, not yet, but there was a charge that coursed over her like the current hanging in the air during a storm. An awareness of how little power she had over his talent creeped over her. Impotent, weak, frail. Just like she had been on the day of her family's execution.

"The princeling. He stole my, *your* dagger."

"Pyre stricken royals." He sat into the indentation Kaianne had let behind in the cushion. "You'll have it again soon, flower. I swear it." His tone was almost endearing.

Kaianne took a step back and another and another until the canvas leading to the tunnel brushed her fingertips and backside.

"Why is there so much blood?" Now the Master sounded frenzied and vulnerable. If anything, that seemed to make him more dangerous. "Where are you hurt?"

Kaianne's fingers glided frantically over the wooden frame for the trigger to unlock it. Everything was going to be fine, she told herself, but the reassurance did not calm her bruising heartbeat. Eybah, the smart girl that she was, was pointedly not looking at her.

"I'm fine now. I'm fine. Please, chichu. Just carry me to my rooms. I don't think I can walk."

The Master made an uncharacteristic grunt but seemed to move to follow Eybah's directions. Until he wasn't, frozen over her, glaring at her wounded arm. Suddenly, Kaianne's body lifted from the ground and thrust into the frame with a thump. The air was knocked out of her. Her head radiated an ache. Worse, an invisible noose was burning through her throat. Her legs thrashed, begging to get just a toe on the ground. It was a curse that her arms could still move, that they raised to her neck to find nothing to pry off her throat, that her fingers dug into the skin and drew blood. Her throat was tearing with the pressure as her face swelled. Her ears rang. Panic set in as she struggled and flailed. It was terrifying to know she was helpless to stop it. Lords, not this end. She should have listened to Eybah.

"You." Kaianne had the Master's full attention, upright and facing her. His nose flared with how clenched his jaw was, but her panicked gaze was on Eybah not him.

"No, Chichu." Eybah rushed to stand from the settee and collapsed just as quickly.

The Master's concentration broke, and Kaianne plummeted to the ground. Air blessedly burned inwards, and she slumped against the painting's frame, coughing between gasps. Tears leaked down her face.

She didn't wait to hear or see what either he and Eybah were doing as she clambered to her feet and drew her family's dagger from her thigh sheath. The blade popped through the canvas. Kaianne applied all her shaky weight on the hilt to drag it down. It tore through the sunrise painting. Quickly she dragged the blade through it again. It took moments, only a handful, but it felt like an eternity as she thrust the canvas aside, panting air through her burning throat and tugged the frame of the stone wall behind it to screech open.

The tunnel's musty air was a godsend as she stumbled into its shadowed haven. Then she ran, wiping away tears as she went. Twice, the Master had nearly killed her. Twice, she had had no defense, and she was beginning to think any mission against them was little more than a fool's errand. It was suicide.

Forty-two

*I*t had taken Rau only an instant to understand what the stitches on Eybah's arms meant. The woman creeping away, like the insect she was, had seen the scarred arm, knew what Eybah was and what they had been hiding for long stretches.

Mistress Tilhold may not have attempted to end Eybah's life, but that only meant she had other sinister plans twisting in her corrupt mind. It made sense now why she had befriended a child half her age. She was a threat that needed to be squashed. No diplomacy, no patience, no mercy. Those only led to weakness, failure and loss.

Mistress Tilhold was having her last breath squeezed out of her — finally, after more effort than expected — when Eybah collapsed into the rug with a yelp of pain. Her smooth features were drawn and exhausted, her skin dull and pale. If Eybah's sweet gentle heart had not pushed her to stand and defend the conniving liar, the woman never would have escaped his talent.

He itched to run after her. Rage boiled inside him. At the royal boy that had dared harm his daughter — the boy had no idea what he had wrought. At the woman that now roamed the castle, free to spread word of Eybah's unfortunate predicament and make demands of him. And he would do and give whatever she blackmailed – he had no choice – until he saw Mistress Tilhold in the flesh again and ripped the life right out of her.

Rau lay his fragile little flower into her bed and kissed her cheek, the salt from her tears transferring to his lips. "Stay here. I'll be back soon."

"Please, Chichu. Don't do it," her soft voice pleaded. The sheets crinkled with her movements.

"You know very well I will let nothing jeopardize your safety. I have no choice. You know that." He massaged her upper arm. "Rest. It will all be dealt with soon."

"She's my friend. Makes me feel normal and happy. She saved me. She wouldn't do anything to hurt me. I promise. Please."

"My innocent child. You don't understand the rules of life's game yet."

Despite the ache in his chest to stay until she was resting, Mistress Tilhold needed to be dealt with as soon as possible. As Eybah cried after him between sobs, he strode out of the room with determination. He had long ago made the mistake to trust in honor and sworn promises, only for them to be turned against him and the Order. Moira had died that way. Never would he make that mistake again. He refused to risk Eybah facing the same fate. He had warned the woman to stay away. This was Tilhold's choosing.

As Rau beelined for the suite's door to the corridor, he ignored the hole in the canvas and the swirl of humid confined air that overpowered the floral scents Eybah liked to spray around the suite. From the glimpse of drynn movement in the air, those tunnels were a maze, one he had no intention of following her through. She needed to come out at some point. That was when he would end her pitiful life. He wrenched the door open.

"Captain Sertrios, good, you're still here. I want your men placed at every exit, and every corridor watched."

The young lordling scowled, hands held fast behind his back. "What is this about?"

"A trespasser is on the loose."

Sertrios peered around Rau, his eyes widening, more than likely fixing on the torn canvas. "Is it wise to leave Lady Hirai and Mistress Tilhold unguarded?"

Rau grunted. Sertrios' softened tone at Tilhold's name did not go unnoticed, but he had larger concerns. "*You* are welcome to stand guard by my door *after* my request has been followed."

"Yes, your Grace," the lordling recited behind clenched teeth with an inclination of the head. Then he marched down one end of the corridor, barking commands.

Rau watched him disappear around a corner before he treaded lightly down the opposite side. His sight of drynn particles took over as he swept his gaze over the walls and open spaces for Mistress Tilhold's signature. Time to find himself a rat.

Forty-three

$\mathcal{K}$aianne was lost. She hadn't had the time in the last bilial to memorize every single secret passageway, and each innumerable twist and turns felt eerily similar in the dark. In fact, she could have sworn she had rushed through this same place thrice already. Acting on fear was the best way to lose her head, Ghedi had once told her, and Lords was he right because she normally had a flawless sense of direction. Her legs ached, her lungs were on fire, and she was coughing up a dust storm into her sleeves which was straining her already battered throat.

Five times already she had found exits to the passageways guarded by kingsmen. Five times she had needed to slither back into the tunnels to find an unmanned corridor or uninhabited room, because it seemed like everyone and their mother was in theirs this afternoon.

She was on the verge of pushing another passage door open when the clicks of approaching boots and an echo of voices had her backtracking. A sliver of light from a gap in the wall's stone veneer provided the sole visibility into the corridor, so she crouched to see through it.

"Did she speak to you this morning?" Kaianne nearly sighed with relief at the sound of Andreiyes' voice.

"No, but she was in the gardens earlier. So lost in thought she did no' hear me calling." Mimsee's high-pitched whisper was even more welcome than Andreiyes'.

The princeling groaned. "'Tis my fault, that. I may have allowed certain misconceptions to go unchallenged." His voice and footsteps were growing closer.

There was a thumping slap. "What in the blazes was that for, woman?"

"Princeling or no, ye're in need of some good sense knocked into ye. M'Lady may have hardened her scales, but that does no' mean nothing can get through."

"Aye, I know that. Which is why I must speak to her, but Master Rau rejected my request."

A glimpse of servant grays and a yellow apron followed by flared trousers buried in leather boots flashed by.

"*Mimsee, Andreiyes,*" Kaianne whispered. Boots scuffled to a stop along the tile.

"Did you hear that?"

"It's me, Kaianne. I'm in the tunnels."

"Oh, m'Lady." There was a little slap of skin on stone as the tumble of Mimsee's skirts blocked the sliver of light through the wall. Mimsee's voice almost resonated. "How did ye get in there? Are ye well?"

"I'm…" Gaia help her, how embarrassing. "I'm lost. All the exits I've found are guarded." Kaianne had to hope no one else was with them. That no one else could hear her.

"We're in the south wing m'Lady, two floors up from the kitchens. The Seer of Events' chamber is three doors down."

And that was one of the reasons why Mimsee held a special place in Kaianne's heart after all those stretches. The woman always knew what was needed and when, whether it was what would end a child's tantrum or calm the nauseating anxiety that was building inside of Kaianne. Mimsee's directions were a balm to her thrashing emotions. Kaianne might enjoy the mysteriousness of a cavern or tunnel, but she never wanted to be a corpse in one.

"Why are you in the passageways?" Andreiyes' voice was not as resonant as Mimsee's, nor as close. "Jereown said you were in the safety of Master Rau's chambers with Lady Hirai."

"If I was still there, I'd be dead." At Andreiyes and Mimsee's silence, Kaianne groaned a sigh. "The Master plans to kill me."

"What did you do?"

"It's not about what I did but what I saw."

"What did you see?"

"I…I can't tell you." Andreiyes' growl was an ugly thing, and she wished she could grab his hand through the stone as a tether. Instead, she placed her forehead to the cold, damp stone. "It's not that I don't trust you. I do, truly. I just can't, not yet, not without permission."

"This secret, he will kill you for it?"

She nodded to herself. "Yes. I have to leave the castle. There's nothing more I can do here with a Master hunting me. I know there's a tunnel that leads out the bottom of the cliffside. I heard you and Grayson once, but I don't know the way. Please, Andreiyes. Tell me how to get there."

"Then what? Kay…When would you return?" Now he was the one whispering, his voice sounding closer than before through the wall, a solemn edge to it. She imagined his breath fanning along the stones like it would her face. Mimsee's gray dress fluttered out of sight, light filtering back into the passageway, only for Andreiyes' legs to take up the space, his groin in her direct line of sight. A smile teased her lips, but she squashed it down quickly.

"I can't. I don't want to leave. Truly I don't. I haven't achieved anything, but that Master…I can't fight him like this. Not right now. Yannic will have to be your liaison now. If we can still count on any hope of an alliance with you, your men, and all of us." She dared not mention the group's name just in case. "Just until I can figure out a way to eliminate him."

"And us?" She almost missed his question with how softly it was spoken.

"Is there an us?" Her heart skipped a beat in anticipation of his answer. The whistling breeze down the tunnel made her shudder. "Is this more than stolen moments?"

His silence dragged for too long, and she felt her heart tumble into her stomach.

"Saying simple words does not seem to be enough," he finally said, his words muffled through the stone. "I wish to hold you to show you my affection, to look into your eyes so you can see the truth behind my words. I was simply taken off-guard earlier."

They were such lovely words, but they changed nothing. Master Rau had somehow seen her through the tunnels the first time his talent had gripped her. He had known it was her when they had met in person, which meant there was nowhere to hide here to continue her research if he was dead set on finding her. If she stayed, if she was discovered, there was a chance it might put her entire plan in jeopardy. That simply wasn't worth it.

"Look at you, turning all poetic." She chuckled despite herself, the soft sound echoing around her like a taunt.

There was a ruffle of skirts with rushing footsteps. "Someone's coming," Mimsee huffed in pants.

"Viper, listen." His voice seemed to rumble through the wall, and she smiled at the moniker. "I just might have a plan. 'Tis as outlandish as dragon and man ever collaborating, but you need to trust me."

If only that was the hardest part in all this because she did, with her life. That was the kicker too, because her life did depend on this if she agreed to whatever his idea was. "I trust you think you have a solution. It won't work."

"It will. We only need to obtain the key element."

"The what?"

The clip clap of shoes on the next walkway over were approaching.

"Trust I will wrangle you out of this." Despite the situation, she tittered with a roll of her eyes at his innuendo. "Meet me in my chambers in less than a sandturn. You too, Mimsee."

"All will be well, dearie."

The shade they created disappeared just as voices and heavy feet crested the corridor. Kaianne did not wait to know if it was the Master or the less threatening kingsmen. Now that she knew where she was and where to go, every step she took was purposeful and careful not to attract attention. After all, it was crumbled stone that had first garnered her the Master's attention. For now, she would meet Andreiyes in his suite, and if his solution was insufficient, at least he had a balcony for her to climb down.

Forty-four

"Father?"

Andreiyes stood in Balliol's study as the crown prince's quill scratched signature after signature on a stack of parchment so high that it made Andreiyes' hand ache from imagining the task. The pages rustled as Balliol handed them off to his personal secretary.

Andreiyes' heel tapped gently against the rug. Already, a quarter of the timekeeper's sand on Balliol's desk had sifted to the bottom half of the apparatus.

Without any candles or incense lit or trays of fresh scented oils put out, the stuffy air made it obvious Father had not aired out the room in some time. He must have forbidden servants from cleaning to immortalize evidence of Edmira's last passage. From the wilted flowers with rotting stems that she had last plucked, the last books she had pulled from his library lain out on her favorite chaise, to the tea set she had gifted Father and always used in this room. It was suffocating.

Father's grunt was barely an acknowledgement that he had heard Andreiyes' call as he continued scribbling signatures. His features were even more drawn than they had been almost a quint ago at Edmira's cremation ceremony. His clothing was wrinkled as though he had slept in them, and his hair was unkempt. It was very much unlike Father's normal pristine appearance.

Andreiyes had been avoiding his father since the ceremony, unwilling to be dragged back into the painful grief that he was digging himself out of. He had one person to thank for that, for the challenge she presented him, the teasing, the laughter, the intrigue. She was the bright light in his otherwise dull existence that was wrapped in spiked gold. And she was depending on him, strong and stubborn as she was.

"Father," Andreiyes called again, satisfied when Balliol's head jerked up. "I only require a few sandfalls of your time. Then you can return to whatever…this is." He waved his hand to indicate the state of the room.

"Forgive me, son. There is so much to do, and we have yet to discuss your new duties and responsibilities." Balliol again buried his head into his pile of documents. "Your sister, may she find happiness in Iltheln, was much more adept at this than I. Come, sit. You might as well start now. There is more than enough for the both of us."

"Tomorrow perhaps." Andreiyes raked a hand through his hair and loosed a breath. He preferred discussing this without his father's secretary present, but Balliol trusted the waif of a man. Besides, come that eve, if all went according to plan, it would be more than just new gossip spouting from every wagging tongue in the court. "Right now, I am in need of the heartstone."

That had Father straightening to get a good look at him. He set down his quill and intertwined his fingers. "Are you certain about this?"

"Yes." And he was. The circumstances prompting his decision were outlandish as reasonings went, but now that he had made up his mind, he wanted this. It made sense and felt right.

"It cannot be undone once the blood seeps in. If this is only infatuation–"

"Is that your only objection?"

"Should there be others?"

Andreiyes stared his father head-on. "I have chosen this. My mind is set, and if I did not *need* your permission to use the heartstone, I would only ask for your best wishes. As it is, I refuse to involve grandfather unless I must, but I am not below finding a means to…entice you to give it to me."

Father chortled behind his desk. "This woman must mean a great deal to you for you to resort to threats, but there is no need for them, son. That was all I cared to know. I simply do not wish my regrets to become your own."

And there was much to regret with Pearle, especially his halfwit half-brother. Or perhaps it was the idea that Balliol had neglected Uncle Deacon's trust when he had entrusted the heartstone to Father for safekeeping, only for him to misuse it during a drunken night. "Seeing as I am far from inebriated and I do not already have it in my possession, trust my actions are my own."

"Right." His father forced a smile and waved to his secretary. "The case, please."

It was not long before the man lay an unopened case on Balliol's desk. Neither Andreiyes nor the secretary made a move to open it. Such a thing was to tempt fate. If the heartstone lay near the clasps and when the case was opened it slipped out slightly, there was an exorbitant amount of risk that the opener might touch it. Even a graze would kill a person without royal blood. For Andreiyes, without it having been properly handed down to him by the royal directly above him in the line of succession, the shock would have probably rendered him unconscious or at the very least, numbed his limbs for sandturns on end.

Father's chair scraped along the hardwood floor as he stood. When he came around the desk, Andreiyes caught a whiff of pungent body odor that had him cringing and turning his face away.

"You need to take better care of yourself, Father."

"I will, once I have caught up." Balliol pressed his thumbs to the clasps on the case. They snapped open. "There is so much to be done first."

"Have a bath drawn for his highness," Andreiyes ordered. The secretary must have agreed with him, because he did not look to Balliol for confirmation before leaving the study to relay Andreiyes' instructions.

"Traitor," the crown prince mumbled.

"Edmira would not want you wasting away."

Father only sighed in response before prying the case open.

Therein, the heartstone gleamed beneath its silver embellishments, catching the sunlight and refracting it into golden beams that speckled the shelves and furniture around the room. It appeared to be smooth in its oblong shape, but looks were deceiving. Father had once described it as prickly as a spined fawneer, the quills on the miniature mammals known to draw blood easily.

"Do you willingly lend it to me, Father?"

Andreiyes held out his hand in the hopes of hurrying this along. It would be so much simpler if he could simply take it.

There were only two ways for a royal to bind their life to another permanently. One involved a ceremony by which the crowned Lenierz drank from a chalice in which the royal wishing to marry and his or her chosen spouse had mixed in drops of their blood. That was out of the question with the influence the Stewards had over King Triunn, especially with Master Rau pitted against Kaianne. Even if Andreiyes caught his grandfather in a moment of lucidity, the King would most likely refuse his choice of woman.

The second option – the only one he saw available to him in their current circumstances – involved spilling the blood of both parties that wished to be joined over the heartstone. That depended only on his father's willingness to hand over the fossilized dragon's heart. Hence this unending visit.

Another quarter of sand grains had vanished down into the lower half of the timekeeper. Their drizzle downward teased Andreiyes' ears. Half a sandturn gone. Kaianne was waiting. If he was late, he did not doubt for a moment that she was going to take matters into her own hands and escape. Out of the castle, Lityoll, Isyldill and his life.

"If we could hurry this along."

"That much in a hurry to bind yourself, son?" Any other moment, Andreiyes would have welcomed the playful lilt to Father's tone, but not today, not right now. Especially not when Balliol slammed the case shut and snapped the clasps down.

"What are you doing?" Andreiyes clenched his fist.

"Calm down, son. I am not refusing you. I simply have a condition."

Andreiyes groaned at the uncharacteristic grin Father was sporting. "What?"

"The heartstone is yours as long as I am present. If this woman truly means enough for you to do what you fought me so vehemently on, I want to meet her."

Gods, now Andreiyes' cheeks were prickling. Should he explain the pressing conundrum of the situation? Could he even reveal Kaianne's Carved status to him? To top it all, the man smelled nearly as strong as a latrine in close proximity.

"Later, I swear I shall introduce you."

"Andreiyes." Balliol pressed a hand on Andreiyes' shoulder, his happy expression wavering. "I need this. I need to see you happy."

Andreiyes sighed. "Fine, but please, for the love of Iltheln, change. Clean below your armpits at the very least, and hurry. I have less than half a sandturn before I need to be in my chambers."

A wallop across the head had Andreiyes wincing. Before he could question the act, he caught the disapproving glare on his father's face. Aye, it had been deserved.

"Sorry, Father."

The glare transformed just as quickly into a wide grin. Balliol squeezed him in a hug that forced the air out of him but had him gasping despite the stench that rushed in. With a final pat to his cheek, Balliol released him and sauntered out of his study with renewed vigor.

"My son. My son is getting married," the crown prince yelled.

Andreiyes blanched at how loud the words were belted. Now, he needed only to inform and convince the bride.

᛭

"Well go on then," his father urged him while he hesitated at his suite's threshold. His guard, Uslan, had a hand to his hilt as if his unease meant an assassin might lay in wait within his suite.

There was an ominous aura to that door, and suddenly he felt the fool because he had planned this, informed his father of it, and taken the man along with him who had then dragged Andreiyes' younger sister into it as well, all while the bride to be had no idea she was engaged. Andreiyes dragged a hand down his face. If she refused him…gods, perhaps he had not thought this through. His collar seemed to squeeze his throat. Tugging at it did not help, nor did clearing his throat.

"Your brother's hesitation is not a good sign," Father whispered to Katheryn. Demure as ever and never one to offend, she simply peeped a little squeak with a cautious smile.

"How…how do you convince someone to marry you?" The moment the words were out Andreiyes wished he might drag them back. How stupidly insecure he sounded. Him, a prince, a commander of men. He was turning into a stumbling simpleton whenever she was concerned.

"You have not asked?" Katheryn looked shocked.

"How much convincing could she need? The lass does know of your affections at least?" Father seemed to be in much better spirits now that he was decently groomed and away from his pile of official business.

"Stop heckling me."

"Ye're a handsome prize for any lass, yer Highness," Uslan said gruffly. "She'll no' say no."

"Thank you, Uslan." Andreiyes wanted to laugh. A prize, as if he were something to be competed for. It was unlikely Kaianne would see that as reason enough to marry him. He turned to his father and sister. "I will just need a moment to speak to her. Privately. If you, Father, would not mind keeping quiet before then."

"Why me?"

"Because we both know you are far more excited about this than even I am, and Katheryn would never."

"Oh, very well, as long as we do not need to remain out here as loiterers."

With a deep breath, Andreiyes gave a knock to the door and turned the handle. What he saw had his breath catching and warmth bubbling into his chest. Mistress Harleston had done fabulously with the little instruction he had left.

Forty-five

*K*aianne felt utterly out of place in the finest gown she had worn since infiltrating the castle. From the peach-colored silk of the dress, the lace, the thin white gloves, the jeweled necklace, the cosmetics to the complicated halo braid Mimsee had insisted on. Too much. It made her itchy with anxiety.

All of it was forced on her by Mimsee's cryptic urging that it was all part of Andreiyes' plan. It was beautiful and soft and elegant – but so very unlike her – and so very problematic if she needed to climb down the balcony and escape unnoticed. Yet she went along with it as she had agreed she would for the sandturn allotted for Andreiyes' schemes. Then vases of freshly cut flowers had been delivered and candles were lit – all arranged under Mimsee's scrutinous guidance – before the servants had left once more. What in the bloody pits was going on here?

Nerves crawled up her skin, especially as time sifted by and Andreiyes did not show. Particularly when Mimsee fawned and oohed over a tendril of hair falling out of place or her dress bunching up or how beautiful she looked. This, whatever this was, was definitely not what she had expected, and if Andreiyes did not show himself soon to free her of this ridiculousness, she was going to come back and risk the Master's wrath only to wring the princeling's neck.

She snapped to attention at the sound of a knock and the creak of the door. Her relief was palpable at the sight of Andreiyes. He had returned after all, and the wondrous awe on his face had her blushing like a maiden on her wedding day. Dressed in his same everyday fineries, she breathed him in, committing every contour of his face, his hair, his stance to memory. If this was the last time they saw each other, she was going to cherish every moment.

"You came," she whispered.

"I said I would."

A throat cleared behind him, and Kaianne's serenity fled. There, behind Andreiyes, stood the crown prince with a case beneath one arm, and Princess Katheryn. Kaianne glanced over her shoulder at the balcony doors. There was still enough time to reach them and flee.

Andreiyes caught her wrist. "No running. Please."

The crown prince barked a laugh. "This union is off to a fantastic start."

"You are not helping," Andreiyes hissed.

The switch from his pleading to argumentative tone made Kaianne take a good look at him. His eyes were wide and alert. His shoulders were tense. He was almost puffing deep breaths, and when he wasn't rubbing his palms, one hand was stroking his chin. Something had him flustered, that much was clear.

"Union?" she asked tentatively, because that word seemed out of place.

With a shaky exhale, Andreiyes gestured to his study. "May we talk for a moment? I have a…proposition for you."

That seemed to amuse the crown prince greatly as he chortled a fit worthy of the mocking lilts she had heard in alehouses. It was such a contrary demeanor to the somber man she had caught sight of the day before. Even the princess appeared amused, judging by the genuine smile cresting her pretty face.

The moment the door to Andreiyes' study clicked shut behind them, Kaianne vaulted to face him.

"Have you told them what I am? Who I am?" she asked, more than ready to get on with whatever the plan was or to simply leave. Drawn out goodbyes were in no one's best interest.

"Of course not."

"Why are they here?"

Andreiyes curled back his lips and massaged the back of his neck. This man who always acted so self-assured with enough arrogance at times to crush his subordinates looked downright distressed. It was almost endearing.

"Well? What is it?"

"They are here to witness a blood oath."

"Of?"

"Of wedlock."

She shook her head. "I've no time to witness a wedlock joining."

"Since it is yours and mine, I was hoping you would make time."

For a moment, Kaianne gaped as his words sunk in. Then, she barked a laugh because what else was she to do after such ludicrous words? But he did not join in. In fact, he looked downright dejected. "Oh, you're serious."

"I will try not to take offense to your reaction." He paced the room twice while Kaianne tried to process what was happening. "Is that your answer then?"

"What was the question?" He came to a stop in front of her. "Because I highly doubt we are understanding each other. You're going to have to clari-"

His mouth colliding with hers stole the words from her lips. He devoured them, ate up every protest, every reasoning her mind could have formed. His kisses were unlike any other she'd shared with other men before. There was skill, but it was because of what it meant – the heady taste of him, his addictive pine and sea-brine scent closer than ever, the possessive feel of his touch. She wanted him and cared for him more than any lover she had ever had before. A pit in her stomach ached at the thought of leaving him. She deepened the kiss, pushing everything she had in it, as if it were their first, as if it were their last.

One of his hands coaxed its way to the back of her neck, drawing them closer together, his thumb massaging her nape. She wasn't ready for it to end when he broke the kiss. Her heart thumped in her ears as she chased his lips for more, but his forehead pressed against hers. Their breath mingled.

"Marry me."

His magnetic amber eyes tugged on her soul. "What?" she whispered with a quiver.

"Will." His lips pressed gentle kisses to her forehead. "You." More soft kisses over her eyes and cheeks. "Marry me."

"But…" She pulled away from his intoxicating proximity. "I'm Carved."

"Aye, I could never forget." He closed the distance between them and nuzzled her head, inhaling deeply. "You wanted an alliance between Marked and Carved. This is me offering it to you."

"That's why you're proposing this?"

He cupped her cheeks. "Do not put words in my mouth, you frustrating woman." His hold kept her trapped, his eyes almost hypnotizing. "Do you not understand? I want you, Kaianne. In my arms. In my life. By my side. However you come. You have buried your fangs so deep in my soul I cannot fathom my life without you in it anymore. It would make me bleed. Marry me. Please."

Despite herself, she was smiling. Tears brimmed her eyes because this was never something she had expected to ever happen, and she wanted it. Wanted it with him. Never mind whether or not it would ever be accepted. On a sob, she leaned in and kissed him.

"That was so lovely, and gods know any normal woman would accept in a heartbeat."

"Then do so."

"Why do you have to make this more complicated? You know I can't. The Master will –"

"As my blood-oathed wife, he cannot touch you. Aethel's curse will extend to you."

"This was your plan?" She swatted his shoulder playfully. "You play a hard game, sir."

He groaned. "Give me an answer, Kay."

"Do you promise never to force me into this sort of assemblage again?" She gestured to the over-embellished attire she wore.

"Yes, damn it."

"I shouldn't have you stew a little longer?"

"No." He grabbed around her waist and flexed his fingers against her sides, every touch excruciatingly vibrant as the silk dress bunched and brushed her skin. It was delicious, exciting, putting every nerve she had on edge. Then the tickling began and snorted giggles escaped her. Her muscles tensed, her body arching into him without control. "An answer, woman."

"Yes. Yes. I'll marry you." She sighed with relief when he released her. "You're evil."

"Then you should not torture a poor man's heart."

"But it's so much fun to see you squirm."

"Oh, one of us will be squirming soon enough. That is a promise," he whispered in her ear. Chills had her shivering and arching her neck. "But not yet. We need to make this official before the Master can intervene. Come."

Those words were the equivalent of falling through an ice-covered lake fully armed and cloaked, the weight and current dragging her down while the burning cold pickaxed her exposed skin. How easily he made her forget reality.

"Doesn't that require a ceremony before the King? Can you even get us an immediate audience with him without the Steward present?"

"No and no." He gave her one last kiss before giving her hand a tug. "Trust me."

The gesture beckoned her to follow him back to the sitting room where her soon-to-be in-laws awaited in prim poses on the couch while Mimsee spruced up the decorations and flowers.

"Oh good." The crown prince rose from his seat and clapped his son on the back. "All is settled then. Convinced her, have you?"

"There was no convincing needed," Andreiyes assured, which made Kaianne snort ungracefully.

Balliol raised a brow and smirked. "I like her. Any woman that can give my son a run for his arrogance is a fine choice by me. I do not believe we have had the pleasure of meeting, although I must say, your face is a familiar one."

"Kaianne Tilhold, your Highness."

He frowned. "I do not recognize the name."

"A peasant's name." She glanced hesitantly at Andreiyes. Did this mean his father opposed their union? "The nobility in my blood was not recognized."

"Father, she is who I chose. No matter if she were highborn or the realm's most renowned criminal, I would have no other."

Balliol chortled. "No need for dramatics. Your choice is your own. I only want you happy, my son. You can have all the wealth and titles in the world and still never be content. You, my dear, appear to give him that, so I would be a poor father indeed to not give my blessing. That said, the King might not share it, so we need to hurry this along, yes?"

That sounded like a wonderful idea. Any moment now, Kaianne worried that the Master would barge inside Andreiyes' chambers and strangle not only her but Mimsee as well, then take out any remaining rage on Andreiyes. The crown prince clicked open the case to reveal an ornate livery collar which held an amber stone embedded in silver as its centerpiece.

"The heartstone is yours for today, Andreiyes."

The heartstone. Kaianne's jaw dropped. The stone was legendary, one of five pieces of fossilized dragon heart said to have been entrusted and receptive only to royals of its designated line. There were so many rumors of its power and legends – who knew which were true – and never once had she ever considered seeing it in person. Nor had she taken the time to consider whether it could be wielded as an asset against the Order.

"How is this done then?" Andreiyes pried the collar out of its case, the metal and jewels rattling together. It clanked against the marble top of the end table he set it on.

"You will each need to make a parallel wound on the other. Your palms or fingers are easiest. Then you need only have your mixed blood drop atop the heartstone. If both parties are willing to be joined in wedlock at the moment the blood falls, the heartstone will absorb it and bind you. A scar will form to represent your uncontestable union to one another. But if either party is coerced, the blood will roll right off and stay off." Balliol presented his palm as proof, two straight-edged 'L's, one for each marriage, each atop a scarred line.

"That's it?" It sounded far too simple. "What about vows?"

"The blood oath is your vow, but if you wish to speak any, they are your choice and for you to uphold. The heartstone simply binds your essence to one another until one of you passes on to Iltheln."

It sounded far more permanent than any union Kaianne had previously heard of. Her parent's bloodsworn marriage had been symbolized by the exchange of vows and tokens, not scars. Even the Allying ceremony's blood oath between Carved was more a promise of allegiance than a binding contract.

"Are you certain this is what you want?" Kaianne searched Andreiyes' eyes for any hint of uncertainty.

"I should be offended you think I do not know my own mind."

"We still know very little about each other. I could come to frustrate you to the edge of insanity and still you would be bound as my husband."

"I will welcome that challenge." The excitement in his gaze was palpable. It increased her own. This alliance could work. It would, by the gods she swore it. "Do you have your dagger?"

Did he realize when asking that he was symbolically including her family with that question? Kaianne unsheathed the heirloom from her thigh, the grooved hilt warm, and took her place on the opposite side of the round table from Andreiyes.

"That's stunning," the princess said softly from over Kaianne's shoulder. "The artistry, 'tis quite beautiful. Do you think, brother, that the same griffin might be sculpted onto a hair comb for me?"

The question had Kaianne feeling even more possessive of the blade. Her fingers tightened along the hilt. It was the last link to her family. Sure, the griffins on the crossguards could be interpreted as a symbol of the royal house, but every noble house of Isyldill incorporated it into their crests in some way. And the 'L' engraved on the blade conveniently did match Isydill's royal line as well as her own family name.

Andreiyes must have taken notice of Kaianne's reaction because his eyes widened and bounced between the weapon and her. "I...will ask."

His unease had Kaianne nodding, which in turn loosened the rigidity of his posture. In the end, what did it matter if people or his family believed he had commissioned the weapon for her? It was probably for the best. Less questions this way. More freedom for her to openly wear it.

To think, only a few cycles before she wanted to wrangle his neck, and now...now she was willingly marrying him, agreeing to a life with him, to...

"Wait, what of children?" Kaianne whispered in a panic.

"What of them?"

"You know I can't..." She darted a glance to Balliol.

"I want this, even knowing that. If anything, it makes this union more appealing."

That had her brows knitting in confusion. "You'll have to explain that one to me."

Mimsee snapped a cloth in the air. "Alright me dearies. Are we to have a union here today or no'?"

"Yes," Andreiyes said with a wicked smile directed at Kaianne and only her. It had her biting her lip and wishing to hurry the ceremony along and get the two of them alone. "Yes, we are."

Pulse pounding, Kaianne took that as her cue and sliced the blade's edge down her palm. She winced from the sting. Warm blood trickled down into her sleeve.

She handed him the dagger and mouthed for no ears to hear, "I, Ynnea Kaianne of House Lyssandre renamed Tilhold, promise never to let your life turn dull from this moment on. And never to poison you...again."

He threw his head back on a laugh before mirroring her wound with a similar gash on his palm.

"I, Andreiyes Xander of Royal House Lenierz, promise to fight in your battles and stand by your side. I promise you a better and brighter future, together."

She pinched her lips together to lessen her grin. Perhaps it wouldn't be so bad to be married to him of all people. Their palms pressed together, the blood making the wounds slip over one another. Their fingers intertwined. His calloused digits molded around hers, his not nearly half as hardened from wielding weapons.

A commotion somewhere down the corridor outside Andreiyes' suite pulled her focus.

"And now for the binding…" Balliol stepped in and forced their hands closer to the heartstone. Their combined blood splattered onto the jewel into red splotches that ran over the stone and its silver encasement.

She watched the blood begin to pool on the white marble below the heartstone, and her stomach plummeted. It was not working. They weren't going to be bound. The joy, elation, hope from moments before – all of it vanished. Perhaps being Carved made this impossible…or perhaps he felt coerced into doing this for her, or maybe she did? Either way, his jaw was tight, his gaze intent and determined when she met his eyes. The uproar in the corridor was growing closer, indecipherable commands thrown about.

"Kaianne," he gritted, as if just saying her name now was painful.

"I should go." There was nothing else to say as she averted her gaze, but as she went to move, he did not release her hand. Nor did he when knocking banged against his door and shouting clamored outside his suite. Nor when her body tightened and spasmed from a hefty tug in her chest that threatened to tear her heart straight out of it. When the door rattled against its hinges, still he held on. But the Master was here now. She felt it. This was her end. She still had control of her arms, so she clutched her dagger, found its balance, and readied her aim.

Andreiyes had to have known what was on the other side of that door because he stepped in front of her. Brave man. She had to remind herself it was unlikely the Master would permanently harm him. And yet, that action took most of the pressure off her chest for a few precious grainfalls. It was relief enough.

With deafening cracks, the door burst into shards. Their volley shot toward them, and though Andreiyes gasped, he did not move away. She should have told him before how much he meant to her. Now they only had the failed blood oath to hold onto.

She faced the incoming impalements with open eyes, but they never reached her. Instead, the wood hit an unseen barrier finger-widths in front of Andreiyes and Katheryn, who had bolted upright from her seat beside their table. The next instant, every shard clattered to the ground. Wood dust rushed in and billowed around them, burning eyes, tongue and throat with oak residue.

"What is the meaning of this?" the crown prince snapped, heading off the Master's entry.

"Hand her over," the Master commanded.

He stood like an immovable shadow among the swirls of dust, and the burning in her chest returned tenfold. Every rip inside she felt, like a claw digging within. Her knees buckled, only Andreiyes' hold kept her standing. Her eyes locked onto their conjoined hands, lost to a pure white discoloration on his palm below the thumb she had not noticed before and to the lack of pain from the gash on her own hand. Probably because nothing compared to the pits dragged agony in her chest.

"What in Nogo's name gives you the right to burst into my son's chambers? This is preposterous." Balliol raged while Andreiyes seethed, "She is under my protection."

That was the problem though, wasn't it? His protection meant little against Stewards. Through squinted eyes and gritted teeth, Kaianne aimed her throw and released. A gasp held in the room as it sailed toward the Master, pivoting end on end, but just like the shards, it never reached its target. The dagger hung in the air, blade glinting with the fading sunlight, mocking her attempt before it flung itself aside without so much as a movement on the Master's part. Another wrenching jerk in her chest. Kaianne screamed.

"You are hurting the girl. Get out." Balliol's protests fell on deaf ears.

"How?" the Master hissed.

How what? How was she still alive? It didn't feel as if she would be for much longer. Especially not as spots marred her vision and turned into a blinding flash.

"Andreiyes." Katheryn's call was as much a gasp as a yell and so very distant. "The heartstone."

Despite the pain, the blotches in her sight and wood dust, the heartstone's unnatural golden glow was difficult not to notice. And unless her eyes were deceiving her, the pool of blood had been wiped clean. Andreiyes released her hand, and she caught a glimpse of that odd discoloration on his palm once more, though the shape had changed.

"What have you done?" Master Rau roared.

The unnatural grip on her heart did not loosen, but the pull vanished. She slumped in relief. That reprieve felt like drinking a jug of fresh water after hours in Nimedor's southern desert.

"You cannot harm a royal's spouse," Andreiyes declared, the livery collar dangling from his hand. "We have sworn the blood oath. The heartstone has accepted it." He held his palm out to the Master.

Kaianne glanced at her own and massaged it as if her eyes were deceiving her. The slippery blood had vanished. The gash on her palm was closed. A reddened line with a thin indent was all that remained as proof the cut had occurred, but even more shocking was the white discoloration that stemmed from the new scar in the shape of a cursive 'L' with the exact same design as that etched onto her heirloom dagger. That was a little difficult for her to process, especially with her mind muddied with pain.

"You think I care what happens to me?"

"And what about Eybah?" Kaianne managed to grit out.

"Do not speak her name."

"Master Rau, this is far from appropriate," Balliol said as Andreiyes yelled, "Get out of my chambers."

Kaianne whimpered against the agony tearing through her organs. "Who will take care of her when you die from Aethel's curse?"

The Master's hold eased. She sucked in shuddering breaths and pressed her point further.

"Do you even know how far Aethel's curse extends? Only to blood-relations? Or to those you've bound yourself to willingly?"

Despite the Master's flaring nostrils and twitching muscles around his clenched jaw, his talent's hold on her slackened further.

"Will Eybah pay the price for it as well? After everything you've done to protect her?" Because Kaianne was certain there was more to what Rau's protection entailed than what Eybah had revealed.

Kaianne grappled a chaise's cushion and forced herself to raise one knee off the ground, then the other before Andreiyes was hefting her the rest of the way to her feet.

"And what of your Order? Are there not Stewards you consider family? Are you willing to risk their lives to protect someone I have done nothing to harm?"

She leaned on Andreiyes' steadfast figure, the pain throbbing in breath-robbing peaks, but it was no longer all consuming. Bone-deep fatigue was dragging her down instead.

"You should be dead already." The Master's words were muffled, but his disgust was clear. His gaze made her squirm as it ran over her slowly as though he were trying to pinpoint something, anything, and found her wanting. She expected his torture to wrench at her innards again, but instead he groaned, and the last of his hold faded. "This is not over."

Kaianne scowled. "I will not harm her. I swear it."

Master Rau tapped his hands together violently and puckered his scarred face as if finding her vow repulsive. She expected no less. His deluded conclusions could not be changed so easily. With a heavy grunt, he turned on his heels and made for the doorway, wood shards cracking underfoot.

"You're not doing her any favors, you know," Kaianne said between pants, "keeping her sheltered and alone."

The Master stepped over two unmoving bodies in the corridor without a care, yet still cocked his head over his shoulder to glare at her. "Be careful, Mistress Tilhold. There are ways to end a royal without igniting Aethel's curse. You would do well to keep that in mind."

Then he was gone. Kaianne heaved a sigh that her entire body mirrored and sunk into Andreiyes' hold, her legs wobbly.

"Are ye alright, dearie?" Mimsee caressed her face, and Kaianne nodded. It was over. This was only one obstacle out of many to come if they truly planned on going against the Stewards, and lingering on the heart-wrenching fear and pain would only hinder them all.

"Do you think that true?" Katheryn whispered in the sudden silence of the wrecked room.

"Whoever knows with those bastards. What in his pompous mind was he after, anyway?" Balliol delicately carried the heartstone livery collar Andreiyes handed off and placed it back in its case. It sunk into the velour.

"Me," Kaianne said with a cringe, her heart still thumping amongst the ringing in her ears. "I'm sorry to have brought this on you. Not my best first impression."

That had the crown prince teetering between a snicker and a chortle. "Oh my dear, if only you knew. Welcome to your trial by immersion into the family." He hugged her close. "We will speak again soon, yes? Perhaps after my son has introduced you to the King and court, though I might suggest doing the former in private to contain his reaction."

"Yes, in the morning. Can you keep the news contained until then?" Andreiyes might have been responding to his father, but his eyes were for her alone. His thumb massaged her cheek, and she leaned into it, desperately wanting the others to leave. Her Marked *royal* husband. Oh, Oidh and Yannic were going to be spitting boars out of their arses when they found out. Kaianne pinched her lips shut to stop from tittering at the imagery.

"Ah, we will try, but since the Master knew where to be, I am afraid my secretary might require a lesson in privacy." Balliol glanced at Mimsee. "Slow the spread of gossip among the servants, if you can."

"O'course, yer Highness."

"Perfect, now if you would not mind, all of you," Andreiyes said, his eyes tacked to Kaianne's lips, "I need to attend to my wife." His wink had heat warming her cheeks.

Mimsee had barely ushered the royal family past the shattered threshold before Andreiyes swept her off her feet and smashed his lips to hers in a kiss that started as a smooth massage and turned deliciously vicious. She met him with the same vigor. Fingers gripping his hair, nails digging into his shoulder, she released all her fears, her hopes, her needs. All of it fell into one kiss, and lords it made her dizzy with anticipation.

As he carried her to his bedchamber, they disrobed in flashes of torn clothing. Gone with the dress, the gloves, the heavy gems. Skin met skin, warm and welcoming. When his hand dipped along the curve of her rear, Kaianne broke the embrace with a hand to his chest. His heart was pounding beneath her fingertips as hard as hers was in her ears, and their breaths were just as labored.

"Did you mean it all?" she asked.

"Every word. Together."

She sighed with elation, her cheek pressed to his chest, her heart fuller than it had been in ages. "This wasn't supposed to happen. So far off-script from the plan."

"I would not have it any other way."

She pressed a finger to his chin and over the day's stubble that would need a shaving come morning. "But I doubt making every Carved a royal is a feasible solution. You'll simply have to meet my crew to devise what can be done."

"Tell me none of them are those I have met."

Kaianne fiddled with his hair. "Oh, come now. I held you prisoner. Now look where we are."

He snorted. "Aye, but I have no intention of forgiving anyone else so easily."

"That was easy?"

Andreiyes gave her an incredulous look.

"Fine, just promise you'll meet them."

"Yes. Very well, anything." He nuzzled her breasts. "As long as I find you naked in our bed at least three times a day."

"Once."

"Twice." He smothered the negotiation with another kiss. "We will meet them, but not today. Today is reserved for that squealing and squirming I promised."

"Lead on, dear husband. How about you show your wife exactly what you're capable of?"

The wiggle of her brows had him tipping his head back with laughter. And lords, he had a glorious smile. She wanted to bask in its warmth for as long as possible.

In the back of her mind, a nagging voice was warning that it couldn't last. All good things came to an end, and the upcoming challenges were bound to steal their joyful reprieve away.

Forty-six

*T*he alehouse was located in one of the dodgiest parts of Lityoll Kaianne had ever had the displeasure of visiting, but this was where Yannic had said Oidh and others were agreeing to meet. Little did they know she had brought a special guest along.

A mix of piss, spilled ale and sweat stuffed the air. Her boots squeaked at each step along the sticky floor. People shoved past Kaianne and Andreiyes, even though the two of them clung to the wall nearest the entrance for any sign of other Carved. Patrons yelled their conversations. The serving lasses were pulled onto laps or had their rears slapped as they passed. Kaianne shook her head at it all. Men were disgusting.

While her new husband – husband, three days later and the term was still shocking – was not a fan of the chosen location for this rendezvous, he had graciously kept quiet about it since exiting the secret passageway at the bottom of the butte's cliffside. Unfortunately, Andreiyes was having difficulty blending in. It would have been comical if it wasn't so dangerous. His hooded cloak and peasant clothes were a simple enough disguise, but his stately posture ruined it.

A three-beat, pause, two-beat and repeat knock pounded through the wall at her back. The signal. Not two grainfalls later,

Oidh's tall figure and shaggy mess of hair that did nothing to hide his cleft chin blocked the entrance. His face puckered in dissatisfaction before turning and leaving the alehouse altogether. Kaianne cursed him loud enough a patron lowered his ale and leered at her.

"So elegant, wife."

"Elegance is not what you married me for."

Kaianne grabbed Andreiyes' hand and dragged him out of the alehouse with her after Oidh's figure. Of course that browbeater had never planned on meeting inside. He had simply meant to subject *her* to that filth.

The fifty-stretch-old man was climbing a wooden stairwell on the outside of the alehouse. The steps were so weathered, they creaked loud enough to be heard over the crowd inside, but she followed him up at a distance to the rooms the alehouse rented. He entered one, and when no other tenants peeked past their doors to spy, she lugged Andreiyes inside after her.

It was tiny and sparse with a lone table surrounded by two rickety chairs that they had dragged beside the solo bed to use as a third seat. The hardwood was gray from overuse, splotched with outlines of large, cryptic stains. There were no colors around the walls, no decorations, and the window had a large crack through which the city's stink and cold whistled in.

"Ye were to come alone," Oidh said as he shut the door behind them. She huffed away the desire to roll her eyes at the grump's attitude.

"Well, *we* have news to discuss." She stepped further into the room, dropping Andreiyes' hand. "And it affects all of us in Isyldill."

With a grunt, Oidh shoved past her to sit at the measly table in the center of the room and nurse his jug of ale. Yannic sat on the bed's edge, face in his jug, shaking his head while Ghedi leaned back in his chair, regarding her and her guest. His expression might have been passive, but she was well aware he was assessing the threat Andreiyes' cloaked form posed.

"Ghedi," she greeted with a nod.

"Howzit kinder?" He never had stopped calling her that. "We've missed you."

She eyed Oidh. "Unlikely."

"If ye're here to tell us of the princeling's secret wedding, we're well aware." Oidh announced without a glance.

"Also unlikely." It may have been three days since she and Andreiyes were bound, but the King and Master Rau had been adamantly attempting to undo it in that time, with the excuse that she was unfit for the role per her lack of nobility and wealth. So far, no announcement of the union had been made. It was merely gossip amongst the servants. But according to a few tomes read on the heartstone and Balliol's own reassurances, there was little or nothing the King or Stewards could do to reverse the process.

"We're here because the princeling wants to form an alliance with Carved."

Oidh barked his laughter. "Nice try."

Yannic said nothing, but unease scrunched his face. Ghedi, on the other hand, emptied his jug in one swallow and tapped his fingers against the jar.

"Why?" he asked.

With her palm held back, Kaianne quietly asked for Andreiyes to wait his turn.

"We share a common goal against the Stewards. He wants to join his men with our crews against them."

"'Tis a trick." Oidh slammed his jug down. "He means to root us out and slaughter us once and for all."

But Ghedi's intense stare had not left her. "What assurances has he given you?"

"None, he can give none," Oidh bellowed. "A royal's word means nothing. Yannic, reason with the damn woman."

"I don't think I can. Nor want to."

Kaianne smirked at him. "The princeling has known I am a Carved since the day he did the honors himself. I owe him my life."

"You never told us." She waved away the pity downturning Ghedi's proud face.

"It wasn't crucial at the time." She looked over her shoulder and into the hood of Andreiyes' cloak, certain those amber eyes were on her. "I trust him. So should all of you."

"Ye're a fool then."

"Is this the princeling's man then?" Yannic asked. "Is it the captain he sent? You two seemed on well-off terms."

"Sertrios is another to be recruited in this endeavor."

She caught the suspicion and agitation in each of her crewmates' faces. For a moment she reveled in it, the excitement of what was to come and the plans to be made building anew.

"This though, this is my husband." For good measure, she held out her scarred palm. "Ghedi, Oidh, Yannic, meet Andreiyes. Together, we're going to raise an army of Carved and Marked against the Stewards. The five of us are the first step."

The thump of Yannic's jaw dropping was worth the dramatics. Ghedi rubbed his chin contemplatively, but by the brightness of his eyes, plans were already swarming his head. And Oidh…well, Oidh remained the leery militant that had survived nearly three decades as a Carved. He shook his head like he hoped she would make better sense.

"Only ye, Kaianne, would be this bloody mad."

To that she grinned, because you had to be a little crazy to go against the powers that be. And everyone in that room was, at least a little. Change was within their grasp. They only needed to reach out and haul it out from the world's cage of stagnation.

Epilogue

*T*he Agorethney Mountains stretched below Nimedor's southern border. No one ever crossed the desert down to the range's base for fear dragons might sail down from their perches in the sierra's peaks and gobble them whole. Yet one man lived there.

Within the recesses of the home he had hand carved into the cliffside of a plateau amidst the red-stoned Agorethney Mountains, Master Chaephren – because yes, he still considered himself a Master despite his centuries long exile from the Order – blinked from his trance. He grinned. He heaved a deep sigh of the acerbic air.

It was time. Finally, a new opportunity to right the wrongs of the past was again presenting itself. It was stronger than the last failed one, the resolution more defined, but there were still so many possible future choices that could affect the outcome.

He traipsed to his window, his walking stick tapping the sandstone in beat with his gait, and gazed over the view of Nimedor's snowy desert horizon and sand dunes to Onlooker's Peak and the surrounding mountains that blocked the view into Lakoldon. Growls and roars drew his attention to the plateau on which he lived. Teenage griffins were tussling against two dragon younglings, while their parents stood sentry over several mountain peaks.

The last time a vision had graced him with the possibility of great change, Chaephren had done nothing but watch. He had let decisions be made and futures set in stone without interference. He had thought it best not to intervene, convincing himself per the scorched brands that marred his entire right forearm that he could do nothing. And the charred marks – of Isyldill's griffin, Lakoldon's basilisk, Nimedor's wyrm and Gyldrise's finfolk, while only his Telfinorian wyvern mark remained undamaged – had seemingly mocked him when it became clear that the slight chance of change was doomed by choices made on all sides.

This time he needed to play a part. For it to come to fruition, he needed to influence the outcome. To be a true Steward was to preserve and enforce the balance, something his brethren had forgotten long ago in their fury. Perhaps doing this would assuage some of his guilt at his part in this mess. If not for those reasons, then it was for his personal freedom.

For too many centuries he had been exiled in the mountains with Nogo's numerous spawn, physically unable to cross a border. Oh, the beasts and he had grown to tolerate one another – he had as close to friendships as possible with some, and quite a few owed him favors – but he missed people, two-sided conversations and physical contact of any sort. He was alive unlike the rest of his family, but he longed for more varied scenery than the constant red stone of the mountains.

Chaephren sat at his handmade desk and delicately pried from his box of stationery items a precious strip of parchment he had pulped, pressed and dried for such an occasion. Everything he owned was of his own making.

He scratched a few words on the vellum, his handwriting sloppy and blotched with droplets of ink. His fingers quickly ached from lack of habit, but he grinned at his successful rendition. It was but a start with more to come, but in time it would help cement the future he needed. Now he had only to convince one of Nogo's spawn to deliver this message to the Lady Kaianne in exchange for one of his favors owed.

Glossary

Bilial = fifteen days

Cycle = thirty days long with a total of twelve in a stretch.
- ℵ Named in successive order : Alpha, Beta, Trien, Quart, Pental, Semest, Septen, Octet, Noven, Den, Adec, Cusp

Drynn = the particles that make up all living organisms and inanimate objects on Taelgir. What the Stewards manipulate.

Grainfalls = smallest measure of time, equivalent to the fall of one grain in a timekeeper

Money = (in order of lowest to highest value) Copper Par, Bronze Slag, Silver Blit, Gold Mig

The Order and its Stewards = organism created by the god Aethel before his ascension to Iltheln to order to create a link between the realms and keep the peace. They were charged with balancing the power between the rulers of the five kingdoms.
- ℵ Transitional – youngsters that have a high drynn retention or erratic drynn tendencies but have not yet reached their twenty-fifth stretch
- ℵ Greenling – Steward entry level and permanent positions of very low drynn retention individuals
- ℵ Mentee – scouts for the Order. Evolutionary position for those of high drynn retention and permanent position for those of low drynn retention

- ℵ Foreman – teachers and guardians of the Order. Well respected position reserved for those of medium to high drynn retention
- ℵ Master – protector and emissary of the Order. One of the highest standings reserved for those of high drynn retention
- ℵ High Master – eleven council member chosen by the Archchancellor at the beginning of his term or at the death of another High Master.
- ℵ Archchancellor – position held by Aroawn for five hundred twelve stretches. The archchancellor is voted on by an assembly of Masters and Foremen at the death or abdication of the previous archchancellor

Quint = six days

Maiesta moon = the moon by which Taelgians determine their cycles, 30 days

Persefin moon = the moon by which Taelgians determine their seasons. The full moon occurs during the last quint of a stretch and the first cycle of the next. The new moon occurs halfway through the stretch.

Sandfalls = measure of time, equivalent to the fall of a handful of grains of sand from a timekeeper

Sandturns = measure of time, equivalent to the emptying of one bulb of a timekeeper

Stretch = total of three hundred sixty days. Each lasts an entire season. There are four seasons:

- ℵ Stretch of Rebirth = season of recovery after the cold season
- ℵ Stretch of Fervor = season of heat
- ℵ Stretch of Gain = season of high harvest
- ℵ Stretch of Blight = season of frost

Talents = two different types (elemental and influential)

- ℵ Elemental (inherited only by royal descendants)
  - ¤ Aquer – able to manipulate water
  - ¤ Cendiar – able to manipulate fire
  - ¤ Molder – able to manipulate the land

- ¤ Souler – able to manipulate and change living things
- ¤ Guster – able to manipulate air
- ℵ Influential (inherited by any line that can be traced back to Aethel)
  - ¤ Augur – able to see the future
  - ¤ Drifter – able to speak to the dead
  - ¤ Hefter – able to move drynn
  - ¤ Mender – able to heal others
  - ¤ Narc – able to heal themselves only
  - ¤ Guzzler – can suction other's drynn
  - ¤ Giver – redistributes drynn either to themselves or someone else
  - ¤ Planer – the ability to astro plane
  - ¤ Sayer – able to speak and read the minds of others

Acknowledgements

First of all, to my husband. Thank you for your amazing support. For reading every first draft of each chapter. For listening to me ramble my ideas for hours on end. For taking care of the kids when I needed some time to get my thoughts typed out. I've been working on-and-off on different novels in this series since 2018, and you've been my rock through every up and down.

Thank you to my kids for allowing me some quiet time to write and being just as excited as I was to receive that first printed copy.

Thank you to my beta readers: Andrea, Emma, and Dad. Your feedback was wonderful and critical in working out the kinks. To Bianca, Myriam, and those at Scribophile who provided critiques on an initial version of what will be part of book three and four of this series, thank you. Your feedback helped cement what I wanted for this book and its sequel.

Thank you to Stefanie at SeventhStar art for the amazing cover design and Florian Cavenel for the illustration of Kaianne's dagger. One day, I hope to have that dagger replicated and on my mantel.

Thank you to Adam at Red Line Editing for all your edits and suggestions that helped polish the novel.

And finally, thank you reader. Thank you for taking a chance on this debut author.

About the Author

Writing has been a part of Mari-Tris' life since the moment she penned her first word. If she could feel it, she wrote it. Born and raised in the Grand Canyon State, Mari-Tris Fontaine now lives in Spain with her husband, kids and dog. Whether it's morning or evening, while she's reading or writing, she's binging on tea and planning hikes to landscapes she and the family have yet to visit.

www.mtfontaine.com